THE TRIUMPH OF THE
SNAKE GODDESS

THE TRIUMPH OF THE
SNAKE GODDESS

KAISER HAQ

INTRODUCTION BY
WENDY DONIGER

Harvard University Press

Cambridge, Massachusetts   London, England

2015

First printing

LIBRARY OF CONGRESS CATALOGING-IN-PUBLICATION DATA
Haq, Kaiser.
  The triumph of the snake goddess / Kaiser Haq ; introduction by Wendy
Doniger.
      pages cm
  Includes bibliographical references.
  ISBN 978-0-674-36529-2 (alk. paper)
  1. Manasa (Hindu deity)   I. Title.
  BL1225.M3H37 2015
  294.5'2114—dc23

                                               2015006997

For Raina and Shumi

CONTENTS

THE TRIUMPH OF THE
SNAKE GODDESS

SYMPATHY FOR THE DEVI: SNAKES AND SNAKE GODDESSES IN HINDUISM

Wendy Doniger

MANASA AND THE NAGAS

Snakes are a sacred and sinister presence throughout the history of Hinduism, and ideas about them and images of them that appear in many early texts resurface later in the tale of Manasa. Hindu snakes are liminal creatures, on the borderline between animals and the anthropomorphic categories of beings (men, gods, and demons). In fact, one word that is usually translated as "snake" is far more ambiguous than a simple serpent; it is *naga,* which designates any of the creatures, anthropomorphic from the waist up and cobra from the waist down, who live in the watery underworld *(patala)* and in deep waters on earth. The translation of *naga* as "snake" is somewhat justified by the fact that nagas are often assimilated to more ordinary snakes or reptiles (*sarpas,* cognate with the English word "serpents," meaning "gliders" or "slitherers"), but they remain creatures betwixt and between. Sometimes they are represented with several serpent hoods; sometimes they take on fully human form, though still with a crest of serpent hoods.[1] And though nagas are often open-handed with the great wealth that they control, and female nagas (*nagis* or *naginis*) are very beautiful and particularly generous with men that they take a liking to, they are and remain cobras, and therefore can be lethal, especially to those same men. In this, as in so many other aspects that we will encounter, Manasa is the quintessential *nagini*.

Morally as well as physically, snakes slither over boundaries. The rope that you mistake for a snake is the central metaphor in the philosophy of illusion, and it is often argued that this imaginary snake still has the ability to kill someone out of sheer terror. The god Shiva wears snakes as his ornaments, and the very fabric of his clothing is woven, warp and woof, of snakes, which express Shiva's power both to poison and to protect from poison. This is an ancient concept in India; the *Atharva Veda*, the ancient book of magic (ca. 800 B.C.E.), has a spell that says, "With poison I destroy your poison."[2] Manasa, the daughter of Shiva, inherits her father's ambivalent power over what Edward C. Dimock terms "destruction and regeneration." Dimock continues: "As a goddess of snakes her power of destruction needs little explication. She destroys ruthlessly and wantonly, the innocent with the guilty, to demonstrate her might. She is full of wrath and violence. But she has a strange and equally wanton compassion. She has the power to bring her victims back to life, and this she often does once she has conquered them."[3] In Bengal, all snakes are believed to have something of this power; fire fails to consume the corpse of a man who dies of snakebite, and such a man "remains alive for at least a period of seven days."[4] Manasa "is like a snake, now striking out randomly and angrily, now spreading its hood over the face of a sleeping child."[5] Her "actions are sometimes snakelike," but she herself has a human form.[6]

Manasa has the ambiguous epithet of "Visahari," which can mean either "holding poison"—as in the poison glance of her eye—or "destroying poison." In this latter aspect she is the guardian of soma, the elixir that destroys the poison of snakes.[7] Shiva, too, "holds" poison, most famously when he enables the gods to obtain the soma from the churning of the ocean (see below) by holding in his throat the poison that threatens to destroy them. Shiva also has an odd number of eyes, not a single one, like Manasa, but three; and that third eye has the power to kill (as he burns Kama, the god of erotic love, to ashes) and to restore (as he resurrects Kama, at the plea of Kama's wife).[8]

The earliest ethnographic evidence of snake worship in India comes from the Greek historian Aelian (second century C.E.), who reported that when Alexander was attempting (in vain) to conquer India in the fourth century B.C.E., he found a snake that the Indians regarded as sacred, kept in a cave, and worshipped.[9] Throughout India today, Hindus worship snakes on various occasions, usually by putting out saucers of milk for them at the bottom of the garden. Women, in particular, visit naga statues that are often placed beneath trees; most of the women ask for the blessing of becoming pregnant. And all over India people observe Nagapanchami, the fifth day of the moonlit fortnight in the lunar month of Sravana (July–August). In Varanasi, on that day, thousands of people crowd into the area around the snake pool, and daring young men dive into the pool from the top of the wall surrounding it, thirty feet above it.[10]

The worship of snakes is always hedged with ambivalence: the snakes are invoked to come, bringing water and fertility, but also to go away without harming the worshipper. Dimock has written about Sitala, another Bengali goddess who is the subject of blessings (mangals) like those dedicated to Manasa, noting that though Sitala brings smallpox and is therefore certainly feared, she is still supplicated for her grace, which in practical terms means either never coming to the worshipper at all or, in the deeper theological reading, coming only through the recitation of the blessing, the mangal, rather than a fever.[11] But the grace of a repulsive goddess can also mean coming through a gentle visitation, not killing the person she touches but leaving scars that are signs of her grace, her kiss, and her promise not to return—for people in India knew, long before techniques of inoculation were invented, that if you survived a mild case of smallpox you would never die of it. This attitude seems to me to apply equally well to snakes in general and to Manasa in particular: the ritual or the poem asks her to come, but with grace and mercy, and then to depart.

The ambivalent attitude to ambivalent snake goddesses can also be viewed as an expression of what Hindus call the "love-hate" relationship with the deity (dvesha-bhakti), more precisely "devotion through hatred." This is the belief that any powerful emotion toward a god or goddess is a form of love, so that mocking, excoriating, even attempting to kill the deity brings the worshipper close to him or her and ultimately leads to a union with the deity in heaven. And since bhakti is always a two-way stretch, any attention that the deity pays to the worshipper in return, even an attempt to kill the worshipper, as Manasa and snakes in general might be regarded as doing, leads ultimately to the worshipper's salvation.

A glance at the history of snake worship in India deepens our understanding of the meaning of the ambivalence of Manasa in the story of Chand the Merchant. The rest of this essay will consider that history.

SNAKES IN THE VEDAS

Stories of Indian snakes begin in the oldest Sanskrit text, the *Rig Veda* (ca. 1500 B.C.E.), which refers only once to serpents *(sarpas)*, in expressing the hope that the funeral fire will make whole whatever a snake might have bitten out of the corpse.[12] But there is an important Rig Vedic myth about a creature named Vritra ("Restrainer" or "Constrictor"), who appears to be a kind of dragon or shoulderless and footless serpent. Vritra is called an *ahi*,[13] which means "snake" but is also connected with the word *amhas* (related to our "anxiety" and the German *Angst*), which means "to press hard, to strangle, to cause distress or anxiety." It signifies a kind of claustrophobia, the uneasiness of being confined in a tight place. Vritra is said to hold back the waters or enclose the rivers[14] until the rain god Indra kills him, piercing him and releasing the flowing waters, which then rush straight down to the sea.[15] This dragon-slaying myth, clearly connected to similar myths in other Indo-European cultures, is retold in many Indian texts, right up to the present day. The myth of Vritra suggests that the authors of the *Rig Veda* were the enemies of people who were already present in India and who worshipped serpents. For Vritra is called a Dasa, a name given to the enemies of the Vedic people. In slaying Vritra, Indra simultaneously slew the dragon of drought and perhaps, on another level, destroyed the champion of serpent worshippers. Nagas appear on Indian temples and shrines as early as the second century B.C.E., "epigraphic and archeological evidence for the worship of *nagas* [supernatural snakes]."[16]

But if that was the situation, it did not last long. Later Vedic texts are more sympathetic to snakes and indeed prescribe serpent worship, which they may have assimilated from the Dasas. The *Grihyasutras* (ca. 500 B.C.E.) prescribe the worship of snake deities by filling a special pot, pouring water on a clean place, and saying, "Honor to the divine serpents."[17] The pot remains an important part of the worship of snake goddesses, particularly Manasa, to this day.

The *Tandya (Panchavimsha) Brahmana* (ca. 800 B.C.E.) tells of a sacrifice by serpents *(sarpas)*; by this sacrifice the snakes "gained a firm support in these worlds" in two ways: First, they obtained poison, together with the quality of biting; this was possible because they sacrificed with ten verses, and the text puns on the Sanskrit words for "ten" *(dasha)* and "biting" *(damshuka)*. And after that, the snakes vanquished death: "they sloughed their old skin and slithered out, for they had vanquished death."[18] The serpents here are identified with the Adityas, sun gods who die and are reborn every day. So first the snakes obtain the power to inflict death, and then they obtain the power to transcend it themselves. This two-edged sword remains typical of the serpents throughout later Hinduism.

SNAKES IN THE *MAHABHARATA*

The Vedic sacrifice *by* serpents is turned upside down in the sacrifice *of* serpents in the *Mahabharata,* the great Sanskrit epic composed over several centuries, perhaps between 300 B.C.E. and 300 C.E. The intertextuality is quite clear: among the dozen priests who officiate at the sacrifice in the *Tandya Brahmana,* several of them later identified as nagas, are one named Janamejaya, the king who performs the snake sacrifice in the *Mahabharata,* and another named Takshaka, the serpent who is the targeted victim of Janamejaya's sacrifice. According to the commentator Baudhayana, the snakes in the *Tandya Brahmana* text were the kings and priests who performed the sacrifice in the *Mahabharata.* The links here are quite strong. The epic gives several recitations of the Vedic lineages of the snakes, treating them as families of individuals like the families of sages, worthy of respect.[19]

Snakes play a major role throughout the *Mahabharata,* but particularly in the *Adi Parvan* ("Book of the Beginning," the first of the epic's eighteen books). As J. A. B. van Buitenen remarks of Janamejaya's sacrifice of snakes, "to the ancient Indians, among whom the non-Aryans must be counted, such a sacrifice must have been an abomination."[20] The snake sacrifice is a dark mirror for the epic as a whole, brilliant, sinister, and surreal. Though Janamejaya's priests tell him that the gods themselves devised a ritual called "the snake sacrifice," they add that no one but he can do it[21]—or, presumably, would want to do it.

The massacre of the snakes is an intentional genocide; the massacre of the Bharatas (the two sets of cousins, Kurus and Pandavas, the humans in the story) is an accidental genocide. Yet the very first story told in this text, even before the listing of the contents, is the story of an intentional genocide: the slaughter of all the Kshatriyas (kings and warriors) by Parashurama ("Rama with an Axe"), a man who once beheaded his mother at his father's request. Though the story is told briefly, in just three verses,[22] it is most vivid: in order to avenge the death of his father, Parashurama filled five lakes with blood and offered his oblations into them. The ostensible excuse for telling this story at this moment is rather thin: several hundred verses earlier, the bard has mentioned the name of the place where the great Bharata battle was fought, and the listeners ask him to tell them about it in greater detail; it turns out to have been the place where Parashurama filled his lakes with blood. The real reason, however, is to set the scene for two other oblations of blood: first the actual ritual slaughter in the surreal snake sacrifice of Janamejaya, and then the metaphorical ritual slaughter (of Kshatriyas again) at the real Bharata battle.

Madeleine Biardeau has demonstrated that the Armageddon depicted in the *Mahabharata* is a representation of the cosmic doomsday *(pralaya)*, and Alf Hiltebeitel has gone on to show how that final battle functions as a ritual sacrifice.[23] This sacrifice that is performed on the doomsday battlefield is reflected in the epic in the unofficial, "black" ritual of witchcraft—the snake sacrifice in book one. (Snakes are an essential element in black magic formulas in many later texts.)[24] Many scholars have been puzzled by the prominence of snakes in the opening book of the *Mahabharata*. Van Buitenen believes that "much of the *Beginning* must be regarded as extraneous to the story,"[25] and that "the structure is loose and associative . . . a presence of Snakes, largely forgotten in the rest of the epic."[26] But the snake sacrifice in the first book sets the stage for the tragedy that is to be the subject of the entire epic to follow, the story of a sacrifice that goes horribly wrong. For not only is the snake sacrifice the wrong sort of sacrifice to undertake; in addition, Janamejaya's sacrifice is never even completed. This latter danger, which is a constant threat in all Vedic sacrifices, also infects the consecration of King Yudhishthira, a ritual that is disrupted by Yudhishthira's envious cousins; only after a long exile and a disastrous battle is Yudhishthira finally able to perform his sacrifice of consecration. And that final sacrifice is bitterly undercut by the snake sacrifice at the very beginning of the text.

After the introductory invocation, the very first words that the bard says are, "I was at the snake sacrifice of Janamejaya the son of Parikshit."[27] The ostensible significance of that sacrifice is, at first, merely to set the stage for the central epic: that is, the reason that Janamejaya is mentioned at all is because it was at his sacrifice that the *Mahabharata* was narrated, and that is all that the listeners ask about: Do tell us tell us the *Mahabharata,* they beg. Indeed, throughout the introduction to the *Mahabharata,* the concern to know the events that led to the telling of the epic seems to outweigh the concern to know the events that led to the experiencing of the epic battle; and Janamejaya is the pivot of both of these concerns: his perverse sacrifice is the end of the experience and the beginning of the telling.

There then follows a 400-verse summary of the epic,[28] a summary that condenses into only two verses the two connecting sets of snake myths: "In the book about Astika are told the birth of Garuda and all the snakes, the churning of the milky ocean, and the origin of Uccaihshravas, the stallion of Indra; then comes the beginning of the story of the *Mahabharata* as it was told to Janamejaya the son of Parikshit at his snake sacrifice."[29] Astika was so named because, at his birth, he said, "It is,"[30] but his name is an obvious contrast with, a kind of back-formation from, the better-known term *nastika,* "one who says it is not," the usual Hindu word for a heretic.[31] Astika's story is therefore the story of the affirmation of good religion (in which one does not sacrifice snakes) against bad religion (in which one does sacrifice snakes).

Only after this summary does the bard return to his original subject, Janamejaya, and begin to tell his story. This story is not told chronologically; it starts in the middle and goes back to the earlier causes of the snake sacrifice, meandering sideways into apparently irrelevant episodes and then flashing back to still earlier causes of the snake sacrifice (such as the churning of the ocean). And this whole labyrinth of snake lore hardly touches upon the importance of Janamejaya's role in the so-called central theme of the epic: the fact that Janamejaya's father, Parikshit, was the only survivor of the holocaust of the Kurus and Pandavas. For, though the historical role of Janamejaya may indeed have been central to the skeletal narrative of the *Mahabharata* (the battle of the Pandavas and the Kurus), the mythical role of the snakes is far more central to the symbolism of the epic, and it is this symbolism that is tangled up in the coils of the *Adi Parvan*. Stories about snakes form a thread that runs through this first book, a thread around which the scattered stories are not so much strung as coalesced, like crystals in a supersaturated solution. The subtle repetitions, never quite the same, reveal a point that is never stated outright.[32] And the relentless volume of those repetitions testifies to the great importance that the author of the great epic placed upon that complex of perceptions.

To unravel the thread of snakes in the first book of the epic by following the order in which the events are presented there would be possible, but rather confusing. I prefer to rearrange the basic episodes according to their historical (or should I say mythical) chronology, in order to demonstrate the underlying structure of the serpentine cosmogony of the *Mahabharata*.

THE CHURNING OF THE OCEAN

It all begins with a creation myth:

> Once upon a time, the gods and demons decided to churn the ocean in order to obtain the soma, the elixir of immortality. They used Mount Mandara for the churn and the snake Vasuki as the churning rope: the gods took hold of Vasuki's tail and the demons took Vasuki's head, and they began to churn. Vasuki belched forth fire and smoke from his mouth, but the clouds of smoke became rain to cool the gods in their labors. A terrible fiery poison emerged from the ocean, but Shiva swallowed it and held it in his throat. Many valuable things came forth, including

Uccaihshravas, the white stallion of Indra, and finally the elixir. The gods and demons fought for possession of the soma, and the demons managed to steal it for a while, but in the end, the gods won the soma for themselves.[33]

A snake, Vasuki, is used as a literal tug-of-war rope; the snake is a liminal figure as always, here in the eternal battle between the gods and the demons. The soma is contrasted with the poison, and Shiva mediates between them. The contrast between the head of the snake, which spews fire upon the demons, and his tail, which is held comfortably by the gods, is a reversal of what one might naturally expect: a contract between the "good" head and the "bad" tail. Reversals of this sort characterized the world of snakes in general, and the benign Vasuki is no exception.

THE FIGHT BETWEEN KADRU AND VINATA

The "Book of Astika"—that is, the section that the *Mahabharata* regards as the start of the story of Janamejaya's sacrifice—begins with the contest between Kadru and Vinata,[34] a seminal myth of snakes in which the horse that emerged from the churning plays a central part:

Kadru and Vinata, sisters, were the wives of the sage Kasyapa. Kadru chose to give birth to a thousand snakes, and Vinata chose to have two sons, Aruna (the dawn) and Garuda, the great eagle, king of the birds.

One day the two women saw the stallion Uccaihshravas; Vinata claimed that he was entirely white, but Kadru said he had a black tail. They made a wager, the loser to be the slave of the winner. Then Kadru ordered her sons to become like black hairs and to insert themselves in the horse's tail; at first they refused, and so she cursed them to be burnt in the fire at the snake sacrifice of King Janamejaya. Brahma endorsed this curse, and in addition gave Kasyapa the power of curing anyone poisoned by snakebite. When Vinata saw the many black hairs in the horse's tail, she agreed to become the slave of Kadru.

When Garuda asked his mother why he and she were the slaves of the snakes, she told him the story of the wager about the horse. Kadru told Garuda that she would set the birds free if he brought the snakes the soma, the elixir of immortality. Garuda carried off the soma, having conquered the two snakes who guarded it; challenged by Indra, Garuda promised that Indra could take the soma back if Garuda ever put it down, and in return Indra promised Garuda that he could have the snakes for his food. Garuda placed the soma on the sacred *kusha* grass and advised the snakes to bathe before drinking it. The snakes set Vinata free from slavery, and Indra scooped up the soma and took it back to heaven. When the snakes returned from their bath, they found that the soma had been stolen; they licked the sharp *kusha* grass but got only split tongues for their pains.[35]

Indra is here, as he was in the Veda, the enemy of snakes. The gift of immortality almost won but then lost is a theme that we have already seen in the tale of the churning of the ocean; there it was the demons who lost the soma, and here it is the snakes. This myth may well be the earliest attested example of betting on a horse; significantly, the horse is "fixed," and not for the last time in human history (nor is this the last crooked wager in the *Mahabharata:* an unfair dice game robs the Pandavas of their kingdom). The opposition between birds and snakes pervades ancient Indian texts. But on the cosmic level, when Ananta ("Endless"), the serpent of infinity, supports the earth, Garuda becomes his helper.[36] Kadru, mother of snakes, is sometimes said to be one-eyed,[37] a characteristic that links her with Manasa.

THE DEATH OF PARIKSHIT

The story then shifts to the human level:

King Parikshit's birth was an ominous foreshadowing of his death: a magic weapon had destroyed all the embryos in the wombs of the Pandava women, and Parikshit was stillborn. Krishna had promised to revive the child, however, and he did.[38]

One day Parikshit went hunting and wounded a deer; as he followed the wounded deer deep into the forest, he came upon a sage sitting in a cow pasture, where he fed upon the froth from the mouths of suckling calves. Parikshit asked the sage if he had seen the deer go by, but the sage was under a vow of silence; infuriated, Parikshit picked up a dead snake with the end of his bow, draped it around the hermit's neck, and returned to the city. The sage thought nothing of this insult, but his son uttered a curse that within seven days Parikshit would be bitten by the great snake Takshaka and die. His father chastised him for this curse, reminding him that it is the duty of kings to commit crimes in the course of protecting dharma, and sent a messenger to warn Parikshit to take measures to protect himself against Takshaka.

Parikshit built himself a platform, carefully guarded by doctors and Brahmins with magic spells, and on the seventh day a sage named Kasyapa came there to cure the king if he were bitten. Takshaka took the form of a Brahmin and met Kasyapa upon the road; he identified himself as Takshaka and demonstrated his power to reduce a tree to ashes, whereupon Kasyapa demonstrated his own power to bring the tree back to life. Then Takshaka promised that, if Kasyapa turned back and did not cure the king, he would give him more money than the king would give him if he did cure him. Kasyapa was impressed by this, and, telling himself that the king was fated to die that day in any case, he turned back.

Takshaka then had some of his snakes, disguised as ascetics, bring Parikshit a basket of fruit; as Parikshit was about to eat a piece of this fruit, he saw a small worm there. Laughing, Parikshit picked it up and placed it on his neck and said, "The sun has set and I am no longer in danger from snake poison; let this worm stand for Takshaka and bite me, so that the Brahmin who cursed me will not prove a liar!" He was still laughing when Takshaka coiled around him and killed him. As the ministers fled,

they saw Takshaka streak away through the sky and the tree
house go up in flames from the virulent poison. Parikshit's son
Janamejaya, still a child, was anointed as king.[39]

The snake sacrifice has at least three causes: the curse of Kadru is the
more distant cause, the death of Parikshit is the central cause, and Uttanka's inciting of Janamejaya is the proximate cause. We have seen the
first and second links in the chain, and will consider the episode of
Uttanka below. Parikshit is a symbol of survival, but a grim symbol
indeed. The text seems most concerned here with ways in which Parikshit's curse might have been averted but wasn't—just as the *Mahabharata*
as a whole is concerned with ways that the war might have been averted
but wasn't. Parikshit's complicity in his own death is quite clear: he was
wrong to mock the Brahmin in the first place and wrong to mock the
Brahmin's curse later by laughing at the tiny worm. The turning point
for the fate of Parikshit is the encounter between Takshaka and a man
named Kasyapa who is a descendant of the Kasyapa who was married
to Kadru and given the power to avert snakebite (right after Kadru was
given the power to curse her sons to be burnt in Janamejaya's sacrifice).
The burning and revival of the tree that stands for Parikshit and his
tree house is a recapitulation of the circumstances of Parikshit's birth
and revival, but not, as Kasyapa intends it to be, a prediction of Parikshit's death and revival.

The bribery of Kasyapa by Takshaka is a sticky point; when the story
of Parikshit's death is retold to Janamejaya, Janamejaya says, "I would
like to know exactly what was said between Takshaka and Kasyapa.
Surely the forest was empty; were there any eyewitnesses? If I can hear
the exact conversation, I will set out to kill all the snakes." The ministers then tell him, "There just happened to be a man who had climbed
up into a tree, looking for kindling wood; that was the tree that Takshaka
burnt and Kasyapa revived, and the man was burnt and revived along
with them. Unseen by them, he heard them talk, and then he came and
told it all here in the city."[40] This final bit of evidence infuriates Janamejaya, the more so as in the eyewitness account Kasyapa does not even
justify himself with the thought that the king is fated to die anyway; he
just accepts the bribe, which makes both him and Takshaka more cul-

pable and direct factors in the death of Parikshit than they are in the version told directly by the *Mahabharata* bard.

This episode may provide us with a clue about the origins of these putatively "interpolated" snaky passages. The story of Parikshit bears a striking resemblance to many folktales, of which perhaps the most famous is the tale of Behula in *The Triumph of the Snake Goddess*. So, too, other folk stories about people saved from snake-bite are often used as charms to save the listeners from snakebite. It may well be that stories of this type, which surely must have been current in the oral literature of India from a time long before the recension of the *Mahabharata,* are the source of some of the snake episodes in the *Adi Parvan.*[41] But it took the vision of the epic poet to see why and how these stories were relevant to the great battle of the Bharatas.

RURU'S SNAKEBITTEN BRIDE

Another episode in this series is connected to our story more by its themes than by its rather loose bonds with our dramatis personae:

The sage Ruru fell in love with a beautiful girl named Pramadvara and asked her father for her hand in marriage. A few days before the wedding, Pramadvara was bitten by a snake and died of the venom. Ruru begged the gods to revive her, and they agreed to do so if Ruru would give her half of his own life span. He did this, but he also swore an oath to destroy all the snakes. Whenever he saw a snake he would grab a club and beat it to death.

One day he came across an old lizard and began to strike it, but the lizard pointed out that, though he was a reptile, he did not bite people: "Lizards share the shortcomings of snakes but have separate uses; we share their sorrows, but we have our own joys." Ruru was frightened, thinking that the lizard was a seer, and he asked him who he was. The lizard replied, "I was once a seer named Ruru, and I had a Brahmin friend named Khagama ['Sky-Goer' or 'Bird']. One day when I was still a child and was playing with him, I made a snake out of straw and frightened him with it when he was performing a fire sacrifice. He fainted, and when he regained consciousness he cursed me to become a reptile, but to regain my true form when I met a man named Ruru. Now, let me tell you that it is not right for a Brahmin like you to kill. Killing is the job of a king, like Janamejaya, who destroyed the snakes at his snake sacrifice, while it was a Brahmin, named Astika, who rescued the frightened snakes." Intrigued by this story, Ruru went home and asked his father to tell him the story of Janamejaya's snake sacrifice.[42]

The story of Ruru is told as part of the extended preface to the tale of Parikshit. As usual, there is a rather loose official thread to tie the story to the central theme: at the end of the episode, we discover that the tale of Ruru is part (a nonessential part) of the story of the telling of the *Mahabharata*. (And it is an anachronistic telling: Ruru is an ancient ancestor of Parikshit who nevertheless tells the story of Janamejaya, which will not happen for several generations!) But the tale of Ruru is more closely related to the story of Parikshit through its symbolic themes: death and resurrection from snakebite, the fight between a snake and someone named "Bird," the artificial snake that leads to the creation of a real snake (just as the harmless worm turned into Takshaka), the auspicious meeting between two people with the same name, and the inauspicious presence of a snake at a fire offering.

The lizard's sermon is reminiscent of the sermon of the sage upon whom Parikshit drapes the snake: it is all right for kings (but not Brahmins) to commit certain violent acts. Finally, there is the liminality of the lizard, who is a reptile but not a snake, as he himself eloquently points out; he is a mediator between good reptiles and bad reptiles. In this he is a heightened form of the snakes themselves, who are, as we have seen, liminally attached/detached to the categories of gods, demons, and men. Like the snakes who refuse to commit the dishonest act of dyeing the horse's tail black, the lizard is unjustly punished at first but ultimately rescued from that punishment.

THE BIRTH OF ASTIKA

The story of Astika is central both to the plot and to the moral issues associated with snakes:

> When Vasuki first discovered that the snakes had been cursed to be sacrificed, he learned from Brahma that the one who would put an end to the sacrifice would be a son born to Jaratkaru and to Vasuki's sister, who was also named Jaratkaru. Therefore Vasuki guarded his sister and kept her safe for the sage Jaratkaru.[43] Jaratkaru had vowed never to marry, but his dead ancestors needed the oblations that the descendants of Jaratkaru would offer to them. So, against his better judgment, he promised to marry, but only if he met a virgin with the same name, Jaratkaru. One day he met the serpent Vasuki, who offered him his sister, who happened to be named Jaratkaru.[44] Shortly after the woman Jaratkaru had conceived a child by the sage Jaratkaru, he picked a quarrel with her and threw her out; she ran back to her brother, Vasuki, and gave birth to her child there. The child was Astika.[45]

The story of the snake sacrifice begins in the *Mahabharata* not with the circumstances that led to the attempt to kill the snakes but with the circumstances that led to the rescue of the snakes. Indeed, the story as a whole is known as the "Book of Astika" (1.13–53), not the story of Janamejaya, though that book actually begins after the narration of the birth of Astika (a story that is retold in three different places).

Jaratkaru's unwillingness to marry leads him to suggest a condition that he assumes will in fact prove insuperable (just as demons often choose conditions for their death that they hope cannot possibly be met): he wants to marry a mirror image of himself, a girl with his name. When he finds that Vasuki's sister just happens to be named Jaratkaru, he is forced to keep his promise. (We have already seen a similarly striking coincidence in the prediction that someone named Ruru will be released from his curse by someone named Ruru.) The unlikelihood of finding such a girl is mocked in the epic; when the bard says that the girl was named Jaratkaru, his interlocutor bursts out laughing and says, "How fitting!"[46] To get out of his promise, Jaratkaru manufactures an excuse to leave his wife. But he has already done both of his duties: he has provided an heir for his ancestors and a savior for the snakes.

Jaratkaru (f.) lives on in the cult of Manasa. In Vipradasa's version of the story,[47] Manasa is called Jaratkaru and also marries a sage named Jaratkaru, to whom she bears a son named Astika before her husband abandons her. But this time a reason is given for his desertion: On the wedding night, Manasa puts on all of her best serpents and lies down beside Jaratkaru, who is paralyzed with fear of the snakes and lies beside her wide awake. Then Chandika creeps into the room and throws a frog among the snakes, who begin to hiss and roar; Jaratkaru jumps up and runs away, declaring that he is abandoning Manasa because he cannot overcome his terror of snakes.[48]

In the *Mahabharata,* Jaratkaru (m.) marries a naga princess, and so do other men in the *Mahabharata*—Arjuna marries Ulupi.[49] In later Indian literature, the sage Kusha marries the *nagi* Kumudvati,[50] and the exiled prince Brahmadatta marries a *nagi* who is a widow, driven by her lust to seek a mortal man for her second husband.[51] In Indian history, too, a number of royal dynasties claim descent from naga princesses, including kings of Kashmir and Manipur, of Chutia Nagpur, and dynasties of Cholas and Pallavas.[52] No matter whether they are regarded as mythical or historical, all of these naga women are alike: "they are of royal heritage; they are fabulously beautiful and sexually irresistible; they have healthy sexual appetites and are often driven to find a mortal man in order to satisfy these cravings; and they are forever fertile, often giving birth to a host of sons."[53]

THE CURSE OF THE DOGS

The episode of the dogs adds another piece of the puzzle:

> When Janamejaya and his brothers were performing a sacrifice, a dog, a son of the bitch Sarama, came near. The brothers beat the dog, who ran howling back to his mother and told her that they had beaten him though he had neither looked at nor

licked the offerings. Sarama then went to the sacrificial grounds and said to Janamejaya, "Since you beat my son when he had not done anything wrong, you will suffer an unseen danger."

Janamejaya then sought a priest who could avert the evil that he had incurred, and one day while he was hunting he came upon a sage named Somashravas who had grown in the womb of a snake woman who had drunk a man's seed. Janamejaya then brought the sage back to his brothers and told them to do whatever Somashravas asked them to do to avert the evil of the curse.[54]

On the narrative level, this episode merely tells how it came to pass that Janamejaya employed a sage very much like Astika and how that sage performed a sacrifice on behalf of Janamejaya. But the sage is a slightly distorted twin or mirror image of Astika, as is evident from the peculiarities of his birth: like Astika, he was born from the seed of a sage shed in the womb of a snake woman. Unlike Astika, however, who thwarts Janamejaya's sacrifice, this sage is engaged by Janamejaya and successfully completes a sacrifice for him. The "unseen evil" from which this sacrifice saves Janamejaya is not specified, but whatever it was, it failed to save him from the evil of the death of his father from snakebite or the evil of the subsequent snake sacrifice.

UTTANKA AND THE EARRINGS

Another link in the chain is provided by the bizarre tale of Uttanka:

One day when the sage Veda was absent, his wife asked Uttanka to sleep with her during her fertile period; Uttanka refused, and though Veda praised him for this when he returned, the wife set him a difficult task: she asked him to bring her the earrings that belonged to King Paushya's queen. When Uttanka asked the queen for her earrings, she gave them to him willingly, but she warned him that Takshaka, king of the snakes, wanted the earrings too. Uttanka assured her that Takshaka could not overcome him.

Uttanka set out with the earrings, but on the way he saw a naked beggar, a polluting sight; hastily Uttanka put the earrings down and went for water to purify himself, at which the beggar took the earrings and ran away; when Uttanka grabbed him, the beggar assumed his true form, Takshaka, and entered a chasm that had suddenly opened up in the ground. Uttanka followed him down into the realm of the snakes. After many adventures, Takshaka gave the earrings to Uttanka, who returned to Veda's hermitage just in time to avoid the curse of Veda's wife.

Veda then dismissed Uttanka. But Uttanka was still furious with Takshaka, and he went to Hastinapura, where he met Janamejaya. He told Janamejaya that it was Takshaka who had killed his father, Parikshit, and that it was therefore the duty of Janamejaya to burn Takshaka as an offering at a great snake sacrifice in order to avenge the death of Parikshit—and also, incidentally, to do a favor for Uttanka, giving him revenge for having been robbed by Takshaka.[55]

This story gives yet another explanation of Janamejaya's decision to undertake the snake sacrifice (after the curse of Kadru and the death of Parikshit—and, perhaps, the curse of Sarama). Uttanka's arrival at Janamejaya's palace mediates between Janamejaya's encounters with two other Brahmins: Somashravas (who performs a horse sacrifice for him) and Astika (who prevents his snake sacrifice). The information about Parikshit that Uttanka gives Janamejaya is quite superfluous, since any of his ministers could have told him the same thing; nor does Janamejaya really need the knowledge of Takshaka's relatively minor offense against Uttanka to drive him (Hamlet-like) to avenge Takshaka's murder of Janamejaya's father. We can best understand the role of this encounter as yet another instance of the narrative that is told in order to explain the telling of the *Mahabharata* war rather than the doing of that war.

In the course of his many adventures in the underworld, Uttanka meets the god Indra mounted on a snake named Airavata. Now, Airavata is usually the name of the elephant that Indra rides upon; but since the Sanskrit word *naga* means both snake and elephant (probably because of the serpentine trunk), it seems likely that the author chose the snakier of the two alternative meanings for this snaky story. The serpentine identity of Airavata is, in any case, confirmed a few lines later, when Uttanka, upon arriving in the underworld of snakes, sings a hymn of praise that begins with a flattering description of Airavata as the lord of snakes and only then goes on to praise Takshaka.[56]

JANAMEJAYA'S SNAKE SACRIFICE

We come at last to the main act, center stage, the snake sacrifice:

When Janamejaya heard the story of his father's death, he vowed to undertake a great snake sacrifice. Even before the sacrifice began, there was an evil omen portending that it would not be concluded; therefore the king ordered that no one who was not known to him should be allowed to enter. The priests put on their black robes and began to drop the terrified snakes into the fire; the snakes darted and hissed and wildly coiled about, screaming horribly. Some were as small as mice, some as big as bull elephants; all of them died powerless, punished by their mother's curse.

As soon as Takshaka learned of the sacrifice, he sought protection with Indra, who granted him refuge. But Vasuki told his sister Jaratkaru to summon her son Astika; at his request, she told him the story of the quarrel between Kadru and Vinata, and Astika promised Vasuki that he would save him and the other snakes. Astika went to Janamejaya's sacrificial ground, but the guards did not let him enter. Then he recited a long poem in praise of Janamejaya, and Janamejaya was so pleased that he not only let him in but was about to offer him a boon. The priests, however, reminded him that, though the sacrifice was almost over, Takshaka had not yet been sacrificed; he was still lurking in Indra's palace.

The priests increased their incantations, and just as Takshaka was about to fall into the fire, Astika demanded his boon: that the sacrifice be stopped. "Stay there," he said to Takshaka, who hovered in the air, caught between the incantations of the priests and the incantations of Astika, until Janamejaya said, "Let the sacrifice end." The king gave Astika many gifts and sent him home, saying, "You must come back when I have my horse sacrifice." Astika agreed to this, and as he went home he was greeted by the delighted snakes, who also offered him a boon. He asked them to grant that anyone who recited his story would never be in danger from snakes. And, indeed, whoever recites this Epic of Astika is never in danger from snakes.[57]

Janamejaya decides to avenge his father, just as the son of the sage mocked by Parikshit decided to avenge his father—and as Parashurama decided to avenge his father, by wiping out the race of the Kshatriyas altogether. And just as Parikshit failed to carry out his "ritual" (of protection from snakebite) because he jumped the gun, relaxing before the day was completely over, so Janamejaya fails to complete his ritual because he offers a boon to Astika before the last and most important snake—Takshaka—has been killed. Takshaka hovers in midair, caught between the black magic of the snake ritual and the white magic of Astika; in this he is the very embodiment of the liminality of the snakes.

THE BURNING OF THE KHANDAVA FOREST

A final episode forms a kind of coda or postlude to the tale of Janamejaya:

One day Agni, the god of fire, took the form of a Brahmin and came to Arjuna and Krishna. He told them that he was insatiably hungry and wished to devour the Khandava Forest, but Indra quenched the fire with rain, in order to protect his friend Takshaka, who lived there. Agni, abetted by Krishna and Arjuna, proceeded to burn the forest. Creatures by the thousands screamed in terror and were scorched; some embraced their sons or mothers or fathers, unable to leave them. Everywhere creatures writhed on the ground, with burning wings, eyes, and paws. The noise of the forest animals was like the noise made by the ocean when it was churned.

Then Indra sought to quench the fire, and a great battle ensued, in which all the gods and demons took sides. As the holocaust continued to blaze, a disembodied voice told Indra that
Takshaka was not in the forest; he had gone to the Field of the
Kurus. Hearing this Indra went away, and Agni continued to
burn the forest unopposed. Finally Agni was sated.[58]

The burning of the Khandava Forest is the final episode in the *Adi
Parvan,* an episode tied to the central story of the epic by the snake/ropes
of the mythology of Janamejaya's sacrifice. It is evident that the
burning of the Khandava Forest is a multiform not only of the great *Mahabharata* battle itself but of the snake sacrifice that is an already
transformed variant of the ritual battle. Agni's insatiable hunger (an
incidental mockery of the hunger of a Brahmin) drives him to devour
not only the trees in the forest (his proper food, an expanded form of the
kindling sticks of the Vedic fire) but all of the living creatures in the forest
(improper food, not a usual component of the Vedic oblation). The torment of the creatures in their death throes in the forest fire echoes the
torment of the snakes in Janamejaya's fire.

The horror inspired by the vivid descriptions of these two scenes of
suffering is a vision of the shadow side of the Vedic ritual and the ritual
of battle. But more than that: Agni functions in the Khandava Forest as
the doomsday fire that sweeps all before him. The death of the creatures
in the great forest fire is an inversion of their birth in the churning of
the ocean, with which the conflagration is explicitly contrasted.

Takshaka is a key figure in both the sacrifice and the conflagration:
at first, Indra protects him from the fire, as he protects him from Janamejaya. Then, however, there is a new twist: Takshaka turns out not to
be in the forest at all; he has gone to that other scene of doomsday—the
Field of the Kurus, where the great battle has taken place. His absence
releases Indra from his one reason for protecting the forest, and almost
everyone else in it is killed.

The rescuing of the snakes from Janamejaya's sacrificial fire and from
the Khandava fire is vividly echoed in another episode later in the
Mahabharata. When King Nala rescues a tiny snake from a forest
fire, the snake turns into the great serpent Karkotaka, whose bite
transforms Nala benignly, enabling him to live safely in disguise.[59] The

transformation of the tiny snake into Karkotaka further echoes the metamorphosis of Takshaka from a tiny worm to a big snake who kills Parikshit. Karkotaka's bite *(damsha)* is effective only after Nala takes ten *(dasha)* steps—the same pun that gave the serpents their immortality in the *Tandya Brahmana*. There is no bottom to Indian intertextuality; it's snakes all the way down.

KRISHNA AND KALIYA

One episode embedded in the Janamejaya cycle spills over into later Hindu snake mythology. It takes place in the course of the conflict between Kadru and Vinata:

> One day, Kadru commanded Vinata to take her and the snakes to the island of Ramaniyaka; Vinata asked Garuda to help her. So Garuda carried Kadru and the other snakes toward Ramaniyaka; as they flew near the sun, the snakes fainted with the heat, but Kadru prayed to Indra, who sent rain that refreshed the snakes. After they had arrived on Ramaniyaka and enjoyed themselves on the island, Kadru asked Garuda to take them to another island.[60]

As in the Khandava Forest, the post-Vedic Indra rains on the snakes. Transporting the snakes to the Ramaniyaka island is a device intended not only to give them a pleasant vacation (flight included), but a way of dealing with an evil that, though it cannot be destroyed, can at least be moved out of the way, if only for a while. The *Bhagavata Purana*, in the tenth century C.E., tells a story in which Krishna similarly transports another group of snakes to the similarly named Ramanaka island:

> At the beginning of each month, all the serpents used to receive an offering under a tree, to prevent unpleasantness; this was agreed long ago by the people in the realm of the snakes. And each of the serpents, to protect himself, would give a portion of this offering to Garuda at the beginning of each lunar fortnight. But

Kaliya, the son of Kadru, was full of pride because of the virulence of his poison, and he disregarded Garuda and ate the offering himself. When Garuda learned of this he attacked Kaliya, who fought back with his poison and fangs, raising his many heads with their hideous tongues and hisses and fierce eyes. But Garuda struck Kaliya with his left wing, and so injured him that Kaliya went and hid in a pool in the river Kalindi. For Kaliya knew, though no other serpent did, that Garuda could not enter that pool because of a previous curse for eating fish there that were protected by a powerful sage.

One day, the child Krishna went to play in that pool in the Kalindi with the little boys who were his friends. As the serpent's poison polluted the water, and people and cows that drank it or even touched it died, Krishna revived them. But realizing that the fire of Kaliya's poison was making those waters boil, Krishna resolved to subdue him. He plunged into the pool and danced on the cobra's many heads until he surrendered. But Kaliya's wives begged Krishna not to widow them, and Kaliya pleaded with Krishna, saying, "We are evil from our birth, dark creatures whose anger endures. And it is difficult to abandon one's own nature, for it possesses people like an evil demon." Krishna did not kill the serpent, but merely banished him, with his wives, friends, and sons, to Ramanaka island in the ocean, promising him that Garuda would not eat him, now that he had been marked with Krishna's foot. And he said to Kaliya, "Whatever mortal remembers my chastisement of you and recites it at dawn and sunset, he will have no fear of you."[61]

This text describes snake worship as a kind of protection racket: "to avoid unpleasantness," people make offerings to snakes. (And, as in human protection rackets, the little snakes make protection offerings in turn to bigger snakes.) But the snakes argue that they cannot help being evil; they cannot change. And Krishna implicitly agrees; he does nothing to them but simply gets them away from his own people. After all, you can't kill death, you can simply keep it away from you.

This is perhaps the most basic attitude to snakes in India. The moral ambiguity of the snakes is an essential point; when the gods ask Brahma, the creator, why he did not stop Kadru, the mother of serpents, from cursing her own sons, he replies, "There are too many poisonous snakes. The mean, evil, virulent snakes who love to bite are the ones doomed to die, but not the law-abiding ones."[62] As soon as the snakes are cursed, one of them, Shesha ("the Remnant"), rejects his wicked brothers and performs awesome acts of asceticism. And when the gods and demons become incarnate as the heroes and villains of the *Mahabharata* conflict, Shesha is the only snake who joins them, and as a hero: he becomes incarnate as Baladeva, the brother of Krishna.[63] Shesha is eventually reabsorbed into Ananta ("Endless"), the serpent of infinity, who supports the earth[64] and, in later mythology, the god Vishnu when he sleeps on the cosmic ocean. The *Mahabharata* also makes a sharp contrast between a bad snake (Takshaka) and a good snake (Vasuki): Takshaka is branded a villain by his various nefarious deeds and cares only to save his own skin at Janamejaya's sacrifice; Vasuki is established as a good guy through his service to the gods and demons at the time of the churning of the ocean, and he is the one who takes measures to save all the other snakes at the sacrifice.[65] When the genealogies of snakes are listed, Vasuki is the author of one line and Takshaka of another,[66] but both sets are sacrificed, which seems to violate Brahma's pious intention.

NAGAS IN EARLY INDIAN BUDDHISM

Nagas are as ambivalent in Buddhism as they are in Hinduism: some begin nasty and become nice, some stay nasty, and some appear to be quite nice right from the start. The naga king Muchalinda is of this last variety:

> When the Buddha achieved enlightenment, he went to the foot of a tree and sat there for a week, experiencing the happiness of being freed from the wheel. But at that time a great black cloud arose, out of season, and for seven days there was cold, wind, and rain. Then the naga king Muchalinda came out of his palace in the tree, surrounded the body of the Buddha with his coils,

and spread his great hood above the Buddha's head, determined to keep cold, heat, wind, hot air, mosquitoes and crawling things from touching the Buddha. At the end of the week, when the sky was clear, Muchalinda unwrapped his coils from the Buddha's body, changed his appearance to that of a young man, and bowed before the Buddha.[67]

At Amaravati, the Buddha sits cross-legged on top of Muchalinda's coils,[68] and cobra hoods appear over many images of the Buddha, representing the story of Muchalinda.

Like Vritra, Muchalinda has the power to hold back waters. But nagas in post-Vedic India generally bring rain and cause waters to flow. Muchalinda here reverts to the Vedic model, as the Buddha, like Indra, usurps the naga's powers. For the Buddha is depicted—at Bharhut, Gandhara, Ajanta, Sarnath, and other shrines—with streams of water flowing from his body, and Buddhist saints are renowned as rainmakers.[69]

Another naga tries, in vain, to become better:

> There was a naga who was ashamed, troubled, and disgusted to have been born a naga. He assumed the form of a young man and went to the monks, asking to become a monk. The monks ordained him and he lived with another monk in a monastery set apart from the other monks. One night, the naga fell asleep and thus resumed his true shape, filling the entire monastery, with his coils sticking out of the windows. Then the Buddha said to the monks, "A naga reveals his true form when he indulges in sexual intercourse and when he falls asleep. Nagas are not capable of understanding the dharma or engaging in the discipline. They must not be ordained."[70]

The number of nagas who sought ordination in actual life must have been very few indeed; but we may read this text as a statement that naga worshippers may not become Buddhists. Buddhists, however, can become, in some ways, nagas. Richard Gombrich has noted that candidates for Buddhist ordination arrange cloths over their heads to resemble a cobra's hood and are called nagas.[71] And it is said that people who stay on the Buddhist path never go to hell or become reborn as animals; they become nagas.[72]

Here again the Buddhists are usurping the territory of the sacred snakes. For, like Hindu snakes, Buddhist snakes are morally complex, sometimes enemies, sometimes allies.

THE AMBIVALENT GODDESS

Let me conclude with a consideration of the ambivalence of Manasa. Edward Cameron Dimock and A. K. Ramanujan have demonstrated how many characteristics Manasa shares with other snaky and nonsnaky goddesses of India.[73] She shares names with the great goddesses Sarasvati, Lakshmi, and Parvati/Chandi. Like Lakshmi and Parvati, in particular, she has the characteristics of "regeneration, association with water and the lotus, the swan and the color white," qualities of goddesses that women worship "for fertility, for husband-finding and the protection of husbands." With Chandi, in particular, she shares "not only terror and the desire for worship, but small details such as metamorphosis into an insect."[74] But unique to Manasa is "the complex of associations snake-gold-pot, and that of death by bite or glance and revival by water fertility."[75] Now, these are precisely the qualities that we have found diffused throughout the mythology of Indian snakes in general and nagas in particular. Dimock and Ramanujan remark upon this too, in a passage so rich in insights for our present project that it is well worth citing at some length:

> Some of the sources of Manasa's snake traits may be found in the Sanskritic tradition; there is sufficient warrant for it also in folklore. Beliefs are attested for snakes guarding treasure, usually in pots, everywhere from South Indian family histories to phrases that occur in Dravidian languages to mean "guard like that of snakes" (sarpakaval) to the Dragon of the Golden Fleece. The association of snake and pot is perhaps a very immediate one: it seems likely that snakes were caught and imprisoned in pots; there is a Tamilian belief that snakes seek out pots in the

summertime because they are cool. One may then speculate
about the possible relationships between these facts and the very
ancient beliefs in the pot of poison and the pot of soma, the pan-
acea. There is no reason to speak further about the well-attested
relationship of snakes to women-fertility-vegetation.

Many of the snaky aspects of Manasa are taken not from goddesses
but from her father, Shiva: "Like Shiva, she is the deity of destruction
and snakes; . . . she has Shiva's eye of death. . . . The inescapable conclusion is that in her triumph over the Shaivite gods of Bengal, Manasa
assumed their characteristics."[76] We have noted how the Vedic people
assimilated the snake worship of their enemies, turning a sacrifice *by*
snakes into a sacrifice *of* snakes; and how the Buddhists assimilated
the power to control rain that had been the possession of the naga
worshippers whom they supplanted. Following in their footsteps, the
worshippers of Manasa in Bengal tell how she absorbed the snaky
male gods of earlier Hinduism, as well as the whole, rich lore of the
nagas and *nagis*.

   As the story of Manasa was told and retold in Bengal over the centuries, the unbroken oral tradition touched down from time to time in a
series of texts preserved in writing. And these written versions were then
read aloud on both sacred and secular occasions, renourishing the oral
traditions from which they were originally derived. After a while, it became impossible to identify precisely which elements were "oral" and
which were "written." Individual storytellers would blend together several different versions to make their own original composition, and that
composition, in turn, would bleed back into other oral and written versions. This new translation by Kaiser Haq reflects the permeable boundaries (to use A. K. Ramanujan's term[77]) between the various retellings
of the story, picking one piece from here, another from there, just as a
traditional storyteller would do.

   Kaiser Haq's version of the tale of Manasa is the very opposite of a
critical edition; one might call it an uncritical edition. The attempt to
winnow out all the "accretions" in order to expose the skeleton of the
"original" (or "Ur" or "basic") version of the *Mahabharata* resulted in a
text that is no one's text, merely a scholarly construct that allows us to

trace certain manuscript traditions.[78] The opposite impulse, to put *back in* the pieces that have been dropped out of one version or another, is one that better approximates the way that individual audiences inhabit the cultural tradition. And this impulse, the uncritical edition, is what Kaiser Haq has achieved in this remarkable translation.

PROLOGUE

THE FEAR AND FASCINATION INSPIRED by snakes have given rise to colorful myths and legends and snake cults across cultures. South Asia, where snakes probably outnumbered humans until recent times, has been particularly fertile ground for snake cults. The most significant of these, centering on the snake goddess Manasa, took shape in the medieval era in Indian history. Manasa's constituency is the whole of eastern South Asia: present-day Bangladesh, Paschimbanga (West Bengal), Tripura, Assam, Meghalaya, Bihar, Jharkhand, Orissa. It is a vast geocultural area, taking up roughly a third of the subcontinent. The largest group of Manasa-related texts comprises verse narratives in Bengali, one of the major languages of South Asia.

Like other North Indian vernaculars, Bengali evolved out of Sanskrit a thousand years ago. Old Bengali emerged from roughly the tenth to the twelfth century C.E. and bequeathed one extant classic, the *Charyapadas,* mystical lyrics composed by Buddhist *siddhas,* or wise men; they are comparable to Old English in terms of accessibility to today's common reader. In the context of the history of Bengal, the equivalent of the Norman invasion was the Muslim irruption, inaugurated by Bakhtiyar Khalji's entry into Nudiya, capital of the Sena empire, in 1204.

The next two centuries were extremely unsettled and produced nothing of literary interest in Bengali. Stability returned with the founding in 1342 by Ilyas Shah of an independent Bengal sultanate, which accommodated the Hindu elite within the ruling classes; this remained a trait of Muslim rule as long as it lasted in the region. The cultural concomitant was perhaps more momentous. Muslim architecture incorporated indigenous Hindu and Buddhist influences;[1] Persian, the language of the Muslim conquerors, impacted on the vernacular to give rise to the Bengali language as we know it:[2] the parallel with the rise of Middle English under Norman influence is obvious.

The fifteenth and early sixteenth centuries, particularly during the reign of Husain Shah (1493–1519) and his son Nusrat Shah (1519–1532), witnessed an unprecedented literary efflorescence. Religio-mystical lyrics and verse narratives proliferated in a Bengali that the modern common reader can access with the help of cribs and a little will power. The key figure in the development of a devotional mystic—or Bhakti—tradition in Bengal was Sri Chaitanya (1486–1533), whose teachings inspired a Vaishnava renaissance throughout eastern India. Its finest literary manifestation is in the lyrics in Brajabuli dialect by Vidyapati, Chandidasa, and others.[3] Vaishnava mysticism and Sufi Islam fruitfully influenced each other, and, as Edward Dimock has shown, in time fostered the living tradition of the Bauls (members of the Bengali cult of mystic minstrels).[4]

The verse narratives, sharing the common label *panchali,* which simply means "tale," may be divided into two categories, the Puranic and the non-Puranic, the canonical and the noncanonical. The canonical tales deal with the major deities worshipped by the orthodox, and include vernacular versions of the epics, like *The Ramayana* of Krittibas (1420) or *The Mahabharata* of Kashiram Das (ca. 1643). The noncanonical tales are folkloric, emanating from the subaltern sections of society, and include popular romances, such as those collectively known as the *Mymensingh Geetika* ("The Mymensingh Ballads") from the eighteenth century, Saiyid Sultan's syncretistic epic *Nabibangsa* ("The Genealogy of the Prophet") from the late sixteenth century, various narratives inspired by the Perso-Arabic tradition, the syncretistic tales about Satya Pir from the eighteenth and nineteenth centuries, a useful selection of which has been translated by Tony Stewart under the title *Fabulous Females and Peerless Pirs*,[5] and the various versions of the legends about non-Puranic deities like Manasa.

The particular poetic mode to which the Manasa tales belong is the *mangalkavya,* which means (narrative) poetry *(kavya)* written and recited to celebrate deities and obtain their blessings *(mangal).* Clinton B. Seely in his essay "Secular and Sacred Legitimation in Bharatcandra Ray's *Annada Mangal* (1732 CE)," astutely points out that besides being popular entertainment, these long poems through their eulogy of "one or another Hindu deity," further "the process of legitimation, both within the narrative world and in the world outside the narrative," and "are a means by which a particular deity establishes power over humans as well as rank vis-à-vis other deities"; from this one can infer "that deities, like people, are political creatures and must compete for status and respect."[6] Seely successfully analyzes the *Annada Mangal* in terms of Propp's morphology of folktales, thus suggesting the scope for further research along these lines. In another essay, "Say It with Structure: Tagore and *Mangal Kavya,*" he shows that Rabindranath Tagore's dance drama *Tasher Desh* ("Land of Cards") is similar to *mangalkavyas* in structure and didactic intent.[7] This is a significant example of the persistence of a precolonial literary form in modern times.

Mangalkavyas are superficially similar to the Puranas, but differ in paying more attention to social reality. Hence it is not surprising that historians have found them of particular interest. David L. Curley, for instance, in his book *Poetry and History,*[8] has shown how a close reading of a single text, Mukundaram's *Chandimangal* (1590), can yield a many-layered historical portrait. Kumkum Chatterjee, in her essay "Goddess Encounters: Mughals, Monsters and the Goddess in Bengal," examines two versions of the *Chandimangal* and Bharatchandra Ray's *Annadamangal* to trace changing perceptions of the Mughals among Bengali Hindus from the seventeenth to the eighteenth century.[9] Another historian who has made significant use of *mangalkavyas,* as we shall see in due course, is Richard Eaton.

Mangalkavyas emerged in Bengal after the Muslim invasion, at a time of dramatic sociopolitical change, and hence their precise sociohistorical location needs to be noted. Following several centuries of Buddhist rule under the Palas, the Hindu Senas (eleventh and twelfth centuries c.e.) vigorously promoted Brahminism, or orthodox Hinduism. Then came the Muslims. The *mangalkavyas* emerge from the indigenous religious cults of the Bengalis as these engage in a double dialectics, with Brahminism, on the one hand, and on the other with the politically dominant Muslims.

The *mangalkavyas* above all else are the poetic record of the compromise or synthesis of the opposed cultural formations. The Indo-Aryan orthodoxy at the time of the Muslim conquest accorded a central position to Shiva and Shakti, representing respectively the male and female principles of divinity, but the way they were viewed underwent rapid indigenization. Asutosh Bhattacarya in his detailed Bengali history of *mangalkavyas* in the language[10] describes how the austere, ascetic Indo-Aryan Shiva, under the influence of Jain, Buddhist, and the non-Aryan Natha cults, morphed into a farmer-god with spectacularly loose habits and was subsequently commemorated in several *Shivamangal* poems. Similarly, the conception of Shakti, equated earlier with Durga, became identified with Chandi, originally a local forest deity, and the heroine of Mukundaram's *Chandimangal* (1590). Numerous *mangalkavyas* celebrate minor local deities like Sasthi, goddess of childbirth, or Sitala, goddess of smallpox, bringing them into alignment with the great deities of the Hindu pantheon. An excellent example of a *mangalkavya* striking a compromise between Hindu and Muslim powers is the *Raymangala* (1686) in which Dakshin Ray ("King of the South") and Badi Gazi Khan, a Muslim adventurer, battle for control of the tiger-infested Sundarbans. The result is a stalemate, which is resolved through the mediation of a personage who is half Krishna and half Prophet Muhammad. The contenders agree to coexist peacefully and jointly rule over the forest. Some versions of the Manasa legends too, as we shall see, deal with the conflict with the new Muslim rulers as a kind of subplot.

THE MANASA CANON

The earliest writer of a *mangalkavya* about Manasa was one Kana Haridatta, who flourished in the Barisal district of present-day Bangladesh sometime before the fifteenth century, but nothing remains of his work save a few tiny fragments. Interestingly, one of these has been incorporated into other versions, including Vijaya Gupta's *Manasamangal*, also known as *Padmapuran* (1494). It purports to be the oldest complete version of the story but has accumulated so many interpolations that it is impossible to ascribe it to him in its entirety. However, it is reasonable to believe that Vijaya Gupta did produce most of the extant text. Vipradasa's *Manasa-vijaya* (1495) seems to have gathered fewer interpolations, though the language on the whole has undergone noticeable evolution by the time the extant manuscripts were produced. Such textual problems, needless to say, are endemic to precolonial Bengali writings. Both Vipradasa and Vijaya Gupta acknowledge Husain Shah as the supreme ruler of the land, an obvious indication of their historical situation and evidence perhaps of royal encouragement, if not direct patronage, of literary efforts in the vernacular.

Sukumar Sen has usefully categorized the Bengali Manasa texts on a regional basis, dividing them, first, into the northern and southern versions. The northern version is subdivided into the North Bengal (including Kamrup in western Meghalaya) and Bihar versions, the latter being in Hindi or Bhojpuri. The southern version is subdivided into the West Bengal and East Bengal versions. Since we are concerned with the versions in Bengali, we may modify this categorization and identify three versions: the North Bengal, the West Bengal and the East Bengal versions.

Vipradasa, who hailed from the 24 Parganas district, was the oldest of the Manasa poets from West Bengal. He was followed by the seventeenth-century poet Visnu Pala and several poets whose works do not exist in their entirety, among them three known by the name Kshemananda. The most important of the North Bengal group was the seventeenth-century poet Tantrabibhuti, who was closely followed in content by Jagatjivana Ghosal. It is in East Bengal that the Manasa cult and its accompanying texts have enjoyed the greatest popularity. As Sukumar Sen notes: "The worship of the goddess of snakes [in East Bengal] has been as popular as almost an item of domestic routine, and so verses or ballads recounting the greatness of the goddess obtained a familiarity unknown in the western part of the country. This is why the names of writers (and singers) of *Manasamangala* in East Bengal are legion and why no work, neither a single manuscript nor a single published volume, bears less than half a dozen signatures."[11] The singers of the legends would often add their names to the text even if they hadn't contributed anything to its content, and this might lead the modern reader to think it was the work of more poets than was actually the case. There is, however, a consensus in identifying the significant poets of this group. Leaving aside Kana Haridatta, who is little more than a name, the earliest of the East Bengal poets was Vijaya Gupta, whose version may well be the most popular so far. Of comparable fame is the seventeenth-century version of Narayan Dev, which is equally popular in East Bengal and Assam and Meghalaya.

A recent addition of great significance to the East Bengal canon of Manasa texts is that of Ray Binod, the nom de plume of one Ram Binod. The latter name is mentioned in Sukumar Sen's history of Bengali literature in a long list of East Bengali writers of Manasa texts, but there is no discussion of his work—understandably, because the work was not available until all the extant manuscripts were collated and edited by Muhammad Shahjahan Mian and published in 1993 as *Padmapuran*. Mian has also published a useful study in Bengali, placing Ray Binod in historical and literary context.[12] Mian describes him as a sixteenth-century poet but cites 1631 as the latest likely date of composition of his poem. Since Ray Binod came after Narayan Dev, the later date is likely to be a closer estimate.

Besides the three regional groups already mentioned, Sukumar Sen identifies a group of six "modern" Manasa poets. They belong to the nineteenth century, by which time Bengali culture had undergone a sea change under the impact of British colonialism. Their works evince the durability of the traditional culture of the region. At least one of these poems, the *Padmapuran* of Radhanath Raychaudhuri of Sylhet, has gained notable popularity with readers, if the ready availability of a cheap edition is any indication. Another popular edition is the *Baishkobi Padmapuran* ("*Padmapuran* by Twenty-Two Poets"), a compilation of episodes by divers hands.

The various titles given to the Manasa stories deserve some comment. Undoubtedly they are all *mangalkavyas*, though the suffix *mangal* isn't used in all of them. Vipradasa's poem, we have seen, is titled *Manasavijaya*. There has been some speculation as to whether a *vijaya* is a distinct poetic mode, but the consensus is that it is simply a synonym for *mangalkavya.* Most of the East Bengal versions are titled *Padmapuran,* Padma or Padmavati being another name for Manasa because she was conceived in a lotus *(padma)* garden. But why *puran?* Since a Purana is a canonical Sanskrit mythological tale, using it in the title can be seen as an attempt to gain respectability for a subaltern narrative. The eighteenth-century Manasa tale by Sitaram Das is titled *Kamala-mangal* or *Kamala-kirtana,* Kamala being another of Manasa's names. Rasik Misra called his poem *Jagati-mangal,* after yet another name of the goddess.

PUTTING TOGETHER A COMPOSITE VERSION

My version is a composite prose retelling of the Manasa legends, rather than a complete rendering of a single text, which is the more common scholarly practice; and hence a word of justification and a brief explanation of the way it has been put together are in order.

If a scholar-translator were to choose a single text from a corpus to work on, it would presumably be one that stood out for literary merit, originality, or authenticity. How far such criteria would be applicable across the board is open to question. Faced with the *Chandimangal* texts a likely choice would be Mukundaram's version, because the critical consensus is that it is the most impressive long poem from precolonial Bengal. But it is not the first, nor can it be called the most authentic. Indeed, the concept of authenticity is of little use in folk literature, unless one is dealing with a fraudster like James Macpherson. The problems proliferate in the Manasa corpus. Vijaya Gupta, Vipradasa, Tantrabibhuti, and Narayan Dev, and perhaps a few of the others, could all claim to be poets of singular merit. But translating one of them would mean leaving out many interesting episodes or narrative elements that occur in the other versions. Besides, the account given above of the textual problems relating to the Manasa texts clearly shows that they have changed over time, accumulating the imprint of a number of authors; in other words, they are composite texts. Why not extend the principle of "compositeness" to attain greater comprehensiveness in the narrative?

Then comes the question of the literary medium: should it be prose or verse as in the original? Prose versions are more reader friendly and also avoid the hazard of churning out imperfect verse renditions. The point I am trying to make will become clearer if we pause to consider the technical aspects of the poems. Characteristically, *mangalkavyas* are split into two segments, a shorter *devakhanda* or *devaparba* (part set in the realm of the gods) and a longer *martyakhanda* or *martaparba* (part set in the mundane realm). In the Manasa stories the latter part is designated *banikparba* (part set in the realm of the merchant). The Bengali texts are in alternating sections in the *payar* and the *lachari* or *tripadi* meters. The first is like the English heroic couplet, with rhyming end-stopped lines and a marked caesura. By way of an example, here is the opening *payar* in Raychaudhuri's version:

> shuno shuno sharbajon karo abodhan|
> srishtir utpatti shuno apurbo akhyan||

A rough-and-ready translation into a heroic couplet (but I can manage only a half rhyme, I'm afraid) would be:

> O hear ye everyone, and hear it well,
> Hear how Creation began, a wondrous tale.

The *tripadi* verses comprise triplets, rhyming *aab, ccb, dde, ffe,* and so on. Each triplet is like a three-ply end-stopped syntactic unit arranged with the first two phrases on two sides of one line and the third phrase centered in the next line. Here is an example, again from Raychaudhuri:

> bidhi boley, harihar,   kiba kori atopar,
>   srishti hetu pranantah hoilo|
> jake srishti kori tay,   sangsar chhariya jay,
>   ki upay kori ami balo||

A rough translation, but this time in prose and hence devoid of the tripping quality of the original, would be: "Brahma said to Vishnu and Shiva, 'What am I to do now? This business of Creation will be my death:

whoever I bring into being renounces the world. Can you suggest a solution to the problem?'"

The triplets, that in performance are sung, accompanied by dance
steps, reiterate and elaborate things that have been recited, chanted, or
sung in the couplets. The two forms of verse therefore complement each
other in performance, but in a complete translation meant for the solitary reader the repetitiveness would be tedious. The ragas to be used in
singing the sections are mentioned at the head, for example, "Bhairava,"
"Mallar," "Sri." In my retelling, therefore, there is not only a change in
the language but, markedly, also in the literary mode of expression. Fur-
thermore, the Bengali Manasa tales are divided into episodes called
palas—Vipradasa's *Manasa-vijaya*, for instance, has thirteen—one of
which was performed in a single session. The whole story therefore un-
folded over the days like a soap opera. I have found it convenient to split
the story into chapters as in a novel.

Prose versions of epics and verse drama, be they translated or retold,
are of course nothing new. Even in the Bengali literary tradition we have
Iswar Chandra Vidyasagar's novella-length Bengali prose version of Kalidasa's Sanskrit play *Shakuntala,* and Dinesh Chandra Sen's 100-page
English prose retelling of the core Manasa story, *Behula: An Indian Pil-
grim's Progress* (1923). Long popular in the Manasa canon has been the
composite *Baishkobi Padmapuran,* a patchwork of fragments from
twenty-two poets. Putting together retellings of mythic tales from divers
sources is also fairly common practice, a recent example in the South
Asian context being William Radice's *Myths and Legends of India*
(London: Folio Society, 2001; and Delhi: Viking Penguin, 2002).

I have drawn upon a number of the major versions in Bengali and
tried to produce a narrative incorporating all the key episodes. It therefore provides a more comprehensive experience of the Manasa legends
than any single Bengali version. I ought to add, though, that I do not
mean to be dismissive of the value of a scholarly translation of a single
text, let us say Vipradasa's, but I do believe that such a translation would
be of greatest value if there also existed a conspectus of the entire Manasa canon accessible to scholars and common readers alike.

I have surveyed important texts from all three regions, the North
Bengal version of Tantrabibhuti,[13] the West Bengal versions of Vipradasa[14]
and Ketakadas-Ksemananda,[15] and the East Bengal versions of Vijaya

Gupta,[16] Narayan Dev,[17] Ray Binod,[18] in addition to the "modern" version
of Radhanath Raychaudhuri[19] and the anthology of the twenty-two
poets.[20] Of these, my chief primary sources have been Vipradasa, Vijaya
Gupta, Tantrabibhuti, Ray Binod, and Radhanath Raychaudhuri. The
sources corresponding to the different chapters are listed separately
after the text of the narrative. Of course in using these sources I have
taken certain liberties, as all *Manasamangal* authors have done, adding
a flourish here and a flourish there and leaving out bits, but keeping narrative consistency in view. I have kept literary interest and comprehensiveness of treatment in mind in deciding which source or sources to use
for a particular chapter.

Among the five principal sources mentioned above, three account for
the majority of the chapters. Since the creation myth and other mythological background material are presented most comprehensively in the
version of Raychaudhuri, I have mainly drawn on it for the first seven
chapters and the ninth chapter. Ray Binod usefully provides an account
of Shiva's marriage with Ganga, which has been utilized in the eighth
chapter; some versions leave out Ganga altogether or include her as one
of Shiva's two wives, without mentioning how they got married. These
tales derive ultimately from venerable Sanskrit sources but have been
brought into alignment with the Manasa story, giving us, one might say,
a naga's–eye view of Indian myths. Vipradasa contributes most to the
middle chapters, from the eleventh to the twenty-first; five out of eleven
are based entirely—and one almost entirely—on him. Vijaya Gupta is
used for one whole chapter and more than half of another. In the book
as a whole some elements have been taken from Ray Binod in eight, from
Vipradasa in six, and from Tantrabibhuti in three chapters. Vipradasa
provides the most comprehensive and powerful versions of some of the
crucial episodes, like the ones involving Hassan and Hossein and the
Sarpa Satra, which are absent from most other versions. From Tantrabibhuti I have taken an exuberant scene that rounds off Part I and sets
the mood for Part II. I have allowed Ray Binod to dominate the last eight
chapters, supplemented by elements from Vipradasa, and Tantrabibhuti,
who contributes the crucial Kausalya episode, which also takes a cue
from Ahmed's *Behular Bhasan*. Ray Binod has been extensively used
here because of his broadly comic and somewhat novelistic treatment

of the closing episodes. The effect is a welcome lightening up of what might otherwise tend to be unrelievedly grim.

THE CORE STORY

What one could call the core story is in its essentials common to all the versions. Like many supernatural beings Manasa is born magically, of semen involuntarily ejected by Shiva onto some object; different versions mention different objects. She is brought up by Kadru, the queen mother of the nagas, or serpents, and hence as the foster sister of Vasuki, the serpent king, who hands over to her custody of the entire stock of snake venom and invests her with authority over all snakes.

Manasa sets off to meet her father, who was unaware of her existence and becomes sexually aroused at her sight. She convinces him about their filial bond after knocking him out with her venomous gaze and then insists on accompanying him home. He rightly fears a hostile reception from his consort Chandi (or Parvati), who believes her husband has brought along a mistress. Chandi gouges out one of Manasa's eyes; Manasa knocks her out with her gaze. Shiva is forced to ask his daughter to set up her own home, and out of his tears of paternal sympathy fashions a sister for her; this is Neta (or Neto) who becomes Manasa's wise adviser. Shiva arranges Manasa's marriage with the sage Jaratkaru. The marriage is short-lived, thanks to the machinations of Chandi, but results in the birth of a son, Astika. Neta is married to the sage Vasistha.

After various adventures in the divine realm Manasa comes down to the human world to establish her dominion. It is child's play to cow the numerous communities into submission through the determined implementation of a carrot-and-stick strategy. The "lower orders" are indeed enthusiastic in their worship. In some of the East and West Bengal versions, the first serious opposition to her from the ruling classes comes when the potentates Hassan and his brother Hossein, representatives of the new Muslim rulers, muster their forces against her, only to be routed and forced into submission. Eventually, only the merchant prince Chand or Chando (short for Chandradhara) holds out, and he is formidably armed with occult power granted by Shiva and enjoys the support of the mighty *ojha* (occultist healer specializing in treating snakebite victims) Shankha-Dhanvantari. Manasa uses her wiles to dispatch Shankha and then Chand's six children. Chand remains resolute, while Sonaka continues with her Manasa worship and wins the boon of another son. But Manasa sets a condition: if he marries, death will inevitably follow on the wedding night.

On Neta's advice Manasa goes up to heaven and persuades Indra to send his favorite dancer couple Usha and Aniruddha to earth. They are to be incarnated, respectively, as the merchant Sahé's daughter Behula (in some versions she is Bipula, but Behula is by far the more popular name) and Chand's new son Lakshmindar. Sonaka is pregnant with Lakshmindar when Chand embarks on a voyage to (Sri) Lanka with a fleet of fourteen ships. This turns into an Indian *Odyssey,* with Manasa brewing a cyclone and wrecking the ships and playing all sorts of tricks on Chand, usually to hilarious comic effect.

When Chand eventually returns home, his son is a youth of marriageable age. In all versions save the North Bengal ones, the marriage takes place as a matter of course. In the North Bengal version the youth's parents decide at first not to get their son to marry so that the fatal prophecy of death from snakebite in the bridal chamber will not be realized. But Manasa's manipulations force them to change their minds. She sends an *apsara* (celestial nymph) to appear in Lakshmindar's dreams as his maternal aunt Kausalya and go on to titillate and seduce him. When he is at the peak of excitement she asks him to make love to her in the daytime world. He then waylays and rapes Kausalya. She goes to Sonaka in a bedraggled state and tells her what has happened. Sonaka tells her husband, who then decides that Lakshmindar needs a wife to cool down his libido.

He arranges a match for Lakshmindar with Behula and orders an airtight bridal chamber, but the architect-builder leaves a hairbreadth chink. In some versions this is due to Manasa's coercion; in others it is done without prompting. I have taken the latter course because by the time we reach this part of the story everyone except Chand has become a Padma devotee, eager to serve her, and the purpose behind the steel chamber is common knowledge. On the fateful night Behula sits up to guard her husband, but Manasa induces drowsiness in her and a *kali-*

naga snake swiftly sneaks in and bites the groom on his toe. As is the custom with snakebite victims, the dead youth instead of being cremated has to be placed on a raft made of banana plants and set adrift. Behula, ideal wife as she is, like Savitri or Damayanti, is determined to persuade Manasa to revive her husband. She insists on accompanying the corpse and embarks on a riverine odyssey. Trying experiences of sociological and historical significance await her at various river bends: a number of men try to seduce or abduct her, a hunchbacked cripple, a hideous old man, some gamblers, and a robber gang among them. At one bend a tiger poises to attack. But the most painful experience is presented in a modern version that I will later discuss; the story of Kausalya from the North Bengal version is used here and Behula learns from an elderly man who turns out to be Lakshmindar's maternal uncle that her dear departed husband had raped his aunt.

Finally, when Behula and the decomposed corpse on the flimsy raft are lost amid swirling waters, Manasa responds to her prayers, restores her husband to life, and the stage is set for a grand reconciliation. When Manasa restores Chand's fourteen ships to him, the stubborn merchant prince agrees to worship the snake goddess. But according to some versions he uses the left hand to make his offering, and that will not do. Then at Shiva's urging he submits unreservedly. Behula and Lakshmindar go to heaven to resume their lives as Usha and Aniruddha. Manasa becomes a part of the universally accepted pantheon. Traditionally the altar for Manasa worship is occupied by her sacred symbol, an earthen pitcher with a twig of the *sija* plant *(Euphorbia nivulia),* which is sacred to the goddess, or a fully blossomed lotus in its mouth. Sometimes a pair of pitchers are used, one representing Manasa, the other Neta. The worship may be a simple and daily practice in one's home, but the annual festival for Manasa puja is in the monsoon month of Sravana (mid-July to mid-August).

This core story is preeminently dramatic and provides the staple for most if not all the performances by folk drama troupes or individual *gayens* (singers). The preliminary episodes that feature in many East Bengal versions begin with a creation myth and move on to Puranic tales of gods, goddesses, asuras (or demons), wars between gods and demons, touchy sages and their curses, the birth of Manasa, her exploits in the celestial sphere and then in the mundane realm. Thus comprehensiveness and continuity is achieved, we are served a conspectus of Indian myths, and the narrative progresses smoothly from mythic time to earthly time and acquires historical resonances. The inclusion of the preliminary episodes turns a drama into an epic. I have tried to follow the epic course while highlighting the dramatic elements at the same time.

FROM PURANIC TO FOLK

But what kind of an epic do we have here? True, our sources present Puranic tales, but in a way that alters them almost beyond recognition. To give a conspicuous example, Shiva is no longer the austere ascetic god of Indo-Aryan Puranas but a randy, cannabis-addicted rustic strongman whose antics create broad comedy and farce. A folk god. And yet, not entirely: the folk god does not replace the Indo-Aryan god but is another, novel divine persona. The folk imagination encompasses both the great Indo-Aryan god and the folk deity without diminishment of devotion. The seemingly vulgar brings within reach of human devotees what would otherwise have remained grand but remote. The devotee addresses the deity as a familiar, and common notions of propriety may be suspended. As Sukumar Sen notes, "Obscenity was once an important feature of magic cults that had gathered round Manasa worship."[21]

As with Shiva, so with his consort. His first wife, Sati, was the embodiment of wifely virtues; she committed suttee because her father slighted her husband, and she was reincarnated as the daughter of Himalaya, king of the mountains, and named Parvati or Uma (lady of the mountains) and Gauri (the fair one), and after her marriage to Shiva, became identified with Durga, the prime manifestation of the primal goddess Devi, Kali, and the folksy Chandi. Like all Indian deities, her names, derived from her multifarious attributes, are legion. Her wedding with Shiva becomes the scene of ribald farce, largely through the manipulations of the mischief-making sage Narada, who keeps popping up throughout the Manasa story to complicate matters. Chandi, as the center of a popular folk cult, is the natural rival of Manasa, a role that is played out through that classic figure of malice, the stepmother. Ganga is Chandi's co-wife and plays a compensatory role as the good stepmother.

Among the other gods, Vishnu and Indra and some of the minor divinities play occasional supporting roles, but it is Brahma, identified with the older god Prajapati, who is quite conspicuous in the role of creator and dispenser of destiny. Since he is usually a quiescent figure in Puranic tales, his dynamism here is significant: as the creator god he is presiding over the formation of a new socioreligious configuration, in which Manasa, the new kid on the celestial block, will occupy a major position. Once the dramatic events precipitated by Manasa's advent reach their finale, Brahma, one imagines, will go back to his long-established life—as the creator god who, once the world gets going as desired, sits back, paring his fingernails. Yama, the god of death, becomes a particularly pesky antagonist to Manasa and has to be put in his place more than once. The opposition is quite understandable, for Manasa as the controlling deity of snakes takes charge of snakebite victims and decides their ultimate fate; and this cuts into the absolute authority over the dead that the hoary Yama used to enjoy.

The portrayal of Manasa's character is of paramount importance in establishing her cult. She is puissant, irresistible, relentless, inspiring awe, fear, reverence. She can destroy and revive like Shiva. She is not only Shiva's daughter but only *his* daughter, being born out of his seed but not in anyone's womb. We might say she is consubstantial with Shiva. She is the controlling deity of snakes, and like her Shiva wears snakes on his body as an adornment. Father and daughter are so close that the incest theme seems to fit into the narrative pattern quite naturally. Introduced, as we have seen, at Shiva's first encounter with his daughter, it becomes a recurrent motif because the jealous Chandi keeps insinuating that there is an incestuous attraction between them.

The manifestations of the incest theme in the Manasa legends fit into two patterns identified by A. K. Ramanujan in his essay "The Indian Oedipus."[22] Ramanujan points out that in the case of incestuous attraction between father and daughter, the Indian stories invariably show the attraction coming from the father's side rather than the daughter's, which is the case in the (Western) Electra complex. This is precisely what happens between Manasa and Shiva. Another pattern described by Ramanujan is that of the man returning home after years in exile to find a youth sleeping in his wife's bed. He mistakes the youth for his wife's lover, unaware that it is his son, who has grown to manhood in his absence. This occurs in the Manasa tale when Chand returns home from his disastrous voyage to Sri Lanka; Lakshmindar, who was born soon after he had left home has grown up into a handsome youth and is discovered slumbering in his mother's bed.

Besides Manasa's encounter with the Muslim potentates Hassan and Hossein, which is discussed below, it is Chand's voyage to (Sri) Lanka that readily invites historicization. It provides literary corroboration to the common belief among historians as well as laymen that Bengal, like the other coastal regions of the subcontinent, was from ancient times a land of seafarers. It should be mentioned that not every Manasa text mentions Lanka as Chand's destination. Vipradasa, for instance, mentions "Anupama Patana," a port of indeterminate geographical location somewhere beyond Simhala (Sri Lanka). Still, the popular imagination has fastened on Lanka, partly because it can be located on the map and, more important perhaps, because of its connection with the *Ramayana*. The details of Chand's trading mission, it is worth pointing out, are comically devoid of realism. His ships are floating gardens, and prominent among the commodities he is carrying is the coconut; needless to say, carrying coconuts to Lanka is like carrying coal to Newcastle. However, the way Chand cheats the king of Lanka in barter trade can be seen as a realistic account of a timeless tendency among merchants.

Much can be gleaned about life in Bengal between the fifteenth and nineteenth centuries from the Manasa texts—and much of what we learn from them is still true of traditional life in the countryside. Caste and class distinctions; varied superstitions; the poverty of the rural proletariat; cowherds; fishermen using nets cast by hand; labor-intensive farming with cattle-drawn plows and painstaking manual hoeing; conspicuous consumption among the wealthy—these aspects of traditional Bengal are vividly portrayed in the Manasa texts. In the episode where Chand's six sons are killed, which I have based on Ray Binod's version, we get a graphic account of a village school run by a pundit, a traditional scholar. The six brothers study there, and understandably enough enjoy preferential treatment. Among their schoolfellows is a poor boy who, when the talk turns to what the boys will eat when they go home in the afternoon, says that the most delicious thing to him is eating *panta bhaat,* or watered stale rice. The six brothers are curious to try this extraordinary dish, which at their insistence is prepared by leaving leftover rice steeped overnight in water. The rich-poor divide comes across sharply, as well as the tendency among the fortunate few to enjoy slumming—in this case what we might call culinary slumming. Precisely this example of the phenomenon is conspicuous today among affluent Bangladeshis, who celebrate the Bengali New Year by feasting on *panta bhaat,* albeit incongruously accompanied by the expensive *hilsa* fish specially cooked in mustard paste.

AN AMBIGUOUS DEITY

Wendy Doniger in her introductory essay has aptly dubbed Manasa as "The Ambivalent Goddess," while Sukumar Sen describes her as "the goddess of life, cure and prosperity, and the demoness of death, decay and misfortune."[23] Another way of putting it would be to say that she controls every aspect of life and, as such, demands to be revered as a supreme deity. That she is powerful enough to be regarded as one is established in the story through the episodes in which she knocks out and then revives Shiva and Chandi and trounces Yama in battle. Routinely in the narrative, she is addressed by both mortal devotees and divine peers in superlative terms, as the mother of the universe and so on. The Indian mind has no difficulty in relating to rapturous rhetoric. But what about the non-Indian readers? It should hardly come as a surprise if they ask: Does Manasa supersede the other gods and goddesses? Who is the boss in this universe, Manasa or Shiva or Vishnu or Chandi/Durga? I think the question is best answered by pointing out an essential trait of Hinduism, that as a religion it is based on henotheism, the term coined by Friedrich von Schelling to signify faith in and worship of one deity while accepting the existence and even worshipping other gods. To a Saivite, like Chand for instance, Shiva is the chief god; to a Vaishnavite, like, say, Sri Chaitanya, it is Vishnu; to a Shakta, a votary of the primal feminine energy in the universe as embodied in a goddess, it is Durga or Chandi or Kali. It is a status similar to theirs that Manasa aspires to and eventually achieves, at least within the fictional framework of the *mangalkavya*.

Like all major deities, Manasa has numerous names, and these deserve some attention. Manasa, or Manasa-devi—goddess Manasa—as she should be reverently referred to, is the best known of the names and was used in a Buddhist text for a poison-removing deity as early as the sixth century C.E. Etymologically, it is related to the Sanskrit word *manas,* or "mind," and is apt in that she was born out of Shiva's mental excitation. Besides the rich associations of meaning it conjures up, the pure sound of the three syllables possesses a certain poetic quality. This is so even if we take the Anglicized pronunciation: Ma-na-sha. I recall a performance by the sound poet Bob Cobbing at Warwick University in 1979 at which he played on just these three syllables, chanting them, spouting them, varying their order, getting the audience to join in, working up a frenzied tempo, then slowing down and mouthing the sounds in a dying fall. He didn't mention any deity or object, it was a play on the sounds alone, and yet the effect was dramatic. Imagine a gathering of Manasa devotees doing it and you have an electrifying spectacle of religious ecstasy.

Almost as popular as Manasa among the goddess's names, at least in East and North Bengal, is Padma, short for Padmavati, lady of the lotus. She is so called because she was conceived in a lotus garden; she is also called Kamala, and since both names are shared with Lakshmi, Vishnu's consort and the goddess of fortune, Manasa's role as generous benefactress is all the more readily recognized by her devotees. The names Padma and Kamala, in a secular context, also suggest extraordinary sexual allure; in Vatsayana's *Kama Sutra* and kindred treatises, the *padmini* ("lotus lady") is the cynosure of feminine sexuality, and "sundari Kamala" ("the lovely Kamala") is celebrated in many a Bengali folk song as an exquisite dancer, probably inspired by a historical Kamala, a famous sixteenth-century courtesan in Bengal. In harmony with these two names, Manasa's sexual attractiveness and sexual freedom are amply demonstrated; divinely amoral, she doesn't hesitate to act like a slut, even seducing Chand to make him divulge and hence lose the great occult mantra that makes one invulnerable, an incident that may perhaps be given a sociological interpretation as an instance of the subaltern female trying to sleep her way to power and acceptability.

Widely used throughout the goddess's domain is the ancient name Visahari, literally "stealer of poison," that is to say, one who can cure a victim of poison. Manasa shares the name Jaratkaru with her husband, the commonality of their names being a condition set for the match in the *Mahabharata*. Brahmani, linking her to Brahma, is another of Manasa's names that is found in every version. Ketaka, Totola, Jaguli or Janguli, Jagati, and Jagatgauri, are some of her other names, but their usage is restricted to one or another region.

The multiplicity of names can be off-putting to a reader who is not familiar with Indian culture, and I believe it is judicious to apply Occam's razor to them. I have used Padma and Manasa (or Manasa-devi) in this version. Similarly, in the case of the other deities, I have used the best-known names. Shiva's consort is either Parvati or Chandi, the latter being the manifestation that is in stark opposition to Manasa: folk deity against folk deity. Shiva is simply Shiva and not Har or Mahadeva or Shulpani or any of his various other names; Vishnu is Vishnu and not Hari or Narayan or anything else; Brahma is Brahma; Indra is Indra; and so on and so forth.

An interesting—perhaps even unique—facet of Manasa-devi is her dependence on her sister-goddess Neta. In some versions, Narayan Dev's or Radhanath Raychaudhuri's for instance, Neta is the elder sister, bound through a curse to serve her younger sibling. This introduces an unnecessary complication: why should she be a happy slave? And why doesn't Chandi react to her with jealous rage as she does when Manasa arrives? It's best to have her as a younger sister whose brilliant mind complements her elder sister's all-conquering power. Manasa in fact comes across as a naïf, childlike, mercurial, utterly lacking the ability to look ahead and calmly make plans. It is Neta who provides the strategies and tactics that eventually results in her triumph. In a sense, indeed, Manasa and Neta are twin goddesses, perfect partners, always together, sometimes even on the pitcher that marks the altar of Manasa worship.

THE HASSAN-HOSSEIN EPISODE

As the two sisters begin their campaign to win earthly votaries for Manasa, after an easy success in winning over a community of cowherds they come up against a formidable enemy, the Muslim rulers of a kingdom, the brothers Hassan and Hossein, referred to jointly in the Bengali text as Hassan-Hossein. The conflict is of epic dimension and ends in the comprehensive destruction of the Muslim forces and the surrender of their king, Hassan. Peace is restored, the dead are revived, and they all become Manasa votaries. Truly remarkable in this episode is the social realism in the depiction of Hassan-Hossein's city; we are presented with an elaborate description of the various social and professional groups and personages in a Muslim capital, as well as the agricultural activities in the surrounding countryside.

Manasa's conflict with Hassan-Hossein is triggered when a contingent of one hundred of their men goes out under the command of a foreman called Gora Mina (a name that suggests non-Bengali origin, since *gora* means "fair complexioned") to plow the land. This seems to be a routine activity. Mina's servant goes to have a bath in a pond and runs into a group of cowherds worshipping the goddess. They chase him away. The Muslims then destroy the votive pitcher of Manasa and provoke her vengeance. This forest episode is historically significant as it is an early literary account—perhaps the earliest such—of the role of Muslims in extending agriculture in Bengal. The process has been magisterially treated in Richard M. Eaton's *The Rise of Islam and the Bengal Frontier*. The essence of Eaton's thesis is that the chief agents of Islamization in the region were Sufi *pirs* and *Shaikhs* (religious and spiritual mentors) who provided both spiritual and practical leadership to Muslim communities, comprising settlers from outside Bengal as well as converts who clear forests and bring the land under wet rice cultivation. This process got under way on a large scale with the coming of the Mughals, for reasons we needn't go into here, but it does not mean that turning forested lands into rice fields was not a common activity, albeit on a smaller scale, even before that. In fact Eaton states categorically that "the advance of wet rice agriculture into formerly forested regions is one of the oldest themes of Bengali history."[24] He cites the Chinese traveler Wang Ta-Yuan, who visited Bengal in 1349–1350, as a witness.

Reading between the lines we may surmise that Hassan-Hossein's men have already cleared forest land and brought it under the plow. That a hundred plowmen are working together suggests fairly large-scale farming. Their fields border the meadows where cowherds graze their cattle. The action of the cowherds in chasing away Mina's servant is significant. They might not have done so under normal circumstances since they no doubt know that he is linked to the local potentates. Perhaps they do so because they have been emboldened by Manasa's patronage. In any case, that they do so indicates that they see the agriculturists as interlopers; the encounter then may be seen as yet another instance of conflict between an expanding agricultural economy and an older pastoral economy.

When Manasa surveys Hassan-Hossein's capital city she is impressed by its splendor and prosperity. Through her eyes we get a vivid picture of a thriving urban center in the days of the Bengal Sultanate. We are introduced to the various administrative and military cadres, the religious personages among whom are the *pirs* who feature so prominently in Eaton's historical reconstruction, the workers in the textile (weaving) industry, the housewives, maids, and concubines. The upshot of the cataclysmic assault of the nagas is that the entire city, led by Hassan and Hossein, acknowledge Manasa and offer her puja. It takes little imagination to see this episode as a dramatic rendering of the social evolutionary process whereby Bengali Muslims accommodated themselves to an indigenous cult like that of Manasa. Sad to say, this is not how the episode would be looked at today by most people. Professor Jamil Ahmed of Dhaka University, who has devoted years of study and theater work to the Manasa legends, has informed me in conversation that all the *gayens* (singers of folk narratives) and folk theater troupes he has come across excise the Hassan-Hossein episode from their performances; the reason, he thinks, is that they fear it might inflame the sentiment of Muslims who would (mis)interpret it as Hindu triumphalism. In his pioneering study of the country's folk culture, *Acinpakhi Infinity: Indigenous Theatre of Bangladesh,* Ahmed puts it more reticently, in a parenthetical comment: "Interestingly, none of the performances I have seen contained the [Hassan-Hossein] episode."[25]

The Manasa texts that feature the Hassan-Hossein episode clearly belong to a historical epoch in which the relations between Islam and

Hinduism (and indigenous cults) were very different from what they have been for the last couple of centuries—this is to say, since the onset of colonialism. It is common to hear it said that religious beliefs and practices in premodern Bengali folk culture evinced syncretism. Eaton complains that "such thinking simply projects back into the premodern period notions of religion that became widespread in the colonial nineteenth and twentieth centuries, and that postulated the more or less timeless existence of two separate and self-contained communities in Bengal, adhering to two separate and self-contained religious systems, 'Hinduism' and 'Islam.'" He suggests that "one may see instead a single undifferentiated mass of Bengali villagers who in their ongoing struggle with life's usual tribulations, unsystematically picked and chose from an array of reputed instruments—a holy man here, a holy river there—in order to tap supernatural power."[26]

Vipradasa in his *Manasa-vijaya* taps the resources of Islamic culture toward the end of his narrative as well. Among the novel tactics employed by Manasa to harass Chand, one involves dervishes. Manasa makes five nagas assume the form of dervishes, who hail Chand and press-gang him into their group, forcing him to don a Muslim-style cap and go begging with them. Of course Manasa makes sure Chand is not treated charitably by the householders they visit. When Chand takes the name of Shiva he is manhandled and sent packing. "Why do you take the name of a *bhuta* [evil spirit]?" the "dervishes" admonish Chand and abjure him to take the name of the Prophet instead.

I wonder if it will be stretching things a bit too much if one were to suggest that this comic episode reflects the tension between orthodox Hindus, such as Chand himself, and indigenous cults. One can argue, surely, that Manasa here deflects the conflict between herself and the Saivite orthodoxy onto another conflict of that age, between Sufi dervishes and orthodox Hindus.

AN EPIC OF CULTURAL RECONCILIATION

In this context several points are worth noting from Eaton's summing-up of the historical dialectics between Indo-Aryan culture and indigenous Bengali cults, particularly that of Manasa. The Manasa cult evolved from around 500 C.E. to roughly 1000 C.E. After the Muslim conquest, state patronage of the Shiva-Shakti cult in its orthodox Brahminical form was withdrawn. The Brahmin establishment tried to appropriate the Manasa cult as well as other indigenous goddess cults "by identifying female divine power in all its manifestations with the Sakti, or pure energy, which is the counterpart of the Brahmanical god Siva [Shiva]."[27] Kinship ties were forged between Shiva and the indigenous gods and goddesses. As we have seen, Chandi became his consort; Manasa and Neta his daughters. However, the degree of assimilation into the Brahminical order varied. Manasa had a tougher time finding a place for herself than her rival Chandi, and remained more of a subaltern deity. But Eaton also found stone sculptures of Manasa in the museum at Chittagong University in Bangladesh and convincingly argues that, since such sculptures must have been commissioned for well-built temples, this is evidence of a degree of acceptance of the Manasa cult among the higher castes. The same argument no doubt applies to the stone statues of Manasa from various parts of the region mentioned by Ashutosh Bhattacharya.[28] Professor Syed Jamil Ahmed cites a pertinent point made by T. W. Clark, that the Manasa cult has influenced conjugal practices among orthodox Hindus: the marriage is customarily not consummated on the wedding night, when the bride is supposed to stay awake to protect her husband from harm, just as Behula does on her wedding night.[29]

It is no doubt heartening that in an age in which many of the world religions are afflicted by the virus of fundamentalism, there are many who still celebrate Manasa and proclaim her continuing fascination. Professor Muhammad Shahjahan Mian, in his Bengali study of Ray Binod declares that the *Padmapuran*, or *Manasamangal*, is the national epic of Bangladesh—one should perhaps add that it is in that case an unacknowledged national epic.[30] That there is substance to Professor Mian's claim is borne out by the fact that even now there are numerous itinerant professional performers who regularly enact the legends in markets and at fairs in the Bengal countryside, and in every Bengali home, whether Hindu or Muslim or Buddhist, a child grows up hearing the Manasa stories. These are retailed, usually by elderly grandmothers or aunts, in the context of various folk beliefs regarding nagas, or snakes:

they possess fabulous wealth in the form of gems that they guard jealously; they are relentless in pursuit of vengeance, should any of them be harmed. A Bengali publisher friend informs me that they are considered so fearsome that to many country people *shap* (snake) is a taboo word, for simply uttering it might invoke the dread creature's presence. There is a noteworthy parallel between the snake cult and the forest cults in the Sundarbans, home to the Royal Bengal tiger, where *bagh* (tiger) is a taboo word and in common parlance is replaced by *mama* (maternal uncle). We have already mentioned the *Raymangala;* another forest cult is centered on Bon-bibi (lady of the forest), a guardian deity of the Sundarbans. Woodcutters, collectors of wild honey, and fishermen, whether Hindu or Muslim, will make an offering to an icon of Bon-bibi to seek her blessings and protection before venturing into the forest.

The snake is not as great a threat as it used to be, not even in the Bengal countryside, and it certainly is not as much of a threat as the Royal Bengal tiger is in the Sundarbans; still, the mythic sway of the snake goddess in the popular culture of Bengal and eastern India in general remains conspicuous.

MANASA IN PERFORMANCE

Syed Jamil Ahmed in his book on Bangladesh's indigenous theater has a long chapter on performances related to Manasa,[31] covering twelve different examples that are described with ethnographic precision, on the basis of performances that the author witnessed between 1993 and 1995 in various districts of Bangladesh, interviews with performers and scholars, and also written sources. Five of the performances were based on unpublished local versions of the *mangalkavya* that included elements not found elsewhere. Nowhere was a script rigidly adhered to, and in every performance there was scope for improvised interpolations. These are clear signs of a vibrant, living tradition of oral poetry and folk theater.

The performances took place usually in the outer courtyard of a farmer's home, with minimal trappings marking the performance space, for example, bamboo posts with an awning stretched over them, and paraffin or electric lights. The audience squatted on hay or mats on all four sides. A nearby hut might serve as the green room. A leading actor, a supporting actor, boys in saris playing female roles, a few musicians, and a group of choral singers would make up a troupe. At one end outside the performance space would be an altar in the form of an earthen pitcher for the worship of Manasa. Some troupes would have female actors. Five of the performances discussed were entirely by Hindu actors and sponsored by Hindus; one was entirely and another mostly by Muslim actors, with Muslim sponsors; five involved both Hindus and Muslims in varying capacities. Even such minimal statistics are sufficient indication that the Manasa cult attracts votaries and fans (who might simply find it an engaging source of entertainment) from both the major religious communities.

Some of the performers could trace their line of gurus back by a number of generations; others were enthusiastic amateurs who earned their livelihood as farmers. There was no caste uniformity among Hindu performers. A remarkable troupe in the district of Khulna was made up of six women of the lowly Namasudra caste and was led by a congenitally blind woman called Kanjika Rani Sarkar. Like many of the well-known *Manasamangala* poets, she claimed that the goddess had appeared to her in a dream and commanded her to compose a poem celebrating her. This she did, in the rhymed verse forms characteristic of *mangalkavyas,* and then trained her half-dozen-strong troupe to perform the composition. Here we have a living example of the way the *Manasamangal* tradition grew from generation to generation. How much longer the tradition will continue to thrive is of course an open question. Jamil Ahmed notes with evident sadness that many forms of Manasa-related performance he has come to know about through his research have become rare if not extinct.

One way of preserving the tradition is to introduce it to the cultural mainstream, as Jamil Ahmed himself has admirably done in his role as a writer and producer. Together with a team of his students, he scoured several Manasa texts and compiled, revised, and edited relevant verse fragments, linking them together with a commentary in a mixture of prose and verse by the *gayen* (traditionally the lead narrator/singer, but here also incorporating the role of the *sutradhar,* or master of ceremonies in classical Sanskrit drama) to create a powerful dramatic performance centered on Behula's riverine odyssey. Titled *Behular Bhasan* ("Behula Adrift"), it has played to critical acclaim in Dhaka, Kolkata, and Delhi.

The play highlights the feminist aspects of the legend and transposes the story of Lakshmindar's rape of his aunt Kausalya into the episode of Behula's encounter with her husband's uncle; I have taken the cue from this in my version. The key characters readily lend themselves to interpretation in terms of gender politics. Chand is the patriarch devoted to the great patriarch-god Shiva; he despises Manasa because she is female and has had an unnatural birth, and hence is lowborn. Chand's wife Sonaka is the long-suffering mother who loses her children because of her husband's unbending stance. Chand blames Behula for his son's death, because she is a woman and can easily be made a scapegoat in a patriarchal society. Behula suffers sexual harassment from a weird range of male characters as she drifts down the river with her husband's decomposing corpse. And yet, Behula can rise above all the anguish and humiliation she suffers to bring about a grand reconciliation. With her resolute personality she is, as Tony K. Stewart puts it, "a prime local example of a woman in a 'take-charge' mode."[32] Fittingly, the play ends with the *gayen* declaring that more important than gender is our shared identity as human beings. This particular adaptation shows how the Manasa story can speak to us in a way that is in keeping with contemporary ideological predilections. Other recent critical appraisals also, and quite rightly, foreground the significance of gender in the story.[33]

LASTING APPEAL

Whether one reads the Manasa texts or watches a performance, the final impression one has is of the tremendous appeal of the human characters. Chand rises to the stature of a tragic hero through his hubristic refusal to bow to a deity whom he considers an upstart, despite the horrendous suffering meted out to him. His reluctant acquiescence at the end is an apt image of the kind of accommodation that the Indo-Aryan orthodoxy made with indigenous cults. Chand's wife Sonaka is an endearing character because of her resourcefulness. She is a loyal wife to Chand but secretly worships Manasa from whom she obtains the boon of her last son, Lakshmindar. We should not forget the minor human characters either, those assigned walk-on roles, the cowherds and fishermen and plowmen, who practice a wise pragmatism and bow before any deity who can help them to get on in life; or comic characters like Chand's servant Tera, whose name appropriately enough means "crooked."

But above all it is Behula who is the central star of this folk blockbuster. At her wedding she wears a magnificent bodice embroidered with representations of key aspects of the whole universe, much like the shield of Achilles in *The Iliad;* like Achilles, albeit in a feminine way, she is heroic. She not only carries the plot forward to a happy resolution but is an embodiment of qualities highly prized in subcontinental culture. She is, on the one hand, the ideal devoted wife, comparable to other mythic characters like Savitri or Damayanti; on the other hand, she is a celestial dancer, whose final performance before Shiva has all the primal allure of a Bollywood item number. This traditional picture of her personality may seem at variance with what comes across in a feminist interpretation, but the two are actually inextricably linked, for the feminist reading is nothing but the deconstruction of the traditional image. In Bengal Behula has upstaged her Indo-Aryan peers Savitri and Damayanti and in the popular imagination is the foremost example of ideal femininity. Even the Internet, which has usurped the position of that social archetype "Mr. Know-all," tells us confidently that "in India the meaning of the name Behula is: Perfect wife."[34] However, one notes with amusement, that an authority on the Bengali language like Sukumar Sen comments rather reticently that Behula "is probably" derived from "*vidhura,* 'a bereaved girl, a widow, a forlorn woman.'"[35] An anthropologist friend living in Santiniketan, the university town founded by Rabindranath Tagore, met a Baul who sang passionately of Behula's wifely qualities. When my friend asked him if a Behula could be found in the contemporary world, the Baul replied with great conviction that there was a Behula in every wife, and even if it was only in a nascent state she would manifest herself under the right conditions.

It should come as no surprise that film and television have not missed the opportunity to make capital of the Manasa story. Manmatha Roy, who wrote and produced a Bengali stage play on the Manasa story, titled *Chand Saudagar* (1927), also scripted a film version of it in 1934. There was another film version, titled *Behula Lakshmindar,* in 1977; and a soap opera on an Indian TV channel in 2010–2011 that enjoyed wide popularity in both India's Bengali-speaking areas and Bangladesh. These may be B-grade productions, but what they lack in artistic finesse is made up for by either piety or the simple human fascination for snaky stories. Other media could easily have a fruitful engagement with the snake goddess; wouldn't children love an animated cartoon series? And as for a graphic book, it ought to appeal to all age groups. I have produced the version that follows in the hope that it will interest students of literature, myth, cultural studies, and anybody who enjoys a chronicle of deaths foretold that ends in happy resuscitation, a rollicking, violent, emotionally charged tale full of utterly unbelievable things and yet making complete sense.

PART ONE

IN THE DIVINE REALM

CREATION

STRANGE AND MARVELOUS is the story of creation.

In the beginning formlessness reigned everywhere. There was neither heaven, nor earth, nor underworld; no land, water, wind, fire, sky. There were no men, women, or animals; nor any supernatural beings, divine or demonic. Only the supreme spirit, Niranjan, radiant and immaculate, extended everywhere as pure consciousness.

A time came when Niranjan was filled with a desire to create. At once the immaculate spirit split into two, the masculine Purusa, and nature's feminine principle, Prakriti. Ever since, Purusa and Prakriti have engaged in ceaseless play. They engendered the three great gods, Brahma, Vishnu, Shiva; each with a Shakti, a powerful goddess, as consort. Brahma became the creator of the universe, Vishnu its preserver, and Shiva its periodic terminator. Each god and goddess also has numerous other names by which their adoring votaries address them.

Brahma set his mind to creation and promptly brought forth a cosmic egg. Focusing his yogic powers, he produced from it the all-encompassing waters of a cosmic ocean. Vishnu observed it with delight and, setting himself adrift on a banyan leaf, went into a profound yogic trance.

Brahma took up residence in Vishnu's lotus-like navel. Vishnu's divine consort, Lakshmi, waited devotedly at his feet. Shiva lodged in Vishnu's body in the form of wrath, while his consort Durga took the form of a tiny birthmark. Vishnu went deeper into his yogic trance. A century went by.

Suddenly, two gigantic demons named Madhu and Kaitabha were born out of Vishnu's earwax. Formidably endowed with supernatural strength, and drunk with vainglory, they bellowed so loudly that Vishnu's trance was disturbed. The demons leapt high into the air and with ear-splitting roars threatened to gobble up Brahma. Seeing their gaping mouths, Brahma shrank in terror, curling up more tightly inside Vishnu's navel.

Brahma pondered the problem at hand and began meditating to call upon the great cosmic feminine force, Mahamaya, for assistance. "Mistress of this illusory universe," said Brahma with palms joined in supplication, "you are the primordial goddess, radiant is your form, and you possess all yogic powers. You can satisfy all we hunger and thirst for, you are the goddess of all creation, the guarantor of peace, the mistress of all divine powers. I beseech you to save us from the demons endowed with supernatural strength that threaten to devour us. Vishnu still dozes in a yogic trance. Awake him and save us by destroying the demons."

Pleased with Brahma's invocation, Mahamaya immediately woke up Vishnu. Now Brahma appealed to the awakened god. "Two demons, Madhu and Kaitabha, have come into being and are on a rampage. Save us from their wrath."

The demons became doubly inflamed when they saw that Vishnu had woken up, and rushed at him with incredible ferocity. The god met them head-on with resolute force. It was two against one. The battle raged for ten thousand years, and still there was no resolution. The limbs of the three combatants flailed and tangled as they fought amid the watery expanse and up in the air.

The demons had come out of Vishnu, shaped by Vishnu's divine power, and hence were invincible. The god thought of an appropriate stratagem and passed on whispered instructions to Mahamaya. She should pour such enchantment into the demons' ears that they would unconsciously wish for death at the hands of the god. Mahamaya entered the very souls of the demons and implanted the fatal wish. At once Madhu and Kaitabha felt impelled to address Vishnu in these words: "We are profoundly impressed by your prowess, for you have single-handedly fought the two of us for ten thousand years, and would like to grant you a boon. We will grant your wish, whatever it is."

"Very well," responded Vishnu. "If you are really serious, my wish is that you will suffer death at my hands."

Taken aback, the demons looked this way and that. There was nothing around but water, stretching endlessly in all directions. They had a sudden inspiration. "Your wish must be granted, for we cannot go back on our word. But there is a condition. You must kill us where there is no water."

With a moment's pause to consider the problem the god Vishnu stretched out a thigh till it reached stupendous proportions and, pinning down the demons on it, swiftly decapitated them with one of his favored weapons, a whirling circular blade. The bodies of the demons slid off and fell into the water. Half of them remained sunken, while the other half stood above the water and was shaped by Brahma into the land on Mother Earth. The demons' bodies were unbelievably rich in fat. It is therefore no surprise that "the fat of the land" should mean the best of everything.

Vishnu mentioned to Brahma the earliest of the numerous incarnations he would assume to fulfill the role of world preserver. First, taking on the form of a fish he would dive into the ocean depths to fish out the four holy Vedas. Next, incarnating himself as a turtle he would carry the earth and its inhabitants on his back. Then he would appear on earth as a boar. He enjoined Brahma to get on in the meanwhile with the business of creation and set off on his quest for the holy Vedas.

Brahma sat down in a yoga posture to contemplate the creation of nature, using his yogic powers to envisage the world's geographical features as well as the configuration of the heavenly bodies. Employing the magical force of yoga, he caused Mount Sumeru to rise, piercing the sky to reach dizzying heights, while the ocean depths were prepared as the dwelling of tortoises and other marine creatures. He demarcated seven heavenly and seven earthly realms; and seven vast regions on Mother Earth. In the ocean's center he created an island rich in *jambu* trees and surrounded it with six other islands. He installed the sun and moon in the sky, the sea god Varuna and the wind god Pavana; the stars that glitter in the dark, and Agni the fire god; and devised day and night, the twelve months of the year, and the six seasons. Mountains, hills, grasslands, rivers and streams, virgin forests, and woodlands decked with myriad blossoms were laid out. In short, all of nature with the exception of living creatures was brought into existence.

Brahma set to thinking of ways to create living beings. He appealed to Vishnu to fashion humankind. Vishnu meditated to call up his yogic powers to create a number of beings modeled on his own form, carrying like him the four distinguishing items: a conch, a discus, a mace, and a lotus. But Brahma deemed these creatures to be useless. He didn't want anybody like Vishnu. Vishnu abashedly withdrew into himself the ones he had made.

Now Shiva sat in meditation and brought forth the Rudras, one by one. They were massive in size and incredibly fierce-looking, and like their maker had ruddy-brown matted hair and bodies smeared with ash. "Oh no, these are no good," interjected Brahma. "Their wild behavior will spell ruin for the universe." Shamed by these words, Shiva at once ceased producing the terrible giants.

Brahma himself now got down to creating humankind, and presently brought forth Sanaka and the Seven Sages: Marichi, Atri, Angira, Pulastya, Pulaha, Kratu, and Vasistha. At once all eight holy men, offspring of the Lord Brahma's consciousness, embarked on spiritual exercises.

"My sons," Brahma appealed to them, "listen to your father and devote yourselves to worldly responsibilities."

"Impossible, Father!" all eight replied in one voice. "We cannot become involved in the affairs of this inane and unsubstantial world. We will spend our time in the practice of holy rites and yogic austerities. We beg you not to create problems by making absurd demands."

With these words the sages took their leave, and setting up ashrams deep in the forests applied themselves to Yoga.

"What a fix I am in," sighed Lord Brahma. "Whoever I have created wants to abandon creation."

In his distress Brahma turned to Vishnu and Shiva and loudly lamented his plight. "This business of creation threatens to put an end to life. Whoever I create turns away from worldly responsibilities. Tell me what I can do now. Asked to be creative, I was pleased to try to build up a world, but no matter how hard I labored, the slightest slip rendered it impossible to multiply the number of living creatures. Who can I confide in or ask for advice, except you two?"

The great god Shiva offered his counsel. "Pray to the divine mistress of this illusory world, the goddess Durga, and the task of creation will resume apace. The grand design that was conceived will then be realized. Everyone knows that the world of samsara is maya, illusory. It is impossible to get on without the help of Mahamaya, its divine mistress Durga. The festival for worshipping her is in *sharat,* the season after the monsoon, when the moon waxes in the month of Aswin; offering puja to her is the sure way to have one's desires fulfilled. Therefore fashion her image in clay, complete with her ten arms, adding the eyes on the first of the ten puja days, and begin the tradition of worshipping her according to the correct procedure. On the sixth day the goddess arrives on earth with her children and is ceremonially awakened in the evening through rites involving the offering of the bel fruit. The night is spent in festivity. The seventh, eighth, and ninth days are spent in fervent worship, and on the tenth day the goddess and her divine children are bidden a sad farewell by immersing their clay images in a river or lake."

The next morning, after a ritual bath, Brahma sat in a yogic posture, while Shiva sat beside him with a leaf of instructions in his hand, so that the puja could begin. A charming image of the ten-armed Durga had been shaped in clay and installed on a magnificent pavilion; all preliminary arrangements had been made. Punctiliously following instructions, Brahma fulfilled all sixteen requirements of the puja rituals and then sat before the idol clapping his hands in satisfaction.

Just then Shiva struck a warning note. "Listen carefully," he began. "The puja will remain incomplete without a blood sacrifice. A living being, beheaded in a single stroke, has to be offered to the goddess. Unfortunately, the world in its present state does not have any goats or buffaloes, which would be the most suitable animals for the sacrifice. But without a sacrifice, let me warn you, the purpose of the puja will not be realized."

These words plunged Brahma into profound anxiety. He cried out to Shiva and Vishnu for help; he wept in despair, for who could rescue him from such dire straits? "I rushed in at Shiva's behest, but the desire to do good has backfired. I have worshipped the goddess with all my heart, only to find that the puja has been to no avail."

"Now, now," said Shiva on hearing his lament, "pay attention and do not be distressed at what I am going to say. There are always hundreds of impediments to the performance of a pious deed. But in your predicament there is no alternative to self-sacrifice. You must chop off your own head and offer it to the goddess. You can be sure that she will in return always look after your welfare. If the laws of dharma in the holy Vedas have any truth in them, you may rest assured that you run no risk in doing as I say."

Reassured by Shiva's words, Brahma agreed to decapitate himself. Washing his head with water from a consecrated pot, he declared that he would gladly make an offering of it to the goddess; then making obeisance to the huge sacrificial falchion raised it and uttering fervent mantras and crying out, "Have it, it's yours, Mother of the Universe," struck himself above the shoulder, sending the head rolling down to her feet.

At once another head sprouted from Brahma's shoulders, a sight that immensely pleased Shiva and Vishnu. "Of infinite grace is the goddess Mahamaya, and whoever receives her mercy is truly blessed," declared an ecstatic Brahma, plunging forward to lie prone at her feet in a complete *pranam*. Then rising he circled her clockwise to complete the puja. He stayed awake through a night of music and songs, he gave a word-perfect recitation of hymns in praise of Chandi, which is another name for Durga or Mahamaya. Still the goddess did not reveal herself to Brahma, much to his dismay.

A distraught Brahma turned to Shiva and Vishnu and lamented: "What shall I do now? All my efforts have come to nothing, for the Mother of the Universe has denied me her boon. What is left for me to do in life, except put a quick end to my existence? My mind is in turmoil. The sin of killing Brahma will be laid on her head."

With these words Brahma picked up the falchion with the intention of thrusting it into his heart. Chanting Durga's name he held the tip of the weapon at his breast, ready to be thrust in. Just then Durga appeared in all her glory. Alarmed at the thought that she would be accused of killing Brahma, she promptly decided to reveal herself. A grateful Brahma abased himself before her, lying prone at her feet.

"Lord Brahma," said the goddess, "rest assured that all earthly sorrows will be removed through my kindness."

She picked up three heads that were lying about the place and installed them on Brahma's shoulders, and ever since he has had a face pointing in each of the four directions. He is lord of the four objects of desire: *dharma, artha, kama, moksha,* righteousness, wealth, sensual pleasure, spiritual liberation. Delighted at this turn of events, with palms joined in salutation Brahma sang praises of the goddess, highlighting her beauty, might, mercy, charity, which made her the mother of the universe, who could build, preserve, destroy, as she pleased. "The burden of my responsibilities I lay at your feet—do as you please."

Turning kindly eyes on Brahma, the goddess replied: "Set your mind at rest. You have nothing to fear, for you can depend on my kindness. I will explain how you can realize your creative ideas. No being can be generated without the power to create an illusion: this is an eternal truth. But those I am well disposed toward will face no difficulties, and I will certainly facilitate your task."

So saying, the goddess altered her true form and took on the appearance of the indescribably seductive Mohini, who inspires infatuation in all creatures in this world. "Fashion a being just like this," Durga instructed Brahma. Going into a yogic trance Brahma called up an exquisitely beautiful female form just like Mohini. He was thrilled and became infatuated with his own creation.

"Now listen," Durga said to Brahma, "whoever you call into being in the presence of this seductress will automatically become infatuated with her." Then with the reassurance that Brahma's wishes would be fulfilled, Durga made her exit. Brahma was overwhelmed, and delighted to learn that the task of creation would be accomplished. After spending the ninth night of the puja in revelry, Brahma ritually immersed the idol on the tenth day.

Again, Brahma put his mind to the creation of mankind. Fixing his consciousness on Mahamaya, the goddess Durga, he sat in a yoga posture and exercised his creative will. In addition to the sages already created he brought into existence Narada, Daksa-Prajapati, Kasyapa, and others. He created four categories of human beings, the four Varnas, or castes. The Brahmins, guardians of the sacred fire, came out of Brahma's mouth; the warriors, Kshatriyas, from his biceps; the Vaishyas, dedicated to business, from his thighs; and the servants, Sudras, from the two feet. These four classes of mankind are the direct offspring of Brahma, and from them branched out various subcastes. Alongside the human beings, Brahma created the other primeval inhabitants of Mother Earth, animals, birds, parasites, insects, snakes, and other reptiles. The creation of all the world's diverse living things, which compose samsara, was eventually completed, thanks to the kindness of the goddess Durga.

Now for the creation of the vast body of supernatural beings.

Daksa-Prajapati, whom Brahma willed into being as his spiritual son, had eleven daughters. The youngest, Sati, became Shiva's first wife. All the others were given in marriage to the sage Kasyapa. Four of them—Diti and Aditi, Kadru and Vinata—are very famous. The gods were born out of Aditi's womb—and in no time at all. Kadru gave birth to all the nagas—venomous snakes. Later, Vinata gave birth to Garuda, the king of all birds.

One day, as they sat bantering and joking, Kadru asked Vinata, "Tell me, what is the color of Indra's horse?"

"A spotless white, of course," replied Vinata.

"Come, come," said Kadru teasingly, "you are pulling my leg. Everyone knows Indra's heavenly mount is black."

Vinata began fuming at these words. Shaking her finger at Kadru, she declared challengingly, "If I cannot show you that the horse is white I will be your slave for all time to come. But if I can, you will be my slave forever. Do you accept the wager?"

"Yes, I do," replied Kadru without batting an eyelid. "We will resolve the question tomorrow."

The two sisters parted, each to her chambers; Vinata in a conspicuously cheerful and complacent mood.

On reaching her quarters Kadru summoned her serpent progeny and told them about the wager. They were dismayed to hear it. "What have you done?" they wailed. "How could you act so unthinkingly? The whole world knows that Indra's horse is dazzling white. What made you claim it's black?"

Kadru hung her head in shame, and her tears of regret flowed in torrents over her breasts.

"You are my only hope," she said at last, making a desperate appeal to her children. "Devise a trick to turn the horse black, or else I am done for."

"Listen, Mother dear, unscrupulous deeds only add to one's burden of sin," the snakes moralized.

But they were moved by their mother's sad plight and held a secret conclave to decide on a course of action. Among them Vasuki was the most evil-minded, treacherous, and full of guile. "Listen, all of you," he began. "Tomorrow when the horse comes to the lake to slake its thirst, serpents black in color will wrap themselves around its entire body, and our stepmother will be utterly humbled at the sight."

Early the next morning all the serpents went to the lake and lay in wait. Soon the horse arrived. The snakes danced and frolicked and the black ones among them playfully wrapped themselves around the horse's body, completely concealing its white coat.

A serpent quickly carried the news to Kadru, who called out to Vinata to accompany her. The sight of the shiny black horse filled Kadru with joy, while a crestfallen Vinata lamented aloud that she was ruined. The frolicking serpents jeered at Vinata. The beautiful Vinata could only cry in sorrow. "The cruel twist of fortune has made me a slave to my co-wife. What a trick has the Lord played on me! Despite all my wealth I must be a beggar all my life. Everyone knows Indra's horse is white. Who knows by what fiat it has turned black today? My misfortune must be the result of sins in another life."

The snake horde kept taunting Vinata. "You have been beaten fair and square. You ought to have thought twice before committing yourself. Now keep your word and go with our mother as her slave."

With tears rolling down ceaselessly, Vinata followed Kadru into the latter's inner quarters to start her life of servitude. All day she did Kadru's bidding, and when she finished working shed solitary tears.

After some days Kasyapa came to see her. "Tell me what's wrong," he said to her. "Why have you stopped taking care of me?"

"Do you have to ask, O sage?" replied Vinata sorrowfully. "I am a victim of fate. Having lost a bet I am condemned to be a slave to my co-wife."

Kasyapa said nothing, for he knew all about the workings of fate. The inevitable had to be faced. It would be natural for anyone contemplating Vinata's predicament to wonder how long it would last.

THE REVENGE OF THE VALAKHILYAS

AMONG BRAHMA'S MYRIAD creations were sixty thousand thumb-sized personages, known as the Valakhilyas. They were all powerful sages whose displeasure could bring down devastating consequences.

Once, as they set off for the woods, basket in hand, in order to gather flowers, they came upon a puddle that had formed in a hollow created by trampling cattle and swam across. Observing this, Indra, the king of the gods, burst into derisive laughter, which sent the tiny sages into a towering rage. It was most unseemly, they declared, with admonitory fingers raised, that Indra should make fun of their miniscule size. Then shaking their fists they declared: "We'll perform retributive rituals and destroy you today."

Struck with fear, Indra rushed to Kasyapa and told him what had happened. Kasyapa, accompanied by Indra, went at once to the place where the irate sages were busy at their deadly rituals. Kasyapa begged forgiveness on Indra's behalf, and Indra himself abjectly put his palms together and appealed to the sages: "I didn't know what I was doing. Please pardon the ignorant."

But the sages didn't relent; they continued with their oblations and mantras in high dudgeon. Their aim was to destroy the heavenly home of the gods. Now the entire pantheon took alarm. The other divinities joined Indra in beseeching the tiny sages to show mercy.

Still, the murderous rites continued; with a hundred invocations and fervent appeals, interlarded with fulsome eulogies to the irate sages, Indra fell prone at their feet, imploring mercy.

But it was Kasyapa whose reasoned and placatory speech succeeded in calming his fellow sages. And since a Brahmin's anger is short-lived, the Valakhilyas, on yielding to the entreaties, at once stopped the rituals. But then, quite suddenly, a pair of large eggs emerged from the sacrificial fire. The Valakhilyas burst into laughter, for here was proof that no effort could prevent something ordained by Providence; the eggs would surely be the cause of great discomfiture to the errant Indra. It was fated. The Valakhilyas knew that the eggs were imperishable, and handed them to Kasyapa, who took them home and entrusted them to the care of Vinata. "Keep them safely till they hatch," he told her. "Two strange and mighty children will be born, and your sorrowful state will come to an end."

Vinata was cheered by her husband's words and carefully tended the eggs. Nine centuries passed by, and yet, to Vinata's chagrin, the eggs wouldn't hatch. In an outburst of rage she picked up one of the eggs and dashed it on the ground. It split open, disgorging a gigantic and terrifying bird. He was named Arun.

But Arun was in a sorry plight, being prematurely born. The air felt chilly, and he shivered uncontrollably. "What have you done, Mother dear?" he lamented. "You have harmed your own fortune by breaking the egg and causing my suffering. Tell me how I can overcome the intolerable chill. But that isn't all my misery. My organs haven't had time to develop fully and I feel terribly weak. What am I to do? If I had a thousand years I would have been born with a handsome appearance. What has happened can't be undone, but tell me where I can find a remedy for my dire straits."

The divine Vinata, overwhelmed by pity and remorse, tearfully replied: "Don't remind me of what I have done. My blunder has been your ruin. It must have been the fault of my karma. But if you go to your father, Kasyapa, who is famed throughout the universe for his wisdom, he will give you advice that will remove your sorrow."

Arun acted on his mother's suggestion and approached Kasyapa.

"Listen to me carefully," said Kasyapa. "Go at once to the sun and take up the job of the sun's charioteer. Your troubles will cease. You will be assured of food and shelter for all time. You can rest assured there will be no deviation from this arrangement."

Arun was delighted with his father's words and was soon on his way to the sun, where he has lived happily ever after.

Now for the story of Garuda. The second egg was safely preserved by Vinata until the thousand years were over. When the time was up the egg split into two, and a wondrous bird, gigantic in size, was born. His wingspan covered five miles, and his height was proportionately great.

He turned to his mother and said in piteous tones: "Listen, Mother dear, I am faint with hunger. Where can I go to satisfy this hunger? Tell me quick, or else I will perish."

"Go to your father, Kasyapa, who is famed throughout the universe for his wisdom. He will find a way to solve the problem."

So the bird hurried to his father and with a *pranam* described his plight.

"Go at once, my bird-child, to the kingdom in the south inhabited by the savage race of Kiratas," advised Kasyapa. "Go there and devour the Kiratas to your heart's content. You will grow to be a mighty hero, and Garuda will be your name."

Garuda was delighted with his father's words and flew at once to the southern land inhabited by countless Kiratas. He fell to without delay, gobbling them up indiscriminately. Among them was a Kirata Brahmin, and like all Brahmins he possessed a special energy derived from Brahma, which gave him immunity from slaughter.

Immediately the bird felt intense pain in the stomach. Unable to bear it, he flew to Kasyapa and narrated everything.

"Hear my sorrowful tale, Father," Garuda began. "I went south, as you advised, and feasted on the Kiratas, but it gave me an intolerable stom-achache. Tell me how I can find relief, for I fear for my life."

The clairvoyant Kasyapa knew at once what was the cause of the trouble.

"You gobbled up a Brahmin along with the other Kiratas and that's why you are suffering," explained Kasyapa. "Go south again and at the exact spot where you ate up the Kiratas, you must throw up what's in your stomach."

The lord of birds obediently followed his father's instructions and found relief. But he came back quickly to complain to his father of unbearable hunger.

"I am so hungry that my entire body seems to be on fire. I could gobble up the whole world."

Kasyapa thought for a moment before replying.

"Go to the seaside where an elephant and a tortoise are engaged in ceaseless combat. Eat them and your hunger will be satisfied."

"Very well," said Garuda. "But tell me, Father, why these two are fighting without respite." Despite his hunger, Garuda's curiosity was aroused. He added, by way of justifying his inquisitiveness: "One shouldn't embark on any venture without gathering sufficient background information."

So Kasyapa narrated the history of the enmity between the elephant and the tortoise.

"These two used to be an extremely wealthy Brahmin's two sons who fell out over the division of their patrimony. The elder brother tried to cheat his brother and appropriate the lion's share. This generated much ill feeling and a bitter squabble. The younger brother put a curse on his greedy elder, turning him into a wild elephant that had to live henceforth in the forest. In retaliation the elder brother put a curse on the younger one, turning him into a giant sea turtle.

"Having thus placed each other under a horrendous curse, the two brothers lived in a state of chronic mortification. One day the elephant went to the seaside to have a dip in the water. It didn't go unobserved by the turtle, which rushed to attack it. The fighting was furious but inconclusive, and ever since the two have met every day to continue their bitter strife.

"If you go and devour these two mighty heroes, your hunger will be satisfied and they too will find release from their unhappy condition," Kasyapa told his son. "You will be doing them a favor, for, according to what has been preordained by Brahma, after being released from their earthly existence, they will immediately enter the heavenly abode called Vaikuntha."

On hearing these heartening words the lord of birds took off again and made for the seashore, where, sure enough, elephant and turtle were locked in tireless combat. Garuda swooped down and, firmly clutching the two with his fearsome nails, flew off again to look for a convenient place to enjoy his meal. This turned out to be an unexpectedly difficult task. The earth trembled under his weight, the branches of the mightiest trees snapped. Not even tall mountain peaks could bear the bird's weight. Chagrined, he turned to Kasyapa again.

"Father, I did as you said," Garuda began, "but after picking up my meal I got into a quandary, for I couldn't find a place that would hold me up firmly, letting me eat in peace. What will I do now?"

"You must go far from here," Kasyapa told him. "You will meet Vishnu in Madhupur, and you can rest assured that his mercy will save you from your predicament."

Garuda set off without delay, flying eastward until his wings began to tire. Just then, Vishnu appeared to succor his devotee, but in the form of a child. "Why roam through space?" he asked the bird.

"I'm looking for a place to sit and eat," said the bird.

"Come, sit on my palm and have your meal," the child said with a merry laugh.

Infuriated by what he took to be a jest at his expense, Garuda landed heavily on the outstretched palm. The impact shook the veins in the hand, setting off thunderous vibrations, but it afforded Garuda the resting place he had been looking for. After pausing to get his breath back, Garuda devoured the elephant and the turtle. His hunger was assuaged, but not satisfied. He told the child of his plight.

"Can you tell me, dear child, how I can satisfy my hunger? You are no ordinary child but a mighty being, so you might be able to help me."

The child good-humoredly replied: "Why not eat my flesh? It will satisfy your hunger."

"Oh no, you are too small," the bird said. "How can your flesh satisfy me?"

The child laughed. "Listen, Lord of Birds, if you eat the flesh on my hand, it will be enough to satisfy your hunger."

Garuda thought he was being put on. He flared up inwardly and tore at the child's palms. How could he know that it was the palm of the lord of the universe? He gobbled all he could and was sated; yet the hand was not consumed even an iota. He felt humbled, for he knew he was in the presence of an extraordinary being.

"Child, tell me who you really are," he begged, and promised: "I will grant you any wish you care to make."

"I would like you to be my mount," replied the child.

"But my speed is awesome," warned the bird. "You won't be able to stay on my back."

"Give me a ride without further delay," the child insisted. "We'll see if I can keep my seat or fall off."

The bird complied and found to his dismay that he was nearly stifled by the weight of the child.

The astonished bird said meekly: "Forgive me for being arrogant and tell me who you are."

The child revealed his divine identity and appeared in all the resplendent glory of Vishnu, bearing his hallmarks—a conch, discus, mace, lotus, and garland of wild flowers.

"My life is fulfilled!" ecstatically exclaimed Garuda. "For I am to be the mount of the lord of the universe."

He made a fervent *pranam,* lying prone at the feet of his master. Vishnu bade him get up and go home, and told him that he would be summoned when needed. With that Vishnu vanished, returning to Vaikuntha, his heavenly home.

Garuda returned home to his mother. One day he asked her about something that had been bothering him: "Why do you have to serve my stepmother like a slave, Mother dear? You must explain the reason to me."

Vinata, overwhelmed by sorrow on being reminded of her abject state, shed copious tears. "My son," she sobbed, "I lost a wager with your stepmother and as penalty became her slave. It must be my bad karma. I cannot even devote time to spiritual matters, nor serve my husband, but must always be at her beck and call."

After hearing his mother explain her sad plight, Garuda went to his stepmother to get her version of the matter. "I hope you don't mind my asking you about this," he said politely, "but could you tell me why my mother has been reduced to slavery?"

"Well, I said to her one day, 'Tell me what is the color of Indra's mount.' She replied indifferently that it's white. I knew the color to be black, so we made a wager: we would take a look at the horse and whoever was proved wrong would be a lifelong slave to the other. She lost the wager and became my slave. That's the long and the short of the matter."

Garuda listened to his stepmother with growing astonishment. How could a white horse turn black, he wondered. He pondered the problem till he hit upon the answer. The cunning snakes must have wrapped themselves around the horse, making it look black. Garuda would take revenge on the snakes; if he couldn't, he would give up his name. But first his mother Vinata had to be extricated from her demeaning situation. Only then . . . only then would he set upon the snakes; he would exterminate those creatures without mercy.

Having reached this decision, Garuda addressed his stepmother Kadru again. "Show some kindess to your helpless stepson," he began in a humble voice. "It is fate that has reduced my mother to servitude, but you can tell me how she can be released from it."

Kadru thought for a while before replying. "In Indra's heavenly abode there is a stock of ambrosia," she then began. "I want to feed it to my children to make them immortal. If you can bring it to me, your mother may be released from her vow."

"Very well, Mother," said Garuda, "if you give me an assurance that you will not go back on your word, I will get it for you."

Garuda left and, after obtaining his father Kasyapa's permission, set off on his mission. Burning with rage and determination he flew at top speed toward his target. He looked so terrifying that he could be taken for the twin brother of Yama, god of death. Whoever saw him trembled in fear. Surely the realm of the gods would suffer an eclipse today. Garuda let out a thunderous shriek to challenge Indra. He blocked the sun's rays as he sped through the sky, and as he neared his target came across the sage Narada, who asked him why he was in a warlike mood.

On hearing Garuda explain the purpose of his mission, Narada hurried to Indrapuri, the heavenly seat of Indra and other gods. Indra respectfully stood up to greet the sage, who was clearly in a state of nervous agitation.

"Garuda is coming here with destructive intentions," Narada warned. "Run and hide, if you want to save yourself."

But the gods were not to be intimidated. Indra armed himself with thunderbolts and mounted Airavata, his flying elephant. Varuna, the sea god, Yama, the god of death, and all the other gods of the old pantheon, thirty-three times ten million in all, came, each on his powerful mount, and joined Indra to do battle with the intruder. The divine army set up a tremendous din as they marched forward. Garuda zoomed in straight to confront the warlike gods.

Indra addressed Garuda. "What brings you here, bird?" he asked firmly.

"I am Kasyapa's son," replied the bird. "I have come for a share of the ambrosia. I regard you as an elder brother. I hope you will treat me as a younger brother. I ask you to help my mother by sparing some of the ambrosia that you have."

Indra, king of the gods, fumed with rage on hearing this and replied sternly. "Aren't you ashamed of uttering such words through your bird's mouth? Being a bird you will eat any and every thing, and now you wish to gain respectability by passing yourself off as my brother. You are brash enough to demand a share of the food of the gods. You are like the unspeakable cur that wants to eat the sanctified sacrificial offerings."

The bird's temper flared at these insults, and he replied in a terrifying voice, "Polite words are wasted on you. You are like the dog's crooked tail—no amount of massaging with butter will make it straight. Saturn's baleful stare is fixed on you. With my talons I will rend you asunder."

With a deafening shriek the lord of the birds flailed at his adversary with his powerful wings. Varuna, Pavana, the wind god, Yama, Agni, the fire god, and the other armed divinities joined lustily in the fray. Undeterred, the lord of birds rushed at them with incredible ferocity, swallowing everything in his path. Flaming with wrath, Indra advanced and aimed a fiery thunderbolt. Garuda gobbled it up promptly, as if it were no different from a locust in flight. But purely as a formal show of respect toward the divine weapon, he plucked a feather from his body and let it fall. Then he gave chase to his foe, grabbed Airavata by the trunk, and with Indra still mounted, spun it round and round in space, and then hurled it to the ground. Both the supernatural elephant and its divine master ran for their lives. The rest of the army of gods too fled in ignominious rout.

There was none to challenge the victorious bird as he entered Indra's palace and made for the reservoir of ambrosia. Garuda drank his fill and put the rest in a container. Indra, who had stolen back from earth, watched from a hiding place but could do nothing to stop the thief.

His mission accomplished, Garuda flew away. Indra and the other gods began to lament loudly. "Listen, brother gods," said Indra between heartrending sobs, "all the ambrosia we had in our store has been stolen by the bird. It spells disaster for the gods, for the ambrosia is the source of our immortal power. The asuras have made numerous attempts to steal it; all were futile, luckily. But we now have yet another adversary to reckon with: the bird, which has gained immortality by drinking ambrosia and has deprived us of what is left. I am at my wit's end, for I can't think of any means to avenge ourselves for such an insult."

✦ ✦ ✦

As Garuda sped homeward with his precious loot, Vishnu was traveling in his flying chariot in the opposite direction. They met before long. Garuda fell prone in a *pranam* at his master's feet and addressed him with palms joined in reverence: "By your grace, O Lord, I have been victorious against Indra and his divine cohorts, and I have captured their stock of ambrosia. Now I beg your indulgence in granting my wish that all snakes on earth be food for me."

"It shall be so," responded the lord of the universe, and he took his leave. A very gratified Garuda resumed his journey. When he arrived he went straight to Kadru with the container of ambrosia. He greeted her with complimentary words and taking her by the hand humbly presented her with the loot from heaven. "Please take it," he said. "Here is the container of ambrosia. Now grant my mother freedom from servitude."

Delighted to get the ambrosia, Kadru blessed Garuda. "May you be immortal," she said. "You need have no more worries about your mother. She is free from this very moment."

Garuda, lord of birds, called upon the sun and the moon to bear testimony to Kadru's declaration and rushed to his mother to give her the good news. Its effect on her was like that of new life on a dead body.

Meanwhile, Kadru excitedly summoned all her snake children and, handing the container of ambrosia to Takshaka, the deadly flying snake, said, "This is for all of you to share. It will make you immortal, and then you won't have to fear anything, you'll be able to defeat anyone you want."

The snakes were delighted to hear their mother's words. Takshaka led them to a river to have a ritual dip before having the ambrosia, which was left in a field of tall *kusha* grass on the bank. But Indra had been on the scent of the ambrosia; finding it unguarded, he quietly made off with it. But first he poured it into another container and tipped over the empty one. All the other gods cheered when they saw Indra return to heaven carrying the precious drink.

The snakes came out of the water and found that the container of ambrosia had tipped over. An accident, they thought. "The ambrosia has fallen on the grass and seeped into the earth," they said, and fell to licking the spot with great vigor. But they couldn't taste any ambrosia. They opened their mouths wide and licked with desperate energy, and became bloody mouthed as the sharp *kusha* grass sliced their tongues into two. That's how snakes came to be fork-tongued. Loud was their lamentation that day as they realized that the greatest of gifts had slipped out of their grasp. They rolled on the earth, crying in despair. "Why have we been cheated of a priceless gift from our kind mother?" they wailed. "Why couldn't we keep it safe? What prompted the folly of coming to the river? How could we be so stupid as to keep the container in the field of *kusha* grass? It must be bad karma that has led to our ruin. What shall we tell Mother; how can we console her?"

Bewailing their fate, crying in bitter self-recrimination, groaning in abject self-pity, the snakes went to their mother and told her what had happened. She became greatly agitated and went to Garuda's quarters to vent her spleen. "Who stole the ambrosia before my children could taste it?" she demanded to know. "Your mother cannot be freed from her bond now—Vinata will remain my slave."

Garuda roared in a mighty rage: "What's that, you sinful deceiver? If you weren't my stepmother, you'd be put to death straightaway. You used deceit to trap my mother in servitude. Now it's time for retribution: watch how I gorge myself on your brood of snakes."

With a terrifying screech, Garuda took off, a veritable Yama, god of death, hell-bent on devouring all snakes. "Why are you crying, you wicked creatures, don't worry, I'll end your sorrow by gobbling you up," he shouted tauntingly.

The snakes were enraged to hear this. They massed together in battle formation and with a deafening hiss spread their hoods, from which dazzling sparks flew in all directions.

This only increased Garuda's wrath. He flew to meet the snakes in battle, circled above them with lightning speed, and swooped down to devour hundreds of snakes at one go, and strike many more with flailing wings and murderous talons, so that they were hemmed in and unable to escape. Seeing what a tight spot they were in, Vasuki, the king of snakes, sallied forth with loud, menacing shouts, and bit into Garuda's body with venomous fangs, while with his tail he tried to strangle the bird.

The stranglehold hurt: with a thunderous roar the bird retaliated by trapping Vasuki beneath his wings and then pecking ferociously at the snake's hood and eyes. Unable to defend himself against the bird's fury, the king of snakes slithered away in ignominious flight, with the lord of birds in hot pursuit.

Failing to make a clean getaway, the snake slipped into a nearby wood. The bird circled over it, unable to land because of the thorny underbrush. The snake hit upon a clever ploy: he took on the appearance of a Brahmin priest and calmly stepped out of the woods. Garuda accosted him and politely enquired about the snake king. "Tell me, revered priest, where is Vasuki now? I would be much obliged if you could direct me to him."

The Brahmin squatted down and scratching some divinatory signs on the ground, looked up open-mouthed, as if he were trying to figure out an interpretation.

The bird at once noticed a forked tongue flickering in the supposed soothsayer's mouth.

"Ah, so that's your trick, you wicked, perfidious creature. Vasuki, you rogue, you have put on the appearance of a Brahmin, have you? That won't save you! Get ready to die."

Casting frantic glances this way and that, the snake king spotted a hole amid a clump of arum plants and slipped in before the bird could strike. It was Vasuki's good karma that saved his life.

Garuda had to give up the chase and return home. Kadru lamented the loss of so many of her children. But she had only herself to blame. Trying to harm another, she had had her comeuppance.

THE MENACE OF TARAKA

A TERRIBLE CRISIS DESCENDED on the gods when the demon Taraka, whom Brahma granted a boon of prodigious strength, went on a rampage, overwhelming Indra and his divine cohorts. The gods abandoned their heavenly abode of Amaravati and sought refuge in the Himalayas. There they prayed fervently to Mahamaya, reverentially joining palms together, singing her praises.

"Listen, O Mother, the gods have been disgraced and tremble in fear of the demons," they said. "Our only hope lies in your kindness and mercy. The invincible demon Taraka has conquered all three realms, the heavens, earth, and underworld. He has usurped the rights of the gods, who are now homeless beggars and have none to turn to but you. You are the mother of the universe, its sovereign ruler, you appear in varied forms: Durga, Kali, Lakshmi. You are the peerless spouse of Shiva; your glory is known to all. You are the guarantor of salvation, the source of all knowledge and wisdom relating to what is right and wrong; the embodiment of serenity, grace, and charm. You are ever in the consciousness of Brahma and Vishnu. We seek refuge at your feet, we vow fealty to your might; for you are the last court of appeal in our distress. Have pity on us, relieve us of our sorrow, deliver us from the scourge of the demons."

The Mother Goddess was pleased with the encomiastic address of the gods. Her divine pronouncement resounded through the skies: "When I incarnate myself in the family of Himalaya and unite with the great god Shiva, the annihilation of the demons will follow as a matter of course."

Reassured by Mahamaya's words, the gods smiled with gratification and said to each other that their hopes would be fulfilled.

THE BIRTH OF PARVATI AND HER
MARRIAGE WITH SHIVA

HIMALAYA, MONARCH OF THE MOUNTAINS, and his beautiful wife Menaka, ardent devotees of Mahamaya, became sick with worry because they were childless. Their devotional austerities greatly pleased the Mother of the Universe, who conveyed a message to Menaka in a dream.

"Cheer up, Menaka," Mahamaya said in the dream. "Very soon a daughter will be born from your womb. She will be a blessing to the world, and both gods and demons will always sing her praises."

So startling was this delightful dream that Queen Menaka woke up. As soon as it was light she nudged her husband awake.

"Listen, my lord, I have been told in a dream that my womb will be blessed with a jewel of a daughter."

Happy to hear such auspicious words, the king sent out invitations to all the Brahmin priests. Together with the mendicants and poor subjects, they were feted and presented with generous gifts. Sacrificial fires were lit and oblations of ghee poured into them. Days and nights passed in festivity. During this time the queen's menstrual period began. She went through the ritual bath prescribed for the event at an auspicious moment, and then ate pomegranates and the flesh of the wood apple. The nights were filled with laughter and merriment. On the fifth day of the new menstrual cycle Menaka went to her husband and passed the night in lovemaking. She conceived at once: Mahamaya entered her womb to begin the process of incarnating herself on earth. Menaka grew big with her extraordinary child. In the fifth month of pregnancy she was ritually fed five sweet things—yogurt, milk, ghee, sugar, and honey. In the ninth month she went through the ritual of eating whatever she craved most. The labor pains started in the tenth month. Midwives took over, cradling the queen in their arms and helping her through the delivery, which was wonderfully smooth and painless.

The newborn child was radiant and lovely as the full moon. All who saw her were charmed. The women in the royal household loudly made the joyous *ulu ulu* sound, wagging their tongues in their mouths. The queen's handmaidens dressed up to carry the good news to the king.

"Hear the good news, mighty monarch of the mountains," they chorused. "The Lord Brahma has sent a treasure to your home in the form of a jewel of a daughter who will cast enchantment over all three realms, earth, heaven, and the underworld."

Thrilled at the news, King Himalaya went into the inner quarters of the palace. He was thoroughly charmed at the sight of his child and munificently commanded that rich gifts be distributed among the people.

Astrologers were summoned to cast the newborn's horoscope. When it was completed and read out, everyone exclaimed in admiration that the queen had borne the king a divine daughter. The king asked everyone to offer thanksgiving prayers without delay.

Festive music played continuously in the palace. On the sixth day of the princess's life, Sasthi, the goddess of childbirth, was duly worshipped. At seven months the child was ceremonially introduced to solid food, to the accompaniment of priestly rites. The first year passed with due attention to all prescribed observances.

When Princess Parvati reached the age of five her education formally began. Gradually she learned to read the various shastras, or holy books, and acquired both knowledge and wisdom. Till she was seven years of age this latest incarnation of Mahamaya happily played with dolls in her leisure hours—dolls that she got married off in the roles of Shiva and his consort.

But when she turned eight her own marital prospects became a cause of concern to her parents. The monarch of the mountains anxiously pondered the question: who among men, or the supernatural gandharvas, or the gods, was worthy of the hand of such a peerless maiden as his daughter?

While King Himalaya worried about getting Princess Parvati married, the gods were similarly concerned about one of their number. One day Lord Vishnu sat deliberating on this with a number of his fellow immortals. "Foremost among us is the great god Shiva," he said. "His home is empty and desolate. He has been single ever since the death and dismemberment of Sati and the end of his manic dance of mourning. But not long ago the great goddess Mahamaya announced she was incarnating herself in Queen Menaka's womb. Now, if we can do a bit of divine matchmaking, a great sorrow will be dispelled forever from our midst."

After this colloquy, Brahma set off for the palace of King Himalaya. On seeing him the king rose and, offering him the throne, squatted down to wash the divine visitor's feet and offer him propitiatory oblations.

"To what do we owe the honor of your visit?" the king humbly enquired. "Do tell us and satisfy our curiosity."

"Your Royal Highness is most fortunate," replied Lord Brahma. "Your greatest fortune is your daughter. She is no ordinary girl, so you should treat her with special care and find a husband worthy of her."

"My lord," replied the king, "why are you saying this to me? What can I do? Nothing can happen unless you ordain it. Therefore, you need not pass on advice through beguiling words. Tell me who is to be my daughter's bridegroom, and I will give her hand to him."

"None but Shiva can have your daughter's hand," said Brahma firmly. "Determine the auspicious time for the wedding and make arrangements for it."

The king was overjoyed. He tingled with excitement; he felt as if heaven had been handed to him. He sent word to Menaka in the inner quarters. It was received with joy, and the ladies of the palace gave themselves up to celebration and merriment. The astrologers came and quickly determined the auspicious time for the marriage ceremony. The king ordered his ministers to make all necessary arrangements and send invitations to all the gods, sages, and ascetics. He bade farewell to Brahma with many expressions of gratitude and words of high praise. Brahma returned to heaven, pleased with his success. His wife Saraswati conveyed the news to Vishnu, who received it with pleasure. But there was a problem, too, Vishnu mused. Shiva was deep in meditation: how to break the news of his imminent marriage to him?

Shiva's fellow gods put their heads together. The problem was quite an intractable one. Shiva was sunk in meditation; his wedding was just days away, and he didn't even know that it had been arranged. Who would approach him and rouse him from his trance? What was the best way to do it? After their deliberations the gods decided to entrust Kama, the god of love, with the task. Kama promptly approached Shiva and loosed his floral darts, bringing him back to consciousness. Shiva reacted sharply and wouldn't heed any plea for restraint. Kama fled in terror, relentlessly pursued by Agni's angry flames, and was soon incinerated. Their fellow gods were mortified and resolved to confront Shiva. Brahma and Vishnu led them as they went in a body to Mount Kailash, Shiva's home in the clouds.

"Pay attention to our words," Brahma and Vishnu said. "Mahamaya has incarnated out of the womb of Queen Menaka as Princess Parvati, also known as Uma and Gauri, because of her radiant complexion, and your marriage with her has been arranged. Prepare yourself according to convention, for the auspicious hour for the event falls tomorrow."

"Why bother with convention and preparations?" Shiva protested. "Take me to the king's palace as I am—we will have our way by hook or by crook. Why make a fuss over inessential matters?"

Vishnu reasoned with his headstrong fellow god. "Brother Shiva," he said, "the rules must be followed. Custom and ceremony cannot be ignored. You are foremost among us gods, you must not court insult. How shameful it will be if people say you are a wretched beggar! So let us go with pomp and fanfare. Gods, gandharvas, yakshas, all will accompany you in a grand procession that will impress the king. Go through the good luck rituals tonight, and tomorrow morning we will set off for King Himalaya's palace."

Shiva didn't go to sleep that night. Early the next morning he woke up Vishnu.

"Let's be off," he shouted happily. "No point tarrying. Let's get dressed and start."

Vishnu was pleased at the bridegroom's eagerness. He called all the other gods and bade Shiva sit down on a special couch so that he could take care of the bridegroom's grooming.

But things soon went out of Vishnu's hands. The ghosts—*bhutas* and *vetalas*—came and applied themselves enthusiastically to the task of fitting out the groom. Shiva for his part took the whole thing in a spirit of fun and piled his matted locks in a knot on his head, smeared ash all over his body, wore around his neck a garland of innumerable skulls, stuck datura blossoms behind his ears, and draped a tiger skin around his loins.

"There! I am ready," he happily proclaimed.

"Wonderful!" whoever saw him would surely exclaim. "What an extraordinary getup for a bridegroom!" they would no doubt add, not without a touch of sarcasm.

Thoroughly pleased with himself, Shiva asked his attendant Nandi to fetch a bull for him to ride. Nandi set to accoutring the bull that would bear the divine rider. All the other members of the bridegroom's party had also arrived and were busy preening themselves in preparation; they were a motley group of gods, gandharvas, and yakshas, and innumerable ghosts, monsters, zombies, and Shiva look-alikes.

Vishnu was mounted on Garuda, Indra on Airavata, Brahma on a flying chariot harnessed to swans. Shiva's two chief attendants, Nandi and Bhringi, had decked themselves out in a hideously incongruous manner. Shiva ecstatically gobbled up some datura fruit before mounting his bull. "Let's go!" everyone called out, and the festive procession moved forward with shouts of joy.

Various instruments played; the ghosts and their cohorts played percussion with their fingers on blown-up cheeks. The continuous din of tabors and horns resounded through space and startled beasts and birds. The Shiva look-alikes and the ascetic women devotees of Shiva danced without a break, chanting the god's name and clapping to keep time. The sinister necrophagous *pisachas* and the *guhyakas,* who attended Kubera, the yaksha king, as well as all the supernatural masters of ascetic practices gave themselves up to riotous drinking and datura eating. There was no pause in their drunken bellows and guffaws. The mighty Rudras made the three realms tremble as they marched forward haughtily, ceaselessly chanting praises for Shiva. The gods, gandharvas, and yakshas in the procession numbered hundreds of millions. The ghosts were in the lead, the gods brought up the rear, and a very pleased Shiva advanced alongside.

It was day's end when the mammoth procession reached Himalaya's capital. On receiving word of their arrival, the monarch of the mountains went forward to welcome them with humility and kindness. The guests responded by reminding him that it was his good fortune that the gods had come to his palace. The king ushered the guests to their seats, and Shiva, the bridegroom, to the throne. The ghosts, however, were not at all inclined to sit down and kept up a relentless hullaballoo.

"Take care," the king advised his subjects, "that you don't get into a wrangle with any of these. That will have dire consequences, for these are not ordinary ghosts, they are Shiva's very own ghosts. They are far more terrifying, each of them is a veritable Yama."

The citizens were awed and quietly watched the ghosts at their weird antics. Now Narada, the mischief-making sage, turned up and joined the assembly. As was his wont he looked for a way to kick up trouble, but he couldn't think of a suitable excuse. He squinted meaningly at Shiva, who took the cue, and with the intention of putting King Himalaya's devotion to the test began to refresh his coat of ash. Right there amid the gathered wedding guests he smeared ash all over his body and face, baring hideously large teeth as he did so. The necklace of skulls and bones around his neck rattled with his movements, and his yellowish-brown beard and whiskers blew in the breeze. The half-moon painted on his forehead flashed dazzling light, and a terrifying aura hung around his mighty trident. From his matted locks Vasuki, the snake king, raised his hood and sparks flew from his mouth. A beggar's satchel was slung around Shiva's shoulders; quilted cloth hung in tatters round his torso. His three bloodshot eyes glowed like torches. Shiva's mischievous antics drew titters from his fellow gods. Citizens invited to the wedding exchanged whispered comments. In whichever direction

Shiva frowningly glanced, panic-stricken guests retreated gasping, "He'll gobble us up!"

"Brahma, you've done a wonderful job of matchmaking," Narada said to himself. He went to see Menaka in the inner quarters to cook up further mischief.

"Your Royal Highness, why are you idling away your time," he chided, "go with your court ladies and receive the groom ceremonially."

The queen was happy to be urged thus; she called the court ladies together and began delightedly preparing the tray for carrying the required ceremonial objects. Then they all trooped out singing auspicious ditties suitable for the occasion.

The queen went forward to greet her son-in-law-to-be and was met with a crooked leer. The court ladies were aghast and rounded on Menaka.

"What a splendid bridegroom you've found for your daughter," they commented. "He's so loony it's embarrassing to look at him. Let's get out of here; it's pointless to hang around."

On hearing this Narada intervened with mollifying words. "Why are you badmouthing Shiva? First come and take a closer look." He picked up a lantern and held it close to Shiva's forehead. Its heat released ambrosial drops from the half-moon drawn on it; these fell on the tiger skin that Shiva wore around the loins. The effect was startling. The supernatural energy of the ambrosia turned the dead skin into a living, roaring tiger, scattering the panic-stricken ladies. Menaka felt trapped; she looked frantically for an escape route. Narada summoned the wind god Pavana and asked him to raise a little whirlwind. In a split second the whirlwind whipped Menaka's raiment off her body. Now both Shiva and his mother-in-law-to-be stood stark naked. A surging tide of laughter rose from the guests.

Menaka streaked away and once in the safety of the inner quarters collapsed in tears of shame and embarrassment.

"Brahma has landed us in such trouble!" she lamented. "I was so thrilled to go out with my friends to receive the bridegroom. We fell into the hands of horrid monsters and feared for our lives. It must be our good karma that saved us. How I've been publicly humiliated! I'm not going to give away my beautiful daughter to this monster—I'd sooner tie a pitcher to my neck and drown myself."

The court ladies openly rebuked Menaka. "Give away your daughter to the worthy groom," they mocked, "but we are all going home. We can't be a part of this monster worship. Is this what Brahma has ordained— that our radiant girl will be given to a hideous monster? We've had a good look at him—his nose is shapeless, he is gap-toothed. His gray hair and beard are like unwashed jute fiber. His eyes droop from overindulgence in bhang and alcohol. His body odor will drive away a dog. He is older than the bride's father—what a shame! Who would advise giving a daughter to such a groom? And if the marriage does take place, think of the incongruity in their relationship. The young bride might address him as 'Father'!"

The ladies went on in this vein. Menaka could only weep in her sorrow. She couldn't get over the humiliation of suddenly being reduced to a figure of fun and having to run away amid the derisive laughter of an assembly of men.

The royal retainers went to the king's chamber and apprised him of the situation. The king was unperturbed. "Don't bother me with such things. You have no idea about Shiva's glorious power. Just observe with humility and devotion, and you will see how effortlessly he removes the queen's sorrow."

Pleased at the king's devotion and trust, Shiva at once assumed his irresistibly seductive form, with a face that surpassed a silver mountain in its radiance. The scent of musk and sandalwood emanating from his pores wafted through the hall. A gold crown glittered on his head, and the gorgeous robes that replaced the tiger skin on his body were embellished with various precious stones. His figure was youthful, supple, his eyes delicately shaped. Everyone who saw him was enchanted.

The citizens went to Menaka with news of the miraculous transformation. "What are you doing all by yourself, Queen Menaka?" they inquired. "Come and see the bridegroom—you will gain merit by doing so."

This only aggravated the queen's distress over her recent humiliation. She simply couldn't bring herself to face the assembly again. The citizens pleaded with her, they swore that all would be well and urged her to reconsider her decision, but to no avail. The citizens thought: "What a quandary we are in. Let's go to the king and tell him about our predicament."

The king went to the queen as soon as he heard about her sulk. He spoke to her in admonitory tones: "Why this delay in ceremonially receiving the bridegroom?"

"To hell with him," the queen returned. "I'm not going to welcome such a bridegroom. I've been so embarrassed and humiliated in front of everyone that I feel like swallowing poison."

"Who asked you to go at that time? I can sense Narada's hand in this. He's always up to such strange antics! He played a prank on you and showed you a hideous monster. Why do you slander Shiva without finding out the truth behind appearances? Go and see how charming he looks: everyone in this world is enchanted. It's sheer arrogance to reproach Shiva. Daksa-Prajapati made the mistake of doing so and paid for it: what reverses he suffered! You forgot all that, or else you couldn't have been so naive as to castigate Shiva. Let me warn you: no good can come of being disrespectful toward Shiva. You'd better go at once with the ladies to receive him ceremonially—just looking at him is enough to make one's life fulfilled."

The queen was filled with nervous apprehension and quickly gathered the court ladies and set off with trays loaded with the ritual articles. But she hadn't yet recovered from the recent shock and placed herself in the middle of the procession.

Shiva was calmly seated on a throne, radiantly handsome, so that the court ladies on setting eyes on him were utterly captivated. "There is no form as attractive anywhere in the three realms!" they declared. "Providence has created a perfect match in Parvati and Shiva—they are like two gems threaded together."

The ladies burst into songs of praise. The presiding priest recited from the Vedas, the sadhus and sannyasis chanted the benedictory *Shantih Shantih Shantih*. The queen performed the ritual of placing an ear of rice and some *durba* grass on the bridegroom's head and happily returned to the inner quarters to carry on with the prescribed observances.

Menaka took her daughter Parvati in her arms and carried her to a seat to give her a body wash. The girl's body was massaged with an oily turmeric paste, scrubbed with a moistened piece of cloth, and finally washed with scented water. She was then dressed in exquisite raiment and seated on a bed made of gold. A number of young maidens artistically

applied makeup and decked her out in splendid jewelry and other accoutrements. Substances that had the magic property of casting a spell of
enchantment on one's spouse were procured and tied in a knot to the
bridal attire. Thus Mahamaya, incarnated as Parvati, became a seductive enchantress.

Menaka sat down with Parvati in her arms, while maids waved over
them fans beautifully fashioned out of yaks' tails. Dancing girls performed in front of them.

The queen sent word to the king that all was set for the wedding ceremony. The king approached Brahma with palms reverentially joined.
"My lord," he appealed, "why delay a felicitous event?"

Brahma was pleased to hear that. He called Nandi and Narada. "It's
time to go to the inner quarters with the bridegroom," he told them.

Nandi asked Shiva to ride on his shoulders and carried the great god,
accompanied by the whole troop of *bhutas, rakshasas, vetalas,* and Shiva's *bhairava* look-alikes.

Good luck chants rose in a crescendo, startling birds and other creatures as the wedding party went with the bridegroom to the inner quarters
where the bride waited with her mother and the bridesmaids: apsaras
accompanying the groom danced to the music of various instruments. The great god was set down by Nandi on a splendid seat earmarked for him, as Queen Menaka came forward to perform the rites
of welcome, placing an ear of rice and *durba* grass on the groom's head
and pouring yogurt on his palm. Joyous tears trickled down as she did
so. Shiva was gratified to see her giving away pretty gems to the guests.
The celebratory *ulu ulu* rose from the mouths of the congregation.

Servants girded their loins and carried the bridegroom to a specially
designated cot. Around him stood his fellow gods, while the *bhutas*
roared as they flew around. The customary friendly tussle ensued between the two sides—the bridegroom's party and the bride's family,
relations, friends, and their cohorts. They pushed and shoved and jostled; such was the din they created that some nervous householders
quickly shut their gates.

As the women gathered in a festive concourse, Narada found another
opportunity for causing mischief. "I'll use the *bhutas* to have some fun,"
he decided. He clapped his hands and cast a spell. At once the ghosts

began dancing wildly. Then they did something more spectacular; they took control of the minds and bodies of the women there. The possessed creatures lost all sense of propriety and decorum: they laughed raucously or danced crazily or flirted outrageously. Some threw off their clothes and deliriously clapped their hands, others jostled and hugged each other, and some just rolled on the ground and howled and wept with joy. This extraordinary spectacle defied description.

"What's going on?" asked dismayed citizens.

"What a nuisance!" Brahma complained to Vishnu. "Narada's antics have become intolerable."

Vishnu sent his emissaries to bring the ghosts under control; then, calling Narada, roundly admonished him.

"Don't be angry," the sage appealed placatingly. "One is entitled to a bit of fun at his maternal uncle's wedding. But I'll do as you say and put an end to the wild revelry. You may get on with the ceremony."

"Fetch the bride!" Brahma commanded. Retainers girded their loins and in a golden palanquin carried by four bearers conveyed Parvati to Shiva's presence. Recognizing her husband, she greeted Shiva with a *pranam*. Then silently invoking the god Vishnu, preserver of this world of samsara, she began the ritual circumambulation of the bridegroom. Attendants made offerings of flowers smeared with sandalwood paste and broadcast powdered dyes of many colors. Gods, gandharvas, yakshas, *bhuta* and preta spirits ecstatically proclaimed the glory of love.

After completing the prescribed seven circumambulations, Parvati made a *pranam* before Shiva, and the two of them left the place. Parvati went in and sat in her mother's lap; Shiva took his place in the assembly; and the king instructed the attendants to take particular care in preparing the space for the rituals to follow. "Go by the book, don't neglect any detail," he said. "Bring the articles for the dowry tastefully decorated and arranged."

As soon as the instructions were issued the men set to work. They set up a canopied dais. Facing seats were placed for the bestower and the recipient. The dowry items were placed in between. Arrangements completed, the men approached the king and requested him to give away the bride without delay. The king got ready after performing an ablution by pouring consecrated water over himself. Meanwhile, Shiva went to the dais and sat down on the seat facing east, which is earmarked for the bestower. A murmur arose at this breach of protocol, and the gathered sages asked Brahma to arbitrate over the matter. Brahma made a pronouncement after a moment's thought. "Assembled guests," he began, "the great god Shiva has inadvertently violated protocol by sitting down in the place traditionally earmarked for the bestower. It should be regarded as an exception that is acceptable for the present occasion. The monarch of the mountains will sit facing west. There is nothing inauspicious in this arrangement."

The king was reassured by Brahma's words and went up to sit down as directed, facing Shiva. Brahma, playing the role of presiding priest, began chanting the relevant mantras. The king again went through purificatory ablutions, then paying due homage to Shiva handed over all the gifts. He held Parvati affectionately and knotted together a corner of her attire with Shiva's. Then sprinkling *kusha* grass and sesame seeds dipped in water and reciting Vedic mantras, the king concluded the ceremony of giving the bride away.

Shiva, the great god, and Parvati, Mahamaya incarnate, went into private quarters set aside for the wedding night, accompanied by a cheerful bevy of bridesmaids who prattled tirelessly, played pranks, and teased the newlyweds.

Shiva happily entered into the spirit of the occasion. He played a game of dice with the bride, while her companions made jokes and teasing remarks. Shiva lost the game; Parvati won convincingly. Her friends declared it was a sign that she would be a devoted wife, like Sati before her.

After the game was over Queen Menaka came and worshipped the great god Shiva with offerings of paddy and *durba* grass. Shiva rose and sitting down on an immaculate couch and calling his bride offered her *panchamrita*, the collective name for five sweet things: yogurt, milk, ghee, sugar, and honey. Parvati accepted them with a *pranam* and left the room. Shiva feasted voraciously on various delicacies, including a dessert of sweet rice pudding. After the meal he rinsed his mouth and prepared to turn in. He summoned Nandi and asked him in a whisper to get some datura seeds and bhang. "I've eaten too much of the sweets," he explained. "I feel like throwing up, and the datura and bhang will act as an antiemetic."

Nandi unobtrusively brought the stuff, and Shiva devoured it with alacrity and felt better at once. He lay down on an exquisitely ornamented bed. Presently Parvati was led in, escorted by a bevy of bridesmaids, who archly urged caution on the great god's part. "Don't start pawing her tender body," they warned. "Let her sleep undisturbed or else you'll have to regret any rash act."

The god smiled mischievously. The ladies spent some time bantering with him before bidding the newlyweds goodnight.

Shiva and his Shakti united again that night, dispelling the anguish of long separation. The newlyweds slept in profound peace.

Meanwhile, the king bade goodnight to the guests who had accompanied the bridegroom. After the rituals, sacrifices, and prayers were concluded, he addressed the gods. "My lords, you are scheduled to leave for home tomorrow morning. Allow me to offer you some refreshments before you turn in. I hope you have a pleasant journey."

Everyone in the bridegroom's party was pleased with the refreshments provided by the king. There were enormous quantities of sweetmeats for the gods and of alcoholic beverages for the *bhutas, vetalas,* and *bhairava* look-alikes of Shiva.

The king then went into his private chambers. He had a modest repast and after vigorously rinsing his mouth, turned in for a night's sleep. Gradually the entire city fell asleep.

In the small hours the koels began to sing. A while after, as the drone of beetles spread in the air, people started to wake up, muttering invocations to the gods. On seeing the rays of the rising sun the sages set off to bathe in a lake. Temples came alive with the music of the cymbals and conch shells of votaries. When the sun had risen, the citizens of the Himalayan kingdom were all up and about. Brahma and the other gods were awake as well.

The bride's girlfriends went in to wake her up and carried her to her private chambers. Nandi went to wake Shiva by tickling the soles of his feet. After rinsing his mouth and washing his face with fresh water, Shiva went to seek out Brahma and Vishnu in the guests' quarters. "It's time to go home to Kailash with the bride," Shiva said to them, "so make the necessary arrangements."

They were pleased to hear this and sent word to the king.

"Listen," the king said to Queen Menaka, "it's time for Parvati to go to Kailash, so make the necessary arrangements."

Though entirely expected, the news struck Menaka like a death-blow. She sat stunned, lost in thought; her soul seemingly stuck in her throat, ready to depart. At last she managed to give orders to servants to get things ready. Then she cradled Parvati in her arms and sobbed uncontrollably.

"How will I live without having my daughter around?" Menaka wailed. "She was born thanks to my good karma. I've given away my golden-complexioned daughter to a stranger. I don't have five or six daughters like others; she is my only child. All the effort to give her a good upbringing has come to this; I'll die of not being able to see her."

Her mother's lament drew a sympathetic response from others. Parvati sobbed uncontrollably; tears deluged her breasts. Her heart seemed to be rent by unbearable sorrow. Her friends were moved to join in, lamenting loudly at the impending separation. The inner quarters were like a house in mourning, filled with keening women.

As Shiva prepared to mount his bull, Nandi went in with a beautifully decorated litter in which Parvati would travel to Kailash.

"You will soon go with your husband to his home on Mount Kailash," Queen Menaka sorrowfully said to Parvati, "but I want to know, my darling daughter, if you will remember your mother."

Parvati embraced her mother's feet and said, "How will I live without seeing you? Please bring me back for a visit before long. Don't forget to do so. Remember me as I will remember you."

With these parting words Parvati made a *pranam* to her mother. She took her seat in the litter and made a farewell *pranam* to her father.

The newlyweds' journey swiftly began with drums playing merrily.

Shiva played percussion on the inflated cheeks of all five of his faces. Hearing this, Nandi and Bhringi began dancing to its rhythm, as did the *bhutas* and others. Apsaras sang in honeyed tones as they danced. The handsome *vidyadhara* demigods beat tom-toms as they danced, and the yakshas danced as they sang praises of Shiva, clapping to keep time. Thus the merry party made its way toward Kailash.

✦   ✦   ✦

Sadness was banished from Kailash, for Shiva and Parvati dwelt there in a state of unsurpassed bliss. They had fervent devotees who offered them puja regularly. Parvati came to be worshipped as Durga or Kali or Chandi, by which name she came to be most widely known. The previously austere atmosphere of the place was replaced by a mood of gaiety and joyous celebration. Shiva's divine peers and the other gods took their leave one by one, but the *bhutas,* demons, and *vetalas* stayed on. Shiva and his Shakti were united in a harmonious spiritual bond.

THE BIRTH OF GANESHA
AND KARTIKEYA

IN TIME, THE DIVINE COUPLE RAISED a unique family. First to be born was Ganesha, whose blessing dispels all difficulties from our lives, and who is famous as the scribe who wrote down the *Mahabharata,* India's great and holy epic, from the sage Vyasa's dictation.

Shiva and Chandi happily passed the first thousand years of their married life in continuous lovemaking. At an auspicious moment Shiva impregnated his wife, but his sperm was endowed with such energy that her womb could not retain it for more than ten seconds. Shiva's sperm of course could never go to waste. The expelled zygote received a further infusion of divine energy from Vishnu and soon produced a son.

Chandi was overjoyed, and when the wind god Pavana circulated the news of the divine birth among the gods they came to see and bless the child—all except Saturn.

Chandi sent Pavana to inquire why Saturn hadn't come. He explained that if he looked at the newborn child his tremendous energy would wreak havoc. But Chandi pooh-poohed the warning and sent an insistent invitation to Saturn. This time he came, but, as he had warned, disaster struck as soon as his gaze settled on the child, whose head came off and was spontaneously incinerated.

Chandi burst into tears and loud lamentation at the horrible sight. "Who gave me the priceless treasure only to snatch it away? Though I live amid powerful gods I have been utterly ruined. I will now lay the world waste. As for the perpetrator of the murderous deed, as of now his life is forfeit."

Vishnu came upon hearing her lament and said rather chidingly: "Why do you cry over the outcome of your own actions? You induced Saturn to come, despite his warning, and that's why his gaze decapitated your son."

Chandi could only hang her head in mortification. Vishnu then instructed Pavana to travel north and bring back the head of the first slumbering creature he came across.

"I'll transplant that head onto Chandi's son and revive him," Vishnu exclaimed.

Pavana set off at once. The first sleeping creature he saw happened to be Airavata, Indra's mount. At once he sliced off its head and flew back with it. He handed it to Vishnu, who promptly clamped it on the bleeding shoulder. At once Chandi's son gave his body a shake and stood up, alive and well but with an elephant's head.

Chandi wasn't entirely pleased. "Now that my son has the head of an elephant, no one in the three realms of the universe will feel inclined to worship him."

"On the contrary," Vishnu reassured her, "he will be worshipped before all other gods. Let his name be Ganesha. His greatness will be universally proclaimed; he will be preeminent among the gods. If anyone prays to another god without first offering puja to him, the prayer will not be fulfilled."

Parvati was pleased to hear this. The gods then went to the spot where Airavata lay lifeless. After going through ablutions they sprinkled consecrated water on the wound—at once a new head sprang up where the old one had been, and Airavata shook itself and stood up, alive again. As for Ganesha's original head, it merged into Vishnu's form.

Once, when they were together in an enchanting flower garden, Shiva and Chandi became sexually aroused and, the spot being utterly secluded, made love with complete abandon. Shiva practiced coitus interruptus, as befitted the great ascetic god, and, the lovemaking over, composed himself and sat down in a meditative posture. Even then, by a divine miracle, his pent-up semen shot out with tremendous force and, landing in a distant lake, began drifting on its waters. By a divinely ordained coincidence a woman went to bathe in the lake just then. As soon as she waded in, the semen entered her womb, impregnating her. The divine semen was impossible for her to bear. Soon she had a miscarriage in the middle of a field of holy *kusha* grass. But the god's semen could not go to waste: instead of an aborted fetus, a son was born with six stunningly handsome heads.

The divine child was discovered in the field by the six nymphs known collectively as the Krittikas. They were charmed by his handsome appearance and, taking him home, brought him up with affectionate care. Because he was fostered by the Krittikas he came to be known as Kartikeya.

One day the sage Narada went to Chandi. "You have a son, miraculously born from your husband's semen, but Vishnu has caused him to be fostered by the Krittikas," he informed her.

Chandi was enraged to hear this and dispatched Nandi to fetch her son at once.

The inhabitants of Kailash were overjoyed when they saw Kartikeya, for he possessed the radiant beauty of the full moon. Chandi was beside herself with joy and ordered a lavish celebration to mark her son's homecoming.

From day to day the young god grew in stature and strength and received training in the arts of war, soon becoming an unerring marksman with bow and arrow. It was quite clear that he was the one destined to deliver the gods from the scourge of the demon Taraka.

THE SLAYING OF TARAKA THE ASURA

IT HAD BEEN AN INORDINATELY long time since the mighty demon Taraka had begun his depredations. He had conquered Indra's heavenly abode, and the gods had fled in terror. Still jealous of the gods, Taraka relentlessly harried them at every opportunity.

A tearful delegation of gods told Kartikeya of their woeful plight.

"There's no reason to panic," the mighty Kartikeya reassured them. "I'll destroy the wicked demon in no time. Take me to his hometown. If he gives battle I'll straightaway dispatch him to the underworld."

On hearing these reassuring words the gods set about making preparations for war. They took Kartikeya's war chariot to Kubera, hometown of Kubera, god of wealth, and had it attractively accoutred. They adorned Kartikeya's battle dress with precious gems, and when the mighty god climbed onto his chariot, they formed up behind as accompanying foot soldiers.

Kartikeya, commander in chief of the divine host, let out a terrifying war cry and led the advance. Thunderous was the din created by the belligerent gods as they rushed forward. Soon they reached the outskirts of Taraka's stronghold and came upon a demon named Raktambuja. Kartikeya hailed him and asked him to carry a message to Taraka: "Go tell your master that he must immediately surrender all pretensions to property belonging to the gods, or else he will face annihilation at my hands. Tell him to come and fight, if he dare."

The demon emissary hurried away and reported everything to Taraka. The mighty hero of the asuras quivered with rage on hearing of the challenge and, armed with bow and arrows, set off at once with meteoric speed, determined to destroy the divine army. Such was his arrogant pride, he ignored the signs of ill omen that appeared. Roaring with anger he marshaled his demon army and advanced in battle formation. At the sight of the army of gods the wrathful Taraka hurled invectives and insults without any restraint.

Addressing the gods generally he shouted tauntingly: "Have you no shame? You keep coming to challenge me and keep getting thrashed. Do you think we would be intimidated by your likes? Who is this Kartikeya who has joined your wimpish crew? Let him come forward and identify himself. Who is the foolish father who has engendered him? Let's see where he finds the strength to defy me."

The demon's words ignited such wrath in Chandi's darling son that his dozen eyes burned like the flaming sun.

"Do you know who you are dealing with, you wicked demon?" Kartikeya said contemptuously. "I am the son of the great god Shiva, who holds sway over the whole universe. You may not have heard of me, but I am going to be the agency of your annihilation. Your vaunted strength I will vanquish in battle."

"Enough, no more about yourself!" the demon exclaimed jeeringly. "I can surmise what kind of fighting you will do. After all, your father has five faces and ten squinting eyes. He is always either drunk or high on bhang. Your mother has ten arms—she looks rather like a spider. She is a fraud besides, extracting sacrifices of he-goats from gullible folk who have been beguiled into believing she can grant their wishes. Your brother has an elephant's head and rides a mount: who would count him a god? You have half a dozen heads and a dozen eyes. What a grotesque-looking family! Who wants to fight with a pesky little brat like you? If you want to live long, go home quietly. You have no idea of my prowess. If you insist on taking me on, you will be like a dragonfly that falls into a fire and is instantly incinerated."

On hearing this insulting tirade Kartikeya roared like a wrathful lion and twanged his mighty bow. Fixing on it a gandharva missile, he launched it with a snap, while gods and demons furiously charged at each other. The missile wrought havoc in the demon ranks. The demon chief twanged his bow with such force that it shook earth, heaven, and the underworld. He picked a special missile obtained from the gods and, as he fitted it to his bow, boomed out a dire warning: "Here's a weapon to take care of Kartikeya. I've had enough of your heroic antics, my child, now it's time to bid farewell, for your end is near."

He launched the missile, and it rose swiftly, releasing a hundred thousand projectiles with flaming tips. In an instant the sky was overspread with deadly darts whizzing toward the invading army. The gods wailed in terror. Kartikeya quickly neutralized this spectacular onslaught by launching the aishika antimissile missiles. He then recited the appropriate mantras and launched a counterattack with the invincible Brahmastra missile. As soon as he fitted the missile in his bow, a wave of panic spread through the enemy ranks. The demons stood transfixed, quaking with fear as flames bright and fierce as a thousand suns emanated from the missile's mouth. In an instant the missile was airborne. It hovered in the sky above the enemy ranks, letting out an ominous roar. The demons lost all hope and burst into wails of despair.

Even the redoubtable Taraka knew the game was up. "What sin has brought me to this pass?" he wailed. "I subdued earth, heaven, and the underworld with the might of my arms, only to lose my life in a battle with a child. I leave behind a tarnished reputation."

Thus did the mighty asura have to pay for the sin of envying the gods. The roar of the Brahmastra missile reduced Taraka to a pale-faced, cowering figure. It then descended like a flashing meteor and instantly decapitated the demon chieftain. Like a mountain destroyed by some cataclysm, his body came crashing down and covered miles of ground where it fell. The demon cohorts burst into loud lamentation, while the gods exulted. The rights and privileges of the gods were restored, and they were assured of an undisturbed reign henceforth.

THE BIRTH OF CHANDRADHARA

LET US TAKE UP THE extraordinary tale of the birth of that great merchant king Chandradhara.

There was a noble sage called Padmashankhya, an extremely pious and contemplative man whose ashram stood beside a sparkling lake. A tree had grown at the water's edge, and a bird had nested in its branches. One stormy night the tree came crashing down, bird's nest and all. A couple of eggs that had been laid in the nest rolled out and nestled on the soft earth.

The next morning the sage went to the lake to bathe and saw the fallen eggs. He brought them home and kept them in a safe place. After some days, to the sage's delight, the eggs hatched. He took good care of the chicks, feeding them on milk and bananas. They grew into a pair of lovely birds. The sage built a comfortable roosting place for them, and in time eggs were laid and hatched. Gradually generations of birds came to share the sage's home, and the air at all hours was filled with their cheery chirping. The sage's ashram became the most joyous of all hermitages.

Once, the sage was invited to a fête. As it was at a distant place, he had to stay overnight. In his absence a host of snakes sneaked in and devoured all the birds, their chicks, and their eggs. The next day the sage returned home to find everything eerily quiet. There wasn't a single bird or even a bird's egg anywhere. He couldn't think of any explanation for their disappearance. He sat down to meditate and through his yogic insight came to know everything. His sorrow couldn't have been greater if he had lost his own sons.

The sage said to himself in self-castigation, "From today mine is an accursed life. I will never be able to overcome my sorrow in this life. I will sacrifice my life to the holy, wish-fulfilling waters of the Ganges and beg from her a life on earth as the enemy of snakes. I will slay all creatures of that loathsome species that I come across."

Having made this resolution, the sage left his ashram. Tears of grief rolled down his cheeks and flooded his chest as he made his way to the holy waters. On coming to the river he waded in, as if he were taking a bath. He recited the appropriate evening prayers and prepared to abandon this life. "Ganga, Ganga," he called out to the river goddess and, with palms reverentially joined, began singing her praise.

"I bow to you, Mother Ganga, goddess who nurtures life on earth. Your glory is indescribable! The great god Shiva bore you in the awesome locks of his hair to make your gifts available to mankind. Whoever enters your sacred waters to make a wish is sure to have it promptly fulfilled. I humbly offer my life in the hope that you will mitigate my grief. I beg you in the name of Shiva to reincarnate me on earth as the scourge of the serpent species."

With many more encomiastic words addressed to Ganga, the sage plunged into the bosom of the river and disappeared from view.

The sage's tale has to be taken up again on earth.

There was a famous city by the name of Champaknagar. It was ruled by King Katiswara, who belonged to the merchant caste and who in his worldly possessions was a match for Kubera, the god of wealth. A pious man, the king was an ardent worshipper of Shiva and his consort.

Our sage was reincarnated as King Katiswara's son. The father was delighted. He offered celebratory prayers to Sasthi, the goddess of childbirth. The child was fair and handsome as the *chandra* (moon) and was consequently named Chandradhara. Like the waxing moon Chandradhara grew rapidly and soon became famous as a most worthy scion of the royal family. He mastered all the arts, from archery to wrestling to swordplay to magic. Observing his son's progress to manhood, the king began to think about getting him married.

A wealthy merchant named Sankhyapati had a beautiful daughter called Sonaka. King Katiswara arranged a match between her and his son. The wedding took place amid sumptuous festivities. Chandradhara was happy to marry a beauty like Sonaka.

Soon after, King Katiswara died. Chandradhara performed the obsequies and, having come into his estate as the new ruler of Champaknagar, carried on his father's religious practices with renewed fervency. Shiva and Chandi were so pleased that they paid him a visit.

Shiva said to him with a smile, "Ask me for a boon, O sage."

The sage—now incarnated as a king and a merchant—replied at once: "If you wish to give me a boon, O great god, let me have the greatest form of knowledge, the Mahagyan mantra, which enables one to revive the dead. It will be of great use to me, for I am, as you are aware, the sworn foe of the serpent species."

The great god was pleased to hear this and imparted to him the greatest of occult mantras in a whisper.

Chandi said exhortingly, "O sage, take up your sturdy staff and let it annihilate the serpent species."

Well armed now, the merchant king was confident of his might. In gratitude to the great god and his spouse he flung himself humbly at their feet in a complete *pranam*. This pleased the divine couple immensely. They urged him to get up and reassured him that they would come whenever Chandradhara prayed for their assistance. Thus reassured, Chandradhara stood up, brushing the dust off his body. With a few more words of reassurance the divine couple returned home to Mount Kailash.

Thrilled with his newfound power, Chandradhara drank cupfuls of snake venom. It had no effect on him, for he was now immune to its deadly action.

The word quickly spread that Chandradhara was a sworn enemy of all snakes. All the snakes in Champaknagar fled in fear. Nor would any snake enter Champaknagar. The sage-king looked in vain for snakes within his domains. He then summoned all the snake charmers in and around his kingdom and bade them scour the wild forests, catching and imprisoning any snake they came across. Hundreds of venomous snakes were caught in this way and were brought to Champaknagar. There the sage-king took them one by one into his viselike grip and beat them to death against a rugged rock.

Thus the sage-king passed his days in Champaknagar. As the years rolled by six sons were born to him and Sonaka. They were named Sarvananda, Purander, Sundara, Vidyananda, Narayan, and Janardana. They grew up into splendid youths, well mannered and well educated, and their proud father arranged their marriages with six beautiful girls of excellent lineage. They were named Lilabati, Kalabati, Padmagandha, Hiramoti, Chandrarekha, and Mohini. They were incomparable in their loveliness, their modesty, and their command over all the domestic arts. After thus settling his sons as householders, Chandradhara continued to look after the welfare of his subjects to whom he was a benign, paternal figure.

SHIVA'S DALLIANCES

SHIVA'S LIFE WITH CHANDI WAS not all bliss. How could it be, when he was Lingaraj, lord of the phallus, the epitome of male potency? Chandi had to bear a lot because of his uncontrollable casual philandering and even had to learn to share him with a co-wife, who was none other than the river goddess Ganga, whose mighty waters Shiva had tamed by catching the torrent in his tangled locks.

As ordained by Brahma, an irresistible attraction sprang up between Ganga and Shiva, and they got married according to gandharva rites. Chandi threw a tantrum when Shiva went home with the new bride perched on his head, but the sage Narada's intervention restored peace. Shiva's conjugal life became a ménage à trois, with his wives consoling each other when he went on the prowl for other females.

Shiva would often escape Chandi's jealous tirades by making for his beautiful celestial park. One day, as he sat there, wondering what to do, he resolved to visit the prostitutes in the red-light district and have some fun. But before he could leave the garden Chandi appeared before him, having discerned his errant desire by exercising her telepathic powers. She had assumed her most seductive form, and Shiva readily suspended his plans. Instead, he drew her to his lap, made love to her, and let her doze off in his arms in postcoital bliss. Then he summoned Nidra, the goddess of sleep, and asked her to install herself in his wife's eyes. Nidra readily complied. Shiva gently laid Chandi on a bed in a bower and, quietly slinging his satchel over his shoulder, mounted his bull and set off for the prostitutes' quarters.

He had to cross a ferry to get there. The single ferryboat there was operated by a woman of the lowly Dom caste—the caste of cremation-ground attendants. "Come quickly, O Dom maiden," Shiva called out, "come quickly and ferry me across, for the fierce rays of the sun have exhausted me, and at my age it's hard to face such an ordeal."

The boatwoman said laughingly as she rowed toward the riverbank: "If you are in a great hurry, why not swim across? It will cool your body, you will get across without delay, and won't have to pay the fare."

"I am carrying a few heavy things, so I won't be able to swim," said Shiva. "Ferry me across and I'll give you some delicious sandesh sweets."

The woman was touched to hear this. She ferried Shiva without delay. Shiva's bull, of course, had to swim across.

Shiva gave the bull a rubdown, saddled it again, and merrily rode it to the red-light district. He stopped at the door of a brothel and played loud and lively percussion on puffed-up cheeks. At once a bevy of garishly decked prostitutes came out running. On seeing the expression on Shiva's face—unenthusiastic, a trifle grouchy—they burst into giggles. Some of them went back inside and gave the news to Heera, who came out without delay and, going up to Shiva, addressed him coquettishly.

"Where have you come from, O lord of all ascetics? What can I do for you?"

Shiva replied with mock solemnity: "I am a homeless wanderer, a mendicant. I have brought sweets for you, as a small token of appreciation, for you are the cynosure of all the ladies of the night."

He took out a large packet of laddoos from his satchel and handed it to Heera, who shared them with all the other inmates of the bordello. In a minute they were all consumed. Shiva smiled to himself, for he had spiked the sweets with bhang; as if to signal that the fun was about to begin, he blew on a horn. Then he started to sing, accompanying himself on a tabor. The women clapped in rhythm, but soon they were completely overwhelmed by the effects of the bhang: some of them just collapsed in a stupor and sat with eyes closed, some danced in a frenzy, and others sang raucously. While the racket continued, Shiva and his favorite, Heera, stole away to indulge in lusty lovemaking. Heera was beside herself with joy as Shiva toyed with her treasure, for he was a master of the erotic arts. For his part, he was highly satisfied with Heera's performance as a lover.

Having pleased himself and his partner, Shiva prepared to take his leave. He stood before Heera with palms joined in a mendicant's gesture of supplication—to the delight of the entire troupe of prostitutes. They plied him with a variety of gifts and saw him off. Shiva rode away on his bull. And thus ended yet another day of gallivanting for the great god.

As for the great goddess Chandi, she awoke from a long, refreshing siesta to discover that her husband was nowhere around. Her inner powers revealed to her all that had transpired. Without wasting any time she mounted a lion and set off for the ferry ghat.

She asked the ferrywoman, "Have you seen my husband, the lord of all creatures? He regularly uses your ferry."

"Listen, divine mother of the divine Kartikeya," said the ferrywoman, "so many use the ferry in both directions that it is impossible to take a good look at everyone. Who can tell if one of them is your husband? There's an old fellow who crosses and recrosses regularly. Around the neck he wears a necklace of human bone, on his body a tiger skin, and he pays me in kind, not in coins."

"That's the one!" exclaimed Chandi. "That's my husband. Tell me where I can find him."

The ferrywoman couldn't help her, but the answer occurred to her spontaneously. All she had to do was to wait with the ferryboat.

"Listen, my friend," she said to the ferrywoman. "If you have any sympathy for me, you'll do as I say. Go home, leaving the boat and paddle to me. I'll exchange my clothes for yours, and the jewelry as well. Leave me your brass bangles and anklets and take all the jewelry you see on me. I'll be ferrywoman for the rest of the day."

The Dom woman was delighted with the arrangement and happily went home with her priceless new possessions. Chandi stepped on to the boat, paddle in hand, and guided the boat to the middle of the stream.

Before long, Shiva came along riding on his bull, Nandi, and merrily drumming with joined fingers on inflated cheeks.

On reaching the bank he called out, "My good ferrywoman, come quick and paddle me across! Chandi sleeps peacefully in the garden, and I must get back to her before she awakes."

Gritting her teeth in suppressed anger, Chandi hissed: "Swim across if you are so desperate. You go back and forth everyday without paying. I'll tie your wrists and force you to cough up if you get on my boat today."

With that stern warning Chandi rowed further away, leaving a forlorn Shiva standing in his tiger skin, clutching his satchel, on the riverbank. He was in dire straits. The ferrywoman would ruin his reputation forever, it seemed: disgrace stared him in the face. The day was nearly done; daylight steadily seeped away. Shiva's tone became humble as he spoke imploringly to the woman.

"Have mercy, I swear my life is in your hands. It is forfeit if you refuse to help me."

The great goddess was thrown into a quandary. She guided the boat slowly toward the riverbank. Plaintiff and defendant were now face-to-face.

"It's terribly unfair of you to resort to such psychological blackmail," Chandi complained. "Besides, if you get on board with your loaded satchel and your other ragged belongings, you'll sink the boat and drown."

"The things I'm carrying are quite light actually," said Shiva reassuringly as he boarded the boat.

"Oh no, see how the boat sinks to the gunwale under your weight. You are a crazy one, old fellow, to cross the river like this."

But I cross the river every day," Shiva protested. "Am I heavier than on other days? Of course I understand that you are concerned about earning some money from your work, but there is reason for making an exception in my case. I am a lifelong mendicant, as you know. When I go home my wife berates me because of this. What can I do but roam with a begging bowl?"

With an ironic smile Chandi began paddling the boat. She began to sing softly, a sweet, melodious air that pierced Shiva's heart like a five-pronged missile, setting it aflame with lust.

"Who is your husband, ferrywoman?" he asked. "He must be a consummate ass to remain complacently at home and let his beautiful wife ferry strangers in a boat. There are so many lecherous rogues roaming around you never know what one of them might do."

"Why do you say such horrible things, Shiva?" the ferrywoman said. "Who can harm me? I paddle this boat because that is my hereditary occupation. If anyone behaves improperly he will have to pay for it."

"What can I say?" Shiva said plaintively. "Your exquisite loveliness has rent my heart asunder. Judging sheer beauty there is no difference between you and Chandi. To my eyes you are the same as Chandi. All men on earth are manifestations of my physical substance, and similarly all women are consubstantial with Chandi. Therefore you are a manifestation of my wife. Come into my embrace and assuage my raging desire."

"Please, not another word," said the ferrywoman firmly. "Has age made you lose your mind? If my husband came to know about this would you escape with your life? How can you have such wicked thoughts in spite of being the lord of all gods? If Chandi came to know she would feel mortified and humiliated. You'd better go home while your self-respect is intact, or else you'll soon land in deep trouble."

At this Shiva joined palms in supplication and declared: "For god's sake, don't turn me down. My body is trembling with desire, my life hangs in the balance. Be kind and grant me an embrace."

In a burst of impatience Shiva took the ferrywoman by force into his arms. At once Chandi assumed her normal form and began berating her husband.

"This is what you do away from home. If I wasn't paddling the boat today your folly would have led to the loss of your caste status."

Shiva hung his head in shame, though he did try to explain away his scandalous behavior as a playful jest.

"I knew all along it was you, I wanted to play a prank on you," he said. "Now let's go home to our children."

Later that day, taking the form of a mouse, Shiva nibbled some holes in Chandi's favorite bodice, at the places that covered her breasts. Chandi was aghast when she saw what had happened. Had it been any other piece of clothing she would have thrown it away without batting an eyelid, but she was deeply attached to the gorgeous bodice that now lay tattered. She sent a servant to fetch an expert darner of clothes. The servant came back with an old man equipped with various kinds of needles and threads. Chandi handed him the bodice.

"Can you mend it so that it will look new again?"

"A very difficult job, but for a price I can do it."

"Anything you ask for."

"Do you solemnly promise?"

"Of course. My word is inviolate."

The darner set to work and miraculously restored the bodice to its original gorgeous form.

"Here," he said, handing it back to a very pleased client. "Now for my payment. You must let me make love to you."

"What! An old man like you? Do you know who I am?"

"Don't you know what happens to those who break a solemn promise?"

There is nothing to do but get it over with, thought Chandi. The old man had his way, but when he got up he wasn't an old darner any more. Chandi saw her husband Shiva in all his resplendent glory and hung her head in shame and embarrassment at being tricked.

Shiva grinned and said, "Now we're quits."

THE BIRTH OF MANASA

SHIVA WALKED INTO THE PARK one day and reposed in a flowery couch in a bower. As wild birds and animals copulated with abandon all around, he was pierced by the invisible arrows of Kama and lay roasting in the fires of lust.

Presently his eyes fell on the branches of a bel tree. Hanging from them were thick clusters of bel fruit. Shiva cupped his hands and called out to the hanging fruit; two promptly landed in his hands. They were exact replicas of Chandi's breasts. The flames of lust burned more fiercely for Shiva; he lost consciousness and rolled off the couch. A little later he ejaculated involuntarily. Instantly awake, he cupped his mighty hands to receive the semen and carried it to a lotus garden. He transferred it to a lotus leaf and returned to his bower.

What had been ordained by Brahma now came to pass. A foraging female bird flew down to the lotus garden and, noticing the syrupy stuff left by Shiva, gulped it down. Inside the bird's belly the potent semen grew intensely hot. Unable to bear it the bird frantically guzzled quantities of water, only aggravating the situation, for the water instantly came to a boil. The bird became panic-stricken; it rose shrieking into the air and, flying to Brahma, fell sobbing at the god's feet.

"Why are you crying?" Brahma inquired kindly.

"I'm in deep trouble," wailed the hapless bird. "My strength and my wits have deserted me. Take pity on me and do something. I'd gone to the lotus garden to forage. I was so hungry that I ate whatever seemed edible. Suddenly, I began to experience an intolerable burning sensation in my belly, as if the fire god had invaded it in force. Frantic with agony, I rushed to you. Help me, O lord of all beings."

Brahma heard the bird's lament and looking inward came to know all that had transpired. After a moment's reflection he told the bird that if it went back to the place where it had eaten the stuff and regurgitated it, the agony would surely vanish.

Solaced by the god's assurance, the bird flew swiftly to the lotus garden and threw up. As soon as the potent semen landed on a lotus, a huge egg took shape from it. The egg promptly rolled away and entered the nether regions, where the sage Kasyapa lived. The sage realized that it was a miraculous object and went into yogic meditation to learn more about it.

He found out that the egg was born of Shiva's semen and had been conceived in the lotus garden. The sage decided to hatch a daughter for the great god out of it. So he placed it in a golden bowl and invited all the gods to witness the divine birth.

To Vasuki, the emperor of all nagas, the sage sent instructions to prepare for a coronation. The great goddess of their species was due to be born out of a magical egg, and thanks to her powers the nagas would receive the adoration of pujas performed worldwide. The naga king set about the task with alacrity and soon arrived with all the items required for coronation rituals.

Sage Kasyapa sat down in the appropriate posture with all the Vedas and began performing a coronation ceremony for the egg. He chanted the relevant mantras aloud, and all the assembled gods chanted along. Presently there emerged from the gigantic egg a ravishing maiden whose beauty would charm all three realms—earth, underworld, and the heavens. She stood, radiantly fair in complexion, triple-eyed, and four-armed, casting an everlasting spell on all who saw her. The gandharvas sang, the *vidyadhari* demigoddesses danced, the apsaras cavorted to celebrate the arrival of the new goddess.

The gods joined in, crying "Hail!" Then everyone joined in sprinkling the goddess with Ganges water. Vasuki presented her with gorgeous clothes and ornaments. She put them on and ascended the throne, a resplendent sight, while her praises were chanted all around.

Born miraculously and not from a maternal womb, an object of adoration to all, gods included, Shiva's daughter, goddess of all snakes and serpents, and matriarch of the whole world, Padmavati—Padma in short—or Manasa or Visahari, the mistress of poison, as she is commonly called, can grant liberation at will, dispel darkness and gloom with the light of her radiant countenance, and satisfy mortal desires with a nod of her head.

Such were the praises the delighted gods sang before they took their leave. Padmavati lived with the sage Kasyapa, who named her Jaratkaru and groomed her for her divine role in the world, and his wife Kadru, who lavished on her all motherly affection.

"My good fellow," Kasyapa said to Vasuki, "you must serve Padma with devotion. All of your venomous brood in the three realms should be ready at all times to do her bidding."

Vasuki spared no effort to ensure Padma's comfort. Chambers of beaten gold were built for the goddess's living quarters and an earthen pitcher was placed in front to serve as the focal point of puja rituals. At Vasuki's command all the snakes in the universe congregated daily to lay offerings at the goddess's feet.

After some days Padma said to Kasyapa, "Master of all sages, I wish to ask you something. I feel an overwhelming desire to meet my father, Shiva, the god of all gods. Where can I find him and how should I go there?"

The sage replied reassuringly. "Pay attention to what I have to say. The honor of all concerned must be preserved. You must go appropriately attired, so that Shiva is pleased to see you."

Kasyapa then turned to Vasuki. "Lay out a luxuriously upholstered chariot," he commanded. Vasuki produced an outlandishly accoutred vehicle. Manasa was massaged with scented unguents and then decked out with snakes that wound themselves around every part of her body. Thus attired, she climbed in to begin her auspicious journey. Four swans drew the chariot through the air.

The gods blew trumpets and played on drums, and showered the air-borne goddess with petals. The chariot eventually landed in Shiva's celestial park. Padma got down, deciding to wait there.

Presently, Shiva sauntered into the garden. What followed was the inexorable dictate of fate, which even the greatest of gods could only blindly follow. It was an evil hour when Shiva set eyes upon Manasa. He was at once utterly distracted and riddled with the invisible shafts of lust. His mind was a welter of prurient thoughts as he addressed the visitor in his garden.

"Where are you from, who are your parents, why are you all by yourself in this garden?"

Before she could reply he continued: "A hundred moons will pale before your radiant figure. Your beauty has driven me to distraction."

Though shocked at these words, Padma tried to compose herself as she replied: "I am your very own daughter, great god, legitimate in birth. I was born in the nether regions, ceremonially invested in my office as snake goddess by a host of gods, and brought up by Vasuki and Kasyapa. I have come to pay my respects to you, my father."

If Shiva were in his senses he would have heeded her words, but in his deranged state he could only blunder on.

"Come, come," he hissed, "cut out the deceitful chatter. The entire universe knows me as the god of gods, don't you dare lie to my face. I have two sons, Kartikeya and Ganesha, but no daughter. Who taught you the cunning ruse of trying to pass yourself as my daughter? You are a ravishing beauty in the first flush of maidenhood. You have driven me crazy. Come into my arms and satisfy me, let me take you home. I have two wives, Chandi and Ganga, but I'll love you more than I love them."

Shiva tried to grab Padma; she evaded him and inwardly called upon Vishnu for help. She kept appealing to Shiva's good sense. "I beg you, Father, don't you ever utter such sinful words. You'll be disgraced in the three realms. I tell you truly, if you don't check yourself you'll only invite ignominy."

Her words fell on deaf ears. Shiva was like an animal in heat.

"There, I've got you," he shouted, lunging forward to grab her. But she slipped out of his grasp. Driven to desperation, she couldn't restrain her rage any longer.

"That's enough," she said to herself, "I can't overlook Father's indecent proposal any longer." She called upon the sun and the moon to bear witness to her actions, for, she concluded, "I will presently use my divine venom to destroy the great god of all gods."

She aimed her venomous gaze at Shiva; he crumpled at once like a rag doll and collapsed on the ground. Padma was overcome with self-reproach and burst into a lament: "I have disgraced my name through the three realms. I came to this lotus garden in all innocence, only to end up as a despicable parricide." She held the inert head of her father on her lap while tears coursed down her cheeks.

"It must be my bad karma," Padma wailed, "or else why did I stop here, and even though I am Shiva's daughter, why did I face such a disgraceful and humiliating situation? I cannot show my face anywhere. Only one course of action is open to me. I'll leap into a raging pyre and immolate myself."

Padma's lamentation reached the ears of the gods, who rushed posthaste to the lotus garden. Brahma was the first to approach Padma. "Tell me, how did this come to pass?" he asked. Padma hung her head in embarrassment and shame, but Brahma used his clairvoyant powers and in a moment was fully cognizant of all the circumstances behind the catastrophe. He became a supplicant before Padma, imploring with joined palms, "Rescue us from this unprecedented crisis, O matriarch of the universe. Shiva is chief of all gods, and by saving him you will help preserve our race. Vishnu, Shiva, and I are the divine embodiments of three primal qualities in nature, and so we have three different forms. But essentially we are manifestations of a single spirit. You are one with us because you are Shiva's daughter, as the whole world knows. I can't bear to think of all that has happened."

Brahma's words of distress drew forth another shower of tears from Padma. "Lord of destiny," she addressed Brahma, "now you know what a disgraceful plight my father has left me in. To my divine peers I am a figure of ignominy. But I won't long remain like this—I'll soon give up my life. Do not ask me to revive the great god, my father. When one's time runs out there's no help."

At Padma's stern words all the gods joined their palms together and addressed her beseechingly. "Drive away the sorrow that preys on your mind. The gods have ever been notorious. Indeed, the nefarious activities of Indra, Yama, Varuna, Pavana, and Agni are too numerous to mention. It is consequently pointless to take such things to heart. The misdeeds of the powerful are not held against them. Who would take Agni, the fire god, to task for being all-devouring? Therefore, we beseech you to forget your grievance and set your mind to saving the lord of the gods."

Such words of consolation and encouragement had a positive impact, and Padma soon regained her composure.

I cannot disregard the gods, nor can I live as a parricide, she reflected. She then told the gods, "Bring me water from the Gandaki River. Be careful, don't spill it. I will bring the great god Shiva back to life in your presence, and afterward face whatever fate has in store for me."

Padma's words infused a flush of hope into the pale countenance of the gods. They brought water from the Gandaki in golden bowls; Padma was greatly pleased. She spread a ritual mat and laid Shiva's body on it. She sat in a posture of meditation and began her crucial ministrations. She sprinkled water on all four sides to secure the area against any form of occult interference and began neutralizing the venom by reciting primordial mantras. Gradually the five vital airs reentered Shiva's body. His body stirred, his eyes regained their glow, his consciousness returned. But he was still sleepy-eyed and his muscles lacked strength. Noticing this, Padma took some water in a cupped palm and splashed it on her father's eyes. At once Shiva sat up and gave his massive body a vigorous shake. The gods, delighted at the successful resuscitation, let out shouts of joy.

Brahma was the first to address his fellow god. "Look upon your daughter, the goddess Padmavati. Take her home and look after her with care and affection."

The words fell on fond ears, as paternal love blossomed in Shiva's breast. Reaching out with his mighty arms he lifted Padma onto his lap and showered her with sweet, affectionate words, dispelling the sorrow that had recently overwhelmed her. The gods looked on with delight and, showering her with sweet-scented blossoms, took their leave and turned homeward.

Padma too, after spending some time with her father in the lotus garden, wished to take her leave. Shiva was saddened at the thought and said in a voice choked with emotion, "You are my beloved daughter, miraculously restored to me. Why should you live all alone in the underworld?

You will go with me to my home in the city on Mount Kailash and my wife Chandi, your mother, will look after you with care."

Padma gratefully accepted her father's offer. Shiva then considered how best to convey his daughter to his home. If she stepped out of a palanquin, the sight would instantly inflame Chandi's jealous rage, and there was no knowing what irrevocable curse would escape her lips—for according to tradition, a palanquin is the conveyance for a newlywed bride. If Padma went on foot, like any humble young girl, she would draw taunts from onlookers.

Shiva was in a fix. Unable to find an elegant solution to the problem, he finally decided to carry his daughter in his cloth satchel.

On his way he came upon Bachhai, Chandi's plowman, tilling a field. He greeted Shiva and noticed that sitting in his satchel was an exquisitely beautiful maiden. He couldn't help indulging in a bit of raillery.

"You have two wives, Chandi and Ganga. Do you need another one? Let me have this pretty girl."

Shiva said nothing in reply and kept a straight face as he continued on his way. But Padma was inflamed with rage.

"Father, I can't tolerate wicked tongues," she said. "Why don't you rest a little under a tree over there? I'll sort out this yokel and rejoin you."

"Very well," Shiva acceded. "Do what you have to do, but use caution. None must know about it."

Padma instantly took the shape of a venomous serpent, but instead of slithering on the ground she became airborne and silently followed Bachhai as he guided the bullocks dragging the plow.

"Hari-Har, Har-Hari," he chanted softly as he plodded behind the plow, invoking the two popular names of Vishnu and Shiva, two brother gods equally matched in power. As long as the names of the gods were on his lips, Padma's powers were useless; she flew behind Bachhai's back, waiting for an opportunity to strike.

An opportune moment had to come eventually, for the dictates of fate cannot be evaded. As the bullocks reached the end of the field, in order to turn them around the plowman paused in his chant of "Hari-Har" and shouted "Whoa!" and at once, in a lightning flash, Manasa injected the snake venom into his bottom.

Instantly, he crumpled and collapsed in an inert mass on the furrowed earth. Seeing this, his fellow plowmen came running and set up a piteous wail. They picked up their dead comrade and carried him home on their shoulders. His mother broke down at the sight of her son's dead body. "Why has Shiva taken you away? Why has fate decreed your death?" she lamented. "You were the child of a poor mother, her sole support and solace. I can't understand for what fault you've been struck down so suddenly. I can't live with my grief at losing you; it's best if I leap into the flames and perish."

Bachhai's mother wailed inconsolably, she hurled herself on the ground, and her neighbors' words of consolation had no effect on her. Padma smiled to herself and appeared before the distraught mother in the garb of a Brahmin lady.

"Listen, dear lady," Padma said to the grieving mother, "sacrifice animals to the snake goddess, for it is her wrath that has cost your son his life. Surely she will relent and restore to you what you have lost."

"I will certainly worship the snake goddess if I have proof of her power. If Bachhai comes alive now I will offer puja to the goddess and sacrifice many animals to her."

On hearing this Padma, directed a benign gaze at the plowman's lifeless body. At once it stirred and began to breathe. His mother exclaimed in delight at this miracle and set about arranging puja for the snake goddess. Brahmins of various sects were invited; the altar was prepared with the earthen pitcher that is Padma's symbol; puja offerings and quantities of milk, sugar, bananas, and various sweets were brought from various places. Herds of buffaloes were sacrificed, and ghee was ritually fed to a fire. The grateful mother prostrated herself on the ground before the altar and loudly prayed to the goddess for protection. Pleased at her devotion, Padma blessed her and conferred generous boons on her before returning to the spot where she had left her father.

Shiva, who had clairvoyantly followed everything, was worried at the prospect of a face-off between his consort Chandi and his newfound daughter. For as soon as Chandi heard about what had happened to her plowman Bachhai, she would be up in arms against Padma. Chandi could be relentless in her animosity, she could be utterly unforgiving, and Shiva too wouldn't be spared: he would be the target of many a jibe.

Shiva gestured to Padma to get into his satchel again and this time hid her completely within its folds.

Chandi came out to welcome him home, fussing over him like a devoted housewife. He went in and kept his satchel in the loft, with an earnest word of warning to his wife. "Under no circumstances should you look inside the satchel," he said, "for that will have dire repercussions falling on my head. You see, it contains certain highly potent substances for use in rites of austerity."

After spending a very pleasant night with his family, in the morning Shiva took his sons Kartikeya and Ganesha to a forest ashram for instruction. As soon as they were gone, Chandi called Ganga and asked her to fetch Shiva's satchel. "There's something he is trying to hide from the two of us," she said. "I must see what it is."

But Ganga ignored the request. Then Chandi pushed one of the large mortars used for husking grain till it was near the open side of the loft, upturned it, and stood upon it so that she could reach the satchel. She brought it down, loosened the strings fastening it, and looked inside.

A scream of rage escaped her as her eyes fell on the lovely girl sitting there. "Ganga!" she cried. "Come and see the latest evidence of the old fool's nefarious activities. He picked up this pretty thing from somewhere and hid her in his satchel, trying to pull the wool over our eyes with a cock-and-bull story about keeping some holy object. My blood boils at the thought of what he has done. Just imagine—picking up a strange female and stashing her away. If we don't kick out the wicked bitch, heaping imprecations on her, there will be trouble in store for us, I'm telling you."

Padma pleaded with Chandi to refrain from vulgar outbursts. "I am the great god Shiva's daughter," she introduced herself. "All gods, gandharvas, and yakshas know this. I was conceived miraculously in a lotus garden. It ill behooves you, my mother, to speak in this fashion. If I am lying let me be struck down at once."

But Padma's words only served to further inflame Chandi's rage. Chandi addressed Ganga and vented her wrath. "Just listen to the little bitch!" she yelled. "Not even in a dream have I heard of the birth of a daughter. How dare she make such a ridiculous claim! I must give her a sound thrashing—that might relieve my feelings."

Ganga, however, counseled restraint and tolerance. "Hear my advice, O great goddess," she began. "Shiva is our lord and master, and even if he decides to have a hundred wives our protests will be to no avail. Besides, since this girl has introduced herself as his daughter it will be improper to make her suffer. Defying the laws of Dharma will only lead to unpleasant complications. Why not wait till Shiva returns home? Let's see what he has to say."

But the impetuous Chandi was in no mood to heed such advice. She took hold of Padma's locks, dragged her outside, and set upon her with vicious force. Padma cried out in pain and called upon Ganga to bear witness to the unfair treatment being meted out to her. This only enraged Chandi further. She beat the wailing Padma black and blue, until the girl passed out. Then she dragged her by the hair to a field of arum plants, gouged out one of her eyes with a sharp reed, and covered her unconscious body with leaves.

Her wrath spent, Chandi washed and tidied herself and went to her chamber to rest. She was still relaxing contentedly when Padma regained consciousness and resolved to hit back. She took the form of a humble fly—but a fly equipped with the most potent snake venom—and innocuously buzzed into Chandi's bedchamber. Without a moment's hesitation Padma injected the venom into the sole of her stepmother's foot.

It was as if she had been struck by lightning: Chandi screamed, calling for her mother. Padma slipped out and hid in the clumps of arum. The terror-stricken Chandi called Ganga: "Come quick, I don't know what's bitten me, but I'm dying. The pain is unbearable. I was resting in bed when some creature got in through some chink and injected poison into my foot. What will I do, what will happen to me? I feel weak, my whole body is racked by pain. My heart's racing, I find it hard to speak."

Ganga came running and took Chandi's head in her lap, but it was impossible to relieve her suffering. Her eyes looked out in despair; presently she lost consciousness and lay inert.

Ganga had the presence of mind to send Nandi posthaste to call Shiva. As soon as the terrible news was conveyed to the great god, he rushed to his wife's side along with his two sons.

"What has brought on this catastrophe?" he asked Ganga in distressed tones.

"What can I say," said Ganga hesitantly. "If you really want an answer I'll have to start with an account of Chandi's ill-treatment of Padma. Without any provocation she beat up the poor girl till her body was one big bruise, blinded one of her eyes, and dumped her in the arum field. I don't know where she is now. Chandi was bitten by an unknown creature that no one saw. She lost consciousness within minutes."

On hearing this Shiva, the lord of the universe, sat down on the floor with a wail of despair. Kartikeya and Ganesha began crying. Presently Shiva, using his clairvoyant powers, learned what had transpired and started calling Padma.

"O my darling daughter, where are you hiding? Do come and see what dire straits I'm in. If you don't stand by your father in times of sorrow people will say you're heartless. And if I die grieving for Chandi you'll become an object of obloquy."

Padma was touched by her father's words and presently appeared before him. But though she felt sorry for her father, her heart was still smarting at the unfair treatment she had received.

"Look! My flesh and skin have been pummeled into a pulp," she complained. "If my stepmother is dead, it is only just punishment for her sin. Besides, death can come only when one's allotted time has run out. Why should you be distressed at this, you are, after all, lord of the three realms, and if you wish I can get you a hundred gorgeous brides to wed."

"O my daughter," said Shiva in piteous tones, "without Chandi I'm utterly helpless. She is my Shakti, my divine power in its feminine form, and everyone knows that Shiva and Shakti are an indivisible unity. By saving Chandi you will keep your father alive. I beg forgiveness for her sinful behavior. Look at her lying lifeless and have pity. After all, she is your mother."

Padma half turned away, still smarting from the pain inflicted on her. Kartikeya and Ganesha came up and holding her hands begged her to spare their errant mother. "We beg you to save your two brothers by saving their mother. Show mercy and relieve our sorrow or else we will yield our lives to the funeral pyre, and so will our father, you can be sure. You will then be censured in all three realms."

The tender voices of the two young gods, Padma's half brothers, touched her heart and dispelled all anger and resentment. She said,

"Forget your grief, my dear brothers, go and fetch water from the Gandaki River so that we can bring our mother back to life."

Delighted to hear this, the brothers flew off at supersonic speed and returned with the Gandaki water before one could say "Jack Robinson." They handed the water to their sister.

Shiva sat down solemnly in a meditative posture, cradling Chandi in his lap, while Padma recited primordial mantras over the inert body and over the holy water. Then she went into a meditative trance and sprinkled the water all over Chandi's body.

As soon as the droplets touched her skin, the venom was neutralized, and Chandi, matriarch of the three realms, regained her consciousness and stood up, fully revived. But on seeing Padma she drew back and sat down in the inner recesses of her bedchamber. Shiva at once thought of a way to defuse the tension and mend matters. He went up to Chandi and addressed her firmly: "Though you and I share the same essential nature, you ignored my warning and went on to inflict terrible pain on Padma. What satisfaction has it given you? You are too obstreperous and quarrelsome, and when you get worked up you lose all sense of right and wrong. For no fault of hers you have assaulted Padma, you have insulted her after she identified herself as my daughter. Your wicked deed would have been repaid with death from the effects of snake venom. It's only at the entreaty of myself and your sons that Padma has brought you back to life. Now you owe it to us to make up with her. Call her and talk to her with motherly affection!"

Shiva's words struck home. Chandi hung her head in shame and said to Padma, "I have hurt you out of ignorance. Please don't take it to heart. I hope you will forgive me and forget this sad episode." Chandi then took Padma on her lap and showered hundreds of kisses on her tender cheeks. Padma was touched; she bent down and made a *pranam* at Chandi's feet. Thus ended the sordid episode of a fight for no rhyme or reason between mother and daughter.

MANASA'S FOREST EXILE

THOUGH PEACE HAD BEEN RESTORED in Shiva's home on Mount
Kailash, and Chandi outwardly showed such affection toward Padma
as one could expect from a stepmother, the situation was not one of
domestic harmony. Having seen Padma demonstrate her power, hum-
bling both her parents, Chandi suffered from an inexorable sense of
insecurity. It was only Shiva's abject entreaty that had induced Padma to
relent and restore her to life. The next time there was a quarrel it might
not be possible to avert a fatality. How could she live in the same house
as this dangerous interloper, thought Chandi. Better go to her father's
home, taking her two sons with her. From what she had seen of Padma's volatile temper there was reason to fear for the lives of Ganesha
and Kartikeya. At the slightest provocation Padma might destroy them
with her venomous gaze or just devour them.

Venting her anxieties in a stream of demented muttering, Chandi
started packing and called to her sons to get ready. Shiva was in a quandary. He decided to play the good husband. Taking his mountain goddess wife by the hand, he said, "This is your home, you stay here. I will
send Padma into exile in the forest."

Shiva led Chandi into the bedroom and by way of sealing his vow
made love to her, dispelling her anxieties at least temporarily.

Then Shiva called Padma and told her solemnly, "My daughter, as long as you are here there is bound to be tension between you and your stepmother. From time to time it may lead to open conflict. It is best if you have your own home somewhere else, on a lofty mountaintop, as befits your divine status."

Distraught at hearing this, Padma pleaded with her father. "I don't understand, Father," she said tearfully. "What's past is past. I have bowed at my mother's feet and I try to serve her and do her bidding. Why should she begrudge me a place in her home?"

Shiva sadly shook his head and said that Chandi saw things differently. To spare his daughter more heartache he said frankly, "You are well aware of Chandi's personality. You will be happier living away from a stepmother like her."

For a moment Padma hung her head in sorrow; then she pulled herself together and said she would take her father's advice. "You know best," she said. "Let me take leave of my mother."

She went into Chandi's chamber, self-composed and calm. Shiva followed a couple of steps behind.

"Mother," Padma addressed Chandi, "I have come to say goodbye. I apologize once again for the pain and distress I have caused you. It was the product of a deplorable misunderstanding. My reverence for you and my father will always remain. You may not wish to see any more of me, but in case you need me, I wish to present you with this ring. If you send a messenger with it I will rush to your aid."

Chandi bristled—"The damn cheek of this waif of a girl!" she muttered to herself—but a stern glance from Shiva forced her to control herself.

"Keep it for my father's sake," Padma said. "He might need me, even if you don't."

Though outwardly calm, Padma was fuming inside. She thought to herself: Chandi is my mother, but she is unnatural in her cruel jealousy. If I had known the parents who brought her into the world I would have destroyed them with a venomous glance.

Chandi bade her a brusque farewell. Shiva, out of shame for his wife's rudeness and affection for his daughter, quickly came forward and took Padma by the arm.

"I will go with you and see you safely into the forest," he said.

As father and daughter made their way silently through the wilderness, Shiva brooded under paternal misgivings. Where would he take his daughter? Towns and large settlements contained diverse people of different castes. How would they behave toward a beautiful young woman who came out of nowhere to live among them? For a first stop Shiva chose the home of a pious Brahmin who worshipped him with intense devotion. Shiva and Padma spent the night there and set off again the next morning. They ran into Chandi who had been driven by her jealous hatred of Padma into following them.

Chandi burst into vile abuse. "Have you no shame?" she screamed at Shiva. "You old lecher, you're now shacking up with you own daughter?"

Padma was struck speechless. Shiva flushed in embarrassment and quickly said, "Go home. I'll see Padma into the forest and come back."

Father and daughter were a sad pair as they entered the dark shade of the forest. Padma was weary from the journey and wanted to rest. They halted under a banyan tree. Shiva asked her to lie down with her head on his thigh. Soon she dozed off. Shiva gazed mournfully at her gentle face in repose. His eyes brimmed with tears, for he knew the time had come to abandon her.

Shiva gingerly raised Padma's head from his thigh and placing it on a heap of dry leaves stood up. A teardrop overflowed his eye and fell on the ground. At once a beautiful girl sprang up where it fell. Shiva was startled but realized at once that he now had two daughters. Since she had been born of a teardrop from his eye—*netra* in Sanskrit—he named her Neta.

With a sigh Shiva reflected on his dire fate: after having a son or two, parents would welcome a daughter or two with joyous hearts. But in his case the birth of his daughter Padma only created domestic strife. What would happen now that there was a second one?

He woke up Padma and introduced her to her sister. "The two of you can live together in the forest," he said. "Neta will make an able adviser and lieutenant to you, Padma." Shiva then empowered Neta with occult knowledge. Both sisters were happy at the way things were taking shape.

Shiva sorrowfully bade his daughters farewell and set off for Mount Kailash. A little while later he was overcome with worry as he thought that the two girls were all alone amid wild creatures. Sweat broke out on his brow. He wiped it with a finger and with a flick magically engendered yet another divine child, a boy this time. He named him Dhamai and instructed him to seek out his sisters in the forest and look after their safety. Dhamai at once set off in search of his sisters. He found them resting under a tree in the forest. They were startled to see a youth suddenly appear in front of them, but he allayed their fears by introducing himself. "I am another son of Shiva, the god of gods, lately engendered from a drop of his divine sweat. You are therefore my sisters and it is my bounden duty to look after your safety. I have been expressly urged by our divine progenitor to live with you and help you in any way possible."

Padma and Neta were delighted to hear this. "We now have a younger brother!" they exclaimed. "Now let us make a home for ourselves, one worthy of our divine status." A site was readily chosen—Mount Sijuya, or Mount Siyoli, as it was also called. It was a lofty peak, with ample ground space around the peak to build a city that would compare with Shiva's Kailash or Indra's Amaravati.

Padma telepathically summoned Vishwakarma (or Vishai in the diminutive form), the master builder of the divine realm. He was deep in meditation by the seaside, and as soon as Padma's message was sent the bowl of holy tulsi leaves he was holding in his left hand fell from his grasp. The message registered at once on his consciousness, and he rose and, mounting the bear that he used as conveyance, set off for Mount Sijuya.

Vishai's strange mount, though clumsy in its movements on land, was capable of swift, graceful flight, and in no time reached its destination. Vishai presented himself to Padma with palms respectfully joined and said, "Tell me, goddess, what I can do for you."

"Have a *paan* first," Padma said to Vishai, and then explained what she wanted.

"Make me a home on top of this mountain," she said, "one that will not shame me and my brother and sister."

Vishai bowed to signify his readiness to carry out the commission. He sent for his brothers and nephews and the redoubtable simian deity Hanuman, so that they would lend a hand. Ax in hand, Vishai went into the forest and felled various kinds of trees that would be needed for building. He fashioned a gilded roof with four sloping parts.

Hanuman brought stones of many kinds and built a plinth five cubits in height. Columns of quartz, stone doorways, steps shaded with peacock feather awnings, precious and semiprecious stones inlaying the doors and walls, and golden pitchers atop every wall and at every corner completed the magnificent palace built for Padma. Interior decoration was not neglected either. Bedsteads, seats, and a throne, all of gold, were made, and the softest and most exquisite pillows and cushions were placed on them. Padma was overjoyed. She rewarded the builder's skills with quantities of gold. Vishai and his assistants went home satisfied.

Soon a new city sprang up around the palace and people of various castes and professions came to live in it. There were learned Brahmins, accomplished ayurvedic physicians, warriors, farmers, merchants, scribes, growers and sellers of *paan,* potters and blacksmiths, oil pressers, wood-cutters, makers of conch-shell ornaments, braziers, goldsmiths, weavers, gardeners and florists, launderers, barbers, carpenters, fishermen (who set up home by the river flowing past the mountain), and many more. All thirty-six professional castes known to human society were represented in the thriving new city presided over by the youngest of divinities.

Delighted with her new abode, Padma had a lively housewarming party with her siblings and friends. With a radiant vermilion spot on her forehead and sandal-paste traceries on her cheeks, her long curly hair trained into a comely bun, sporting beautiful earrings, and with her eyebrows drawn like the love god Kama's bow, Padma was naturally the cynosure on the occasion. A deadly Kalkuti snake encircled her neck like a choker, and an ivory necklace dangled on her breast. Anklets jangled sweetly as she moved about on her shapely legs.

Padma and her friends went to a lake to sport in its waters. Flocks of ducks, geese, and swans and various other aquatic birds enlivened the place with their calls and their playful movements. Padma's companions splashed each other with the clear, sparkling lake water; they dived for lotus and water lilies and showered each other with their petals. While such gaiety prevailed in Padma's glittering new city, portentous events were under way elsewhere.

THE CHURNING OF THE SEAS

THE BEAUTIFUL GANDHARVA Vinalata appeared before Brahma. Instantly and intensely aroused, Brahma ejaculated. Out of his semen emerged two youths, composite in physique, with godlike torsos and seven heads, but a bestial lower part sporting a tail. They begged the gift of immortality from their munificent father, who then directed them to report to Mount Sijuya. There they found employment as Padma's bodyguards and scouts; their task to go in front and clear the way for her whenever she went out.

Then Brahma poured water on the spot where his semen had fallen, and at once a pair of ferocious tigers, a male and a female one, sprang up. The owners of cattle herds were stricken with anxiety, but Brahma allayed their fears with a reassuring prophecy: the tiger couple would meet their end before long at the hands of the calf born to Kapila, the heavenly cow, and would then be metamorphosed into gandharvas and sent to dwell in Indra's heavenly city.

This is how Kapila had come into being. Brahma wished to perform certain rites for which he needed flowers, so he called one of the celestial sentries and ordered him to fetch the wife of Indra's gardener. The sentry went and called out for the woman, who appeared without delay.

He explained that she should hasten to gather flowers for Brahma who was waiting impatiently to begin certain puja rites. The young woman, who was in the bloom of youth, sashayed away like a she-elephant in heat and picked forty-two varieties of flowers and carried them to the god in a wicker tray. Brahma gladly accepted the tray and was all set to start the rituals when he discovered a spider amid the blossoms. Infuriated, he laid a curse on the careless woman: she would turn into a cow and live on earth. The curse took effect even as it was being uttered, and the attractive young woman turned into a beautiful, yellowish-brown cow. She came to be known as Kapila since the word signified the color of her bovine coat. She wandered away, browsing desultorily as cows are wont to do.

To go back to Brahma's tiger children: the divine father sent them flying to the shores of a lake, where they found Padma and, introducing themselves, asked her leave to stay there. Presently the gods planned a grand sacrificial feast at which Chandi would be asked to take charge of the cooking. Brahma set off to tell Chandi about it and found the goddess fast asleep in her chamber, with only a little finger showing from beneath the sheets. The exquisite beauty of that finger was enough to induce an involuntary orgasm in Brahma: the semen promptly found its way into the womb of the goddess. On waking up she became aware of what had transpired through exercising her divine clairvoyance. She went to cook for Brahma and the other gods. They were charmed to see her, but the god and guru Gorakshanatha, bent on mischief, entered her nether parts and closed the mouth of the uterus so that she might not be able to deliver the child. Overcome by extreme discomfort she waded into a river in the hope of finding some relief, only to have a miscarriage; and ever since this has been a common mishap in the world.

The aborted fetus mingled with the water. Presently Kapila, thirsty from her wanderings, came to the river to drink and in the process ingested Brahma's potent seed. As a result she became pregnant and over the months grew huge with child. It was a full ten months before the calf was born, a big and strong bull calf that rampaged with such vigor that the earth trembled in alarm. Kapila would need a lot of nourishment herself to be able to produce enough milk to feed her mighty son, whom she named Manoratha, which means "the heart's joy." Kapila then wandered far in search of adequate nourishment.

Along came a thieving cow who urged Kapila to help herself to the lush fields growing various crops. She led Kapila to the home of the sage Bharadwaja. On its grounds grew succulent leafy vegetables. Kapila, who was quite famished, fell to with alacrity. Unfamiliar with the jealous code of private property on earth, she had no sense of guilt. Her worldly-wise companion, on the other hand, paused in her feast every now and then to raise her head and look about in every direction. And when, in a while, she espied the sage heading home, she quietly made herself scarce. The unsuspecting Kapila was still munching innocently when the irate sage burst upon her and with unholy imprecations proceeded to tether the offending animal with a strong rope made of jute. He didn't stop there; as if by way of a fine to compensate him for the loss of his vegetables, he snatched away Kapila's golden cowbell and replaced it with a wooden one.

All alone and helpless, Kapila lamented her humiliation while ample tears rolled down her face. "Why has Brahma brought me to such a pass?" she sobbed. "I have traveled to this distant land only to be humiliated in this manner. Meanwhile my poor son is starving, with none to turn to for succor. It breaks my heart to think of his plight. Why did I have to fall into bad company and commit a misdeed? To think that I, goddess of three realms and mother of the earth, could forget myself and do such a thing! It's nothing but excessive greed that has brought me to ruin."

Sage Bharadwaja came round to inspect his captive and was astonished to see a cow talking to itself and shedding tears that turned into precious gems as they fell to the ground. He knew at once that she was a divine being, and, overwhelmed by remorse, he prostrated himself at the animal's feet and begged forgiveness for his haughty act. Then he asked Kapila to reveal her identity and once again apologized for unwittingly committing a sinful act. He set Kapila loose and replaced the ludicrous wooden cowbell with the golden one he had confiscated. Kapila let him have the gems from her tears that lay on the ground and set off homeward at a trot. Sage Bharadwaja, bidding her a respectful farewell, gratefully gathered up the gemstones.

Kapila hadn't gone far when two ferocious animals, a tiger and a tigress, appeared, blocking her path. Kapila halted and addressed an appeal to the heartless beasts. "I gave birth to a calf only last night, and it hasn't been suckled all day today. My son will die if he doesn't get some milk soon. Let me go home and suckle him. I will return before long and you will be able to feast on me."

Her piteous tone moved the tiger couple, particularly because they too had a pair of cubs by now. They agreed to grant Kapila the respite if she would first swear that she would keep her word.

"I give you my divine word of honor," Kapila reassured them and hurried home.

Meanwhile, Manoratha had been waiting for his mother until he had become so thirsty that he went to the seashore and drank up all the water, putting in jeopardy all the varied creatures of the deep. Many of them came ashore and wandered disconsolately about the fields and villages.

As Kapila neared her home Manoratha ran forward excitedly with his tail happily up in the air to greet her. As he reached eagerly for his mother's udder he noticed that her eyes were tearful.

Manoratha had just taken a teat in his mouth. He let go and raised an anxious face. "What's wrong, Mother?" he asked.

Kapila told him everything that had happened, adding, "It's not the prospect of imminent death so much as the thought I won't ever see you again that brings tears to my eyes."

"Enough, Mother! I don't want to hear any more. I won't touch your sweet milk till I've killed those scoundrels." And off he went in search of the tiger couple, ignoring his mother's cautionary words. His muscles swelled in his fury and the earth shook under his hoofbeats. His mother followed him to the place where the tiger and tigress were waiting.

Seeing Kapila return the fierce beasts came forward with drooling mouths, but they were stopped by Manoratha.

"Just a moment," he thundered. "You will have to beat me in battle before you can eat up my mother in my presence."

The tiger and tigress flew into a rage. "Who in the three realms can stand up to me?" they roared in a terrifying duet. "You are like a locust that is flying into the fire. Our breath will blow you to kingdom come."

Boiling with wrath, Manoratha assumed a form of cosmic proportions. Grunting repeatedly as his muscles quivered in excitement, he
generated a gale around him. Goring the earth, he tossed sods to the
heavens, startling Indra and the other primal divinities. Breathing fire,
he dug his knees into the earth, making it tremble with a noise that
stunned the inhabitants of the three realms, then pawed the earth to let
fly a storm of dust and whirled his tail to set off a gale that tore away all
the plants growing thereabouts. With a bellow that resounded through
the earth, the heavens, and the underworld, he leveled his massive horns
to charge.

On the other side, the tiger and tigress, veteran fighters both, were
fiery with anger at the sight of the challenger. Seven cubits high they
stood, with flaming eyes as terrifying as Yama and nails sharp as diamonds. They bared their large, sharp teeth, strong enough to crush rocks,
till they reached up to their whiskers. Pricking up their ears, leaping
fearsomely, with tails upraised above their heads, with eyes blazing,
they advanced on Manoratha. Kapila watched nervously as the battle
commenced.

Manoratha, massive in size and confident in his stride, advanced with
horns ready for action. The fierce tiger met him head on, grabbed the
horns and roaring thunderously, pulled with all its might. Manoratha
gave his horns a mighty shake; the tiger leapt away and crouched at a
distance.

Manoratha jeered. "Shame on you—running away like a timid fox!"

The tiger crept forward, then with a deafening roar leapt on to Manoratha's back and dug in with its teeth and plowshare-like nails. Blood
streamed down his sides as Manoratha shook off the ferocious beast
and lunged with his lance-like horns. The tiger closed with Manoratha,
and the two rolled over and over in a fierce bout of wrestling. With un-
diminished strength the tiger then leapt onto Manoratha's hump and,
clamping its jaws on the bull calf's neck so that its mouth filled with
blood, swung round and round in an attempt to break it. Overcome with
intolerable pain, Manoratha gave a desperate shake and threw the at-
tacker to the ground. Pinning it down with his knees, he drove his
horns all the way into its chest. The tiger was done for and lay prostrate.
Manoratha stamped on its body, bellowing in a fiery rage, then scooped

it up with his horns and hurled it to the skies. It fell to earth miles away, all its bones broken and without any sign of life.

The bereaved tigress sprang into action, boiling with rage, but was promptly dispatched to kingdom come with a few well-directed kicks. The two tiger cubs, which were watching the fight, fled in terror. But just then Brahma's promise was fulfilled, and the entire tiger family was metamorphosed into gandharvas, who happily headed for Indra's heavenly city. Their ordeal over, Manoratha and his mother Kapila went home.

Brahma, accompanied by Shiva and a cheerful band of sages, went to bathe in the sea. But when they reached the beach, their high spirits gave way to bewilderment. There was no water in the sea, and fish and other deep-sea creatures lay dead everywhere. The gods went into a clairvoyant trance and found out who had drained the sea and why. Shiva asked Narada to fetch Kapila. She came at once, along with Manoratha. Mother and son were warmly greeted by Shiva, who then proceeded to sing her praises and appeal to her for help.

"You are the mother of the three realms," Shiva declared. "It's up to you to preserve this world. Your affection toward the world is immeasurable and none can deny your glory. Millions of creatures who live in the sea have either perished or face death, all because our mighty hero Manoratha was forced to satisfy his thirst with seawater. There can be only one remedy, Kapila: fill up the sea with your milk and a disaster will be averted."

On hearing Shiva's words Kapila hung her head in embarrassment and replied that she would redress the situation at once. She let her milk flow in a steady stream till the sea filled up once more. The gods sang her praise in gratitude and enjoyed a pleasant dip in the rejuvenated sea. Kapila and Manoratha returned to the world of householders and dairy farmers where they are the reigning divine beings.

Life resumed its normal course. The creatures of the sea who survived began to multiply. People began going down to the sea to bathe or fish once again. The sage Durvasa resumed his habitual ascetic practices by the sea.

One day Brahma brought a strangely shaped brass container to the seashore for washing. First he wanted to scrub it clean and summoned all the birds and asked who among them would like to go on a mission to fetch something that he needed. Everyone was eager to oblige the god, but when he told them that they would have to fly to Lanka, the kingdom of Ravana, and fetch the tamarind fruit from there, the enthusiasm ebbed away. Only one bird remained that was still willing to hazard the flight—the parrot. Brahma waited for the parrot to bring the tamarind, whose astringent pulp was excellent for scrubbing brass to a shine. In time the parrot came flying back, carrying the tamarind in its beak. As it flew over the spot where Durvasa sat, the sage called out to ask for a share. But the parrot ignored him, provoking the temperamentally irate sage to hurl a curse: at once the tamarind slipped out of the parrot's beak and fell into the sea of milk, which presently turned into yogurt.

The gods were dismayed for they wouldn't be able to bathe in the sea again, but Brahma didn't mind; a break from the routine marine rituals wasn't unwelcome to him.

Durvasa finished his routine of austerities and decided to amuse himself with sightseeing in Kailash, Shiva's exquisitely charming celestial city, where Brahma and other gods came to rest, and great sages like Bhrigu and Parasara sat in a contemplative trance. In one spot the celestial *vidyadharas* sang to the accompaniment of stringed instruments and apsaras danced with well-choreographed movements. The wish-fulfilling tree, the *kalpataru*, grew here and there, as did medicinal plants of great potency; aging, death, grief, and sorrow were powerless before them. At night ambrosial moonlight bathed the landscape. Serpents, deer, and dancing peacocks abounded. Durvasa savored the delightful sights and sounds. He stopped to ask a group of *vidyadharis* for one of the garlands of heavenly *parijata* blossoms and left for his ashram. On his way he ran into Indra and presented him with the garland.

Indra received the present with profuse thanks but a little later draped it around the head of his elephant Airavata. After a while the garland slipped to the ground unnoticed, the result of intervention by Fate; and Durvasa, who later recalled that he had forgotten to do something, retraced his steps and came upon the fallen garland.

Durvasa exploded in rage. "How dare Indra insult me like this!" he thundered. "I will ruin him and his tribe of gods. Who can undo my curse? Lakshmi will desert him this moment." He cast an angry glance at Lakshmi, as if to confirm that his curse had begun to take effect. All the other rishis sadly shook their heads, anticipating a cataclysm. Indra fell at the sage's feet, together with all the other gods, gandarvas, and *kinnaras;* they begged for mercy and loudly sang the sage's praises; but to no avail. "You have brought disaster on yourself," Lakshmi told Indra. "Durvasa's curse is driving me away from you and your domain, and with me all the boons and blessings that are mine to bestow on deities and people. Nothing can undo Durvasa's curse—he's such a stubborn one! Now chaos will reign in the world. The gods will not receive worship from devotees, clouds will lose their moisture, Kubera, the god of pelf, will lose his fortune, the sun and moon will not rise, the wise will lose their wisdom, the sages will lose the ability to meditate, the farms will lose their crops, rivers will lose their water and fish, the earth will be gripped by anxiety, trees will lose their fruit, priests will forget the scriptures, the chaste will become wayward, the wicked will hold sway, Sudras will challenge the higher castes, none will respect rank and status, everything will be reduced to the same lowly state."

Everyone was stunned by the graphic picture of disorder given by Lakshmi. Indra, overcome by a sense of guilt, wept ceaselessly. All his fellow gods were woebegone and even the great deities Brahma, Vishnu, Shiva became morose.

Lakshmi left heaven in search of a suitable place where she could exile herself. First she went to the forest and sought sanctuary from the forest king, but was politely turned down. "You are goddess of the three realms," he said, "and I am only a tree. What resources do I have to keep you in concealment?"

Next Lakshmi went to the mountains and again had no luck. "We do not have the power to keep you hidden," the mountains pleaded. "You will have to forgive us, great goddess." So Lakshmi went down to the sea and addressed the tossing waves of yogurt. "A sage's curse has driven me out of the heavenly city," she said. "I ask you to conceal me in your depths along with all the beings who owe me fealty—grains and crops, moonlight, Indra's two mounts Airavata, the elephant, and Uccaih-shravas, the horse, the heavenly *parijata* flower, and many others." The sea responded warmly and made room for Lakshmi and her variegated retinue.

The gods were now in a quandary. Lakshmi is the goddess who ensures prosperity. With her disappearance, poverty and scarcity threatened the three realms. The three chief gods, Brahma, Vishnu, Shiva, put their heads together and came up with a plan. They would arrange to have the yogurt sea churned till it yielded Lakshmi and the other things that had followed her to the deep.

For a task so stupendous, extraordinary equipment would be needed. For the churning stick the gods chose Mount Mandara, while the rope would be Vasuki, the serpent king. Hanuman, the monkey god, was assigned the task of uprooting the mountain; he accomplished it neatly, with the mountain's acquiescence.

In order to pull the "rope" from both ends, the gods and Hanuman would be on one side, but the asuras had to be recruited to take care of the other end. Indra went to the underworld to persuade the demon king Bali to join in with his cohorts. Indra lured Bali with a promise to share the ambrosia that would be decanted as a result of the churning.

"Gods and asuras will both get the ambrosia," Indra assured Bali.

"Half-and-half?"

"Half-and-half."

The deal was sealed, and the demon host trooped to the seashore to join the desperate army of gods. In order to steady the earth for the task Vishnu incarnated himself as a tortoise that swam with the earth on its back. Vasuki wound himself around Mandara; the gods and Hanuman took hold of the serpent's head and left the tail end for the asuras.

But the asuras objected. "Why should you have the head and we the tail?" they cried. "It shows that you consider yourselves superior."

The gods gladly swapped places.

They had wanted to take the tail end all along and knew that if they wanted it first the asuras would suspect it was the relatively advantageous position and demand it. Now, with the "superior" end in their hands, when the churning began the asuras were showered with noisome froth ejected from the serpent's mouth.

The churning was a tremendous affair: the whole of creation groaned and trembled. The yogurt quickly lost its consistency and a tower of foam rose skyward. As the churning speeded up to a climax, Uccaihshravas emerged from the depths and was handed over to his master Indra. The second round brought the moon to the shore: it went to Shiva. Rice and all other grains emerged next and were given away to the human race. Airavata followed and was handed over to Indra. Then came the apsaras, who livened up the scene with songs and dancing; they went home to Indra's court. The next round of furious churning yielded Lakshmi, whose retrieval was the chief aim of the exercise. She emerged in all her radiance, bedecked with *parijata* blossoms. She handed the *parijata* to Indra and went to her consort Vishnu's home. The curse on Indra now stood neutralized. But one more object remained. A final, vigorous round ended with the appearance of a man bearing a large cup filled with the much desired ambrosia. He had been miraculously born as a result of the churning; and the great gods Brahma, Vishnu, and Shiva named him Dhanvantari. He appealed to the gods to teach him the science of medicine. The gods were pleased at his thirst for knowledge and instructed him on antidotes to snake venom. "As you know," the gods told him, "if a venomous snake on earth bites someone in the chest at dawn, death follows instantly. But even that has a remedy. Listen carefully. The juice of the scented *salyavisalyika* plant will revive the victim. Another antidote, to be applied directly to the wound, is the froth of the sea of milk."

Dhanvantari thanked the gods profusely and took his leave. He began applying his knowledge on earth and gained great fame as an *ojha,* a medicine man whose speciality is curing snakebite victims.

The ambrosia brought by Dhanvantari became a bone of contention between gods and demons. Brahma said to his fellow gods, "Let us partake of the ambrosia, which can protect us from old age, death, and rebirth." The demons said to each other, "The gods want to appropriate all of the ambrosia, in violation of our solemn agreement. Our hard work will come to nothing if we don't do something about it." They snatched the cup of ambrosia and made off with it.

"This will threaten us with ruin," cried Brahma. "If the demons imbibe the ambrosia they will become immortal." He urged Vishnu to use deceit to get the cup back.

Vishnu appeared as another of his incarnations, that of Mohini, the enchantress, most ravishing of females in all three realms. Her gorgeous curly hair was bedecked with oleander blossoms, both white and red, interspersed with glittering gold foil in stellar shapes. Vermilion *sindur* glared from the middle parting in her hair, and a neat dab of sandalwood paste adorned her forehead. Beautiful earrings hung from the two sides of her head, and pitch-black *kajal* added mysterious depth to her eyes. Her eyebrows were excitingly animated: they were like cannons in the arsenal of Kama, the love god. Pink lips pouted from her lotus-tender face; variegated jewels adorned her throat, and armlets, bangles, and conch-shell bracelets graced her arms and wrists. Her prominent shapely breasts were repositories of sex appeal. A girdle set off her ravishing hips; anklets with tiny tinkling bells beautified her feet. As she walked she was flamboyant as a peacock; enough to distract the most assiduously meditating ascetic. She wore her sari in a provocative style.

Mohini sat down with the demons and spoke seductively in a brief exchange of pleasantries. Then she grew solemn, broke down in tears, and sobbed uncontrollably. The demons crowded round her, asking what was the matter. They were all smitten with desire for the ravishing female and would do anything to win her favors. Mohini drew the edge of her sari to half cover her face in a titillating show of modesty and said in a mellow, sorrowful voice, "My beloved lord abandoned me and came this way."

The demon king at once offered to take her home with him. "Come and live with me," he said plainly.

"On one condition," said Mohini. "You must swear not to do anything against my wishes. If you do you can be my lord for all time." The infatuated demon swore at once and went home with the ravishing Mohini in tow.

All the demons gathered at their leader's home to imbibe the stolen ambrosia. But Mohini intervened. She said to the demon king, "My lord, everything should be done in a proper way. Leave the cup of ambrosia with me and go and have a bath. When you come back you can sit down in a circle and divide the ambrosia among yourselves."

"Why wait so long; let's have it now," the demon replied.

"If you want to go back on your sworn word, very well, you'll fry in hell, and I'm off."

The demons agreed to do as Mohini wanted. When they left she made off with the ambrosia and gave it to the waiting gods. Now Shiva saw her for the first time and such was her allure that he became uncontrollably aroused. He began making love to her and was met with vehement protests.

"Brother Shiva, it's me, Vishnu," came the remonstrance as Mohini started changing back to the original form. But Shiva was too excited to stop and consummated his desire on the god. Thus what had started as heterosexual ravishment ended up as homosexual rape.

Shiva then seemed to distance himself somewhat from his fellow gods. "Share the ambrosia among yourselves," he said to them. "We will have another round of churning and I will drink the ambrosia that it produces."

Brahma tried to dissuade him, saying chidingly, "Don't be difficult, Shiva. There's nothing else to get from the sea. Another churning tomorrow morning will only bring up poison."

Seeing that there was no response from Shiva, Brahma took him by the hand and tried to reason gently. "There's plenty of ambrosia for us all. If you want you can have it all. But another churning will spell disaster—now, don't contradict me. Excessive greed has always had dire consequences in the three realms."

"We will churn out everything that's left in the sea, the good and the bad," Shiva replied bluntly.

The demons, who had been deprived of a share of the ambrosia, came grumbling to the seashore, making the gods apprehensive. Shiva addressed them: "The other gods have taken everything, but you all and I have got nothing. Let us resume churning without delay. You will be able to satisfy your desire with what we find."

The demons took hold of Vasuki's head again—but with suitable caution, for the violent exhalations from his mouth were extremely noxious—while Hanuman grabbed the tail. On Shiva's instructions vigorous churning began once more. Hanuman and the demons strained with all their might while the gods kept beseeching them to stop. At one point Shiva's fiery eyes exuded balls of flame that fell into the sea and turned into the *kalkuta* poison.

Some, of course, say that the poison had originated from Brahma. It happened, they say, when Padma had been turned out of Kailash at the instigation of her stepmother. Brahma ran into her on his way to the seaside to perform certain austerities. Padma decided to tag along. The sea god came up to greet Brahma, who then asked him to help him wade some distance. The sea god obliged by creating a long strip of sandbank on which the water was no more than knee deep. Brahma waded in, and behind him Padma followed, raising the skirt of her sari to her thighs. Just then sudden gusts blew from the four corners, and Brahma found that meeting the goddess Padma had stirred a strange excitement in him. He looked back and his eyes fell on her shapely thighs. At once he had an involuntary ejaculation; his semen fell into the water, but his intention to practice austerities had impregnated it with the deadly *kalkuta* poison. The floating sperm crept up Padma's thighs and entered her womb, but the effect of the poison was too agonizing to bear. She had a painful miscarriage, the embryo rending her loins as it slid into the sea. Brahma fashioned a gourd-shaped earthen pitcher into which he transferred all the poison. He hurled the pitcher into the ocean depths, where a large *boal* fish swallowed it and thrashing about in pain came on shore. Brahma slit open its belly to relieve it of the poison pitcher and gave it a boon. As for the poison, Brahma asked it to go back and remain in the ocean depths. The poison asked him, "Father, how long do I remain confined to the ocean depths?"

"Till the gods churn the ocean and produce you out of its depths," replied Brahma.

Be that as it may, the indubitable fact is that the world's entire stock of *kalkuta* poison was mixed with the water in the ocean depths; now it was violently expelled into the atmosphere. It destroyed everything that it came into contact with. Even though it was a cloudless day, everything grew dim and flames shot this way and that like lightning. People ran for their lives, the demons fled to the underworld, and Vasuki slithered to an underground shelter. Mount Mandara hurried back to its original location. The gods too vanished in no time, leaving only Hanuman and the bull Nandi beside Shiva. The yogurt sea calmed down, while land and air had to deal with an impending apocalypse.

Hanuman, son of the wind god Pavana, pontificated to Shiva: "Friends, kinsfolk, allies are always around you when the going's good. Come adversity, they won't even acknowledge you. See how the gods abandoned you and disappeared. But what is the remedy? You ignored Brahma's warning and generated the ruinous poison. Now the decent thing for you to do is to swallow the poison and save the world. Even the sun and the moon have fled the skies in fear, and everything on earth is withering at the touch of the poison."

Shiva gulped down the entire quantity of the fiendish poison. Within moments he was seized with involuntary trembling; then he lost consciousness and collapsed in a heap. Narada went to inform Chandi. The sky seemed to fall on her head; she clutched her two sons and with a piercing cry, "My lord! My lord!" set off for the seashore. She felt that her breast had been rent asunder as she bent over her husband's lifeless form. "Without you, my lord, my life is nothing," she wailed, and tears streamed down her face. She cradled Shiva's body in her arms and in a pathetic monologue recounted his tragic end. "It must be the outcome of my karma," she wailed, "or else why should you come to the sea and, ignoring the warnings and entreaties of Brahma and other gods and without a thought of the consequences, willfully generate poison and swallow it, leaving my poor Kartikeya and Ganesha fatherless? You were always a bit crazy, abjuring jewels and proper attire to deck yourself with a garland of bones, a half-moon painted on the forehead, carrying a trident and a tabor, a mendicant's staff and a begging-bowl in a beggar's cloth satchel, and wearing only a tiger skin wherever you went."

Chandi made a grave resolution, which she declared to Brahma, Vishnu, and Indra. "You will have to bring up my sons," she told them, "I leave them to you, for I have no desire to continue in this world of illusion. I will accompany my lord, so prepare the funeral pyre for us." She tore off her necklace and flung it to the ground.

The gods erected a grand funeral pyre of the finest sandalwood on the sea beach. They gently laid Shiva's body on it and poured ghee all over. Before mounting the pyre to lie down beside the lifeless form of the great god, Chandi took off her jewelry and handed it to Ganga. As she pulled off the last of the rings on her finger she recalled how it had come into her possession. "Listen," she said to Brahma and the other gods, "this ring was given to me by Padma as a parting gift. It is studded with five different gemstones. Padma told me when she gave it that if ever Shiva was in mortal danger I should send for her, for she could bring him back to life."

On hearing this, the gods sent Narada to fetch Padma without delay. The snake goddess had in the meantime learned about her father's plight by invoking her clairvoyant faculties. She knew that an embassy would soon come to her asking for her help. She prepared to receive it by covering her magnificent city with a veil of illusion and putting in its place humble dwellings made of leaves and twigs and with heaps of refuse in the yards. Padma sat in the dirt dressed in a tiger skin. When in due course Narada arrived, Padma gave him a respectful welcome, bringing water to wash his feet and humbly offering him presents and refreshments. Narada told her about her father's sad fate. "Now come without delay and revive your father," he urged the goddess.

Padma sat like one struck suddenly by a thunderbolt. Neta came and sat hugging her; tears coursed down their cheeks. "Just think of our plight if our father dies, Brother Narada," Padma said in piteous tones, "We were compelled to leave Kailash in his presence. In his absence we will not even be allowed to go there on a visit."

"Why waste time in lamentation? If you wish to resuscitate the great ascetic god, come quickly," urged Narada.

"But how can I go in this half-dressed state?" rejoined Padma. "Ask my stepmother to bring me suitable attire so that I can appear without embarrassment before the gods."

Narada went back to Chandi and told her about his meeting with Padma. "She is living in great hardship in the wilds," he said, "and didn't come with me out of embarrassment. If you took her a decent set of clothes she would come at once to her father's aid."

Chandi went immediately to her chamber but couldn't bring herself to pick a decent sari. She chose the coarsest and shortest she could find and set off with her retinue for Padma's home. Padma, who had kept her clairvoyant faculties awake, was prepared to receive her stepmother. She had returned Mount Sijuya to its actual splendor. Padma sat on a gem-studded throne, surrounded by maids-in-waiting who waved yak-tail fans over her head; some of them chatted and giggled, some sang to the accompaniment of small drums.

Chandi was awestruck at the sight of golden walls studded with rows of pearls and galleries with dazzling glass roofs. Padma rose at the approach of her stepmother, greeted her with many pleasing compliments, and gratefully accepted the sari Chandi had brought. The two mounted a chariot and set off for the seashore where the gods were waiting with Shiva's corpse. They greeted her warmly.

Padma addressed the gods. "I have a strange tale to tell you first. My stepmother cruelly turned me out of heaven, forcing me to live on a forested mountain. Narada must have told you how I live. My stepmother brought me this present so that I could come to you decently attired."

She held up the cheap sari she got from Chandi. Brahma, Vishnu, and Indra stepped forward and counseled her. "This is no place to take your stepmother to task," they said, "but if you set aside your personal sorrow and bring your father back to life all of us will forever hold you in the highest esteem."

However, Chandi, who had been listening to her stepdaughter with growing anger suddenly lost her temper and raised a fist to strike her. Padma responded by shooting a venomous glance at Chandi, who instantly collapsed in a lifeless heap.

Padma turned to her father, gently raising him and, as the other gods looked on with delight, revived his consciousness. At her command the poison in Shiva's body rose to his mouth. She placed a golden bowl to collect it as it was spewed out. A little residual poison remained stuck in his throat, which as a result turned blue; and hence he got the appellation Neelkantha, the blue-throated one.

Shiva opened his eyes and saw the prostrate body of Chandi. "O my darling daughter," he said in anguished tones, "why have you revived me when my Chandi lies lifeless? How can I live without her?"

"Forgive me for being the cause of this, but I can make amends—I will get you a hundred new wives."

"What good will more marriages do to me? Chandi is half of my being, without her I am crippled."

Padma relented and with her life-giving look revived her stepmother, who got up as if from slumber. But her anger too revived as she saw Padma. The gods stepped in and induced her to keep quiet.

Everybody profusely thanked Padma, who then wondered aloud where she should keep the poison. The gods said, "None but you can safely keep it."

Padma telepathically called all the snakes. They came from everywhere like rain clouds that darken the skies.

First to arrive was the serpent king Vasuki. There followed, from all points of the compass, a host of his fellow nagas and *naginis* in all sizes and hues. The speed with which they answered their goddess's call and their overwhelming presence struck terror in the gods. With palms respectfully joined in *pranam* they asked Padma what was the reason for summoning them.

"The poison that rendered my father unconscious is now in this bowl," Padma explained. "It is too lethal to leave around. I will distribute it among the nagas and other creatures that bite and sting."

After distributing poison among all the venomous nagas and *naginis* there was still about ten pounds left. Half of it Padma stored in her eye; the other half was for all the creepy-crawlies. The scorpion dipped its tail in the lethal stuff.

The gods were impressed by the way Padma dealt with the situation and loudly sang her praises. Clearly she would henceforth be a mighty figure in their pantheon. They felt it was now time to find a groom for her.

THE MARRIAGES OF MANASA AND NETA

SHIVA DISCOVERED IN A MEDITATIVE TRANCE that Padma's destined groom was her namesake, the young sage Jaratkaru. He went at once to the spot where Jaratkaru sat meditating. The sage was thrilled at Shiva's appearance. For this was a much longed-for epiphany.

"My efforts at meditation, mantra chanting, and austerities have borne fruit today," he said with tears of joy and a quiver of excitement shaking his frame. Pleased at his reception, Shiva wasted no time in making his wish known.

"Come with me to my home," he said. "I have two daughters whom I will give to two blessed sages in marriage. Let's go, there's no point dillydallying over an auspicious act."

At the mention of marriage the sage went pale.

"I beseech you not to bring up the question of marriage," he said. "It prevents one from receiving the fruits of ascetic practices. To me the supreme knowledge pertains to austerities, mantras, and meditation; nothing else matters. O king among gods, your affection is misplaced, for I am not interested in marriage. By divine grace I had a miraculous birth: I wasn't conceived in a human womb. Since birth I have engaged myself in continuous ascetic practices here by the waters of Lake Balluka. My aim is to attain immortality, and if there is a break in my efforts Brahma will deny me this boon. Most of the time I am doing a headstand with unblinking eyes. I have never set eyes on a woman's face. I have never experienced sexual pleasure or touched a woman. How can I give up my ascetic pursuits and marry?"

Shiva dismissed his misgivings and said reassuringly, "I am foremost among gods; I can grant you the desired boon. You can marry and then get on with your mantras and meditation."

The sage stood with bowed head and silently called upon his ancestral spirits to counsel him. In one voice they urged him to marry and beget children. "Otherwise we cannot rest contented," they said.

At this the sage turned to Shiva with a quaking heart and declared, "I am ready to marry."

In the twinkling of an eye Shiva conveyed himself and the prospective groom to Mount Kailash and set about making preparations for the wedding. Musicians came playing on horns and drums and other instruments, and Brahma and Vishnu accompanied by the other gods and heavenly denizens: Indra with his consort Sachi, the musically gifted *vidyadharas* and *vidyadharis,* gandharvas, *kinnaras* and other heavenly ladies, and also rishis and maharishis, and the *vetalas.*

A long canopied area was decorated with golden pitchers and fringed with pearl-studded ivory. Lightning created beautiful traceries while apsaras sang melodious benisons. The great god Shiva himself recited the scriptures through the mouths in his four heads as the planets aligned themselves to signal the auspicious hour for the wedding.

Brahma cheerfully chanted Vedic mantras and the married ones among the divine females went to Padma's chamber to prepare her for the wedding ceremony. They massaged sandalwood oil on her body and tied a sacred thread round her left wrist. Other divine ladies went round the rooms with golden watering cans. The air resounded with music from vinas, cymbals, drums, and conch-shell trumpets. The community of sages rejoiced because one of their number was wedding Padma.

At dawn the sixteen female deities known as the Matrikas offered flowers to Shiva as they honored him with a puja. Then they recited Vedic mantras to signal the start of the wedding rituals and made auspicious vertical marks with ghee on the inside walls of all the rooms.

The divine ladies smeared Padma with turmeric paste mixed with amla oil and gave her a comprehensive wash. Before the wedding rites began Shiva received her with presents of rich garments and sweet perfumes. The divine ladies escorted Jaratkaru to the inner chambers where the great goddess Chandi herself joined them in performing the rites specifically meant for womenfolk. Some of the ladies sang joyous songs while others helped Padma get ready, with a gorgeous coiffure decked with glittering jewels and sweet-smelling flowers. Her attire was of colorful silk, and a corner of it was knotted with a corner of the groom's dhoti so that the seven perambulations of the bride around her lord could commence. Padma performed the rite with concentration and slow steps. Then bride and groom entered a canopied area made of flowers. The groom was carried on the shoulders of a demon as Padma sat on a low wooden seat, ringed by cheering ladies. Presently Shiva held Padma aloft and radiated benediction in all four directions. The music was frenzied as bride and groom sat down on the ground. Indra rained petals on them.

Another wedding followed immediately, with the sage Vasistha as the groom for Neta. The final ritual of the gifting of bride to the groom took place in a temple. Then the two newlywed couples were showered with opulent gifts and feted on delicacies.

The divine ladies prepared the flower-bedecked bridal beds for the couples. The great goddess Chandi took Jaratkaru aside to give him some well-meaning advice. "Your bride, our daughter, is the snake goddess incarnate," she said, "and so she abjures jewels and decks herself with snakes, so you should behave with appropriate caution."

Then she approached Padma. "The sage will find you more attractive if you discard clothes and jewelry and drape yourself with beautiful snakes."

Padma accordingly decked herself with snakes and serpents of various sizes and colors, including a few that wound themselves in her hair to create a novel coiffure. Smiling, she presented herself before her husband in this extraordinary form. Jaratkaru lay frozen with fear. Padma, tired out by the wedding rituals, which according to custom had to be gone through while fasting, soon dozed off. Jaratkaru, equally tired, lay sleepless.

Chandi crept up to the window and tossed in a huge bullfrog. All the snakes and serpents began hissing in the most frightful manner as they gave it chase. Jaratkaru jumped up with a start, leapt to the door, and opened it with trembling hands. A serpent on guard barred his way. "I can't take it anymore, I'm scared to death by you serpents," Jaratkaru wailed, "she's all yours, let me quietly slip away."

Seeing the terror he was in, the serpent let him pass. Jaratkaru bolted and didn't stop till he reached the ocean. He dived in and took refuge in the womb of a seashell.

Padma woke up and saw that she was alone in bed. She went into a clairvoyant trance and saw what had happened. Sorrow mingled with humiliation made her weep without pause. Her flower-strewn bridal bed was a desolate spot; she sat sobbing and poured out her heart to Neta. "What weird karma has brought me to this pass," she wailed. "I followed our stepmother's wicked advice and went to bed draped with snakes. How could I not see through her trick? Unknown to me, my lord the maharishi took fright and vanished. What will I say to him now? And why didn't I follow him without delay? Now I am the laughingstock of the divine realm. I was born to experience misfortune, it seems."

Word of the catastrophe reached Shiva. He went to Padma with affectionate words of reassurance and then set off to bring back the fugitive son-in-law. Taking the form of a regal eagle he flew over the ocean waves and called out to the seashell that had harbored the terror-stricken sage. Hearing him, the seashell emerged from the waters and lay on the sand. At a word from the divine eagle the shell disgorged Jaratkaru.

Shiva assumed his normal form and, taking his son-in-law by the hand, spoke reassuring words and led him to a temple where Padma was waiting. Jaratkaru said to his wife, "Please give me permission to return to my own place because I cannot neglect my vocation as an ascetic."

"I am lonely," replied Padma, "and I have no children. Where will you go, leaving behind this divine realm?"

Jaratkaru caressed his wife over her womb and said, "You will give birth to a son whose name will be Astika. He will grow to be a handsome and worthy youth and will rescue Indra from danger."

Vasistha likewise gave Neta the boon of a child. Then the two sages took their leave and returned to their ascetic life.

Padma and Neta soon gave evidence of their pregnancy and in due course gave birth to two sons. Indra, Brahma, Vishna, and the grandfather Shiva were delighted and showered the newborn with blessings. Padma named her son Astika in accordance to his venerable father's wish and handed him to Vasuki for his education. Vasuki taught him the shastras, the holy texts, and then took him to his home on Mount Sijuya. Before long, Astika would give evidence of his sagacity by saving the nagas from extermination. Meanwhile Neta gave birth to a strapping boy whom she named Dhananjaya.

THE SARPA SATRA

THE STORY OF THE SARPA SATRA, or the snake sacrifice, begins with the ultimate curse put on King Parikshit. Once on a deer hunt he came upon a stag and a doe making love. He let fly an arrow that killed the stag, while the doe escaped. He gave chase and came upon a sage in the state of contemplative trance called samadhi. Determined to discover and kill the fugitive doe, the king roughly asked the sage which way it had gone. The sage remained unmoved, his trance undisturbed, his eyes calmly shut. In an outburst of rage, the king pricked the sage's throat with the fine point of an arrow. The sage's eyes instantly opened wide, blazing with anger, and he laid a fatal curse on the arrogant king: "Seven days from now you will die of snakebite."

The king was stunned. His hauteur crumpled, and he turned homeward with his men in a state of anxiety and foreboding. He told his courtiers about the curse and asked for their advice. One of them confidently said, "Set your mind at rest, Your Majesty. There is an *ojha* now known as Shankha-Dhanvantari. His original name was just Dhanvantari, but after he trounced a famous *ojha* called Mahashankha in a contest his fame spread even to the underworld and the name of the vanquished was prefixed to his own. This peerless *ojha* is the man who can rid you of your fear and protect you from snakes."

King Parikshit immediately sent for and employed Shankha-Dhanvantari to safeguard him against snakes. He kept to himself within his palace walls and waited out the seventh day since the meeting with the sage.

Meanwhile the naga Takshaka on whom fell the responsibility to execute the curse was all psyched up for the mission. He set off, single-minded in his determination to get at the king and finish him off. On his way he overheard people say that the *ojha* Shankha-Dhanvantari had with an angry roar hurled a challenge at all snakes.

At the suggestion of the sage who had laid the curse on King Parikshit, Takshaka assumed a calm demeanor, took the form of a mendicant Brahmin, and armed himself by loading his eyes with *kalkuta* poison. He made caste marks on his forehead with sandalwood paste, put on the attire of a priestly novice, slung a serpent around his neck in lieu of a scarf, and wound other snakes around different parts of his body.

On entering the *ojha*'s hometown he looked about to see if he could spot Dhanvantari. He accosted passersby to ask if they knew the *ojha*'s whereabouts. "I have come to take him on in a fight to the finish. I want to test the extent of his much-vaunted knowledge. I have defeated all comers on earth and I will teach Dhanvantari a lesson he will never forget."

As word of the belligerent Brahmin spread, some went to Dhanvantari with the news. He flared up in rage, ordered ten to twenty of his disciples to accompany him, and set off to confront the challenger. As the two contenders faced off under a tree, hundreds of all ages, both male and female, gathered round to witness the contest.

"What is your name and your caste and who are your parents," Dhanvantari asked the stranger, "and what is the purpose of your visit to this place?"

"I have come to challenge you to a contest," replied the stranger. "All the *ojhas* on earth, whom I have defeated, acknowledge you as the greatest master, so I'd like to test your powers. Hurl a missile at me. I will stop it and retaliate with one of mine. As for my identity, my home is on the bank of a holy stream. I am a Brahmin's son and I am known far and wide as the *ojha* Shiromani. I have traveled over all kingdoms but I haven't found an *ojha* who can match my prowess. Hearing of your boasts and your reputation has drawn me here. It's time for a battle between us. If you survive it you can consider your life blessed."

Dhanvantari responded with a piercing battle cry. "Why do you make false boasts? It's only because you are a Brahmin's son that I have tolerated your company so long; otherwise you would have been packed off to the underworld. I am putting up with you even though I have the Brahmastra with which I could dispose of you in a flash."

"You have as good as admitted defeat," countered the Brahmin, "for you are trying to fool me with a show of kindliness. Let the people and the god Dharma bear witness as I declare that I defy your Brahmastra. Attack me with all you've got, I'm not afraid."

Takshaka's words sent Shankha into wild fury and he shouted, "Let all the people, Dharma, Chandra, the moon god, and Surya, the sun god, be my witness. I can't be blamed if the Brahmin falls dead."

The two contestants sat face-to-face under a tree and hurled vile abuse at each other. Takshaka then demonstrated his power by casting a venomous glance at a large tree with lush green foliage. At once it was reduced to ashes. Everyone was awed. The *ojha* Shankha took a little of the ash on his left palm and going into a meditative trance uttered some mantras. Instantly, the tree sprang back to life. The gathering applauded and pronounced the contestants to be equally matched.

Takshaka and Shankha no longer felt any animosity toward each other and talked cheerfully as equals. Takshaka took Shankha aside and told him the true purpose of his visit. "If you help me achieve my aim," he whispered, "I'll give you riches beyond your wildest dreams. All you have to do is to let me get to the king."

Dhanvantari fell for the bribe and let Takshaka approach King Parikshit. Takshaka, in his Brahmin guise, humbly offered a bowl of plums with a muttered word of blessing. The king accepted them with pleasure, for plums were out of season, and raised the bowl to his nose to sniff the ripe fruit. Concealed among them was a venomous snake that was very small and thin as a common thread. The sage's curse could not go in vain: the snake entered one of the royal nostrils and before anyone had any inkling of what was up the king had departed this world.

Lamentation arose around the king, among soldiers and their commanders, among the common subjects, and, as word reached the palace, among the king's wives and concubines and the servants and courtiers. Prince Janamejaya became hysterical with grief and fell unconscious to the ground. The weeping courtiers and servants controlled their own grief and rushed to the prince's aid, gently lifting him off the ground and reviving him with splashes of water. They comforted him and reasoned with him to get a grip on himself. "Your father has ascended to heaven," they said reassuringly. "It is now your duty to perform certain tasks."

Janamejaya composed himself and with shaven head and in mourning garb fulfilled his role as a son by cremating his father's body. On the eleventh day after the death the memorial sraddha ceremony was held with due solemnity and expenditures commensurate with the lofty status and dignity of the deceased. All the rulers of neighboring kingdoms were invited and feted, as were all the subjects and countless Brahmin priests. Hundreds of thousands of cattle were given away to the mourning populace, and the priests were loaded with rich gifts.

All guests left at the end of the day, leaving Janamejaya with the kingdom's councillors to deliberate the future; they urged the prince to assume the throne without delay. Astrologers determined an auspicious hour for the coronation at which Janamejaya was crowned and took in his hand the scepter of royal office.

He proved to be as astute and wise a ruler as his father, fair as a judge, mighty as the sun god, punctilious in religious observances. He was formidable in battle and stern when necessary in exercising power. Surrounded by councillors, allies, generals, and soldiers, he had no end of pomp and ceremony. But he could not get over the grief at the loss of his father. Seeking distraction, he went deer hunting in the forest, accompanied by his courtiers and a detachment of troops. Deep in the forest he had a fateful meeting with a Brahmin priest named Jaya.

The priest was almost demented from grief because his wife and children had been killed by snakes. Now he roamed the forests and jungles mercilessly hunting the species. In reply to the king's queries, he said through uncontrollable sobs, "My entire body is bitter from the tears I shed for I cannot get over the death from snakebite of my wife and children. I roam the wilds seeking revenge."

The priest's words revived the king's grief in all its intensity, and he told the story of his own loss due to a similar cause. Finding a fellow sufferer, the king asked, "If you know any remedy for the abiding sorrow don't hesitate to reveal it to me."

The priest reflected solemnly for a few moments and said, "There is only one effective answer. You are a powerful monarch and if you join hands with me you can perform the Sarpa Satra, a complicated and terrible rite of snake sacrifice whose aim is nothing less than the extermination of the species in all three realms. If you are willing, start preparing for it without delay; I will be the officiating priest."

The king was elated to hear this. "This is indeed a lucky meeting," he told the priest. "I have found a true ally. Come with me to my capital and let us start preparations for the great event at once."

The bereaved priest could have hoped for nothing better. He accompanied the king as the entire royal entourage turned around with pennants flying, war drums beating, mahouts shouting to their elephants, which trumpeted aloud like the crack of thunder.

The king paid a brief visit to the queen in the inner quarters before busying himself with the Sarpa Satra. The king and the priest Jaya came to share a growing obsession with the planned rites. King Janamejaya got his friends and courtiers together, sent invitations to many priests and all the great sages, including Vyasa, who would compose the epic *Mahabharata*.

The priests all gathered at a spot outside the city, and citizens, officials, servants, and soldiers stood ready to execute their instructions. They cut down trees for firewood, built rows of altars and attractive cottages, put up a shade of thick fabric over an area about three kilometers square: space for the grand assembly that would witness the rites. Messengers continuously ran to the king to update him on the progress. At one point he went to bathe and then accompanied by Brahmin priests went to the prepared site. By then it had begun to fill up with guests of various sorts—royalty, priests, sages, merchants, and citizens of other professions. The king received the sages and priests with gifts of clothes, rings, and garlands. The gods too came to watch—Brahma, Vishnu, Shiva, Indra.

The king seethed with rage against all snakes and serpents as Jaya began the rites. First he prayed to five deities—Ganesha, Surya, Vishnu, Shiva, and Chandi. Then he lit a tremendous fire in a hollow in the ground. Dipping sandalwood fagots in a reservoir of ghee, he fed them to the flames. All the priests recited potent mantras as they poured more and more ghee onto the fire. The king, dressed in a gem-studded costume performed a number of pujas according to appropriate scriptural prescriptions. The air became heavily scented from the crackling sandalwood. The fire roared as the king lavishly fed it with ghee and sandalwood. The roaring flames shook the three realms, drew the attention of the great gods, Brahma, Vishnu, Indra, who turned up to witness the proceedings.

The rites had already struck terror among the various clans of venomous snakes. Starting with the snake king Vasuki, they all fled every which way. Some slithered into heaven, others dived into water. Vasuki ran to Shiva and clung to the god's chest, securing himself in that position with a belt. The superlethal *kalinaga* rushed in panic to Padma and, rolling piteously at her feet, narrated all that had happened, including the tale of the curse and the motive of revenge in bereaved king and sage.

Padma lost no time in dealing with the crisis and sought Neta's counsel. "The sacrifice has to be stopped if the serpent race is to survive, and your son Astika can do it if you send him at once," Neta said.

Padma briefed Astika about his momentous task. "Janamejaya is set to exterminate the entire naga race. You must go at once and take over control of the king's sacrifice and save your mother's followers. Only you can accomplish this task."

Astika set off without delay, a handsome youthful Brahmin with an aura of power comparable to the sun's and of learning comparable to that of Brihaspati, preceptor of gods. He arrived at the venue of the Sarpa Satra softly chanting Vedic hymns. Hearing these being perfectly recited by one so young and comely, the king and the assembled priests welcomed him warmly. The king humbly washed his feet in homage and inquired about his antecedents and the purpose of his visit.

Astika blessed the king and replied, "I have come in the hope of receiving a gift from Your Majesty."

"Tell me what you would like," said the king, "and if it is within my powers it will be yours." He then narrated the tragedy that had befallen his father and led to the Sarpa Satra.

"For the sake of your father's soul there is one gift you ought to give me promptly. For I know how to conduct the horse sacrifice and the cow sacrifice and *rajasuya* sacrifice, which makes one an emperor holding sway over many kingdoms. All these I can conduct for you if you grant my wish."

The youth's quietly confident words were like a balm to the king's ears. He said, "Tell me what riches will please you, O twice-born priest."

Astika replied, "If you promise to satisfy my wish I will gratefully accept your gift."

"Rest assured I will not deny your request," said the king.

Pleased with the royal pledge Astika promptly said, "Your Majesty, I would like you to put an end to the sacrifice."

The king reacted like one struck by a thunderbolt. He thought for a while and said, "Ask for something else and I will give it at once."

"You have everything," responded Astika, "wealth, a kingdom, and power of life and death over millions of subjects. Still, you cannot ignore certain rules. The consequences of not keeping a solemn promise are grave indeed, as you well know. Disaster will strike your kingdom—it's inevitable."

The king gave in gracefully, though he realized that he had been outwitted. He said to the young man with a chuckle, "Now do tell us who you are; who are your parents?"

"The sage Jaratkaru is my father, the goddess Padma is my mother, and I am Astika. I came with the approval of Brahma, Vishnu, Shiva, and Indra to prevent the annihilation of the race of nagas."

The king sighed. "But what am I to do now that the sacrifice has been stopped?'

The young sage said reassuringly, "Before I take my leave let me give you a magnificent all-around boon. You will live long and happily, ruling as a mighty emperor and after that ascend heaven."

Astika returned to his mother's highland home, where the nagas gave him a rousing ovation, hoisting him on their heads and dancing with joy. Padma and Neta were proud of the young and wise sage and lovingly took him on their laps and showered him with kisses. They lived happily on Mount Sijuya.

LOOKING EARTHWARD

AFTER SOME DAYS PADMA BEGAN to feel restless. She had had a difficult time since her birth but had overcome all impediments and won the respect of all the great gods, including her father, the most awesome of them all. She had demonstrated that as a deity she was second to none in power and majesty. But what next? Spending eternity doing nothing, even in her heavenly abode on Mount Sijuya was not an attractive prospect. Would she just wait for another crisis to erupt so that she could exercise her power? Even in peaceful times the other deities had their divine vanity pampered by devotees who offered puja and lavish sacrifices. Why shouldn't she as well?

She confided her dissatisfaction to her sister, counselor, and confidante. "Neta," she said with a sigh, "the mortal world down there is controlled by a few gods, goddesses, and sages, all of whom have ardent worshippers and devotees. Now look at me. I am the goddess of the deadly race of nagas, I have power over all the venom, I can kill with venom and revive those who have been killed, and yet I am not worshipped in the human world. What should I do to be acknowledged as a great deity and have puja sacrifices offered by all kinds of people? Do pick up a piece of chalk and drawing divinatory diagrams tell me who is the earth dweller I should first make my worshipper."

Neta made diagrams representing the three realms, including the deserts, all movable and immovable objects, animals ranging from lions to gazelles, birds and their nests and all other forms of dwelling. After thus taking note of the whole of creation she opined that the person Padma should direct her attention to was one Chandradhara, or Chando or Chand—to use the diminutives—who lived in great splendor in the city of Champaknagar. A merchant prince whose single-minded devotion to Shiva was legendary, he had no time for any other deity and feared none, for the great god had gifted him the greatest of boons.

Chand had everything by way of worldly success. He ruled over a vast domain and a large, contented population that never knew want. His treasury was filled with gold and precious gems: he was wealthy as Kubera. His barracks were full of disciplined soldiers commanded by able generals. His stables were full of pedigree horses and his chariots were numerous. His trading ships traveled far and wide, carrying valuable cargo.

And yet, Chand's greatest desire was otherworldly. He had obtained from Shiva the boon of moksha, spiritual liberation, and the Mahagyan mantra, which raised one above aging, death, and rebirth.

At once a lock of matted hair had sprung from his scalp, palpable sign of his promotion to the status of a *siddha,* a liberated being.

Chandi had taken the grateful Chand aside and whispered conspiratorially into his ear. "Remember one thing—beware of Padmavati. She is always up to wicked deeds, always plotting mischief from her perch on Mount Sijuya. Never give in to her demands, never offer her puja or sacrifices."

Chand had solemnly assured Chandi that he would never bow to the one-eyed snake goddess. Chandi's caution was of course quite unnecessary, for Chand had inherited an inveterate hatred of snakes from his previous birth as the venerable sage Padmashankhya.

+   +   +

"You must win over Chand," Neta told Padma, "for his is the most resolute opposition to the spread of your influence. The rest are pushovers. As long as he refuses to bow to you, the world will remain unconquered. Make him surrender and you have the whole world at your feet."

Padma was delighted with Neta's advice. It gave her a strategic focus for her efforts to become established as a significant deity on earth.

"What would I do without you," she gushed, giving her sister a warm hug. "Now let me visit Father and obtain his sanction for our plan. Without his blessing nothing will come of our efforts."

Padma flew to Mount Kailash and greeted Shiva by touching his feet.

"You look troubled—is anything the matter?" Shiva asked in affectionate tones.

"Father, you know my situation—I don't need to explain in detail. My husband has left me and though I have a wonderful son and eight naga children and do not lack any comforts, I remain a nonentity on earth. I have no devotees, nobody worships me, nobody offers me sacrifices."

Padma raised a woebegone countenance whose sight made Shiva smile reassuringly. "The people on earth will offer you puja in the monsoon month of Sravana. This is bound to come to pass by and by, so you should relax and live happily. Only stay away from Chand, because he is dead set against you." Padma pouted in a pique and complained, "That's not fair, Father. He is devoted to you but so is everyone. Besides, how can he call himself your devotee and yet insult your daughter? For he does say terribly insulting things about me. Doesn't he by doing so insult you? You must promise me that he too will worship me."

Shiva pondered the matter briefly and then pronounced, "He will—eventually."

"Thank you, Father," Padma enthused, hugging the great god's feet.

Now in a celebratory mood, Padma leapt onto her swan and began dancing in ecstasy as the splendid bird flew swiftly over the earth until it reached the seashore. Merry as its mistress, the swan dipped its wings in the tossing waves and flew in a crazy zigzag course. On the shore the sage Asanavasana sat in rapt meditation. A drop of water from the swan's wing fell on his head, disturbing his trance and lighting the short fuse of his rage. Dancing in fury, he aimed a fist at the swan. The bird swerved, breaking the rhythm of Padma's aerial dance. Now the goddess burst into rage and let loose a curse.

"For twelve years you will have to stay away from your home," she told Asanavasana. "You will roam from one land to another."

Knowing that a goddess's curse was irrevocable, Asanavasana sadly walked away and roamed many lands. But he came back to Padma not long after and fell at her feet.

"Let me spend the rest of my exile in your company. Your curse has caused me profound sorrow, but it will be mitigated if you let me make myself at home beneath your feet."

Padma was pleased with the sage's words and counted him as the first of her human counselors. This made him very happy, and at Padma's request he began to sing a cheerful ditty to entertain her.

After a while, though, the mood of the song produced an opposite reaction in the goddess and tears rolled down her cheeks.

"How am I to find worshipful devotees in the coming age of wickedness, the Kali Yuga?" Padma lamented. Despite her father's assurance that she would receive universal worship the delay was driving her to despair. "The gods and goddesses who are well known are worshipped by all, but none turns to me with offerings."

"Have patience, divine mother," Asanavasana gently counseled her, "and listen to this prophecy of mine. As the years go by, the nagas through their devotion to you will make you known throughout the seven continents. At the end of the brazen age, the Dwapar Yuga, you will go down to earth and find devoted followers among cowherds, and you will trounce the Turki forces who try to persecute them. You will go to Champaknagar, and though the rich and powerful will be loath to recognize your status, two humble people, Jalu and Malu, will pay you unstinting homage, and you will reward them with kingdoms. You will then cast your spell on Chand's home. Chand will defy you and you will slay his ally, the *ojha* Dhanvantari, and then Chand's six sons. Chand's fortunes will decline when you wreck his trading fleet of fourteen ships. By employing a trick you will cause the heavenly couple Aniruddha and Usha to be born on earth, the former as Chand's son Lakshmindar and the latter as Behula. They will marry and one of your nagas will kill Lakshmindar. Behula will accompany her husband's body on a raft, and, eventually reaching the realm of the gods, she will appeal to Shiva. You will relent and, reviving Lakshmindar, bless both husband and wife. In return Behula will promise to bring her stubborn father-in-law around. And so, eventually, Chand will worship you. You will then restore Behula and Lakshmindar to their true identity in heaven."

Padma was thrilled to hear this and rewarded Asanavasana with gold-embroidered clothes.

PART TWO

IN THE REALM OF THE
MERCHANT KING

WINNING OVER COWHERDS

PADMA ACCOMPANIED BY NETA BEGAN reconnoitering the earth, looking for an opportunity to initiate its inhabitants into her worship. One day they espied a group of cowherds tending their cattle in the fields. The two sisters were both in the guise of Brahmin widows. Padma approached the cowherds and said, "I am so thirsty from the ordeal of traveling that I won't be able to go any farther unless you let me have some milk to drink."

One of the cowherds jeeringly replied, "Since we don't know you the question of giving you credit doesn't arise. You must pay if you want milk."

"I am a widowed Brahmin without any money," Padma said, "but I am dying of thirst and must beg some milk from you."

"Wandering through forests and begging for milk," sneered the cowherd, "you must be a woman of bad character."

He smirked and said, "If you want milk without paying you'll have to spend the night with us—how about it?"

"You are making fun of two helpless Brahmin widows," Padma said indignantly. "Do you want to lose your lives as punishment?"

She turned to Neta and lamented: "Just see how I have been insulted and humiliated. How can I expect to receive worship from such people? Let me finish them off instead."

"Wait!" Neta counseled her irate sister. "First listen to what I have to suggest. Instead of killing the cowherds you should make their cattle vanish. Let them search frantically and when they are at their wits' end they will be ready to worship the one who can bring the animals back. After all, they are as good as dead without their cattle. When they start tearing their hair in despair I will gently tell them what they must do to set things right."

"Brilliant!" exclaimed a beaming Padma. "Brahma has given you limitless intelligence."

Padma instantly used her magic to make the cattle vanish, every one of them. Suddenly finding them gone, the cowherds set up a wail. They called out frantically to each other. "Where could they have disappeared?" shouted one. "I've looked everywhere," shouted another. "Let's comb the forests," suggested a third.

The cowherds ran this way and that, peering into bushes, examining every clump of trees, weeping as they searched in vain.

"When we refused to give her milk to drink, a widow cursed us and went away, and then our cows and calves were stolen from under our noses," lamented a cowherd.

Neta approached him and asked what the matter was. He told her in detail everything that had happened since their encounter with the Brahmin widow. "And now we are without our means of livelihood; we can only cry in despair," he concluded.

"Listen, young fellow," Neta told him, laughing, "how could you be so foolish as to make fun of a goddess, not seeing through her widow's disguise?"

"We are not spiritual adepts," the cowherd humbly explained. "Nor are we clever; we are just simple folk living in the forest and tending cattle."

"Then stop sniveling and I will tell you what to do to remedy your unfortunate situation."

"We will do whatever you say."

"Worship the goddess Padmavati, offer her puja sincerely, and what you have lost will be restored to you," Neta advised.

"What do we know of puja rituals?" the cowherd bewailed. "But if you tell me what needs to be done I will do it."

"Steady your mind and listen carefully," said Neta. "Prepare a plot of land and build a roofed structure; then make an attractive platform to serve as the altar. Draw *alpana* designs on the platform and place on it a pitcher, which you should stuff with mango leaves and twigs. Then you need sweet-smelling flowers, sandalwood, incense, votive lamps, clothes, and ornaments. Shower the pitcher with petals, with fresh milk and ripe bananas, for these are great favorites of the goddess. After making the offerings you should complete the puja with songs and dances. After that a ritual sacrifice will greatly please the goddess and induce her to grant a boon to her worshippers. Do as I say and I can assure you the goddess will restore your cattle by way of a boon."

The cowherds lost no time in setting up the altar for the puja and decorating it in a befitting manner. They offered a mixture of honey, ghee, yogurt, and sugar as an oblation; also milk and bananas, and sugar-sweetened sandesh; and scented wild flowers. Some of them soaked the flowers and sprinkled the altar with the scented water. This was a wonderful new experience for the cowherds. So taken were they with the rituals, which under normal circumstances members of their lowly caste would not be allowed to perform, that they went through them over and over again, singing and dancing with gleeful abandon.

Nor did they neglect the grimly serious side of puja either. One of them ecstatically came forward to be sacrificed to the goddess. Another volunteered to play the officiating priest; he wielded a heavy, curved machete and chanting the names of the goddess—Manasa, Padmavati, Visahari—sliced through the bowed neck. The head of the sacrificed cowherd leapt some distance and fell to the ground.

Padma filled a bowl with the spurting blood and drank it with consummate satisfaction.

"I am pleased with your devotion," she told the cowherds, "so pleased that I will offer you a boon. What would you like?"

In one voice the cowherds replied, "We'll be ever grateful if you restore our cattle to us."

"That's easily done," said a beaming Padma, and as the cowherds leapt in joy at seeing their animals materialize around them, the goddess continued: "I also grant you good health, long lives, relief from the aches and pains of aging, and protection from my snakes and serpents."

The cowherds shouted in unison: "Jai Visahari"—"Victory to the goddess who has power over poison."

Neta gently drew Padma's attention and whispered: "I think you should restore the sacrificed cowherd to life at once. Seeing you perform the miracle will strengthen the cowherds' devotion to you."

"Wonderful idea!" enthused the goddess, and with a wave of her hand and a sprinkling of water she brought her secret occult power over life and death into play and restored the dead cowherd to life: his head flew through the air and joined his neck again, his limbs stirred, his eyes and face became animated again. His friends again loudly cheered the goddess. They vowed to offer puja to Padma on a regular basis. They felt elated as a community because they had been adopted, so to speak, by a deity whose tremendous power had been demonstrated right in front of their eyes. Manasa too was pleased at having made ardent converts of an entire community. Before taking leave she used her divine powers to clear a broad stretch of forestland and build a beautiful hamlet around a venerable banyan tree. This she gave as a gift to the cowherds, naming it Rakhalagacchi, which literally means "cowherds and a tree," or perhaps "wooded home of cowherds." She then showered her blessings on her devotees and took her leave along with Neta.

The worship of Padma became a daily festivity in the newly built village of the cowherds. The air resounded with their songs and dances, as after a bath in the river at the end of a day's hard work, they gathered in their Manasa temple and gave themselves up to the ecstatic worship of their guardian goddess.

THE BATTLE WITH HASSAN
AND HOSSEIN

THE MOST POPULOUS HUMAN SETTLEMENT close to the pastoral hamlet of the cowherds was home to two brothers, King Hassan and Prince Hossein, who were the powerful rulers of an expanding domain; hundreds of peasants toiled for them, felling forest trees and clearing jungle to bring more and more acres under cultivation.

The foreman in charge of the peasants was called Gora Mina. One day he entered the forest with a hundred peasants and a large flock of bullocks to plow a tract of freshly cleared land. At the end of the day, while the men rested and smoked their coconut-shell hookahs, Gora Mina's servant set off to have a bath in the nearby river. As fate had ordained, the path he took led him to the Manasa temple where the daily puja was in full swing. Startled at the sight of the rapturous devotees, he stopped dead in his tracks. The cowherds too noticed the stranger and, overcome with self-consciousness, froze into silence—for a moment. One of them shouted, "Catch him!" And another, "We'll sacrifice him to the goddess." At once all of them erupted into action and rushed at the interloper. The latter was no more than a split second late in reacting and ran for his life. Stumbling through the scrub, he barely managed to avoid getting caught and arrived panting at Gora Mina's base.

"The cowherds have gathered at a makeshift temple under a huge tree to worship a spirit," he explained when he got back his breath. "They put an earthen pitcher with a sija bough stuck into it and salaamed it repeatedly as they danced around it in a crazed manner. When they saw me they charged wildly at me. Who knows what they would have done if they had caught me."

Gora Mina listened to the account with mounting rage. He ordered his men to prepare for a fight and asked his servant to guide them to the cowherds' haunt.

"Let's get the bastards!" they screamed as the cowherds came within their view. By now the puja was over and the cowherds were getting things ready to cook their evening meal. Realizing that they were woefully outnumbered by their attackers they quickly melted into the forest.

Gora Mina marched up to the altar and with one blow from his staff shattered the neck of the earthen pitcher. Unbeknownst to all, Padma had been quietly observing everything. She had enjoyed the sight of the simple cowherds paying their daily tribute to her at the temple, she had laughed at the sight of the cowherds chasing the interloper, and also at the sight of the cowherds fleeing before the attacking mob. To her both the chase and the retaliatory attack had seemed to be a childish game, but the blow to the pitcher was another matter. It was an attack on her. She flew into a deadly rage. Curled up in her hand was a deadly *bighatiya,* a slender snake just a *bighat,* or handspan, in length. She turned it into the much prized *kanchpoka,* a green beetle whose gemlike glittering wings were used as *bindis,* and secreted it into the pitcher.

Gora Mina's servant took it into his head to examine the contents of the broken pitcher. He turned it upside down, pulled out the twigs and leaves, and on sifting through them found the pretty *kanchpoka.* He gave it to his master, who was glad to have it, for it would make a surprise gift for his wife. He tucked it into the waistband of his trousers. Feeling squeezed, the *bighatiya* assumed its natural form and bit into its tormentor's belly. Gora Mina felt as if lightning had seared his flesh. He clutched his abdomen and collapsed. Padma ordered the snake to kill all but one. It struck down the men one by one but in accordance with instructions spared one—a simple fellow nicknamed Bharu, which means "clown" or "dolt."

Bharu fled crying to Hassan and Hossein, who were presiding over their court. With a salaam he sobbed out the whole story—how a servant had stumbled upon the cowherds' puja, how they chased him, the retaliatory raid and how the altar pitcher was broken and a green beetle discovered within turned into a *bighatiya* that killed all in the party except him.

Meanwhile, Padma positioned herself at the ghat where maids from the Hassan-Hossein household went to fetch water. Placing a pitcher in the middle of the landing, Padma sprinkled water and showered flowers to perform a puja to herself. Just then seven maids carrying pitchers on hips came down the path. They frowned at Padma and spoke harshly.

"Move out of the way, you witch. How dare you go through your abominable Hindu rituals in a public place!"

"Why don't you walk around my pitcher?" Padma advised.

The maids rushed at her in anger, and she once again played the trick of turning a *bighatiya* into a green beetle and dropping it into the pitcher. The curious maids sifted through the twigs and leaves in it and were delighted to find the beetle.

"Our mistress will be very pleased with this and will tip us well," they said to each other.

One of the maids had the prized insect but held it so tightly in her anxiousness not to lose it that it felt squashed, reverted to its true shape and nature, and bit her. And five more after her, leaving one called Togri to go home bearing the tragic tale.

Padma boarded her flying chariot and headed for Hassan's city. Hovering over it she surveyed it in detail. Its affluence was obvious: clearly, Hassan and Hossein were wealthy as well as powerful potentates. The streets glittered, well-built houses lined them on both sides, and there was much gaiety among the citizens. One could hear singing and see people dancing. Those who were seated wore expensive jewelry and contented expressions. The absence of poverty or anxiety was striking. Hassan lived happily with a hundred wives. Their harem was a model of elegant living. The ladies chewed sweetened *paan* while maids massaged their bodies with sandalwood oil and musk. Other attendants waved yak-tail fans over their heads. Servants guilty of inefficiency or misdemeanors stood with palms supplicatingly joined, begging to be let off this once. Some piously invoked the names of God. There were others whose duty was to clean and load golden hookahs with fragrant tobacco and proffer them with a smile to the ladies. Yet others were entrusted with keeping things properly arranged so that everything was always in apple-pie order.

At the law court the *kazi* sat with his papers and books and the Koran, conducting the interrogation of suspects and litigants. Hundreds of messengers, footmen, bailiffs, and horsemen, all armed to the teeth, stood by awaiting orders.

The syeds and maulanas, ever with Koranic verses and religious precepts on their lips, instructed new converts to the faith on how to perform ablutions and pray. They taught at the *maqtabs* attached to mosques and were always on the lookout for competent recruits to serve their master. The most pleasant task they performed was conducting weddings, which took place frequently and would be followed by sumptuous feasts. Pious Muslims often recited prayers for the dead and visited *pirs* and paid them tribute in cash or kind.

Everyone in the city was happy with their lives—until the maid Togri and the servant of Gora Mina came bearing shocking news. They went up to Hassan as he sat in assembly and in their distress, repeatedly striking their foreheads with their palms, narrated how plowmen and maids had perished.

Hassan sent out spies who came back and corroborated the stories of mayhem. He snorted and quivered with rage, wrung his beard, and, fiercely rolling his eyes, ordered the mobilization of all his troops.

Hassan's errand boy carried the message to the *kazi* at whose court were assembled a large number of armed soldiers, including many famous warriors. On hearing the details of the recent disasters, the men, among whom there were eunuchs as well, formed up and marched to meet their chief. Ready for action was an entire division of troops, comprising 109,350 foot soldiers, 65,610 cavalrymen, 21,870 soldiers mounted on elephants, and another 21,870 on chariots. The brothers Hassan and Hossein came out to review the army. Their faces set in expressions of wrath, they kept twirling their mustaches as they ordered everyone to look sharp. The men responded with obedient "Yes, sirs" and set about getting things ready.

The elephants were outfitted and guided through their drills by their mahouts; the war horses were equipped with protective mail; the cannons were loaded with cannonballs and gunpowder and mounted on carriages by efficient gunners; the mules and camels were fitted with their accoutrements.

The standard-bearers formed up, holding aloft tall bamboo poles from which various colorful pennants fluttered in the breeze. Archers and musketeers ringed the two brothers who angrily bit their lower lips: they made a formidable pair of opponents. Hassan gave the order to move forward. "Go get me this bitch of a demoness," he growled.

The band struck up: drums of varied sizes and shapes, flutes, war trumpets. With thousands of weapons glinting in the sun the troops moved forward. Bringing up the rear, in palanquins, were armed officials and the *kazi,* holding the Holy Koran in one hand and a weapon in the other. Their subordinates, clerks and suchlike, accompanied on foot, similarly armed. There were also holy men accompanying the army, some of them famed for possessing astonishing occult powers; for instance, they could discharge urine that would fuel lamps.

The ground shook beneath the trampling men and beasts of the punitive army. Before them now came a royal lady, Champa Bibi, wife of the Raja Hassan. She appealed to her husband to call off the campaign. "Manasa is a Hindu deity, the goddess of nagas, possessing such powers that Muslims also are in awe of her," she said. "It is folly to tangle with her for she can besiege your domain with countless serpents. They will sow terror and confusion in the people. Can you imagine a worse calamity?"

But Hassan was not to be moved. He had been informed that his opponent had appeared in the guise of a Brahmin widow. He could not imagine a being more timorous and feckless, and he blustered, "What can an old Brahmin widow do to a magnificent army like this?" He waved his wife aside and signaled his men to advance.

Padma soon appeared before the army in the deceptive guise of a feeble Brahmin widow, but before anyone in the army could react she vanished. The cry went up, "There she is, nab her," but it was too late. She appeared again a little later in a different place. Again the cry went up, and again she vanished. Padma amused herself for a while by playing this game of "Catch me if you can."

King Hassan responded with rage, gritting his teeth and shouting at his men, "Go get the hag." The elusiveness of Padma only increased his anger. When the army came upon a pitcher meant for offering puja to Manasa-devi, Hassan rode up and smashed it with his sword and, picking up some of the sweet-smelling tulsi leaves that had been offered by devotees, rubbed them on his neck. As he did so they turned into nettle and pricked his skin painfully. Hassan picked up cooling sandal-wood paste offered to the pitcher and rubbed it on his cheeks; it turned into flames that singed his beard and mustache. An itch spread over Hassan's skin. He picked up some of the small, ripe bananas left at the pitcher and peeled them and rubbed them on his body. But instead of the expected emollient effect they caused his limbs and joints to swell painfully. He rolled on the ground and slapped his burning cheeks in the vain hope of obtaining relief. He picked up champak blossoms and touched them to his beard; they became stinging wasps. Utterly helpless, he called upon God to come to his aid, vowing to do penance for sins committed and to stay away from sin in future. But the next moment his pride and rage got the better of him again, and he thundered: "Bring me the Brahmin widow at once, I will force her to eat beef and give her in marriage to a maulana."

Padma smiled wryly and decided to bring on her nagas in force. They rushed to her from all three realms, each more fearsome than the next. They were like doubles of Yama, the god of death. When they reared up and spread their hoods it seemed they could devour whole mountains. They were so numerous that they covered the entire surface of the earth.

"What do you want us to do, divine mother?" they asked.

Padma gave a résumé of everything that had happened since she began her campaign to win worshippers—her encounter with the cow-herds, the conflict between the cowherds and Hassan's men, Hassan's campaign against her. She then gave commands.

"Go and massacre all the Turks, spare none."

The nagas hissed most thunderously and flew away to fulfill their dread mission. Their hooded heads covered the whole sky as they laid siege to Hassan's army and his city. In their millions they came, snakes and serpents of all sizes and shapes and hues, and formed a wall around the Turks. Their hiss was a thunderous apocalyptic gale that struck terror in Hassan's heart and even made the gods and demons nervous.

Hassan kept up his bluster, though inwardly he was in abject terror. Death was inevitable, he thought, yet such was his royal pride that he kept urging his men to slaughter all the snakes. The nagas were doubly enraged to hear this and redoubled their attacks. One of the bravest fighters in Hassan's army hurled a heavy spear at Takshaka: it not only slipped off the target but splintered into fragments. Others followed his example and attacked the snakes with staffs and scimitars. The result was laughable: the snakes devoured both attackers and weapons. Padma, who was watching the fray from her celestial chariot, was in stitches.

Next, she deployed the deadly *bighatiyas* in large numbers. Their first victim was Prince Hossein. A *bighatiya* slipped into the waistband of his trousers and sank its fangs into his belly. A lightning strike couldn't have been more sudden or devastating. Hossein clutched his abdomen in terror; his body seemed to be consumed by flames. Gasping, he called on God for aid, then crying for his brother, fell dead with his head pointing to the north.

The *bighatiyas* went berserk, attacking whoever they came upon, chasing whoever tried to escape. Leaping on to elephants they bit the soldiers on the howdahs. They bit soldiers in the chest, on the neck, on the throat, inside their turbans on the skull. Their victims called upon God, begged forgiveness for their sins, they gasped, cried, tottered, and fell to their deaths. Those who jumped into the water in an attempt to escape fell to deadly water snakes. Those who squirreled up trees fell to the lethal bites of tree snakes and dropped with a thud like heavy fruit. Those who clambered up to the rooftop were bitten by snakes that dwell on roofs and dropped to the ground like pumpkins. Cries of panic and terror rose from the men until they all fell to the snakes and an eerie silence settled on the dead bodies of the entire division mustered by King Hassan. Only he was spared, a lonely commander of an army of dead soldiers.

Dust swirled around him, entered his eyes and nostrils. He put a hand over his nose and burst into lamentation. "There was a lone Brahmin widow somewhere around here, playing nasty tricks on people, but where have all these terrifying serpents come from?" he cried. "Why did I go after the widow, ignoring my wife's warning? And now I have lost my only brother, not to mention all my soldiers and noble officials and judges and religious scholars. All my veteran fighters fell to the snakes, which surround my city and continue their depredations." His tears fell like monsoon rain, and even if he shut his eyes his consciousness teemed with images of fearsome snakes. As if to give himself a respite, he fell unconscious.

Presently Padma herself appeared on the scene, in her characteristic form, draped with venomous serpents and holding her favorite *kal-bikal* snake duo, one in each hand. She seated herself on a cushion formed by a huddle of massive serpents. She smiled languorously. Serpents dancing around her waved yak-tail fans. The tableau she and her serpents composed was huge and terrifying. In this form she appeared in front of Hassan, who surfaced into consciousness and on beholding her broke into a sweat while his limbs trembled with fear. He shut his eyes again, then made a desperate dash to escape. But whichever way he turned he saw only more snakes; there was no escape. Seeing a pile of straw he quickly hid inside it. There too it was not safe: a chameleon faced him, shaking its head meaningly. "O my God!" he cried. "Even this lizard is shaking its head to point me out to my pursuers." Gritting his teeth, he stood up and shook his fists at the reptile.

Padma watched his antics with a wry smile playing on her lips. Ordering a troop of nagas to form a ring around Hassan so that he could not move away, she assumed a venerable soothsayer's garb and went to Champa Bibi to sow mischief.

Padma spun a veil of illusion around Champa Bibi so as to render her completely pliant and told her, "Take it from me, all these soldiers died because of hostility from *bhutas*. One of these malignant spirits will soon come this way. Don't hesitate to torch it."

Manasa then telepathically instructed the nagas guarding Hassan to make an opening for him toward the path leading up to his palace. The terrified king at once seized the opportunity to make a dash, running noisily and clumsily. The noise drew Champa Bibi, who thought it was the *bhuta* mentioned by Padma. The darkness made it impossible to tell who it was. Champa Bibi had a brand ready and attacked the oncoming figure with it, setting robes alight and singeing beard and flesh.

"O God, O my God," cried out the figure, and to her shock and dismay Champa Bibi recognized the voice of her husband. She explained with profuse apologies how she had been put up to it by a soothsayer. She took her husband by the hand and led him indoors.

She sat him down, washed his feet, made him change his clothes, offered him refreshments; and all the while she lamented the loss of her trusted maids.

"Kalaphuli is gone," she wailed. "She was excellent at cooking meat dishes. The young one called Bulbuli wasn't spared either: she was such a charming chatterbox. Where is Hoolhooli, who was such an expert at dressing my hair? Zafari had magic fingers when it came to preparing *paan*. They are all gone."

Hassan joined in the lament. "All my good men are gone too. All the learned maulanas and syeds, old Gora Mina who was such a dependable assistant. All my brave warriors are no more, foot soldiers, horsemen, and elephant-mounted soldiers, and even the horses and elephants haven't been spared. But above all, I am devastated by the loss of my brother Hossein." In despair, he struck his forehead repeatedly with the palm of his hand.

Throughout Hassan's city pervaded a mood of defeat and despair. From every household rose the ululations of lament. "O my son, he was the sun and the moon to me—he's gone," came one voice. And another mourned a brother: "He was my alter ego, how can I live without him?" Some slapped their foreheads to curse their fate, cried "Father, O Father mine," and rolled on the ground. "My wise uncle is no more," said some, and others wept for their nephews. Many sobbed disconsolately for their husbands. But their grief was mingled with anger, and loud were the vengeful curses hurled at Padma, "They say she came as an old hag; why doesn't she come again? We'll catch her and stuff her mouth with beef!"

Padma, on her flying chariot, heard the angry voices with mounting anger, and finally ordered the *bighatiya* brigade to attack the city people, showing no mercy to anyone. Cold, methodical, and irresistible, the *bighatiyas* went from house to house, biting all living things. They would come upon a venerable patriarch and with a springy leap sink their fangs into the neck; the next moment his beard would be rolling in the dust as he shook in his death throes. A prosperous householder would be attacked with lightning speed and left dying with the name of God on his lips. Seeing him collapse, his manservant, thinking this was his chance to make fantasy come true, would make a grab for his mistress; but the next moment, fatally bitten, he would be clutching his throat, as would be the object of his lust. A child at play would be bitten without warning and would fall down dead. Its mother, rushing to pick it up with a loud cry of distress, would fall next. A hen crossing the path would be instantly put down, and the woman, its owner who picked it up crying that it was about to start laying eggs, would then bite the dust.

Thus the mayhem continued. The *bighatiyas* came upon the weavers' colony, a large settlement that contributed substantially to the economic prosperity of Hassan's city. Everyone there was busy all day, dyeing yarn, weaving at the loom, folding and piling cloth bundles. The *bighatiyas* struck without warning. Men, women, and children at work fell one after another, hardly getting a chance to cry out. A weaver wearing a skullcap was bitten through its cloth right on the skull and with a stifled cry of "O God" fell dead. An elderly weaver plying his loom and nodding his head in rhythm was bitten on the neck, touched the spot, and swooned on finding blood oozing out. In a moment he was dead. One by one the clattering looms fell silent, until the entire locality became a village of the dead.

Hassan-nagar, the capital city of King Hassan, was completely taken over by snakes. They were the only living beings there—except for Hassan himself and his wife, two lonely, traumatized people. But even in this extreme situation the demands of hunger eventually made themselves felt.

"I am weak with hunger," Hassan moaned. "Cook me some rice."

Champa Bibi went to the kitchen and selected a pot of the right size. But when she tried to lift it off the bamboo shelf where it had lain, from within came an ominous hissing. She hurriedly put it down; a deadly snake reared its head and menacingly flicked its tongue this way and that.

Champa Bibi flopped down on the floor and wailed like a baby. Her husband joined her, crying, "There is no hope—death is sure to come now."

Hassan had lost his entire army, and then his city had been overrun and its inhabitants killed, yet his fighting spirit had somehow survived till now. The incident in the kitchen was like the proverbial straw that broke the camel's back; it brought home to Hassan the futility of all opposition to the rampaging forces of the new goddess. Now he could only lament: he was utterly overwhelmed by the death of his brother Hossein. "Why do I live, why did Hossein have to die?" he wailed. "His death hit me like a stake through my innards. O how I miss my brother! O Hossein, Hossein!" Overcome by grief, Hassan fainted. Champa Bibi took him in her arms and, laying him down, sprinkled water on his face to revive him.

Presently Padma and Neta arrived in their flying chariot, which hovered over the desolate scene. The sight of the defeated and helpless King Hassan aroused their sympathy. They called out to him and addressed him in affectionate tones.

This sudden change from intemperate wrath to affection might strike one as odd if one forgot that Padma's aim was not merely to strike terror but to win converts. There might be a hidden reason as well, one based on kinship ties, for some say that Hassan and Hossein too were the progeny of Shiva. They say that when Shiva took Padma home, Chandi left for her father's home in a huff, accompanied by her sons Ganesha and Kartikeya. Brahma tried in vain to dissuade her, then told Shiva what had happened. The great god disguised himself as a Muslim soldier, complete with turban and scimitar, and waited in a hovel along the route taken by Chandi. As she came into view Shiva caused a tremendous downpour that drove Ganesha and Kartikeya one way and Chandi toward the shack where Shiva was waiting. He offered her some refreshment—*chira* and sweets—and then ravished her. Hassan and Hossein were born as a result. Padma and Neta with their divine clairvoyance would therefore have recognized their half brothers.

Be that as it may, Padma and Neta felt kindly toward Hassan as he sat propped up by Champa Bibi's helping hand.

"Listen to me, you silly boy," said Padma chidingly, "I am Padmavati, Manasa-devi, and all you have to do to get back what you have lost is offer puja to me. Offer me puja with sincere devotion and whatever boon you ask will be given at once."

Hassan sat up hurriedly and raised a tearful face at the sky. "But I do not know how to offer puja," he lamented. "Now what am I to do?"

"Don't worry," Champa Bibi said reassuringly, "I will pick the *vavaya* flowers for you to offer the goddess."

Hassan quickly had a bath and came all fresh to pay homage to a deity whom he had till now considered alien. Sitting composedly he offered the flowers and clean water with these words: "Take the water and these flowers, O Brahmin lady, and bring my brother Hossein back to life."

Padma replied with a laugh, "Listen carefully, Hassan, and do as I say. First comes the pitcher, my prime symbol, which will be the centerpiece on the altar and the focus of your devotion in the puja. It will naturally reflect the wealth and social status of the worshipper. A humble earthen pitcher will please me when the worshipper is a simple, humble cowherd, but in your case it must be commensurate with your royal status. It has to be beautifully crafted out of gold. As for the puja offerings that have to be placed with utmost devotion at the foot of the pitcher, you must have ten different fruits, sacred tulsi leaves, water lilies, and the hundred-petaled lotus. Pray to me with single-minded devotion and your brother and all your soldiers and people will come back to life in an instant."

Hassan listened with rising joy and excitement and without delay set about getting things ready. He went and fetched fresh water from a holy river, gathered the fruit and flowers and leaves, and took out the most beautiful golden pitcher from his treasure hoard. The fruits and vegetables he got were the banana, gherkin, palmyra palms, melon, coconut, rose apple, date, jackfruit, areca nut, and mango. Beating a roll on the drums he placed a sija bough in the mouth of the pitcher, and began the puja in earnest. Padma presently showed that she was true to her word by producing Hossein, alive and well, before his brother—to the latter's ineffable delight. Others close to Hassan and Hossein were then revived, one by one. Quickly appraising themselves about the circumstances of their revival, they joined their king in paying homage to the goddess who had so dramatically established a claim on their devotion. In time the entire army that had been destroyed and then the city's entire population came alive and joined in the puja.

Padma manifested herself atop the pitcher; she was hugely gratified at the devotion of her new and numerous worshippers. To the chief of them, that is, to King Hassan, she said, "I have been pleased to restore all that you lost and I will protect you from all dangers in the future. Now tell me what other boons you wish to have from me."

Humbled, contrite, and brimming with gratitude, Hassan prostrated himself at Padma's feet and said in fervent tones, "O mother of the universe, forgive me, for I have offended you, my sinful mouth has uttered vile words about you, who is the source of the three realms of heaven, earth, and underworld, and of all beings, animal, plant, and inanimate. I am an ignoramus who could not recognize your greatness and glory."

Overwhelmed by guilt, Hassan continued, "Why do I cling to life? I am a lowly creature, sunk in wickedness, whose only hope lies in your mercy, so I beg you to bless me with your touch—kick me on my head and I will be saved."

These words touched Padma, increasing her goodwill and affection toward Hassan. "You will be blessed and raised above other earthly rulers," she promised. "Devote yourself to statecraft and consolidate your kingdom. My blessings will diminish the grip of aging, death, and sorrow on your people. You will have thirty-six palaces to dwell in with your wife and concubines. Spread the word about my power and encourage my worship on earth and be assured of my undying blessings."

Padma laughed with pleasure, gently pressed down on Hassan's head with her foot—inducing in him a mystic ecstasy—and vanished.

Hassan set about proselytizing the cult of Padmavati, Manasa-devi, and commissioned the finest builders and artisans to build a magnificent temple for her worship. The men began work at once, measuring out the land with ropes, putting up stone walls, painting various scenes and figures, and sculpting lifelike statues of stylized and distorted proportions depicting gods and demons, apsaras, kinnaras, rakshasas, and gandharvas. In addition there were countless examples of flora and fauna, either painted or sculpted in relief. Soon it was time to put up the roof and add finishing touches with decorations of silver and gold and ivory and precious stones, diamonds, emeralds, rubies. Awnings of peacock feathers surrounded the entire structure so that people seeing the temple from afar were bedazzled and thought they were looking upon a grand palace on Mount Kailash.

Hassan amply rewarded the builders and artisans and ordered them to construct thirty-six ashrams, the chief among which would house five of the wisest Brahmins. He called a conclave of his allies and subjects and declared his intent to spread the worship of Manasa in kingdoms near and far.

Soon his emissaries were on their way to different countries carrying invitations to their rulers and citizens to make a pilgrimage to Hassan's Manasa temple, particularly on the coming occasion of its commissioning. The response was overwhelming. Not only did kings, princes, courtiers, and citizens come to pay homage to the goddess, they were preceded by cartloads of offerings: the choicest sweets, milk, yogurt, cream, ghee, extra-sweet honey, ten varieties of fruit and colorful and sweet-smelling flowers, incense, drums of varied sizes, wind and stringed instruments.

Music crashed like thunder as the five Brahmin priests got ready to conduct the temple's inaugural puja. At an auspicious hour, accompanied by Vedic chants they set up a gem-studded throne at the center of the floor, placed a golden pitcher on it, and into its mouth inserted a luxuriant sija bough.

By way of preliminary, the priests offered puja to Ganesha. Then began the elaborate rituals of Manasa worship. With their scriptural cribs in one hand, they chanted mantra after mantra while pouring libations on the pitcher with the other. The gathered devotees were transported into a state of ecstasy and prostrated themselves repeatedly at the pitcher. Presently the goddess appeared in her resplendent form atop the pitcher, and the devotees nearly swooned with delight.

Padma addressed Hassan, who sat with eyes closed and palms joined in rapt devotion.

"My son," she said, "I am well pleased with your devotion. You may ask for any boon and it will be yours."

In tones of utmost adoration Hassan apostrophized the goddess as the be-all and end-all of the universe in whose all-encompassing being all other gods and goddesses and demigods and demigoddesses were unified.

"But how can I, a humble sinner, comprehend your greatness?" Hassan bewailed. "My life is a series of sinful activities. Only you can rescue me from this iniquitous existence."

Padma was moved by Hassan's words and felt ever more affectionate toward him. She reassured him with kind words and declared, "Your lineage will thrive from generation to generation, your kingdom will wax prosperous, you will enjoy good health and a long life." This was no more than what she had already bestowed on Hassan, but the reiteration before distinguished guests and the populace enhanced the prestige of both bestower deity and human beneficiary and doubly sealed a special bond between them. Much gratified by the pomp and circumstance of the puja and the adoration of her devotees, particularly Hassan, Padma left in her flying chariot in a mood of exhilaration and returned to her celestial home on Mount Sijuya.

JALU AND MALU

EMBOLDENED BY HER RECENT spectacular successes, Manasa decided to embark on the great trial awaiting her—the campaign to humble Chand, the merchant prince, so that he would perforce worship her. The time she chose was when Chand was preparing to hold the sraddha ceremony for his recently deceased father. It would include prayers and rituals marking the end of the period of mourning and a feast, which, in keeping with Chand's status and wealth, had to be lavish and open to all. Chand commissioned two fishermen brothers Jalu and Malu to trawl the river for the huge quantities of fish that would be required.

Padma mounted her flying chariot and on reaching earth assumed her favorite persona, that of an aging Brahmin widow. She approached the river where the two brothers were fishing with nets from their boat and hailed them beseechingly.

"I beg you, my good brothers, please ferry this old Brahmin widow across and earn merit. I am on my way to Champaknagar to go begging from the good citizens."

"Listen, old woman," one of the fishermen replied, "we have been ordered to catch fish, huge quantities of fish, for the sraddha feast in honor of the merchant prince Chand's late father. We cannot afford to waste time. As it is, we are nervous lest we fail to catch enough fish for the feast. See if you can find someone else with a boat—or swim across."

Padma implored them again. "There isn't another boat in sight, and I am too old and infirm to swim across. Have pity and ferry me across, and on my way back in a few days I will give you a part of what I get from begging. You will also earn the blessings of a grateful old Brahmin widow, my sons."

The two brothers lost their temper at the importunate widow, a manifestation of their frustration with the poor catch so far. "Are you really a Brahmin widow?" they said jeeringly. "More likely, you are the demoness Hidimba in disguise, plotting to drink our blood," they said and cast their nets. Padma seethed with rage but controlled herself. The two brothers cast their nets with increasing desperation; each time they came up empty. Finally they put two and two together and realized why their efforts were frustrated. They went up to Padma with palms supplicatingly joined. "We haven't been able to catch any fish because we have offended you," they said. "Please forgive us and let us ferry you across. With your blessings we'll be able to catch the fish we need."

They touched her feet in reverence and carried her to their boat. When they reached midstream they decided to try their luck again.

"Cast your nets and see what you get," Padma urged them.

This time so many fish were trapped in the net that the two brothers found it difficult to pull it on to the boat. The fish filled the boat to capacity.

"Cast your net again," Padma urged.

"But there's no more space on the boat," the brothers complained.

"That doesn't matter; see what luck brings you this time." Realizing that the Brahmin widow wished to show them something special, the brothers cast a net again. It didn't catch any fish, but entangled in its web were a couple of glittering golden pitchers. Jalu and Malu were wide-eyed in amazement. They fell at their unprepossessing passenger's feet and begged: "You are no ordinary Brahmin widow, please reveal your true identity."

"I am Manasa-devi, Padmavati," said the passenger—now a resplendent divine figure. "I will manifest myself in the pitchers, so take them home and offer puja to them with appropriate devotion, and you may ask any boon of me if you do as I say."

"Let this boat turn into gold," the brothers begged, groveling happily at the goddess's feet.

Padma laughed and said, "You'll have that and more." At once the boat became glittering gold and a shower of gold nuggets fell on it as well as on the brothers' humble home in the nearby village.

Their mother, Nichhani, came running excitedly to give the news to her sons and got a double surprise on seeing the gold-laden golden boat. On learning the whys and wherefores of the miracle, Nichhani carried the pitchers home and with her two daughters-in-law began singing ditties in praise of Padma. Jalu and Malu brought along drummers and musicians and soon the air resounded with festive music.

Just then Sonaka, wife of Chand, the merchant king, was on her way to the Gungari River for a ritual dip in fulfillment of a vow she had made. She was accompanied by the wives of her six sons. Suddenly they were startled to hear the sound of loud music from the home of Jalu and Malu. Evidently, a large number of expert musicians and drummers were giving an enthusiastic performance. Where had the two poor fishermen found money to hire so many musicians, wondered Sonaka. She asked her maid Jhawwa to go and find out what was going on. Jhawwa went and saw the glittering pair of pitchers at the center of the fishermen brothers' puja room. Various objects were being offered to them in worship, and all around the once humble home was resplendent with gold. She came and reported everything to Sonaka, whose curiosity led her to go at once and see everything for herself.

Nichhani received Sonaka warmly, reverentially bending down to touch her feet, and offered her a magnificent seat.

Sonaka went straight to the point. "Tell me, Nichhani, who is this new deity you are worshipping? You were struggling with poverty till yesterday, and now that you have a new deity to offer puja to, suddenly fortune has smiled on you. I am curious about this god or goddess."

"We have become ardent worshippers of the goddess Manasa," replied Nichhani. "The pitchers came out of the water entangled in my sons' fishing net. By the grace of the goddess our home is now glittering with gold."

This account inspired devotion in Sonaka. She said to Nichhani, "I wish to learn the songs of praise and the rituals and join you in worshipping the goddess."

Nichhani was delighted to instruct Sonaka on the procedure for Manasa puja. But that was not enough to satisfy Sonaka; she now asked for one of Manasa's pitchers so that she could start offering puja straightaway in her own home. "Let me have it till I can get one of my own," she said.

Nichhani was in an embarrassing bind. She owed fealty to Sonaka, but she didn't relish the thought of parting with a gift from Padma. But the goddess herself intervened to resolve Nichhani's quandary. From her flying chariot came her imperious voice, "Let Sonaka have both the pitchers so that she can have a grand puja in her palatial mansion."

Nichhani obliged at once, but Sonaka, noticing that she was down in the mouth, comforted her, saying it was only a temporary arrangement, and gratefully picked up the pitchers, balancing one on a hip and carrying the other in one hand.

Back home, Sonaka set about with great enthusiasm to get everything ready for the puja, which she then performed together with her daughters-in-law with fervent devotion. The servant Jhawwa took it upon herself to go and tell Chand about the worship, accompanied by the singing of panegyrics to the strange, new goddess.

Chand was thunderstruck. Without wasting a moment he rushed quivering with rage to the place of Manasa worship and with repeated blows of his sturdy *hintala* staff cracked and dented the golden pitchers. Shocked and hurt at her husband's manic behavior, Sonaka rebuked him roundly. "By such a stupid act as striking the goddess's ceremonial pitchers you have only ensured the loss of your wealth and prosperity," she shouted. Nichhani came running to retrieve the battered pitchers and Manasa, who was invisibly hovering about, flew home.

NEUTRALIZING CHAND'S OCCULT POWER

PADMA WAS DEEPLY CONCERNED at the unbending arrogance of Chand and consulted with Neta on the course of action to adopt.

"Sister," said Neta, "I told you that after our parents imparted to him the great occult knowledge that guarantees immortality Chand lost all fear and became overweeningly arrogant. His greatest passion now is a garden containing every variety of flowering and fruit-bearing plant or tree. He loves to spend his leisure there, gazing at the natural loveliness. You should take your nagas and destroy the garden."

No sooner said than done! Padma mustered her nagas and arrived at the gate to Chand's garden in the twinkling of an eye. With its well-ordered rows and clumps of exquisite plants it surpassed in its beauty Indra's heavenly abode of Amaravati. But that didn't prevent Padma from ordering its prompt and all-out devastation. The serpents systematically poured venom on the plants and trees, causing them to shrivel and die instantly.

The head of the garden guards rushed to inform Chand about the ongoing destruction. He came quivering with fury and draping over his shoulders a scarf symbolizing triumph silently recited the magic mantra he had been taught by Shiva and Chandi; instantly the garden was revived in all its pristine glory. Then, puffed up with arrogance, he let loose a volley of abuse at Padma.

The goddess was shaken and turned to her sister and counselor.

"Assume the form of a sexy nautch girl and seduce Chand to make him yield the great occult knowledge. Once he does that it will lose its potency."

"But I am Shiva's daughter," Padma objected. "How can I stoop so low in order to get the better of a human being who has the gall to call me unsavory names."

Neta pointed out that instances of compromises dictated by exigencies were not lacking.

"You are being inordinately finicky," she said. "Remember that Vishnu in his incarnation as Krishna lived with the lowly cowherds, sharing their food and sleeping under the same roof because it was a necessary part of his stratagem to kill the tyrant king Kangsha. Think of another incarnation of the god, Rama, who formed an alliance with hanumans— with monkeys, Padma!—because their help was indispensable in the rescue of Sita. Then there is the example of Damayanti and King Nala.

Neta's words dispelled Padma's qualms and she prepared for the mission—dressing to kill, as the saying goes. She scented her hair by blowing incense fumes through it, then drawing it firmly, fixed it in a tight bun; put on large round earrings; a nosepin as charming as the sesame blossom. Her dark-rimmed eyes sparkled with the allure of blue lotuses. She massaged a mix of musk and sandalwood essence on her body, and put on bracelets and armlets and tinkling anklets of gold. A garland of never-fading amaranth hung round her neck. As for the formidable nagas she habitually draped around herself, they were set aside. She was now feminine beauty incarnate, the epitome of seductive power, ready to humble her foe. Equipped with drums and pipes, a combo of gandharvas and *vidyadharas* came at her command to accompany her on the mission. Neta gladly became her handmaid, and a troop of nagas in disguise appeared as escort. Of course Padma's divine peers observed the preparations with amusement and gossipy whispers—"Padma has become a courtesan!"—and her stepmother Chandi couldn't contain her laughter.

The seductress and her entourage set off, borne along in their celestial chariots by a compliant wind, and they sang various ragas as they flew over fleecy clouds and reached Champaknagar. The music was wafted to Chand's ears; it gave him an exquisite thrill. The drums resounded like distant thunder in a clear sky, and Padma's voice rang like a koel's. Chand felt his body tingle in response to the jaunty rhythm of drums reinforced by clapping of hands and the beguiling tone of the singer's voice. He called his servant Dhona.

"That's a marvelous singer," he said. "I'm sure she's a celebrity in her country. Go and ask her to come—I'd like to listen to some songs."

"Yes, master," said Dhona, laughing meaningly. He went at once to the group of performers and taking the comely singer by the hand led her into the presence of his master.

Chand's interest and curiosity became greatly inflamed at the sight of the artiste who stood before him in a graceful dancer's posture, eyeing him with a sidelong glance as a teasing smile played over her lips. Many were the seductive wiles at her command. As Chand's eyes roved over her figure, she had a telepathic conversation with Kama, the love god.

"You are Lord Krishna's child," she said to Kama "you are all-powerful in the realm of intimate relations. Now is the time when you can help me. Enter Chand's mind and render him incapable of sober reflection. Just as the lotus is supposed to blossom when moonlight falls on it, let his heart become restless when he notices my physical charms."

Kama, who is more powerful than the mightiest hero, chuckled with delight at Padma's words. He enjoyed every opportunity to employ his powers, and it was particularly gratifying to be able to help out a fellow deity. He let loose his five arrows, which are invisible and yet—or rather, hence—irresistible. These are named after the effects they produce in the victim: enchantment, mania, emaciation, heat (that is, libidinal arousal), and stupefaction.

Kama's arrows bore immediate result as they homed in on Chand. As the ravishing Padma sang and danced, he was seized with uncontrollable lust. The words of Padma's songs ceased to convey any meaning to Chand; they were simply enchanting sounds. He stared mesmerized at her, he was beyond shame or embarrassment; and Neta smiled to herself for she knew her plan would work.

Dhona sidled up to Padma and, with a wink and as sweet a smile as he could manage, said, "My master is burning with desire for you."

"Nothing doing," replied Padma with a laugh. "I am a singer and a dancer, I perform in many cities and towns, but I am chaste."

Chand was like one in the throes of a fever, dry-mouthed, tongue-tied. Padma addressed him directly.

"My lord," she said, "I am not one to indulge in sinful sensuality, yet I do wish for a gift of great value."

Chand found his voice now. "I promise to give you the gift you desire," he said over and over, and then added in a hoarse, tormented whisper, "if you agree to reciprocate."

Padma parried this with a sweet-toned reproach. "Aren't you embarrassed at your own words? You ought to be," she said. "I come from a distant land, and singing and dancing is the profession of my caste. But I haven't deviated from the laws of dharma, my heart has no room for anyone but my husband. I perform before audiences only to win praise for my art. My father was a celebrated artiste, praised and rewarded by many kings. He toured many lands and was acclaimed wherever he performed. He had won many titles of honor when he suddenly died, bitten by a black cobra. My grief-stricken mother died soon after. I was beside myself with grief. Even at the best of times I am restless, unable to think calmly. Now I took a rash vow, not knowing what an ordeal it would entail. I will leave home and country this very day, I said to myself, and though I am an ordinary woman I will seek the great occult mantra that will give me the power to revive the dead and hence defy the most venomous of snakes. My grief gave me courage and a few friends too who decided to accompany me. We traveled far and wide, through many kingdoms, but nowhere did we come across anyone who possessed the great mantra. Then somewhere I heard people say that you possessed it. I came here straightaway and started singing in the streets to attract your attention. It is against my nature to yield to adulterous desire, but I can make an exception if you first pass on the mantra."

"Save me from drowning in the ocean of desire," Chand appealed to Padma, "and I will reveal the mantra to you. The mantra in exchange for the honey of your body—it's a deal."

"Done," said Padma, "just tell me the mantra and I will be yours till your desire is sated."

It is well known that when the gods turn against us they deprive us of our wits. Such was Chand's state now. He put his arm around Padma, who didn't resist, and whispered the mantra into her ear, unaware that he was thereby surrendering his superhuman status—for the great mantra had given him power over death—and becoming an ordinary mortal again.

"You are like the *kalpataru,* the celestial wish-fulfilling tree," Padma said by way of thanks and added coyly, "You will no doubt give other gifts to this performer so that she stays as your mistress."

Such words were manna to Chand's ears.

"Just excuse me for a while," Padma said, "I must go for a number one." She picked up a *lota* of water to wash herself after urinating and left the room. Delighted at the successful conclusion to her mission, Padma paused outside and said aloud for Chand to hear, "You are utterly stupid, Chand, you have lost everything because you gave in to lustful desire. I have used deceit to take away your mantra and now you will be at my mercy."

At these words Chand seemed to wake up with a start. The fire of sexual desire was instantly doused in the turbulent water of rage. In his anger he was like a locust fluttering frantically after flying into a flame. He picked up his *hintala* staff and ran out shouting, "Stop! Stop!" His flaming eyes looked in all directions and spotted—as he gasped in despair—Padma taking off in her flying chariot. He stretched out his hand in a pathetic attempt to stop her flight. She responded with a kick that knocked out six of his teeth and left him with a bleeding mouth.

"I have been shamed by the one-eyed upstart," wailed Chand. "If only I could catch her! She'd be like a doe caught bleeding in the relentless jaws of a tiger."

The next moment Chand's mind turned to his own plight. "How will I go home," he cried. "What will I tell Sonaka, what will she say when she sees my wounded mouth, how will I show my face to my people?

From the sky came Padma's jeering laughter.

"You one-eyed bitch," shouted back Chand, "I taught you the greatest of mantras, and you paid your guru with a kick! You are crowing with delight because you have robbed me of my special power, but remember, Chand will not surrender even if he loses all his powers."

Padma said from up above, "You savage!"

Chand composed himself; even without his superior power he remained steadfast in his refusal to bow to the new goddess.

THE SLAYING
OF SHANKHA-DHANVANTARI

PADMA KEPT UP THE PRESSURE on Chand, appearing to him in dreams in her fearsome serpent form, entwined with numerous swaying, hissing snakes that seemed at the point of striking.

"Why have you defied me, foolish prince? In a day or two I will raze Champaknagar," Padma threatened.

Chand woke up in a sweat. As soon as daylight broke, he sent word to friends, counselors, and allies to come for an emergency meeting.

"That wretched serpent-draped serpent woman has tricked me out of my occult power and now threatens to destroy me," he told them frankly. "Tell me how I can preserve my domain."

The gathered advisers were unanimous in recommending that Chand employ the *ojha* Shankha-Dhanvantari. One of them apprised him of the dramatic rise of this powerful medicine man.

"There lived on the snow-clad Mount Dhavala a powerful *ojha* called Mahashankha, or Shankha, in short. His fame spread by word of mouth and reached the ears of the rising young *ojha* Dhanvantari, who at once resolved to challenge his senior to a test of their powers.

Dhanvantari set off with his disciples and halted on the banks of the icy cold Hima River that flowed down Mount Dhavala. He sent one of the disciples to Shankha as a confidential messenger.

The messenger told Shankha about the challenger who was waiting to engage him in a contest and added, "Your rival is openly declaring that nothing can stop him from defeating you."

Shankha fumed with rage and, bidding farewell to the messenger, summoned his disciples to accompany him to meet his arrogant rival. They found Dhanvantari and his disciples gathered in the cool shade of a large *bakul* tree that spread shade and the sweet fragrance of its blossoms by the swiftly flowing Hima.

Shankha greeted Dhanvantari with these words, "May I know your name, your family background, and where you are from?"

"Dhanvantari is my name and I was born of the ocean," came the reply. "I have proved my superiority over *ojhas* in Ganda and other ancient kingdoms. Having heard of your prowess from many people, I have come to test your skills. You may be covered in glory and puffed up with pride and arrogance, but if you survive this day you will be able to boast that you have cheated the god of death."

Shankha became livid with rage as Dhanvantari finished and replied with withering contempt. "Pure hubris has put such irresponsible words into your mouth. I am Mahashankha, my powers hold sway over all three realms, and I will presently send you to Yama's realm with a deadly mantra."

Dhanvantari cheekily dismissed the threat. "Are you trying to scare me with empty boasts? Let's see how potent your mantras are—hurl them at me and see what happens."

But after the vicious outburst Shankha's temper had cooled and he made a more humane reply. "Taking a human life is the greatest sin in this world," he said, "and that is why I have desisted from using any fatal mantra so far. Now listen to what I propose in a calm frame of mind. This river is continuously fed by the melting snows of Mount Dhavala. Let us see if you can completely dry up the waters of the Hima. If you do, I will fill it up again. In this contest the winner will be the one whose powers prevail. The price of defeat will be grave. Promise me, Dhanvantari, if you lose you will go to the underworld with all your disciples. If I lose, I will give my only daughter, Kamala, to you in marriage and withdraw to the underworld along with my wife and sons."

Both contestants swore to abide by the rules, and the gathered disciples stood witness to the agreement. The *ojhas* sat facing each other; each was of formidable figure and fearsome visage, like an avatar of the fire god Agni.

"Now dry up the river," said Shankha.

Dhanvantari muttered a secret mantra: at once, the river went dry, its bed became parched, and all the fish and other creatures in it lay dead. A gasp of awe went up from the gathered disciples.

Shankha countered with a rejuvenating mantra, but Dhanvantari prevented it from taking effect by using the great occult mantra, the Mahagyana. Not a single one of the dead creatures, not even a single aquatic insect, came back to life.

Shankha was startled at his failure, but lost no time in uttering a mantra to bring back the flowing waters of the Hima River. Dhanvantari aborted his move by using a fiery mantra that canceled out the attempt to recreate water.

"Mahashankha's failure is self-evident," Dhanvantari declared. "Now it's up to him to admit defeat, give me his daughter's hand in marriage, and leave for the underworld."

But Shankha set another condition. "Fill up the Hima River, with all its thriving creatures, and I will do what I promised."

Dhanvantari used the Mahagyana again to restore the river to its sparkling glory. He married the lovely Kamala and began to dwell on Mount Dhavala, having prefixed the name of his vanquished and exiled rival—and now father-in-law—to his own.

Chand's counselors urged him to send for this great *ojha*, now known as Shankha-Dhanvantari—or, in short, as either Shankha or Dhanvantari.

Chand wasted no time in sending his men with an invitation to the great *ojha* to stay at Champaknagar and protect it from the depredations of the snake goddess. Chand's emissaries found the *ojha* discoursing with his disciples in the pleasant shade of a tree on the bank of the Hima River.

"Our master, Chand, the merchant king of Champaknagar, has an urgent job for you," an emissary told Shankha-Dhanvantari. Another explained the circumstances that had necessitated this move. The *ojha* needed no persuasion. Here was a challenge worthy of the most exalted *ojha*; it came not from a snake but from the goddess of snakes. If he came out successful he would be no less than a god. If not . . . well, it was make or break. Dhanvantari quickly bade his wife farewell and set off with his band of disciples.

When they reached Champaknagar, Chand was sitting on his throne, holding court. He and his courtiers rose to greet Dhanvantari, and Chand gave a flattering address of welcome.

"It is our immense good fortune that an incomparable *ojha* such as yourself should agree to help us in our hour of need. Manasa has deprived me of the great occult power and laid waste my beautiful garden. When I collapsed in bed to mourn my loss I was visited by hideous nightmares. A snake maiden surrounded by fearsome serpents sat at the head of my bed. I woke up in a sweat, only to faint. You must not waste any time in dealing with the threat. Start by reviving my garden; the sight will bring me some solace."

"No problem at all," boomed Dhanvantari, overweeningly confident. Chand escorted him to the devastated garden. It revived in front of his eyes, regaining its former loveliness, as Dhanvantari silently chanted the great occult mantra. Chand was overjoyed and heaped presents on the *ojha*.

Dhanvantari, attended by a hundred disciples, set up domicile in Champaknagar and made a great show of his power over snakes by putting on a continuous snake-dance display accompanied by ear-splitting drums. The *ojha* and his chelas even draped themselves with giant serpents they had subdued into tame pets.

The noise of this entertainment reached Padma on Mount Sijuya. She felt it as an insult and a provocation and lamented her plight to Neta. That Chand would not be cowed after the loss of his occult power was bad enough, and now with Dhanvantari undoing all she had achieved and flouting her openly, she was in a desperate situation. Quivering with rage, she flew in her aerial chariot to Champaknagar and saw the *ojha* and his retinue of chelas strutting around. They quaffed snake venom with great ostentation, to the wonderment of the populace and even more spectacularly brought back to life snakebitten corpses that had lain dead for as long as six months. Powerful serpents that they had subdued danced like nautch girls to their pipes and drums and obediently served as their mounts. The citizens watched with awe and amusement. The message they were getting was clear—and devastatingly discomfiting for Padma: the nagas were no match for the *ojha* Shankha-Dhanvantari, and by implication neither was their goddess.

Padma returned to Sijuya and held earnest conference with Neta.

"This fellow has overstepped all bounds and must die," Padma said. "Tell me how I can get at him."

"Use your powers of illusion," advised Neta. "Disguise yourself as a comely flower seller, arrange the various sweet-scented blossoms in your basket. Where the flowers store their nectar, infuse the most potent venoms at your disposal. Then go to Dhanvantari's home and let the poisons finish him off."

Padma assumed the form of an attractive flower girl, with ample braided curly hair, bright *sindur* in the hair parting, lips slightly parted to reveal dazzling pearly teeth, large earrings, swaying hips, and shapely thighs whose contours were evident, thanks to the clinging style of wearing the sari. A faint, seductive tinkle rose from her anklets, while her sidelong glances could be fatal to romantic hearts. She swung the basket up onto her head and transported herself from Mount Sijuya to Champaknagar. She made her way toward Shankha-Dhanvantari's home, pausing for a while in the shade of a tree with the basket before her. Passersby were charmed by her beauty and stopped to ask the price of her flowers. Since she did not want to harm all and sundry, she cited utterly exorbitant figures. The people grumbled and went away, and Padma resumed her journey with the basket on her head.

Eventually she came to a beautiful lake surrounded by large shady trees. Here she sat down with the flowers prettily displayed in the basket and reinforced the venom infused into them as she waited for her quarry.

In time a hundred of Shankha's disciples came gallivanting down the road and stopped on seeing the comely flower girl. They were in high spirits, many of them had deadly snakes draped around their shoulders and loins and made them dance and hiss for their amusement. They flirted with the flower girl and tried to impress her by displaying their mastery over the snakes. Padma forced a smile, though inwardly consumed with rage. The way the snakes were being humiliated amounted to flouting her authority over them. Like the others Padma had met, these disciples of Shankha asked the price of the flowers. Padma cited an absurdly high price. The *ojhas'* chelas decided to teach her a lesson; they simply picked up the basket and made off with it, sharing out the loot and ostentatiously wearing the garlands round their necks. The hidden venom began to take effect and the youths stumbled down to the lakeshore, hoping the cool water would relieve their agony. There they fell dead and lay scattered.

Padma waited, knowing that their master would come that way sooner or later. Dhanvantari eventually appeared and found a beautiful flower girl sobbing disconsolately. An overturned basket lay before her; around it a few dismembered blossoms mingled with the dust.

Before Dhanvantari could inquire of the flower girl why she was crying, she bewailed her fate loudly to him.

"A hundred young men robbed me of my flowers, refusing to pay the modest price I asked for them."

Dhanvantari knew she was referring to his chelas, who were on an outing for pleasure. He paid Padma the sum she mentioned and comforted her with kind words. She thanked him and quietly disappeared from the scene.

Dhanvantari went down to the lakeshore and was shocked to see his disciples lying dead at the water's edge. He knew at once that it was Padma's doing, and that the beautiful flower girl was none other than the one-eyed one. He recited a rejuvenating mantra and waved his magical victory scarf over the dead bodies. His chief chelas, Dhona and Mona, who had accompanied him, helped by holding the edges of the scarf. Presently the dead youths stirred, and they sat up yawning and rubbing their eyes. They looked befuddled but soon recovered their memory and reported what had happened.

Dhanvantari went to Chand and reported on Padma's latest incursion.

"After her!" exploded Chand. "Scour the city for this flower girl. If only I can lay my hands on her!"

Of course it was all to no avail. Padma was back on Mount Sijuya, disconsolately telling Neta how their latest plot was foiled by Dhanvantari.

"And the worst of it is the abuse hurled at me—at me, a powerful goddess!—by the *ojha* and his wretched employer."

"Don't let mere words bother you," Neta counseled. "Calm down, stop moping, and do as I say."

Padma perked up; she knew her clever sister had thought of another trick.

"Assume the form of a milkmaid who peddles yogurt and buttermilk and pats of butter. Make friends with Shankha-Dhanvantari's wife, who is your namesake—she is called by one of your names, Kamala. I will accompany you as your aunt, a chaperone and assistant: I will carry your pot of yogurt. Make yourself even more attractive than the last time."

Padma needed no further encouragement. She seemed to have a natural affinity for the role of femme fatale. In no time she became a young, attractive woman with all the physical endowments and accoutrements loved by writers of erotic literature—large, well-rounded breasts and buttocks, thighs like banana trees, eyebrows arched like bows—and shooting fatal glances, long curly tresses, a smile with tantalizing naughty hints, eye-catching golden earrings and necklace, bracelets that drew attention to beautiful hands with slender fingers, toe rings attached by chains to anklets with tiny tinkling bells.

Kamala—for this is the name that would play a key part in this manifestation of Manasa—walked with swaying hips, followed by a sturdy but visibly aging woman—her aunt, as she told whoever asked—who carried on her head a pot containing rich yogurt.

They wended their way through the posh part of Champaknagar, where the *ojha* Shankha now had his home.

"Yogurt! Rich yogurt! Anyone for yogurt?" Kamala, the milkmaid, called out in the tones of a koel with a somewhat husky timbre. At the same time, she had cast a veil of illusion around herself so that she would appear in an irresistibly attractive light to anyone who came across or even heard her.

Kamala, the wife of Shankha-Dhanvantari, was in her house, going about her everyday chores, when the advertisement for yogurt reached her ears. She dropped everything and stood at her front door calling to the yogurt seller to stop. Kamala, the milkmaid, with her "aunt" in tow, came and stood before Shankha's wife—who was so struck by the yogurt seller's charms that she was dumbstruck and just stared.

"What's the matter?" asked the dairymaid in a soft, coaxing voice. "Tell me if you want to buy yogurt or not."

"Yes, or course," said the lady of the house, struggling to regain her composure, "first tell me what's the price of your yogurt."

The dairymaid mentioned an absurdly inflated figure.

It seemed to bring the lady of the house to her senses—it certainly brought out the sharp-tongued worldly woman in her. Smiling meaningfully, she said, "Never heard of yogurt at this price, I don't want any. You may carry on peddling it—I must say, selling it doesn't seem to be your purpose. Peddling yogurt is probably just a cover for dealing in sex. I think I have seen through you, young woman with ravishing looks. But I must warn you, if you keep mentioning such an impossible price, someone will teach you a lesson by taking away your yogurt by force."

The dairymaid replied in a hurt voice, "You have said nasty things about me, perhaps because you tend to judge everyone in the light of your own standards. But as far as the safety of my produce is concerned, my mind is at rest, for as long as the *ojha* Dhanvantari is in this city none would dare to rob me."

The dairymaid said these last words in tones of such innocent seriousness, that the lady of the house was utterly disarmed and burst into delighted laughter.

"Everyone is full of praise for my husband," she said. "Isn't that a good reason for you not to be proud and haughty in your dealings with me?"

"Forgive me if I have offended you," replied the dairymaid. "How could I have known you are the wife of the great *ojha?* You may have as much of the yogurt as you wish, whether or not you are willing to pay me."

"Very well, now tell me your name and whose daughter you are."

"My father's name is Maheswara Ghosh," the dairymaid said with a chuckle, "my mother is called Gauri, and I am Kamala. Accompanying me is my aunt, an elderly dairymaid."

Shankha's wife exclaimed in joy, "Why, my name is also Kamala, we are namesakes, we must formally pledge our friendship to each other." The two Kamalas hugged each other. Shankha's wife ordered her maidservants to fetch sweets and scented flowers with which she would bind herself in eternal friendship to her namesake. Unbeknownst to herself, she was preparing the ground for the certain death of her husband.

Padma—let us go back to a more commonly used name for the snake goddess, to distinguish her from her namesake—asked her friend's permission to visit Shankha-Dhanvantari's private temple.

There the *ojha* saw her when he came home after Chand's royal court adjourned for the day. She sat rapt in meditation, yet when Shankha entered the periphery of her vision she shot at him a dazzling sidelong glance that pierced his heart, arousing uncontrollable desire.

"Who is this in the temple, Kamala?" Shankha inquired of his wife.

"That's right, Kamala," his wife replied with a laugh.

"Then I can ask her to come into our bedroom."

"Of course, she is a dear friend of mine."

As such bantering continued the *ojha* got to learn the circumstances that had brought the seductive stranger into their house.

Shankha's wife asked her friend and her friend's aunt to come and meet her husband.

Padma bashfully drew the edge of her sari over her face, while Neta played her aunt's role by sitting stolidly beside her like a dependable chaperone.

"We are dairymaids from a village called Kanchigram," Padma said by way of an introduction.

Shankha felt the imperious rise of sexual excitement.

His wife Kamala busied herself making arrangements for dinner. "You must stay with us tonight," she said to her guests.

Padma complained, "My husband is very strict and if I don't return home he will throw a fit."

"Have no fear," Shankha reassured her, "I will put a spell on him so that he will dote on you, no matter what you do."

Padma quietly used her own magic powers to raise a storm that raged all evening.

As if this was just the excuse she needed, she said with a smile, "Now I will have to stay with you, it seems."

"Make yourself at home," Kamala told her, adding with a wink and a laugh, "and if you feel the desire for pleasure, feel free to spend the night dallying with my husband."

Padma coyly fluttered her eyelids and bit her lip, as if to suppress a smile.

Daylight drained away swiftly and evening settled in. The appetizing smell of cooking filled the house. Soon the meal was ready, and they all ate their fill. Shankha withdrew to his bedchamber, where he lay down in a state of mounting excitement as his mind filled with fantasies involving his wife's new friend.

Kamala and her friend chatted over *paan* and betel nut after the dinner things were cleared away.

"You must feel very proud of your husband," Padma said, "for he is universally regarded as the greatest *ojha* of all time."

Kamala beamed with pleasure.

"You are indeed lucky to have a husband like him," continued Padma, "for he must have taught you many valuable things, like powerful mantras and Tantric secrets. Teach me a little of what you know, and I will always be your faithful slave."

"But I know nothing!" exclaimed Kamala.

Padma put on a pained look.

"Why deceive me?" she asked bluntly.

Kamala swore she was telling the truth.

"Then you are the most foolish woman in all creation. Let me explain why you ought to have acquired some of the crucial occult know-how. Your husband is always dealing with deadly snakes and you cannot deny that his is a hazardous profession. He has many disciples whom he is instructing in his art, but should disaster strike there will be no sign of anyone. They will run for their lives—it's human nature. But you will not—for you will be true to your wifely dharma. Therefore it is imperative that you know which snake or snakes might deal him a fatal bite, where the bite will be fatal, and what are the effective antidotes. You should learn these things and remember them."

Kamala resolved to follow her friend's advice and to ensure success put on alluring clothes and jewelry and, entering the bedchamber, sat down on the bed beside her husband.

Padma hovered invisibly and magically induced intense sexual excitement in Shankha.

Trembling with excitement he drew Kamala toward himself and whispered, "Come let us enjoy the utmost delights of prolonged lovemaking."

Kamala, thoroughly brainwashed by Padma, bade him pause. "There is a serious request I must first make," she said. "You are the greatest *ojha* in the world and your knowledge of occult lore is vast. But it is important that you teach me certain things, for in any great danger, when a man is abandoned by others, he can still depend on his wife. I should know which snakes can kill you and where they must strike to cause death and what are the effective antidotes."

Shankha was annoyed at this strange request.

"All the shastras say that a man should not share secrets with his wife," Shankha said. "Why do you want to know these things?"

Kamala was piqued. "You and I are one, I see no boundary between the two of us. If your love is based on differentiating between us then what pleasure can I expect from lovemaking?"

Shankha took a moment to ponder the point, during which Padma further turned up his libidinal excitement. Divested of his wits as a result, Shankha blurted out the secret information.

"I value you more than life, so I will tell you what you want to know. Listen carefully, for I will speak very softly. If Padma steals my magical victory scarf and my spiritual adept's satchel, and then if I am bitten in the chest, close to the heart, by an Udaykala naga, I will face sure death. There are two antidotes. One is the sal bisali plant that grows in Gandhamadana, the other is sea foam. Either will save me from death if applied directly to the wound. Without these antidotes, not even the great gods Brahma or Vishnu will be able to save me. Not a word of this to anyone, for if Padma gets to know I am done for."

Padma smiled and stole away to confer with Neta. They summoned a Udaykala naga and explained what it must do.

The naga slipped into Shankha's bedchamber and found him deep in postcoital slumber. His robust body was bare and in repose, his handsome face relaxed, with a beatific calmness. The naga hesitated to strike, struck by the good looks of the man and the thought that if he fulfilled his mission the lovely Kamala would become a widow.

Padma violently intruded into the naga's thoughts and conveyed an urgent telepathic message.

"Don't you know what vile abuse this fellow Shankha hurls at me? Stop this sentimental nonsense; it's not for you to feel sorry for him. Just bite him in the chest—it will be just punishment for his pride and his haughty defiance of me."

The naga could not think any more thoughts. It struck like lightning, shooting the venom into the sleeping body. Padma snatched it up together with the victory scarf and the mystic adept's satchel and vanished with Neta.

Shankha sat up with a twitch, as if electrocuted, and called his wife.

"The gods have conspired to deprive me of life," he said to a startled Kamala. "The Udaykala naga has bitten me and death is near. It was Padma who came disguised as a dairymaid and used her powers of illusion to get at me. I lost my senses and uttered dread secrets that she overheard, and you were completely taken in by her charms and became a pawn that she could manipulate at will. Now call my best disciples, the brothers Mona and Dhona, so that I can send them for the antidote."

The two brothers hurried to their master's bedside, as did a hundred other wailing disciples. Shankha explained to Dhona and Mona what to do.

"Go with the speed of the wind to Gandhamadana and fetch the white medicinal sap of the sal bisali tree. Its flowers and fruit are red, its roots yellowish. To make sure you have identified it correctly kill a cat and take it along. As soon as you touch it to the right tree it will spring back to life. Beware of Padma's wiles. Now hurry, for if you can't get back before daybreak it will be too late."

The brothers touched their master's feet in salutation and left. The first cat that crossed their path was pounced upon and had its throat promptly slit. When they reached their destination and after a frantic search found a tree that matched the description, they held the cat to its trunk. At once it came alive and with a yowl bounded away. They obtained a quantity of the medicine and started on their way back. When they entered the deserted thoroughfares of Champaknagar it was the twilight hour before daybreak. They were hurrying along when on taking a turn in the road they saw a Brahmin widow, gaunt with age, wailing loudly.

"What's the matter, why cry like that at this hour?" they asked.

"The great *ojha* Shankha is no more!"

"No!" the two brothers exclaimed.

"Alas, yes, he was such a good man—used to give me something everyday, my sole means of support in old age."

"No!" the brothers exclaimed again, and, tearing their hair in grief and in the process tossing the precious antidote to the ground, they ran like madmen to their guru's house.

Shankha was waiting expectantly, seated on a Garuda-shaped chair. When the two brothers burst in, their eyes popping at the sight of their guru, he said, "Quick, give it to me."

"Oh no, what have we done?" the brothers wailed.

Shankha gasped, turning pale with apprehension. The brothers stammered out their tale.

"The one-eyed one has tricked you," Shankha said disconsolately. His words were faint, his face ashen with despair.

"Wait, we will get the sea foam, there's still time," the brothers shouted and bounded out of the room. They reached the seashore in good time; the darkness was still lingering, though clearly it was thinning fast. They scooped up the sea foam into an earthen pot and set off. This time, as they entered Champaknagar, there were one or two early risers whom they passed on the streets. They were within sight of their guru's house when they saw someone running frantically toward them. Presently they recognized Kamala, their guru's wife. Hair awry, clothes disheveled, she came running and asked, "They are getting the funeral pyre ready. Have you got it? Let's see."

In a moment she had taken the pot into her hands. But the next moment she was up in the air, laughing, getting into a flying chariot. She had taken on the fearsome serpent-clad form of Padma, and with a blow shattered the earthen pot with its magical contents, making the froth come down in a fine shower of useless droplets.

The brothers Dhona and Mona ran howling into the *ojha*'s house. Kamala was gently fanning her husband's pain-wracked skull.

Shankha looked up and just whispered, "Again?"

Dhona and Mona beat their breasts in an outburst of penitential feelings and amid uncontrollable sobs described how they had been deceived a second time.

Shankha-Dhanvantari raised a feeble hand to quiet them. They fell sobbing at his feet.

"The end has come," he gasped, "and all through my fault. Sheer pride led me into open conflict with the goddess Padma. My successors will be Dhona and Mona, and I have something to say to them. My death is the outcome of my karma, so I cannot complain against anybody. But I had contracted with Chand, the merchant prince, to protect his domain against Manasa. Since my death is imminent, I wish to make this request to you, my dearest disciples. Do not cremate my body. Instead, cut it into eight pieces and plant them at eight different points around the city so that they may act as a deterrent against intruding nagas. This way I may yet be able to fulfill the task I undertook in this life."

The great *ojha* fell silent. His heroic dedication to duty, even in death, would remain as an object lesson to all his disciples, who stood with heads bowed in reverence while tears streamed down their faces. Shankha's frame trembled, his hands twitched, then he became still. Loud keening filled the air. Kamala wept uncontrollably, her grief heightened by self-recrimination because of the way she was taken in by Padma's wiles.

Chand paid a handsome tribute to the departed who in the course of his work to protect the merchant had also become a close friend. But after a while Chand pulled himself together and advised everyone to do so as well.

"We must face facts," he said. "Death is final, the dead do not come back in their old form, we will never see our beloved Dhanvantari again. Let us therefore prepare him for the funeral and take him to the cremation ground."

Here he was interrupted by Dhona and Mona who mentioned their guru's dying wish that his body be dismembered and planted in the ground to deter nagas. But Chand promptly overruled his dead friend's request.

"His wish is an awesome testament to his integrity and devotion to duty, but I cannot allow it to be executed. Since I employed his services in my struggle against nagas and their upstart deity, I can claim the last word on this. I want my friend to have a decent cremation. He has done all he could for me and gave his life in trying to help me. I will not allow his mortal remains to be disposed of in any but the time-honored way."

There could be no more argument after these words. Shankha's disciples carried their master's body, accompanied by his widow, Kamala, and Chand and his courtiers.

Meanwhile Padma and Neta watched the proceedings from their chariot high in the sky. Padma was immensely pleased with the turn of events, but Neta pointed out that the Shankha-Dhanvantari episode could not be closed yet.

"His body rightfully belongs to you, Padma," Neta said. "You can revive him and keep him to do as you please. All people killed by snakes become your property. It's not proper to cremate them—then you cannot claim them, you see."

"What should I do?"

"Go there at once, assuming the form of a venerable sage. Ask who is being cremated, how he died, pretend you knew him, and tell them what they must do—since he died of snakebite his body must be cast adrift on a raft made of banana trees."

Shankha-Dhanvantari's body was ritually washed, the funeral pyre was prepared with sandalwood doused in ghee, and the priest was ready with a firebrand. Just then a sannyasi entered the cremation ground.

Everyone was struck by his imposing appearance; people muttered that he must be a maharishi.

"Who has died, may I ask?" the sannyasi inquired.

"The great *ojha* Shankha-Dhanvantari."

"That is sad news. I knew him well but hadn't seen him in a long while as I was away many years visiting holy sites. How did he die? He was not old or infirm."

"A naga bit him."

"Then why the preparations to cremate him? He must be placed on a raft and cast adrift. It is possible a wise man well versed in occult matters will come upon his body and bring him back to life. I have known of a case like this where six months after a person's death of snakebite he was revived by a wise man down south."

Chand objected that this would be no more than a gamble. And what if no powerful occultist was forthcoming? In that case Shankha-Dhanvantari would decompose and be reduced to a skeleton and be denied a proper funeral.

Kamala supported the sannyasi's proposal, arguing eloquently that as long as there was even the slightest chance of her husband regaining life, she as his devoted wife would have to give her assent. She said many sentimental things that swayed public opinion.

In the end, therefore, Shankha was sent downriver on a raft, all decked up like a prince; and he was promptly claimed by Padma, revived in the form of a ram, and then thrust into the underworld. There was raucous celebration among the nagas in the underworld, and on Mount Sijuya Padma danced like a demented and drunken slut.

THE KILLING OF DHONA AND MONA

PADMA AND NETA CAME DOWN to Champaknagar to find out what Chand would do after Dhanvantari's death. One thing was clear: he was not ready to bow to Padma. There was only one way to find out how long he would hold out: keep up the pressure.

"There is a sandalwood tree in Chand's palace courtyard," Neta told Padma. "It is very special because Chand offers puja to our father, the great god Shiva, in its shade. Reduce it to ashes with your venomous glance. If Chand can find someone to restore it to life, kill whoever restores it; that will curb Chand's pride."

Padma wasted no time in carrying out the suggestion. Destroying the tree had the desired effect: Chand was mortified at the sight and felt intimidated. He called his friends and allies and asked for their advice on how it might be possible to revive the tree.

"Make an announcement inscribed on a gold tablet, carried throughout the kingdom and proclaimed aloud, offering large rewards to whoever can bring the tree back to life," they advised in one voice.

Dhona and Mona saw the chance of a lifetime in this announcement; they would receive royal favor, their reputation as *ojhas* would be made, if they brought the tree back to life. They declared openly that they were not afraid of the one-eyed goddess and would revive the tree, and they boasted of all the powers they had learned from their guru.

"We can levitate, annihilate, paralyze or cure paralysis, immobilize, bewitch, summon serpents at will or disperse them, revive the dead with a powerful mantra, and you will see how in an instant we can revive the sandalwood tree," they boasted.

Dhona whispered a word of caution to his brother: "Don't you think we should experimentally test our powers before applying them to the king's tree? Failure will mean humiliation and the end of our aspirations."

"Very well," Mona said in an undertone. "We'll do that presently."

The two brothers excused themselves for a little while and found a tree in a lonely spot. Taking up a meditative posture they concentrated their consciousness on a potent mantra and beamed all its force on the tree. At once all its blossoms and leaves withered and fell, and the entire tree down to its roots shriveled and díed. Then they redirected their consciousness to the mantra of resuscitation and focused its power on the tree's miserable remnants; at once the tree regained its lush, thriving shape.

"There you are," said Mona, "we have nothing to fear. Now let's deal with the sandalwood tree."

The *ojha* brothers were sure they would revive the king's tree with great éclat. In anticipation, they glanced triumphantly about; and summoning various snakes and serpents draped them round their necks, wore them as bracelets, made them rear and run, and rode them like tame mounts. They quaffed snake venom and revived six-month old corpses of snakebite victims. In short they proved themselves worthy heirs of their dead guru, whose hundred disciples now acknowledged them master and with much noise and clamor and raucous music followed them in a joyous procession around the city.

Dhona and Mona matched their dead guru in arrogance and braggadocio, which elicited much ironic comment: weren't they as eager to bring death upon themselves? Their mother was alarmed at the dramatic alteration in her sons' demeanor. "Why get into a dispute with a goddess?" she asked them and, when the question elicited mocking laughter, appealed to them to curb their pride. What tears she shed as she reasoned with them!

"Your guru, the greatest *ojha* in all three realms, was no match for Padma," she pointed out. "Why are you courting death even after witnessing his fate? You are all I have in this world, and if necessary I will be able to support you by doing what our father and your ancestors did—growing and selling flowers. Why are you making empty boasts when you know that even other gods and goddesses are powerless against Padma. What chance do mere mortals like you have against her?"

The sons paid no heed to their mother's words. Instead they tried to reassure her that there was no need to worry.

"Our divine guru met his end through his own carelessness," they declared, "but we will be alert and cautious all the time and Padma will not be able to get at us."

They added with a gleam in their eyes, "Just think of the royal honors that will be heaped on us. We will never want for anything, Mother."

With that they went to the royal court and asked for an audience. Chand recognized them no doubt, but for form's sake asked, "Tell me what your names are, who your parents are, what is your caste."

"Dhona and Mona are our names," came the reply. "Our parents are gardeners and flower sellers by profession, and we are disciples of the late, lamented *ojha* Shankha-Dhanvantari, who taught us all the sixty-four arts of which he was the greatest master. We hear you have suffered the destruction of your beloved sandalwood tree. Just give the command and we will revive it at once."

Chand took them personally to the blighted tree and watched with delight as they restored it to its luxuriant glory with a dramatic display of occult powers: first, they withdrew into meditative silence and concentrated on the great occult mantra, then opening eyes wide they let out an explosive roar, at which, as if at a command in a military drill, the tree stood up, alive and healthy once again.

Chand was delighted to have the services of these two worthy disciples of his deceased *ojha*. He loaded them with many precious presents and resumed making abusive remarks about Padma at every opportunity.

Neta and Padma were monitoring all these developments from their aerial chariot and decided on prompt action. Dhona and Mona must be killed without delay: that would deal a salutary shock to Chand's resurgent arrogance.

It would be a repeat of the way Shankha-Dhanvantari had been dis-posed of. Padma would again assume the form of a comely dairymaid; this time she would visit Kajala, the mother of Dhona and Mona. As on the previous occasion, she dolled up—smart coiffure, pearls and other jewels, a pretty sari, sandalwood paste on forehead, and crimson *sindur* in hair parting—and with pots filled with ghee, milk, and yogurt, she arrived once more at Champaknagar. Heads turned as she made her way through the streets calling her wares. Before long she reached Kajala's home and stopped outside where the flower woman had laid out her gar-lands and bouquets for sale. Padma sat down beside her and without asking permission picked up a bouquet and sniffed at it ostentatiously. Annoyed, Kajala said tartly, "Why are you sniffing my flowers, you wretched dairymaid?"

"Come, come," chided Padma in reply, "why get angry over a little thing—I'll pay for the bouquet, don't you worry." At the same time she cast a veil of enchantment over the irate flower woman, who mellowed instantly and inquired in a kindly tone, "Where are you from, who are your parents, and what's your name?"

Once again Padma could put one of her many nicknames to good use.

"My mother's is called Gauri, my father is Maheswara Ghosh, I am from the village of Sugandha, and my name is Kajala."

Kajala was delighted at this coincidence. "Why, you're my namesake!" she exclaimed. "Let's become friends—sealing our bond in the proper way."

Sweetmeats and other goodies were brought, musicians hired to liven up the occasion, and the two women sealed their friendship by exchanging bead garlands, for flower garlands were considered inappropriate for the purpose. The friends warmly hugged each other, and Kajala, the flower woman, led her new friend into the house and asked her to relax while she finished cooking the midday meal.

Padma asked, "How can you live alone in your pretty house?"

"Why, my friend, I have two sons who live with me, both handsome youths. They were the chief disciples of the great *ojha* Shankha-Dhanvantari, and they have learned everything he knew. Unfortunately he defied Manasa-devi and paid with his life. My sons work for the king now and will soon come home. Why don't you take a dip in the lake while I get the meal ready?"

On her way to the lake Padma knew telepathically that two young men were now on their way home and instructed a *bighatiya* she had hidden in her hand to bite them. The tiny but lethal snake went and lay hidden in the dust and first bit Dhona in the foot. Dhona cried out, "Snake! Snake!" and sat down in the road, holding his bleeding foot. Mona kicked at the dust to find out what snake had done the deed and was bitten in the toe. The brothers embraced each other, crying helplessly.

"We will both die today," said one brother to another. "Yes," replied the other, "it was stupid of us to defy Padma."

Soon they felt their bodies becoming numb. When they tried to speak no sounds emerged from their mouths, and a mist fell over their vision as they collapsed in the dust.

Padma went to Kajala and in a concerned voice reported what had happened.

"On my way to the lake I saw two good-looking young men lying in the dust and a few passersby mentioned your sons' names."

Kajala clutched her heart and sat down as if thunderstruck.

"O my sons!" she shrieked. "They are all I have in this world. I warned them not to anger the snake goddess, but they wouldn't listen."

Kajala picked herself up and ran like a demented creature toward the lake. Seeing her dead sons, she cradled them in her arms and howled disconsolately.

Padma came up in a little while and put a comforting hand on Kajala's shoulder.

"Crying will not help, my friend," she said, "but I may be able to. My father is a wise man with knowledge of occult matters and taught me some things. I have never tried out the lessons, so I cannot guarantee if I can revive your sons, but there's no harm in trying."

Kajala laid her sons down and fell at her friend's feet in supplication.

"Come, my friend, I'll try my powers presently," Padma reassured her, "but you must promise to give up your claim on your sons and let me take them with me."

The bereaved mother readily agreed, for anything was better than living with the knowledge that her sons were dead.

Padma at once sat in the yogic *padmasana* and employed her occult powers to resuscitate the two youths. The *bighatiya* that had taken their lives reappeared and sucked out the venom from their wounds. Padma gave a shout, at which the faces of the two youths twitched with life, and they sat up as if awoken from slumber.

"Now, my friend," said Padma, "the day is drawing to its close, and I have far to go. Bid me and your sons farewell, for I must take them home with me now."

Kajala, who had watched with elation how her sons were brought back to life, was stricken with heartbreak again. "Friend, leave me one of my sons," she begged, clutching Padma's feet.

"You must learn to let go," advised Padma, "for your sons have grown up and must leave home."

"But not being able to see them is too much to bear," Kajala lamented. "Leave me the younger son, and I will forever sing your praise."

Padma could sense that Chand was coming that way and decided to cut short this pathetic parley.

"You know what can be the karmic outcome of not living up to one's promise," Padma warned, and left with Dhona and Mona in tow. Kajala continued to lament, a heartbroken mother.

Chand came up and learned all the dramatic details of the tragedy. But instead of offering commiseration to the unfortunate mother he mocked her.

"The one-eyed one has become your daughter-in-law. Don't you know that on her wedding night the bridegroom ran away from the bridal bed? Now she has fallen for your handsome sons and wants to make them her husbands."

The flower woman reacted with a stern rebuke.

"My sons are gone because of your pride and arrogance. What an irresponsible and obdurate ruler you are to speak ill of a great deity. You are responsible for bringing grief and suffering to those you are supposed to protect and help."

Kajala went indoors to nurse her grief, leaving an unregenerate king fuming at her doorstep. Meanwhile Neta and Padma were back on Mount Sijuya, where Dhona and Mona became their personal attendants, ever at their beck and call. As for Chand, his power was proving to be ineffectual, but his arrogant defiance remained intact. Neta and Padma sat down to plan the next move.

ELIMINATING CHAND'S SIX SONS

"WE DESTROYED HIS PROPERTY, he got help to restore it, we eliminated those who restored it, and yet he keeps badmouthing you," said Neta to Padma, summing up their campaign against Chand so far. "Now we get at those he holds dearest. His wife worships you and is our ally. We will go for his six sons."

"Yes!" exclaimed Padma. "You have hit upon the right idea again. Let me summon all the deadly nagas and designate a volunteer to carry out the mission."

"Right, but the volunteer has to be instructed carefully, for any slip will awaken the household and that will not only abort the mission, but Chand's family will become more security conscious and that will make future missions even less likely to succeed."

Padma summoned the nagas, who came from all over the world and the underworld, a fearsome horde whose hissing sounded like a roaring cyclone. Padma felt proud of her host of serpents, they appeared in such an impressive array. She called for silence and addressed them to explain the purpose behind calling the assembly. She delivered a fiery speech, extolling the lethal power of serpents and decrying the stubborn refusal of an earthly king, Chand, to pay homage to her.

"You have shown him how powerless he is against us," Padma told the nagas. "You have put an end to the earthly existence of masterful *ojhas* who were hired by Chand to protect him from you. And yet he adamantly refuses to offer me puja. Now it is time to attack his family. His sons, all six of them, must die. They will die through the action of one of you. Who is it going to be? Who wants to snatch the honor of bringing Chand to his knees?"

Padma's voice had risen to a crescendo. She expected that a universal hiss of willing volunteers would respond. Instead there was total silence. The mighty serpents that had stood with flaring hoods, aggressively flicking their tongues, now lay timidly coiled in the dust. They shrank further as their goddess glared at them.

"What, no volunteers?" Padma screamed.

One of the nagas, distinguished among his peers for his intelligence and wisdom, answered.

"O goddess of the naga race, matriarch of the three realms, you in your omniscience will surely understand our discomfiture. Dealing with the *ojhas* was a walkover, compared to what you propose, for Chand is a favorite of your great father, and even you were put to flight when you provoked him into a *hintala*-wielding rage."

Padma fumed as she heard these words. "Don't try to find lame excuses for your cowardice," she said cuttingly. "And let me tell you, my father has assured me that Chand will eventually bow to me like everyone else, no matter how obdurate he may seem now."

At this point the assembly of nagas was joined by a *dhora,* an easy-going member of the race.

"Why is the air so tense?" he inquired, feeling that he was a misfit in such highly charged situations. Someone clued him in with a few hisses in an undertone. "Oh, is that all?" he commented and then, raising his voice, declared confidently, "O great goddess, set your mind at rest, I will take care of the matter. What are half a dozen spoiled brats? No big deal."

Padma beamed at her unlikely knight.

"But I will need a swift chariot," the *dhora* added, "so, mighty goddess, if you would instruct Dhamai to bring one round I will set off at once."

"That's the spirit," said Padma, and ordered Dhamai to convey her champion to Champaknagar at once. The others looked on, a little ashamed of themselves, and more than a little skeptical of the martial abilities of their fellow snake.

Padma gave the *dhora* a handsome parting gift and saw him off. He cut a colorful figure on Dhamai's chariot as it flew toward Champaknagar. It was the first of the month of Ashar, the earlier of the two monsoon months, and a ceaseless downpour from dark clouds was under way when they arrived. The fields were brimming with water, dykes and canals had flooded, and people came out in droves with various kinds of fishing nets and traps and spears. They raised a loud clamor for their excitement and enjoyment lay in getting wet in the cool shower as much as in the prospect of a good catch.

The loud human voices made the *dhora* nervous. He lost his wits, dismissed Dhamai—who was only too glad to return to Mount Sijuya—and leapt into the water. He felt better now that he was concealed underwater and, finding shoals of fish swimming about, got into the spirit of the fishing crowds and gobbled up as many as he could, which—such was his nature—was considerably more than he should have. Full-bellied, he drifted in the current and got sucked into a fishing trap. He had eaten so much that he felt a nap would be a good idea, and the space inside the trap was as cozy as he could wish. The day declined; he still slept. The owner of the trap, a peasant who had been working in the fields, came to check his catch and eagerly picked it up. The abrupt movement woke up the *dhora,* which reared up with a loud hiss. The peasant dropped the trap, screaming "Snake! Snake!" His friends came, brandishing heavy sticks.

"Let's smash the bamboo trap and the snake with it," one of them suggested.

This would be a sure way to kill the snake, but the owner of the trap demurred; he had bought it just the other day, it was new and shiny, and buying another one would be a drain on his purse.

"Let's open the hatch of the trap's rear exit and wait with upraised sticks," he suggested. "As soon as the snake comes out we'll fall upon him. We'll finish him off in no time."

The peasants waited, sticks at the ready, but the *dhora* wouldn't come out. The day was drawing to an end, the peasants were hungry. They looked up at the sky to make out if it was time to go home. While their eyes were gauging the light in the sky, the *dhora* seized the opportunity to slip out of the trap. He didn't look back once nor surface till he had cleared a hundred yards or so. Once at a safe distance he grew anxious thinking of what the goddess would do to him.

He made his way to Mount Sijuya in a state of gloom and trembled from head to tail tip as he appeared before Padma. The trembling worsened as he told his story.

"I couldn't even reach Champaknagar," he said. "It was impossible to see through Chand's designs. He laid cunning traps and before I knew what was happening I was a prisoner. It's through pure luck that I managed to escape alive."

Padma's anger flared at the *dhora*'s cowardly lies, her eyes flashed, she dealt him ten to twenty lusty kicks and took away all his venom; and ever since he has been despised or ridiculed as the most harmless of water snakes.

The assembled nagas laughed uproariously at the *dhora*'s humiliation, but they were silenced by a fierce glance from their goddess. But beneath her rage lurked profound sorrow; her serpent host realized that the cause for it lay in their own inability to rise to the challenge posed by Chand, and they felt ashamed.

Just then a somewhat matronly black cobra, who had been delayed by household chores, joined the assembly. She quickly found out the reason behind Padma's despondency and decided to act.

"O goddess of the three realms," she said, "set your mind at rest. I will fulfill your wish—the six youths will be eliminated. I have never failed to remove a human who made a nuisance of himself."

Padma cheered up instantly and hugged the quietly confident serpent, praising her devotion and her proven skill in injecting poison into a foe.

Neta briefed the black cobra on her mission.

"If the alarm is sounded, you may not come out of this alive. You must do the job at the dead of night, when everyone is fast asleep. You may try to bite the brothers one after another, I know that would give you the greatest satisfaction, but I would warn you of the risks: a single cry from one of your victims can spell disaster. My advice is this: squirt your venom into something the brothers will eat for breakfast. That way, you are sure they will all be poisoned, and when that happens you will be safely back home."

The black cobra listened attentively and then made a query.

"But do we know what they will have for breakfast? The six of them may eat six different things, and whatever they eat, even if it's one thing, will be cooked in the morning. Where will I pour the venom at night?"

Neta smiled.

"You will go to Chand's palace tomorrow night. In the kitchen you will find a pot of leftover rice steeped in water. The six princes will have it for breakfast. Just pour your venom into the pot and withdraw."

"Six princes breakfasting on water-soaked leftover rice! Never heard of such a thing—it's poor man's fare."

"Don't worry, you'll find the pot of rice and the princes will eat it—for a change. Now prepare yourself for the mission and be in Champaknagar tomorrow night."

The black cobra nodded and took her leave, but went away shaking her head, as if she were saying to herself, "Really! Is such a thing possible?"

Neta and Padma went into a huddle.

"Work a little magic so that things turn out the way we want," said Neta to Padma and whispered her suggestions.

The following morning the six princes went for their lessons to Pandit Somai's school. They were six strapping youths who had been born in quick succession and were exemplary in their physical prowess as well as their pursuit of scholarship. Their father's chest puffed up with pride when he saw them. He had got them married to six charming girls from the best families in the region and happily contemplated a future in which large kingdoms would be ruled by his descendants.

The school lessons went on for six hours and the students were hungry and eager to go home. They requested that the pandit call it a day. Usually a stern disciplinarian, he relented when he saw that Chand's six sons too had lent their voice to the appeal.

The students, who came from diverse social backgrounds, chattered about what they would love to have when they got home. One said he would have various drinks. Another said he would feast on ten different dishes. A third said he would eat a little later. A fourth said he was so hungry he would gobble some *chira* (flattened rice) and bananas. A fifth said he depended on charity and consequently had no choice in the matter. A sixth said he hailed from foreign parts and according to the custom of his land—or, perhaps, it was a necessity owing to his poverty—wouldn't eat a meal until dusk came.

There was a fatherless student named Govardhana, who lived with his mother, a widow called Abhoya. Ever cheerful, Govardhana laughed as he gave an account of his miserable life.

"I am so poor one can only curse my life. There's no food at home, Mother has to go begging. If the gods are kind she gets something. She lets me eat first and eats whatever is left. Many householders give her a handful of uncooked rice. She cooks a pot of rice in the afternoon, steeps it in water, and leaves it overnight. The next day it is soft and cool and wonderful at assuaging hunger.

"I didn't eat yesterday afternoon and shivered through the chilly night. In the morning Mother told me to have a bath and eat before coming to school. She had kept a whole pot of rice steeped in water and served it with some leftover radish that had been cooked in mustard oil and was drowned in this sour gravy. I began to salivate at the very sight of the meal. The stale watery rice gave off the scent of fermentation and tasted like manna from heaven."

The six brothers eagerly swallowed Govardhana's words; they found his account of a poor man's feast literally mouthwatering. When they reached home the sun was in decline. They went up to their mother and said, "Tomorrow there's no school, as it's the eighth day of the lunar fortnight, so we'll get up late and eat a special breakfast."

Sonaka was delighted to hear this; nothing satisfied her maternal instinct as much as preparing a feast and then watching her sons eat with a good appetite.

"Tell me what you fancy," she asked.

"Stale rice steeped overnight in water," the brothers replied.

Sonaka burst into laughter and called her daughters-in-law.

"Come and hear what your husbands want," she said, and told them about their strange wish.

"No problem," said the eldest son's wife, "all we need to do is cook some extra rice and pour water over it."

"Quite," said Queen Sonaka. "But tonight's dinner will be a regular meal and you will have to help me cook the usual variety of dishes. The boys can have the leftovers with the stale rice in the morning."

The daughters-in-law busied themselves in setting out the vegetables, fish, and meat to be cooked, which servants brought fresh from garden, pond, and market, together with the condiments and other necessary ingredients.

Sonaka had the customary bath before she went in to cook. She found everything laid out within easy reach, and her daughters-in-law standing in a semicircle, ready to carry out her instructions. It wasn't every day that the queen did the cooking, and she wanted her dishes to be surpassingly delicious. First she placed the firewood in the twin earthen stoves, then two brass pots on them, and lit up with the help of fast-burning kindling. She then circumambulated the twin fires, praying to the god Agni that he make her dishes as tasty as ambrosia.

The cooking began—rice on one stove, accompanying dishes of vegetables, fish, meat on the other. Once the rice was done both stoves were used to cook the latter—of which there was an enormous number. There were sixteen vegetable dishes—various leafy vegetables, plantain, eggplant, the cucurbitaceous *jhinga,* pumpkin, kidney bean, varieties of lentils, arum, all cooked in best-quality ghee, some also with coconut added. For the fish dishes there were carp, catfish, tiger fish, eels, prawns, small varieties of fish. A dish of tender goat's meat was the last course before several kinds of dessert, rice pudding, sweet cakes, some of them steeped in thickened milk. A whole cookbook could be written about Queen Sonaka's creations of that evening. She sighed with satisfaction when the last dish was cooked and waited for her husband and children to come in to eat.

Chand came and sat down in the center. Sonaka sat down beside him, the better to serve him, as custom dictated. Facing them, their sons sat in an arc, like six stars around the moon. Their wives attended on them. Everyone ate their fill and were full of praise for the queen. Then servants poured water from jugs into large brass bowls so that they could wash their hands and rinse their mouths.

Chand got up, slipped his feet into silver slippers and went to his bedchamber. The six princes followed, each to his room, and waited for their wives to join them.

Now it was the ladies' turn to have their meal. When they finished Queen Sonaka put away the leftover dishes, pouring water into the rice pot till all the rice was well soaked.

Meanwhile the black cobra had arrived at Champaknagar and was cautiously reconnoitering the palace precincts. It didn't take her long to locate the bedrooms of the princes. She concealed herself behind a massive wooden chest and waited till the lamps were turned down and silence descended on the palace.

Though instructed by Neta and Padma to poison a pot of rice, the black cobra resolved to attempt direct strikes against the princes. That was the best way to ensure success, she reasoned. She made for the eldest son Sarvananda's room. The prince and his wife were asleep in each other's arms, a sight that aroused compassion in the cobra's heart. She moved on: the second son, Purandar, was merrily playing dice with his wife. She couldn't bring herself to strike at such a moment of conjugal playfulness. The third son, Sundara, lived up to his name: he was surpassingly handsome, and he was jesting and bantering with his charming wife. The cobra felt affectionate toward the handsome couple and moved on. The fourth son, Vidyananda, was making love to his well-endowed wife; striking at such a moment was unthinkable. The fifth son, Narayan, was chatting with his wife as they chewed *paan*. Again, the cobra desisted. The youngest son, Janardana, was sharing sweet dreams with his pretty wife. The cobra sighed and gave up the idea of sinking her fangs into any of the sons.

She went to the kitchen, still skeptical about Neta's assurance that there would be a pot of watery rice there. But there it was, just as Neta had said. The cobra emptied her sacs of *kalkuta* venom into it, stirred the pot to spread the poison evenly, replaced the lid, and slunk away. She went straight to Padma and reported what she had done. The goddess smiled with satisfaction.

At daybreak the six princes woke up and after completing their toilet sat meditating on Shiva. Then they got ready for breakfast.

Meanwhile their wives went in a body to Sonaka and told her about a bad dream that they had had just before waking up. What made it extraordinary is that all six of them dreamt exactly the same dream; all were equally distraught. The eldest of them narrated the dream, and the others nodded in confirmation.

"We saw a fat, hairy, dark-complexioned man with hair, beard, and mustache like copper wires, a long spike in one hand and an iron bow in the other, but without any clothes. He bound and marched off the six brothers like prisoners toward the south. Seeing him roughly manhandling them, I cried in my sleep, and saw the *sindur* on my head flake off and fall on the ground. My golden bangles slipped off my wrists, and the pair of conch-shell bracelets broke into smithereens. A Brahmin widow with large, crooked nails and teeth appeared out of nowhere and, taking hold of me, turned me out of the house. That's when the dream broke and I woke up with a feeling of apprehension and utter desolation."

Sonaka listened to the account with growing apprehension but didn't let it show and tried to assuage their anxiety.

"Calm down," she said, "you have no reason for worry. Don't you know that whatever befalls you and your dear ones in dreams is transferred to others in real life? The evil you witnessed will be the fate of your enemies. I don't want to hear any more of this. Let's go in, cook rice and fish and have it for breakfast. Have a bath, all six of you, and offer puja to Shiva, greatest of all gods."

The six sisters-in-law went in obediently. Sonaka sat lost in anxious thought. Her reassuring words, which had set the minds of her daughters-in-law at ease, could not assuage her own anxiety. There's no knowing what fate has in store, she thought. Her sons had followed their father in opposing the nagas: could any good come out of it? She resolved to keep them at home as far as possible to minimize the chances of getting into trouble. But where were they now, she wondered; they hadn't eaten breakfast yet, though it was several hours since dawn, and the sun was shining fiercely.

The six brothers came presently and told their mother that they were eager to try their special stale-rice breakfast.

Sonaka served it to them on golden plates, together with leftover dishes of vegetables, fish, and meat. The summer heat had fermented the wet rice, making it a heady brew, and the six youths slurped it up with relish. Padma's divine powers seemed to have rendered the rice as delectable as ambrosia. The brothers ate till they had their fill.

What it meant was that they had their fill of food as well as poison. And the poison was *kalkuta*, so potent that people dubbed it *mahakalkuta*, the great *kalkuta*. None could withstand its fatal force, not even gods. Hadn't the great Shiva collapsed under its action? For the six youths, therefore, death was inevitable and imminent.

The fierce poison entered the bloodstream and spread throughout the bodies of its victims. Their lips and palates felt numb, their eyes rolled and began to lose focus. One of them said, "There was something the matter with the food." Another slurred, "I feel sleepy, I'm too tired to talk." A third added, "Me, too, my tongue feels heavy." "My body is burning all over," cried a fourth. "Padma must have poisoned the rice to kill us," said a fifth. "The raging *kalkuta* is killing us," said the sixth. Their mouths dribbled red blood, no more words came. Their bodies turned blue, they tottered and fell.

The strange sight caught Sonaka's eye. She came running, screaming desperately, "My sons! My sons!" She cradled them in her arms, one after another; they were all lifeless. She tore her hair and beat her breast and rolled crying in the dust for a long time.

She tore off her necklace and all other ornaments, hurled them on the ground, struck her forehead with her fist.

"I have lost six sons in one day, why should I live another day?" she wailed. "What will their wives do now? The lives of six pretty girls have been ruined." Once again she blamed her husband. "He has sinned by insulting Padma, and all this is the fruit of his sin. I don't want any more of this world, I'll drown or drink poison." When word of the catastrophe reached Chand, he came running, crying disconsolately, calling out the names of his sons. Without a son he would be helpless in the afterlife; who would sacrifice to his ancestral spirits?

Worse still, Chand had none to turn to for comfort and sympathy. Beside herself with grief, Sonaka turned on him in fierce accusation.

"You are stubbornness personified," she said to him, "or else why should you insult a deity? Through your own arrogance the conflict doubled and redoubled in intensity. Couldn't you swallow your pride? No, you've behaved like the madman annoyed by a mosquito who goes berserk and sets the mosquito net on fire."

Chand had nothing to say in reply; he could only skulk, staying away from the inner quarters of the palace. Sonaka and her daughters-in-law took to fasting and wept day and night. A pall of gloom settled over the palace and the city. Friends, relatives, servants, court officials, Pandit Somai, all were swollen-eyed.

Of course grief cannot last indefinitely with the same intensity. It gradually blends with various reflections, and in time the usual rhythm of life reasserts itself. Champaknagar was stunned by the sudden deaths, but soon the grief of the populace was mingled with awe, terror, and reverence, inspired by the author of the carnage, Padma, or Manasa, goddess of the nagas.

Gauging the intensity of this dangerous mood in his people, Chand reacted by hardening in his defiance. And so when Sonaka upbraided him yet again, accusing him of indirectly causing the deaths of their sons—"If you had offered puja to Padma, would she have killed the boys?"—he responded with a show of callousness.

"If the gods will the deaths of our sons, what I do or don't do can be of no avail. So let's get over our grief. If we remain in good health we can have a son every two years. I will go practice meditation and austerities and obtain a boon from the gods so that in twelve years we have another six sons."

His words only exacerbated Sonaka's grief, and she burst into fresh lamentation. This in turn provoked another callous outburst.

"There's no point in dillydallying with the dead bodies," he shouted. "Make some rafts quickly so that we can cast these adrift, for this has become the norm whenever the one-eyed bitch kills her prey."

Friends and priests counseled Chand to cremate the bodies according to the dictates of the holy shastras. Chand responded with an insult.

"You are worried about losing your gifts," he sneered. "But I won't let smoke from bodies marked by the one-eyed upstart pollute the air of my city. Call the gardeners and order half a dozen rafts made with the largest banana trees."

The gardeners carried out the order with alacrity. The bodies were ritually washed and decked with flowers and jewels before they were placed on the rafts and set adrift on the Gungari River. From the villages people came to have a last look at the bodies of the princes. Wails of lamentation rose from both banks of the river.

Presently, the black cobra that had carried out Padma's order of execution swam out and took charge of the rafts. Before long she guided them to Padma's presence. The goddess was delighted with her new possessions and with great care put them away in the underworld.

"Well, Neta," said Padma to her wise sister, "what next? I'm not any nearer my objective than when we began this campaign. Chand is more obdurate than ever."

"He may seem hard, but all hard things eventually turn out to be brittle. We must use a more elaborate stratagem. This is what my fertile brain has come up with."

"I'm all ears."

"Go to Indra's court and use some trickery to abduct Aniruddha and Usha. Let Aniruddha be born as Lakshmindar out of Sonaka's womb, and Usha as Behula out of the wife of Sahé, the merchant of Ujaninagar. Before Lakshmindar is born, send Chand on a trading mission to Lanka and make him go through all the torments you can dream up. When he is back home, get Lakshmindar and Behula married, but on the wedding night have a subtle snake dispose of the groom. Behula will accompany her husband's body on a raft and after many trials reach Amarnagar. You will then revive Lakshmindar and send him home with his wife. Chand will be overwhelmed with joy and will finally offer you puja."

Padma was thrilled.

"You are a wonderful scriptwriter," she complimented her sister.

USHA AND ANIRUDDHA PRESS-GANGED
BY PADMA

PADMA FLEW ON HER swan-drawn chariot to Amaravati and was warmly greeted by Indra, king of the gods, who sat with his consort Sachi in assembly along with a host of other deities and demi-divine beings. They were enjoying an entertainment arranged by Indra. The great gods Brahma, Vishnu, Shiva were there, the first two with their consorts Saraswati and Lakshmi. Other powerful gods were there too, like Yama, the god of death, Pavana, the wind god, Surya the sun god, Ganesha, Kubera, the sea god Varuna, not to mention the various categories of demi-divine beings, the apsaras, kinnaras, gandharvas, yakshas, rakshasas. They all sat chewing *paan* and enjoying the songs and dances by various performers.

"Come and join us," said Indra to Padma, offering her a seat beside his own. "I hope you will enjoy this little entertainment, and if there is anything you have come to ask of me, I don't have to tell you that your wish is my command."

Padma thanked him and sat down. Then leaning slightly toward Indra's ear she said, "You have read my mind. There is a favor I would like to ask you. I need your star dancing couple, Usha and Aniruddha, for a spell on earth."

A cloud passed over Indra's face. "Won't any dancing pair serve your purpose, must it be Usha and Aniruddha? I have become very fond of them."

"Others won't do, I'm afraid," said Padma. "The way they are bonded to each other is crucial to the realization of my plan to humble that arrogant fellow Chand. If I have them, this will be their third incarnation and after that they will be truly liberated and attain moksha. They will then be here with you for eternity."

"Very well, then," Indra agreed, "but how can I expel them without any reason?"

"Ask them to come and dance. I will make them miss the beat and that will be reason enough for you to pack them off to the mortal world. You don't even have to lay the curse on both of them. If one of them is exiled the other will go voluntarily, such is their attachment to each other."

Indra snapped his fingers to summon the nymph Chitralekha and asked her to call Usha and Aniruddha to come and dance.

"Usha!" Chitralekha called. "Aniruddha! Put on your dancing attire and come. Indra and all the assembled gods and goddesses want to see you perform."

The response from these two star performers of Indra's court was unusually and uncharacteristically lukewarm.

"I am not in a mood to dance," complained Usha. "I woke up sneezing this morning and I fear my performance will be flawed."

"My dear," said Aniruddha, "I dreamt last night that it was morning and saw large trees come crashing down and the sea drying up. The thought of dancing makes me nervous. My left eye is twitching and my body gives a start every now and then. I fear there may be a mishap if I'm not extra cautious."

"Oh, put away these irrational fears," said Chitralekha. "Indra has sent me to fetch you, go put on your dancing gear and come quick."

Despite her anxiety Usha took care to make a stunning appearance. She massaged her entire body with essence of agar-sandalwood, changed into colorful attire, decked herself in bedazzling jewelry, dabbed a bright circle of kumkum on her forehead, let fall her braided hair to swing over her back, and in tinkling anklets stepped in subtle rhythm into the performance hall, followed by the well-groomed, handsome Aniruddha and a troupe of *vidyadharis*.

While making their way from their living quarters, Usha was startled by several ominous sights—a vixen on the right, a serpent on the left, vultures sporting on one spot, and a woman with hair hanging loose who crossed her path. Usha's brows became creased with worry. Noticing this, Chitralekha reassured her with words of comfort.

"No harm can come to you if you are steadfast in your faith. Concentrate your mind on the great god Shiva and his mighty consort Chandi and seek their blessings."

With the names of Shiva and Chandi on their lips, Usha and Aniruddha appeared before the grand assembly. Once she was on the dance floor, Usha banished all worrisome thoughts and gave herself up to the subtle movements of her art. Placing a plate of fired earth on the floor she stepped onto it and made it more forward and back while she cavorted effortlessly, as if she were light as a feather. Aniruddha and Chitralekha kept time on small drums, and the *vidyadharis* danced around Usha.

The drums speeded up. The *vidyadharis* danced, making lightning-swift gestures, and Usha executed more and more complicated figures and then made the plate whirl like a potter's wheel while she writhed like clay under the shaping fingers of the potter. It would be a fitting climax to her performance and demanded utmost concentration. Just at this point, as the audience was about to burst into wild applause, Padma caused a flicker in Usha's mind. In a split second she lost her balance and hurtled to the floor.

"Damn you!" growled the thousand-eyed king of gods.

Usha was hurt and not only physically. She turned pale and sobbed as Indra pronounced the curse that Padma had scripted for him.

"Off to the mortal world!"

Usha cried uncontrollably, blamed herself for not heeding the ominous signs, fell at Indra's feet, as did Aniruddha.

All to no avail.

"How can we gain reprieve from the curse, O lord?" they wailed.

"Come, get a grip on yourselves," Indra replied. "It is not eternal exile. You will return after you have helped Padma solve a little problem."

The disconsolate pair rolled wailing on the floor.

Chuckling to herself, Padma took them by their hands.

"Your father, King Bana, is like my brother," said Padma to Usha, "so we are kin and your welfare is naturally my concern. You will only sojourn on earth for some time and as soon as I have succeeded in winning general devotion, with none defying me, you will be brought back safe and sound to this heavenly city. What's more, at the end of your earthly existence you will have attained moksha."

Realizing that there was no getting away from a divine curse, Usha sought further assurances from Padma that she would not be utterly helpless during her stay on earth.

"What is unavoidable has to be faced," she said. "I will go to the mortal world, for I must, but I have two requests. First, that I retain memories of this heavenly existence; and second, that you will come to me whenever I want your help."

"Very well," said Padma with a smile.

"I would like you to declare aloud what you have said so that all the gods here can bear witness."

"No problem," said Padma, and announced the concessions she had made.

Padma took leave of Indra and Sachi and the other gods and goddess and led Usha and Aniruddha out of the grand hall. She said to them matter-of-factly, "Get ready to leave this body and come with me to the mortal realm."

"We are ready, but I hope you will not begrudge us a small favor," Aniruddha said. "Let the flames that will consume our bodies be cool and not painful to the touch."

Padma readily agreed. A huge pyre of agar-sandalwood was set up and to its cool flames the loving couple abandoned their heavenly bodies. The flames burned through the night, gently reducing the material aspects of Usha and Aniruddha to fragrant ash and the remains of their skeletons.

As usually happens when someone dies and the flames of the funeral pyre dies down, Yama's minions—two in number—arrived to seize the dead and take them to the underworld. They were gigantic, hideous-looking creatures with fang-like teeth, dressed in leather and carrying heavy clubs. Without any ceremony they stepped onto the pyre, grabbed the remains of the dead couple, and, binding these with leather thongs, set off for their dark realm.

Padma observed all this from the sideline and commanded four nagas to take appropriate action. They promptly snatched away the prisoners and dragged Yama's minions before Neta and Padma.

"You are not acting wisely, Padmavati," the senior of Yama's servants said. "None has the power to take away our master's prisoners."

"Damn your impertinence!" Padma replied. "Do you think I am in awe of the god of death?" She turned to her nagas and gave commands. "Take these fellows by the hair and hack them to bits with a cleaver."

The deed would have been accomplished in no time if Neta hadn't intervened.

"You will achieve nothing by getting these wretches killed," she pointed out to her sister. "Better to turn them into a laughingstock and send them packing. Get their heads shaven and their faces painted with chalk and ink."

Padma was hugely tickled by this novel suggestion and assented readily.

This took a little longer for the nagas than simply chopping them up would have, but the results were far more satisfying. Everyone except the two victims was in stitches.

"Now go to your master Yama and tell him he is free to gamble his life, but if he loses it I'm not to blame. Has his dominion over dead sinners made him haughty enough to challenge me? I'll crush his vanity. Why isn't he content to rule over his own domain, why does he claim my vassals? I'll ravage and burn his realm and set the imprisoned sinners free, and see what he can do. Now go, you two."

Yama's ludicrous-looking minions cut and ran.

Events like this never escape the notice of the sage Narada, who is always on the lookout for ways to cause mischief, for no reason other than that it amused him to stir up strife.

As soon as Padma's nagas set upon Yama's minions, Narada descended into the underworld. Yama's city, built on an island and called

Sanjamini, rivaled Indra's Amaravati in splendor. It had four gates on four sides and around it circled the Vaitarani River. Its water, warm with human flesh and blood, flowed in a swift current beneath which lurked large omnivorous worms. The dead sinners brought from earth stood trembling on the bank where Yama's minions strode, knocking them into the river with heavy blows from clubs on their heads. They tried to swim across and were set upon by innumerable gnawing worms. Their cries filled the noxious air and struck terror in the new arrivals. Parts of dismembered bodies floated in the river.

Narada spirited himself straight to Yama's city and went around its four gates. First, at the western gate, he found Yama in a sober, serene mood, receiving householders who had lived a life of piety, practicing truthfulness, avoiding sin. They were directed to the heavenly realms. Next, Narada went to the eastern gate and found Yama in an equable temper, receiving those who were devotees of Vishnu, charitable toward Brahmins, honest workers who shunned sinful activities. They too were directed toward the heavenly realms. Then, at the northern gate Narada found Yama himself as a devotee of Vishnu, receiving mendicants of the great protector god's order, whose consciousness was always focused on their lord, and who practiced kindness toward all. The world-renouncing sannyasis were sent at once in flying chariots to Vaikuntha, Vishnu's abode. Narada couldn't help complimenting Yama on how well he was spending his time.

Finally, Narada went to the southern gate. Here, Yama was terrifying in aspect and stood grinding large, jagged teeth, growling and screaming at the sinners who came up trembling all over and were packed off to hell. The sinners thus punished included these categories: Brahmin men who had married low-caste women; high-caste men and women who drank to excess and committed other vices; those who stole gold ornaments; those who seduced their gurus' wives; liars and perjurers (they had their tongues sliced off a hundred times before they were cast into hell); those who indulged in backbiting (they had stakes thrust into their mouths and up their backsides before they were cast till eternity into pools of excrement); those who were irreverent toward their parents and spoke harshly with them (eternity in a pool of excrement was their punishment); men in positions of authority who looked with lust at subordinates (first they had their eyes gouged out with pincers); adulterous Brahmin women (they were thrust till eternity into dark wells); those who abducted and raped underage girls (they would hang upside down forever); those who refused to offer puja to a deity even after being asked; and those who ate sweets without sharing with anyone. The punishment in each case was proportionate to the sin. Some had red-hot irons thrust repeatedly into their mouths (and elsewhere); some had their flesh fed to dogs and jackals; some were impaled, others rent asunder; some suffered repeated decapitation but without death intervening; some were clubbed on their heads. Whatever the punishment, it went on and on as long as sun, moon, and stars showed in the sky; taking a deity's name at this stage was of no avail.

At the sight of the torments of hell Narada covered his eyes and invoked Vishnu. Around him swirled the thick, foul-smelling Vaitarani River with its screaming sinners. He addressed a lament to these unfortunates: "How could you act so unthinkingly, giving yourselves up to greed and other sins and ignoring the inevitability of life after death. You wouldn't offer puja to the gods and sinned without experiencing remorse, and the result is this unspeakable, endless torment."

When Narada had completed his round of the gates of Yama's city, the god greeted him with joined palms, offered him gifts, and ordered servants to wash his feet.

"I am blessed by your presence," Yama said.

"I have dropped by to see you and also to bring certain events to your notice," Narada said and briefly described how Padma's nagas had snatched away Usha and Aniruddha from Yama's minions and Padma had heaped insults on Yama himself.

Just then the two minions with shaved heads and faces painted black and white turned up and gave a detailed account of their encounter with the nagas and then with Padma and Neta. For good measure they added: "The nagas bit us and the venom drove us crazy with pain and we fainted." After describing the shaving and painting they ended on a note of pique: "Such an insult is intolerable. We can't go to fetch the dead unless the nagas are taught a lesson."

Yama turned to Narada with a request that he mediate to resolve the brewing tension.

"Go to Padma and ask her why she wants to stir up a conflict by abducting my prisoners. If she doesn't release them—in which case her prestige will remain intact—I will annihilate the nagas to get them."

Narada got on his magical wooden mount and by applying a switch to its hind parts sent it flying toward Padma's palace, where the goddess received him with due reverence, giving him gifts, having his feet washed, then offering him a comfortable seat.

Narada went straight to the point, "Listen, Padmavati, why are you provoking a conflict with Yama? I won't repeat all the boastful things he said, but the upshot is that you won't be able to hang on to the two prisoners, for you will be powerless if he annihilates your nagas. If you don't want to be humiliated hand over Usha and Aniruddha to me so that I can deliver them to Yama."

Padma's temper flared. "Who can take away my vassals?" she cried. "Anyone else coming to plead for Yama would have been roundly punished. Let him keep his boasts to the sinners in his power. He will suffer humiliation if he tries them on me. Go tell him to muster his forces and come if he dare. I will destroy him and set free his prisoners."

Padma respectfully touched Narada's feet and sent him on his way. Off he went to Yama and told him everything. The god of death sprang to his feet and angrily ordered a general mobilization.

The war elephants, the cavalry, the chariot-borne warriors, formation commanders, infantry units, all were ordered to get ready for battle. Yama got on his mount, a buffalo, and with his death-dealing staff in his hand, gave the order to march. Serried ranks of hundreds of thousands of his forces moved forward, with the commanders heading their units; and all the minions of Yama whose primary job was to go as the god's representatives and fetch the dead: they were a hideous-looking lot, some with bloodshot eyes, some hoarse-voiced, some jackal-faced or lion-headed, and many more odd-looking types.

As important as the soldiers, if not more so, were the host of ailments under Yama's command. Fevers, coughs, aches and pains, colic, cramps, gout and arthritis, and many more were the invisible terrors that crossed the Vaitarani River with Yama's army headed toward Mount Sijuya. The three realms shook under the footsteps of Yama's host.

Padma was fully cognizant of Yama's maneuvers and at an appropriate moment ordered all her naga forces to prepare to meet the invaders. Countless war drums rolled, and nagas came hissing to form a massive army. From Mount Sumeru came the redoubtable commander Takshaka, sporting five hundred hooded heads, with ten million nagas following him. Vasuki, powerful as the sun, chief of the nagas, sported seven hundred hoods in which a thousand gems glittered. Blinding rays shot from his eyes. These and many other naga stalwarts, each with millions of followers, hissed and thundered and shook the three realms with their aggressive clamor.

Their words were equally aggressive as they sped forward to meet Yama's minions. "Let's go get them!" shouted the nagas as they clashed with the enemy and easily pinned down their forward elements. Yama's side retaliated with their clubs but were overwhelmed. The nagas entwined themselves around the enemy soldiers and shot lethal venom into their bloodstream. Yama's advance guard was routed. Yama retaliated by releasing a combination of painful and mortal ailments. These began taking their toll, but Padma used Dhanvantari's art in good time (she had absorbed the *ojha*'s secret knowledge after annihilating him). The diseases dispersed. Yama's elephants and cavalry turned tail and fled.

The nagas went into a victory dance, whooping with joy. Yama joined the fray, shooting arrows with phenomenal speed and killing a large number of nagas. But Takshaka, Vasuki, and other veteran nagas—eight in all—rounded upon Yama and perforated him with arrows and lances. The mighty *Shankha naga* opened its giant mouth till it was wide as the sky and seemed about to gobble up Yama together with his buffalo mount. The god was visibly shaken but managed to summon Garuda, who swooped down on the nagas, with lightning speed. Terrified, the nagas scattered, slithering into holes or leaping into the water.

Padma came forward, using her divine weapons to good effect. Now the supreme leaders of the opposing armies—a god and a goddess—were face-to-face.

A verbal duel ensued.

"You don't know what you've got yourself into," scoffed Yama. "You'll surely lose your life to one of my secret weapons. Run if you want to live or become my prisoner, Padma."

"I'm warning you," Padma retorted. "My divine weapons will rend you into pieces. Your much-vaunted power over three realms will be reduced to nothing."

Padma couldn't resist the temptation to boast of her deadly record.

"Why have you come here to die?" she taunted Yama. "You know very well that I am the mistress of poisons, the daughter of the most powerful of gods. There's no escape from my missiles or my magic power. You have grossly overestimated your own strength; you should have stuck to lording it over miserable sinners in the underworld. Don't you know that even my father collapsed under the force of my venomous glance? The great gods, Brahma, Vishnu, Shiva, who have installed you in your little underworld job live in fear of me. I can cloud the universe with poison; it's child's play to destroy your petty pride. You'll regret leaving the safety of your little domain."

Quivering with rage, Yama fitted arrows to his bow but didn't shoot till he had replied to Padma's verbal onslaught.

"Padma, there's no escape from my shafts today. See, here they come."

He had fitted ten arrows to his bow and let fly at once: they glanced off Padma's chariot. He fired ten more; they were intercepted in mid-course and broke into splinters.

Padma retaliated with ten of her own: these struck home, drawing blood from Yama's chest and throwing him into a swoon. But he recovered shortly and, picking up his death-dealing staff, shot a Brahmastra, which is impossible to intercept or deflect—or to survive.

Padma fell. Yama let out a victory whoop. Neta urged Padma to recall the great occult mantra, the Mahagyan, which she did with her flickering consciousness just before it would have been too late. The next moment she was back on her chariot, radiating venom from her eye: it struck home, making Yama feel suffocated. Padma chanted the Brahma mantra and let fly her naga missiles. At once eight million fierce nagas entwined Yama and injected into him their deadly venom. Yama lay unconscious, a helpless prisoner. The nagas whooped and hissed and joined together in a wild victory dance.

Padma crowed over her fallen foe: "What gave you the audacity to cross swords with me? With my nagas I have made you my prisoner, held fast from head to foot, the laughingstock of the three realms. You are merely one of the ten deities assigned different functions in the running of the universe. You have your portfolio, but don't try to overstep its limits."

Yama said nothing; his head was bowed in humiliation. Padma returned home, taking him prisoner, with the famed eight nagas mounting guard over him.

Word of the battle and its outcome reached the other gods, vastly amused them, and also roused some concern, for the underworld without its big boss and his minions would before long threaten the stability of the universe as a whole. Brahma mustered his fellow gods, great and small, and led them in a delegation to Padma's home on Mount Sijuya.

Padma received them warmly, with traditional gifts and by having their feet washed. Brahma opened the dialogue. "There's a purpose behind this visit," he said. "All the gods are voluble in praising you, for there is none greater than you. Yama provoked a conflict with you unwittingly and I would—we all would—request you to pardon him and set him free."

Padma addressed all the visiting gods in her reply: "Yama came personally to abduct my servants after my nagas had prevented his minions from taking them away. He came with a fully equipped army and on losing the battle became prisoner to my nagas."

The gods laughed at this droll account. Padma asked the three great gods to acknowledge the justice of her cause. "Let the three realms of the universe be told clearly that Yama has no right to snatch away my servants."

"Yama has no authority over Padma's people," Brahma, Vishnu, and Shiva declared.

Padma was delighted and ordered that the prisoner be produced and set free.

Yama addressed Brahma with palms conjoined in reverence: "When I heard that two persons who were being transported to the underworld had been snatched away and my servants insulted, I became furious because it was unthinkable that anyone would dare to do such a thing without your sanction, for it was you who invested me with authority over the dead. I beg to be relieved of my responsibilities, appoint someone else to my wretched job, for I have become the laughingstock of the universe."

"Oh dear," sighed Brahma, who then proceeded to explain the finer points of power relations as well as eschatology. "Why did you declare war against Padma," he said, "don't you know that she is Shiva's daughter, held in high esteem by him as well as Vishnu and me?"

"Be that as it may," interjected Yama in piqued tones, "but you can restore Usha and Aniruddha to me. That will salvage my prestige and I can go back to my wretched job."

"Now, now," chided Brahma, "you are not getting the point. It is not a simple case of conflicting egos. In the first place, you shouldn't take your job description too literally. True, you have been appointed to deal with the dead—and how you relish doing it! But there are the dead and then there are the dead, as you know. Snakebite victims are Padma's property. As for Usha and Aniruddha, they are not your average dead man and wife. They were denizens of Amaravati who agreed to be translated into an earthly existence to fulfill a noble purpose that involves Padma. So she keeps the two of them, and you can forget the unfortunate imbroglio and go back to your cheerful job in the underworld."

Yama had nothing to say after that and took his leave, still grumpy, but resigned. Padma thanked everyone with a smile and with Neta at her side set about realizing their grand design.

THE BIRTH OF LAKSHMINDAR
AND BEHULA

"I MUST PUT ANIRUDDHA INTO Sonaka's womb and make him come out in due time to begin his earthly existence," said Padma to Neta. "How do I go about it?"

"Things are a bit problematic," said Neta. "Listen carefully while I explain and suggest a solution."

"I am all ears."

"Sonaka has not got over the loss of her six sons. She hardly eats, her clothes are always untidy, her hair disheveled, she wears no jewelry, and she doesn't share Chand's bed any longer. You see the problem: unless she sleeps with her husband you can't make her conceive the son who will be Aniruddha's earthly incarnation."

"So what do we do?"

"You have to do some acting again. Here's the script: you assume the form of Sonaka's aunt—her mother's widowed sister, who, having lost her sons to snakebite, has been reduced to penury—and by casting a spell make her feel drawn to you as a fellow sufferer. You will help her cope with her bereavement and eventually get her into bed with Chand. I don't need to spell out the rest."

"You are a genius," enthused Padma, giving her sister a warm hug.

She got into her new role without delay, willing her body to change in a highly convincing manner. Her body shriveled, her teeth fell out or broke and became discolored. Wrinkles scored her face, her hair turned white, and her emaciated breasts became elongated and hung low. She needed a staff to steady herself as she walked; but even then her knees shook when she stood up, took a step, or sat down. She put on a white sari, the widow's traditional garb, and set off for Champaknagar with Neta as her traveling companion.

Padma stopped at the pond ghat where Sonaka's maids went to fetch water. The maids turned up in due course carrying brass pitchers and as they dawdled over filling them up engaged the stranger in conversation.

"Where are you from?" asked one.

"Where are you headed?" asked another.

The old woman smiled and said, "Why, I am a visitor to your town, and I am the aunt of your queen, Sonaka."

"What a coincidence," said the maids, "we work in Queen Sonaka's household and we will tell her that we have met you."

They went away carrying full pitchers of water balanced on their ample hips and said to Sonaka, "Guess who we have met today: an old woman has come to town who says she's your aunt."

"Go and bring her here," said Sonaka. "She's probably my mother's sister, whom I haven't seen in years."

The maids went back to the ghat and said, "Our royal mistress requests you to go to her palace."

The old woman got up and was escorted to Sonaka's presence. Aunt and niece shed tears of joy as they hugged each other. Sonaka respectfully touched her aunt's feet and bade her sit down. She ordered her maids to fetch water and washed her aunt's feet. Then the two of them sat down. Sonaka served snacks to her aunt and fanned her as she ate.

"Tell me how you've been faring, Auntie," Sonaka inquired.

"Fate has been unkind to your aunt. Your uncle suffered long from a chronic ailment and then passed away. All my sons died of snakebite, and now I am a destitute old widow."

Sonaka gave a start on hearing about the deaths from snakebite. Tears flowed down her cheeks.

"Auntie, now hear about my condition and the sad coincidence that makes us fellow sufferers. I lost all six of my sons to the venom of the nagas. My grief has unhinged my mind. It's a stroke of luck to have you here now. Live with me for the rest of your days and let me look after you."

Tears of relief and gratitude sprang up in the old lady's eyes.

"We will share our grief and console each other," she said.

And so the old lady became a member of Sonaka's household, a permanent guest. She would always be with her "niece," chattering away in such a way that Sonaka's grief lightened gradually. Not only that, instead of Sonaka looking after her, she took care of Sonaka's needs, feeding her at mealtimes, and groomed her—dabbing her forehead with sandalwood paste, streaking her hair parting with *sindur*—so that her appearance became normal again. After meals she put a bowl of *paan* before Sonaka, so that chewing the stimulating leaf with accompanying lime and condiments she felt her mood became more equable, less susceptible to swings.

The kind "aunt" did not neglect housework either. She took care of all the chores and the cooking, directing the maids so that everything was efficiently accomplished. She worked so hard that Sonaka felt she was overdoing things, considering her age.

"If you work like this at your age you'll strain yourself," Sonaka said anxiously. "You need to take things easy."

"Quite the contrary," the old lady reassured Sonaka. "I'm fortunate to have found you. Looking after you has relieved me of my sorrow. Life must go on."

In time Sonaka's menstrual period came on, and on the fourth day a ritual bath was called for. Sonaka went through with it as a matter of habit, without a thought about its significance in one's conjugal life, for it marks the beginning of the fertile spell. Her "aunt" would not let such amnesia persist. She cajoled Sonaka over her lack of realism: "Here you are, living away from your husband's bed, sleeping with your widowed daughters-in-law, wallowing in grief. I too have suffered bereavement, but I can't bear to see you prolong your agony like this. Where there is life, there is death, and yet life must go on. It's unreasonable to stay away from your husband."

"But you don't understand," Sonaka rejoined. "It is my husband's adamant defiance of Padma that led to the death of our sons. When I remember this it becomes impossible to contemplate sharing his bed again."

The "aunt" gently took Sonaka's hand and said, "Keep this old aunt's request. For my sake, go to your husband tonight. But first offer puja to Manasa-devi and ask her for a boon—a son. I have a feeling it will have a happy outcome."

The "aunt" brought her special powers into play, inducing a change of mind in the "niece."

"Very well," Sonaka said, and added coyly, "but I am such a sight."

The "aunt" became a beautician and in no time transformed a morose, mature lady into an attractive woman. She combed Sonaka's hair and tied it in a bun, applied *kajal* to her eyes, *sindur* in the parting of her hair, massaged sandalwood essence over her whole body, and led her by the hand to Chand's bedroom door.

"Not so soon," Sonaka said to her aunt. "Let me first offer puja."

"A puja is always a good idea."

Sonaka withdrew to her private chamber and, as she often did, secretly offered puja to Padma. The goddess appeared before her; she was awed. "What do you want?" Padma asked bluntly.

"A son, great goddess."

"Very well, you will have another son."

Sonaka prostrated herself before the goddess in gratitude.

"But there's a catch."

Sonaka sat up apprehensively; she had seen enough of the world to be wary of all "buts" and "catches."

"If this son marries, he will die of snakebite on his wedding night."

"Oh no, O mother of the universe, change this terrible curse."

But Padma had vanished.

Shaken by this divine visitation, Sonaka didn't know what to do. She told her "aunt" what had happened.

"Don't worry about the curse," the "aunt" said reassuringly. "Why does your son have to marry? Let him remain a lifelong bachelor and your lifelong companion."

Padma let her "aunt" escort her to Chand's bedroom.

After the long period of enforced abstinence, the sight of a well-groomed and trim Sonaka—her grief-induced loss of appetite had much improved her figure—acted as an instant aphrodisiac on Chand.

Chand showered Sonaka with endearments, making her blush like an adolescent. Their lovemaking was vigorous; or rather, Chand's was, much to their mutual satisfaction. Sweat beaded his face and chest by the time he rolled off her body. At that point, unbeknownst to either, an invisible Padma inserted Aniruddha's life into Sonaka's womb.

That night, as Chand sank into deep sleep, Padma assumed the form of her all-powerful father and appeared in his dreams with a special message. To ensure credibility Padma paid attention to every detail of appearance characteristic of Shiva. Her facial features and figure perfectly matched his; she wore matted hair exactly like his, carried a conch-shell trumpet like his, wore a garland of bones like his, and rode a bull that was a spitting image of Nandi.

Chand saw his favorite god appear at the head of his bed and at once with clasped hands prostrated himself in veneration, awaiting any pronouncement that might ensue.

"I have been moved to pity at seeing all you have suffered at the hands of my daughter. I have therefore devised a way for you to recoup your losses. Go on a trading mission to Lanka. There I will teach you the great occult Mahagyana mantra once again so that you will be able to revive your six sons as well as the *ojha* Dhanvantari and Dhona and Mona. Not least, you will gain a huge fortune that will guarantee your family perennial prosperity."

These words fell on Chand's ears like raindrops on parched soil. He woke up the next morning in a state of exhilaration and summoned a royal assembly after breakfast. He took the throne resplendently attired and accoutred, with a golden crown sparkling with gems, as well as sacred symbols like tulsi leaf in the hair and sandalwood paste dabbed on his forehead. Courtiers, councillors, and ministers sat quietly and noted a change of mood in their royal master. Of late, since the loss of his sons, his defiance of Padma had taken on an air of desperation— desperation with an underlying tinge of depression. Today, he looked quite upbeat.

"Friends," he began his address, "as you have observed, the death of my sons has profoundly affected me. But grief and impotent rage will get us nowhere. We must be proactive, positive, in order to set things right."

A ripple of applause played around the audience.

Chand continued; "I have decided to set off on a trading mission to Lanka." Those in the assembly were visibly taken aback; glances of befuddlement were exchanged, followed by a confused murmur.

"It seems the idea comes as a surprise to you. Does anyone have any objections?"

A veteran courtier stood up and after some hemming and hawing said, "I was wondering if it was quite appropriate for a ruler, a raja like yourself, to go personally as a trader to another kingdom. Isn't it . . . well, um . . ."

"Demeaning?" Chand completed the sentence for him.

"Well, er, no," fumbled the courtier, breaking out into a sweat, for Chand clearly wasn't pleased with his comment. Then he had an inspiration and regained his fluency. "Actually, it's quite the contrary, that's what I was trying to get at. Trade and commerce are the economic backbone of a nation, the source of *artha*, wealth."

"Now you are making sense," said Chand with a touch of sarcasm. "I belong to a race of merchants. All my ancestors bought and sold merchandise in distant lands. Without the wealth they acquired through trade they wouldn't have been able to raise an army and set up a kingdom. Even now our ships sail regularly to distant ports with our exports and bring back precious things that we need. Why shouldn't I lead a grand trade mission?"

"Your Royal Highness, your knowledge and wisdom are palpable in what you say. Your father, King Katiswara, himself once led a fleet of thirteen ships on a trading mission." The courtier had another brainstorm here: "That's why I was asking if it's appropriate for a king of your stature to go on a trading mission of the ordinary sort—that's what I had in mind. Shouldn't you command a huge fleet that will be the awe and admiration of all who see it in foreign ports? Since your father led a fleet of thirteen ships . . ."

"You should have fourteen," interjected another courtier.

"I shall have fourteen ships then," said Chand. "It's going to be a very important mission, urged on me by the highest authority in the universe." Here Chand smiled and raised his eyes heavenward, and a murmur of awe and admiration spread throughout the assembly, for everyone knew of their king's adoration of Shiva and the special connection he had with the great god.

Chand ordered the building of a brand new vessel, his flagship, and the repair and refitting of thirteen others including some that his father had sailed with on his last famous voyage. It would mean a wait of up to six months. This was a cause of some chagrin, for after the epiphany in his dream he felt his youthful taste for long sea voyages coming back, if only because they would get him away from the wretched Padma.

Getting the fleet ready and loading it with necessities and merchandise were time-consuming tasks. Then there was the job of hiring the crew: so much depended upon selecting the right people. They had to be well trained, experienced, and reliable. Chand ordered his personal assistant Tera to press-gang if necessary at least seven hundred expert carpenters.

"Right away, Master," said Tera. This Tera was quite a card, given to practical jokes, as the denizens of the village of carpenters presently discovered.

For Tera rode into their village wielding a long-lashed whip and shouting threateningly. Everyone scuttled into their huts and looked out nervously from their windows. Tera dismounted and went from hut to hut, turning out all the sturdy-looking and experienced carpenters among their dwellers. The poor fellows asked what he wanted of them but got no answer. He carried on with the job of press-ganging carpenters, counting out their number aloud, and stopped when he reached seven hundred. Then, to their consternation, he produced a long rope that had been hanging in a coil from his saddle and proceeded to tie the wrists of the press-ganged carpenters. Confused wails arose, and they all begged, "Forgive us for whatever we have done," or humbly asked, "Master, what will you do with us, where will you take us?"

"Shut up!" Tera screamed, and all seven hundred fell silent—though their children and womenfolk kept up a loud lamentation in the background.

Tera added brusquely, "The king wants you," and led them out of the village in a long, straggling line behind the robust haunches of his mount. As they shuffled along they had ample time to review their recent petty misdemeanors, which the king's spies might have reported to him.

Before long the strange procession entered Champaknagar, attracting curious onlookers and waggish comments, and made for the royal palace. The tearful carpenters fell at their king's feet and begged: "Have mercy on us, whatever we have done wrong."

The king, almost as surprised as the carpenters at their being under restraint, asked Tera, "Why are they all tied up?"

"Master, I'm setting them free at once. I just didn't want to take any chances. What if I brought them here and on counting found that there weren't seven hundred in all because one or two had quietly slipped away? Wouldn't you have me roundly thrashed?"

Chand knew at once this was one of Tera's practical jokes, for he was chuckling as he gave his explanation—instantly cooked up, no doubt.

"Anyway, let's get down to business," Chand said, assuming a sober tone. He called Manik, the seniormost of the carpenters, and as the man stepped forward gave him a *paan* from the royal *paan* tray—a great honor for a member of the toiling castes—and said, "I need you and your fellows to help me build a magnificent seagoing ship, sturdy, swift, beautifully appointed, and comfortable. I hope you will give me your best, for then I will recompense you with gold coins and gifts of handsome clothes for you and your families."

The relief and delight on the faces of the carpenters can easily be imagined.

"Hail Raja Chand! Long live Raja Chand!" they chanted in unison.

"After you have built this ship you will carry out necessary repairs and refitting work on thirteen other ships that I have inherited from my noble father. Then I will have a fleet of fourteen splendid ships with which I will sail to distant Lanka. A lot depends on you. It is your expertise and dedication that can ensure that I will have a really magnificent fleet at my command, proudly flying our flag across the deepest waters."

The carpenters again loudly cheered their king and employer.

They got down to work as soon as the royal audience was over. They felled the best trees to obtain timber. These were sawed into planks and rafters and seasoned by a special process to make them strong and resistant to corrosion.

Chand offered a special puja to Vishwakarma, the divine engineer, seeking his blessings for the work under way. The god appeared in person to give his blessings. Not only that: he promised to guide the hands of the carpenters while remaining invisible.

Manik began laying out the frame of the ship with renewed confidence. The keel was laid straight as a die, accurate measurements of each part were taken, the masts erected, side benches fixed, cabins constructed. The work went on steadily, and when the ship was completed, it was named the *Madhukar*—the "Honey-Filled One," a name that betokens wealth, plenty, the sweet life.

The older thirteen vessels were next refurbished and refitted, so that they shone as if absolutely new. All fourteen were then launched into the Gungari River after puja and the sacrifice of hundreds of buffaloes and he-goats. Final preparations began. Chand's cabin on the *Madhukar* was paneled with sandalwood; another large cabin was furnished to serve as a floating royal court; the kitchen was equipped with cooking implements, plates, tumblers, and stocked with tinder and firewood. To top it all, earth was loaded in large pots in which were planted various flowering plants—for offering flowers to deities was an essential part of pujas—and fruit-bearing trees and plants and vegetables.

There were special varieties of orange, lemon, mango, and even jackfruit; *amlaki, karamcha,* jujube, chillies, pepper, *paan,* turmeric; among flowers the champak, varieties of jasmine, *kinshuk, ketaki, toggor.* The *Madhukar* and its companion ships became a veritable floating garden. Even a number of peacocks and koels were introduced to enliven the air.

Chand next commanded Tera to load the merchandise. Huge quantities of things were taken on board the ships and stacked in neat rows. There were plates, tumblers, pitchers, pots, bowls, basins made of gold and also of brass, finely woven cane mats, spices and condiments, and loads of other items that would be in demand in foreign parts.

Before setting sail there were puja rituals for Shiva and his consort Chandi. Herds of buffalo and flocks of he-goats were sacrificed, a pitcher was set up and filled with Ganges water and mango leaves. Burning incense scented the air. Just then Padma appeared at the puja altar and, positioning herself on the pitcher, hectored Chand: "Offer me puja at least once and I will recompense you with wealth and many sons."

Chand retorted angrily: "You have devoured my six sons, you one-eyed bitch, and yet dare to beg me for flower and water offerings! Make yourself scarce before I come charging with my *hintala* staff."

Padma vanished, only to reappear disguised as a Brahmin widow skulking behind the door.

After completing the puja to his adored god and goddess, Chand had his meal, followed by *paan*. As he sat chewing the leaf and the sweet-scented condiments wrapped up in it, Chand spoke to Tera: "Pick up my *hintala* staff and drive away anything that seems unpropitious."

Tera waved the staff with shouts that were more comic than threatening. But it was enough to make Padma vanish again, having realized that it would take a lot more to bring Chand around.

It was time to make the final farewells and board the ship. Chand went into the inner quarters of the palace. Sonaka came, eyes bashfully averted, and said, "My lord, I think I am pregnant. You will leave us now, but you can't say for sure when you will come back. I am filled with anxiety. I would like to have something from you in writing establishing the identity of the child who will be born."

Chand said with a laugh, "What a time to ask," and added gently, "Set your mind at rest, and look after the household while I am away. And here, let me set down in writing my thoughts about our child if one is born after I leave." He took up pen and palm leaf and began writing.

"There you are," he said, handing the palm leaf to Sonaka, "if we have a son let him be named Lakshmindar, if it's a girl call her Bipula."

Sonaka smiled in anticipation.

"Now cook some of your special dishes. I want to have a good meal before boarding the ship."

Sonaka busied herself, cooking some delicacies with loving care. Chand ate his fill, chewed *paan,* and got ready to leave. Sonaka bent low, picked up his foot, and placed it on her head in a gesture of absolute devotion. Chand stepped out of his home, left foot forward, chanting the names of Shiva and Chandi, while priests recited benedictions.

Chand boarded the *Madhukar* and, taking his seat in the sandalwood scented cabin, gave the command to cast off. Conch-shell trumpets sounded on each of the fourteen ships, oars splashed and set up a regular rhythm timed by drumbeats, and sailors prepared to unfurl sails. People on the riverbank cheered loudly as the fleet shot past them and headed south toward the Bay of Bengal.

Meanwhile Sonaka entered her fifth month of pregnancy and on a suitably auspicious day sacramentally consumed five specified sweet things: curd, milk, ghee, sugar, honey. By the seventh month she had lost weight everywhere except the midsection. She experienced odd sensations. She complained to her "aunt," who had stayed on to see her through her troubles: "My hands and feet feel hot, as if they were burning. My body seems useless for any practical activities. I feel like rolling on cool earth."

She expressed a craving for certain foods: "The leaf of jute plants cooked in gravy with coriander, salt, and tamarind; small fry cooked in sour gravy with edible creepers; and soft rice to go with these."

A maidservant called Rati went around collecting the items Sonaka craved. Sonaka examined them like a connoisseur and relished them when cooked. In this manner the days went by until ten months and ten days of pregnancy were over. A son was born at an auspicious hour, a handsome infant who brought a blissful smile to his mother's lips.

As the newborn's umbilical cord was severed, Sonaka took him into her arms, and the womenfolk of the palace set off a joyous trilling by wagging their tongues. The inhabitants of Champaknagar jubilantly hailed the birth of their prince, and the royal astrologer forecast an immortal life for the child. Sonaka presented him with a gold chain and distributed ample largesse among all citizens.

On the sixth day of the child's life Sasthi Puja was offered. On the seventh day Sonaka came out of confinement and had a ritual bath. After a month Sonaka's period of impurity came to an end and she could resume all normal activities. When the child was six months old he was ritually introduced to solid food—that is, rice—and given his name, Lakshmindar. Thanks to Padma's blessings he was free of childhood ailments and grew rapidly. At five he was given his first lesson. A rapid learner, he had soon mastered the scriptures and at seven could take on learned men in debates. Even at this age one could tell he would grow into a handsome, trim-waisted, deep-voiced, deep-chested youth with hands and feet comely as lotuses.

It was now time for Padma to arrange the birth of Lakshmindar's life partner. The place chosen was Ujaninagar; the family, that of the king who ruled from that city. Sahé was the name of the king; his wife was the lovely Sumitra.

As Sumitra's monthlies came round, Padma got ready to impregnate her. On the fourth day of menstruation Sumitra had her ritual bath and her attendants groomed her, made her up, dressed her so that she looked like a youthful beauty queen. She was then led to the royal bedroom to await her husband.

At Padma's instigation Kamadeva, the god of love, brought king and queen to the pinnacle of desire, and while they gasped and panted in the throes of lovemaking, Padma invisibly inserted Usha's life into Sumitra's womb.

The signs of pregnancy began to show in four months. As with Sonaka seven years back, all the rituals were observed until, ten months and ten days after conception a beautiful girl child was born.

The king and queen were overjoyed and with great fanfare and lavish hospitality observed all the rituals related to bringing up a child. The child was named Behula. At five she had her ears pierced and grew up fast, so that it soon became obvious that she would be a great beauty; the question on the minds of those who saw her was whether she would far surpass the heavenly apsaras, Menaka, Tilottama, Urvashi, of whom they had heard so many legends.

Her face was like a fully blossomed lotus on which a playful pair of eyes shone with a seductive light. Her figure was like a golden statue sculpted by a god. Her lips were cherry red and her lush hair fell in dancing curls down her back. Her wasp waist accentuated the flare of her broad hips. Her hands were delicate, her nails sparkling clear, with well-defined moons. The nose was delicately shaped, the teeth shone like pearls. Her voice was sweet and mellow and she walked with swan-like steps, to the tinkling music of anklets. But we anticipate: we have been describing her as she becomes in the years of maidenhood. Let us also mention the piety and devotion she would bring to her worship of Padma. Thus, with Usha and Aniruddha incarnated as Behula and Lakshmindar the stage was set for Neta's master plan to unfold into a spectacular crisis.

THE ADVENTURES AND MISADVENTURES OF
CHAND THE MERCHANT KING

AFTER SAILING SOUTHWARD for six months, Chand and his fleet reached the river port of Srinagar. He decided to halt here for some time, for the southerly wind blowing from the sea was too strong to allow steady progress. When the monsoon had blown over he made ready to resume his journey, and with the onset of autumn and a fresh northerly wind conditions were ideal to set sail again.

The ships skimmed over the sparkling waters and soon reached the confluence of three holy rivers, the Ganges, the Yamuna, and the Saraswati. Chand had a ritual purificatory bath at this spot and gave away gold coins as alms to Brahmin priests. The fleet sped on to the river bend at Kedar, where Shiva was sporting in the water with Chandi. Nearby was a structure with a quadriplanar roof specially built by the divine engineer Viswakarma; it was ringed by champak and *nageswara* plants. Chand purified himself with a bath and taking along many gifts went to offer puja to his adored god and goddess.

He brought back their blessings and took his seat in a cheerful frame of mind in the cabin hung with many colorful paintings that was his command post. The next stop was at the famed stretch of water called Kalidaha, home to the Kaliya naga. Chand bathed and performed puja, meditated, gave away alms, and sped away again.

The rivers debouched into the sea, widening till they were indistinguishable from the latter. The ships could expect unimpeded progress, but to everyone's dismay they slowed down rapidly and became immobile. Millions of leeches, smelling blood, clung to the ships and rocked them like seesaws, inducing abject fear in Chand. He ordered lime to be poured over the stubborn creatures; at once they let go and sank into the depths. This was only the first of several extraordinary holdups.

After a couple of days of smooth sailing the ship again slowed to a halt and was rocked dangerously from both sides—this time by millions of prawns and lobsters, frolicking, pushing, splashing water. Chand shouted out, "We're sinking," then collected himself and commanded experienced fishermen among the crew to cast their nets. The sight of the nets scared away the menacing creatures.

Next came all varieties of cowries, which surrounded the fleet in such large numbers that the ships lay still, as if stuck on a sandbank. Chand ordered steel fishing traps to be lowered into the water to capture the cowries. About half were caught and buried on the bank to be dug up on the way back. The rest disappeared and didn't return.

After another couple of days the fleet was waylaid by millions of crabs. They crowded round, heaved and pushed, crawled up the sides, and struck terror in the crew, so large and fearsome were they. Chand ordered burnt sheep and goats to be thrown overboard. The crabs abandoned the ships and began devouring the carcasses. The fleet made a swift getaway.

After a few days they entered a mangrove forest inhabited by tigers, bears, wild boars, rhinoceroses, elephants, and of course herds of deer. The river narrowed and split into numerous distributaries. Negotiating them was dangerous: the wild beasts roaring, grunting, trumpeting all around could easily hop onto the ships for a ride. Chand ordered his men to destroy the forest on either bank and massacre the beasts as the ships glided along. He didn't want to take any chances.

Once they were out of the forest, on the coastal shelf, picking their way through numerous islands, the conch shells in massive numbers waylaid them. They had to be picked up, put in wicker baskets, and cast back into the water. While the operation was under way Chand got off the *Madhukar* and went to a temple on shore to pay his respects to Shiva and Chandi.

The fleet was now poised to sail clear of the last of the islands and sandbanks and into the wide sea. Padma asked Neta, "Is there anything we can try while Chand's fleet is still in this no-man's-water between sea and river?"

"The village of Bachhai, the merchant, is right on Chand's path," said Neta. "He is your devotee and is offering a grand puja right now. He will be thrilled if you appear there in person. Grant him any boon he craves but set him the ultimate condition—you know what I mean—and when it's fulfilled, perform a miracle and reverse it. It will get you more devotees and greater devotion from the ones who are already your devotees. Who knows, one of the new devotees may be Chand. At least it's worth giving the plan a try."

"Right," agreed Padma. "We must continue our efforts until he gives in."

Padma decorated herself with a variety of snakes—one became a choker, two hung on either side of her head as eardrops, a tiny one that was bright crimson became innovative *sindur,* a pair of rattlesnakes became tinkling anklets, long dark ones swung like braids on her back. Padma mounted her swan-drawn chariot and flew to her devotee's house.

"O Bachhai," she called. Hearing her voice Bachhai ran to receive her and reverentially touched her feet. The goddess's getup of course terrified him; he broke into a sweat. With joined palms he knelt before her, awaiting her commands.

"I am very pleased with you," Padma said. "I will be even more pleased if you worship me by sacrificing to me your eldest son Sripati. Cut off his head with your own hand and offer it to me."

Bachhai nearly had a heart attack. "Let me be the sacrifice," he begged.

"Your blood will not satisfy me," Padma bluntly replied. "Sacrifice Sripati and offer me puja."

"I have a younger son—let me sacrifice him," said Bachhai.

"Let your younger son live with you. Give me Sripati and I will be satisfied."

Bachhai went and told Sripati everything. Sripati replied, undismayed, "Don't be mournful about it. If Manasa-devi wants me you must do as she says. How can you keep me if she wants me? If you go against her wishes she will leave none alive in our family."

Bachhai resigned himself to the inescapable and had a sacrificial altar put up on the seashore. It was decorated with auspicious *alpana* designs, and a gem-studded throne was placed for the goddess. Bachhai took a ritual dip in the sea and sat down to go through the puja. First he offered sweet-smelling flowers and the incense burning in a bowl; then a gorgeous sari and gem-studded jewelry. He placed a garland of fragrant flowers around the goddess's neck and declared, "I am your obedient slave, happy if you give me a place beneath your feet."

Sripati too came after a purificatory bath and, sitting down with joined palms, sang paeans to Padma. He was in a state of ecstasy; tears of joy ran down his cheeks. Bachhai picked up some *kusha* grass and dedicated his son's life to Padma. Then raising a large, curved cleaver he decapitated Sripati in a single stroke. Manasa smiled with pleasure and accepting the proffered head drank the blood that flowed in a torrent from it.

"See what an ardent devotee you have in Bachhai and his son," commented Neta. Padma smiled with satisfaction, smacking her blood-wet lips.

"Now if you revive Sripati, everyone will be thrilled and happy and grateful, and you will gain many more ardent worshippers. Chand will hear of the incident and, who knows, may realize that it would be wise to give you your due."

"Right," agreed Padma, and at once, like a magician, made a flourish or two, held up the headless corpse, placed the lifeless head on the truncated neck, and, whispering the Mahagyan mantra into the dead boy's ear, snapped her fingers before the closed eyes. At once, to loud cheers, the boy's eyelids fluttered open, the limbs moved and he opened his mouth to say, "Come, Father, let us prostrate ourselves at the feet of the great goddess."

Padma was greatly pleased and granted them a boon after their hearts, then enjoined them to perform her puja regularly. The entire population of the village, which had gathered there, pledged to do so and chanted slogans proclaiming her greatness.

After offering puja to Shiva and Chandi, Chand came sailing down with his fleet and noticed the puja altar set up by Bachhai. His curiosity was aroused by the sound of conch trumpets, cymbals, drums, and other instruments playing at the puja. He ordered the ships to drop anchor so that he could go and take a look. He asked the people coming from the puja whom they had worshipped.

"The great goddess Padmavati," the simple villagers answered in tones of awe and reverence. "Whoever worships her in a spirit of humility is sure to receive her blessings and her protection."

Chand's anger flared up at the mention of Padma. "Only ignorant rustics like you worship that one-eyed bitch," he thundered. He ordered his crew to accompany him as he marched up to the altar and smashed the pitcher at the altar. He commanded his men to dismantle the puja pavilion and cast it into the sea. He stood and watched with satisfaction as the act of vandalism was carried out and then resumed his voyage. Padma's rage was explosive: Chand had overstepped all limits; he must die. If she had her way he would be dead in a moment, but Neta calmly counseled patience. "If you kill him," she pointed out, "you lose the contest, for he will die without having worshipped you." Padma simmered down.

Chand's fleet headed out into the open sea, sails billowing in the steady northwesterly wind. Soon he was out of sight of land, out of range of the one-eyed upstart. Or so he thought.

✦   ✦   ✦

The voyage was pleasant and uneventful. The fleet sailing precisely in the direction of the wind sighted the coast of Lanka one sunlit morning. Chand and his lieutenants watched from the roof of the *Madhukar*. As they drew closer they could make out the buildings of a port. Chand asked, "Does anyone know the name of this port city?"

A lookout answered, "It is known as Kanakpaton."

The name means "Golden Port" and the view of the city gave evidence of its appropriateness.

"I don't want to sail any further," said Chand. "We will dock at this port."

The fleet made for the port in formation, with the *Madhukar* leading.

Word of a large fleet approaching spread through the port city like wild fire. Was it an invading fleet, and if so which king's, people wondered. Many panicked and fled inland with their families; among them some police officers, city functionaries, and even the wharfinger.

As Chand's ships entered the dock, one of the king's spies ran to the royal court. So nervous was he that he just stood with quaking knees, unable to articulate any words. Eventually he managed to blurt out: "An alien king has come to the port with fourteen ships, each as high as a hill. I fear they might try to conquer the land."

The king was concerned and asked another spy to go and find out more about the strangers. He found a constable and briefed him on what to do. The constable went to the wharf and called out to the approaching ships: "Don't draw any closer. Tell us the name of your commander and why you wish to stop at our port."

"I am a merchant from Champaknagar, Chandradhara by name, and we come not with any evil intent but to engage in peaceful trade."

This was relayed posthaste to the royal court and promptly came the reply: "There is nothing to fear from us either. You may dock your ships at the wharf."

Disembarking, Chand engaged one of the wharf guards in conversation. "Tell me about this land of yours," he said.

"Our king is Chandraketu, of the Kshatriya warrior caste. He is a man of integrity and piety, ever engaged in good works. He is wealthy and generous and like a father to his people, so that the police officers and administrators don't dare oppress anymore."

"I have indeed come to your country at an auspicious time," said Chand. He offered the guard a few oranges, saying, "Take these fruits from my land as a present. Eat them and see how tasty they are."

Chand decided to go on a walking tour of Kanakpaton. It was incomparable in the way it was built, he thought. The roads were broad and smooth and clean, the houses sturdy and well designed. There were large ponds to provide clean water, imposing temples in every locality. It was as if Viswakarma, the divine architect, had a hand in building the city.

Chand rented a comfortable house and settled in. The bedroom was well appointed, with a large, cozy bed. Chand's cooks prepared a delicious meal for him. He ate his fill and lay down to sleep.

Nor far away, King Chandraketu too turned in for the night in his grand palace. He had just dozed off when he had a dream in which Padma appeared in her most fearsome aspect—for she had followed Chand in her airborne chariot—and warned the king that the arrival of the merchant in his kingdom with fourteen ships boded ill. Wherever Chand went, disaster struck: famine stalked the land or people dropped dead without warning. He came from a strange land: there humans grew on trees, matured as they hung and died. Chand had brought their dried heads in his ships with the intention of passing them off as a delicious fruit and bartering them for precious commodities. But whoever ate the so-called fruit would die, for it was poisonous. If Chand was allowed to sojourn in Kanakpaton the land would soon become desolate. It was best to confiscate his wealth and cargo and send him away.

King Chandraketu woke up and spent a sleepless night. The next day he told his councillors about the dream and gave a peremptory order to his chief of police: "Arrest this man at once, confiscate all his riches and his cargo, and deport him."

Meanwhile Chand had got up, breakfasted, and begun an elaborate process of prinking so as to make a good impression on King Chandraketu, whom he intended to visit. He massaged himself with sandalwood essence and was dressed to the nines. By way of exotic presents he took sandesh sweets, *paan,* and sweetened areca nut, and coconuts. He rode in a palanquin with four bearers, with attendants in front and following behind. They made up a cheerful party that proceeded at a leisurely pace, observing the attractive sights of the city.

Suddenly they were set upon by the king's men. The officer in charge of the contingent shouted at Chand, "Get off the palanquin, you bastard, the king has ordered us to take you to prison." The constables dragged him out and bound him around the waist and chest with a rope—so tightly that he feared he might faint.

"I am no thief or miscreant," Chand begged, "I was on my way to pay my respects to your king."

The constables responded by slapping him hard, right and left, on his cheeks. This was the first time ever that Chand had faced this kind of treatment. Shocked and startled, his instinctive response was that of a child.

"Ouch! Papa! Papa! Help!" he cried, as the constables buffeted, pushed, and shoved him, like any petty criminal being manhandled on his way to the lockup.

However, Chand had the presence of mind to offer money to the policemen.

"A small present," he said. "I ask only a small favor. Please take me to the royal court and tell the king that I would like to have an audience with him. Let me have an opportunity to plead my innocence before him. For I am innocent, I assure you." Here Chand handed out some more money to his captors and then continued: "I am terribly distressed at being harassed in this fashion without a trial."

The officer in charge of the police detail went up to the king and said, "Your Majesty, the alien who came with fourteen ships is under arrest. But he claims to be innocent and begs for an audience. He was on his way here to pay his respects to you when we nabbed him."

"Show him in," the king commanded. "I will give him a hearing and decide what to do."

Led up to the king's throne, Chand bowed and offered the presents he had brought. The king accepted them one at a time and asked for their names. When he was handed a coconut he gave a little start and handled it gingerly, turning it round and round and examining it from all angles. He recalled what Padma had said to him in his dream. The object in his hands was too much like a human head for it to be coincidence. The goddess had warned him about this. So this is what a dried human head looks like, he thought, a human head that grows on a tree and is poisonous. He thundered, "This man is dangerous. Take him away to prison and deal with him in an appropriate way. All the plant products he has brought are poisonous. He has come with evil intent."

Rough hands propelled Chand out of the king's chamber. So astonished was he at this turn of events that he could not even utter a faint word of protest. He rued his decision to embark on this voyage, recalled that

Sonaka had entreated him to stay home with her and wait for the birth of their son, and desperately invoked the help of Shiva and his consort.

But there was no escaping the routine torments undergone by "dangerous criminals" in police custody. He was at the receiving end of what he had so often inflicted on others with a curt word of command.

Beaten black and blue, aching in every limb and joint, that night in his miserable cell in prison Chand prayed with all his heart and soul to Chandi.

"You are the mother of the universe, the energy that drives all three realms, the mainstay of all householders, you are the day and you are the night, you are consubstantial with the great god Shiva, you are the great protectress, the savior of her devotees, and to you I turn for help, rescue me, O goddess supreme."

So heart-rendingly full of humility and submission were Chand's words that Chandi appeared before him at once and with open hand upraised in a gesture of reassurance inspired calm. Without a word Chand prostrated himself at her feet.

Chandi addressed Chand affectionately: "My son, have no fear, tomorrow morning you will be out of here. I will presently appear before Chandraketu in a dream to counteract a previous dream in which Padma poisoned his mind against you with lies."

And so Chandraketu was visited in sleep by the second goddess in the span of a couple of days. Chandi in all her divine splendor told him, "You must set Chandradhara free first thing tomorrow morning or else your city will be leveled and you and your family will be exterminated."

Chandraketu broke into a sweat and begged forgiveness with palms joined in supplication.

"Chandradhara is my spiritual son," Chandi continued. "Unfortunately, he has a running conflict with Padma, who told you some cunning lies to poison your mind against him. But no matter, you can set things right by befriending him."

Chandraketu promised to make amends, and Chandi left on her flying chariot drawn by winged lions.

As soon as it was light King Chandraketu got up and ordered his guards to go and fetch the merchant Chandradhara from prison.

The king greeted Chand with palms supplicatingly joined and pro-fuse apologies on his lips.

"You must forgive me for the suffering I have caused you," he said. "I was misled and am filled with remorse. I hope we can become friends now. After all, you are my namesake, for both our names derive from Chandra."

"Of course," agreed Chand, "and since you are my namesake, I can frankly complain to you about all that I have undergone."

All his pent-up pique came out in a sentimental torrent.

"I huddled all night cursing myself for having embarked on this voyage. Just look at these bruises, the ache is awful."

Chandraketu made conciliatory gestures and ordered his aide-de-camp to fetch the court physician.

"My doctor will take care of you," he reassured his guest.

Chand continued: "My father was called Katiswara, my name is Chan-dradhara. We are of merchant stock but have become rulers of our land. Champaknagar is my capital city, and it is known far and wide. I came with a fleet of fourteen ships to pay my respects to you and to do some trade—only to be paid in insult and injury. I don't feel like spending any more time here. I will sail from port to port, selling and buying, then go home."

"My dear friend, forgive me," the king entreated. "Let us put all the unpleasantness behind us and build on our newfound friendship. Ah, here is the good doctor. Let us have breakfast and then you'll see how he makes you feel fresh and strong again with a few emollients and tonics."

The delicious repast and the doctor's medicines worked wonders. Chand was himself again as he sat down with his namesake and fellow king.

Chandraketu again apologized for allowing himself to be misled by a dream.

"Padma is deeply antagonistic toward me," Chand explained. "That's why she showed you the dream that led to my misfortune. If only I could lay hands on her—with one blow of my *hintala* staff I'd crack open her skull."

"Tut, tut," Chandraketu chided him, "let us not speak harshly of the goddess. Go to your quarters and relax. Tomorrow morning we shall meet again."

After Chand took his leave, King Chandraketu asked his servants to produce the fruits that his visitor had presented him with the previous day. He wanted to find out what they were like—by having them tasted by one of his subjects. He called one of the palace guards, Vijay by name, and ordered him to taste a coconut.

Vijay fell at his master's feet, crying, "Your Majesty, I have a large family to support. I have served your family for long years, I began as an errand boy for your great father, how can you place me in such danger."

"Danger!" expostulated the king. "It's only a fruit, albeit an exotic one. I just want to find out what it's like."

None, of course, had the temerity to suggest he could best do so by tasting it himself, though the thought must have crossed everyone's mind.

The king continued: "I was misled in a dream by Manasa-devi into thinking the fruit is poisonous. The great goddess had her reasons for doing this. But then the great Chandi, the great god Shiva's consort, corrected my view. Therefore there is no danger."

Still, Vijay wanted some kind of insurance. "You know best, Your Majesty," he said, and added, "but just in case the fruit is poisonous and the poison is fatal, will you not in your infinite kindness look after my wife and children?"

"Yes, I will look after your family if you die after tasting the fruit," the king announced. "Now open your mouth and taste it."

Vijay opened his mouth, tilted his head back, and shut his eyes. He winced as the coconut was split open and a bit of its watery contents poured into his mouth. He didn't swallow it immediately; he let it play around his mouth, stirred by his tongue, as if he were a wine taster trying out a strange vintage. He opened his eyes, which clearly reflected pleasant surprise. Then he gulped audibly and smiled.

"Give me the rest of the coconut milk," he said, "I need to taste more of it to be able to pass judgment."

He drank the rest of the stuff with evident enjoyment and said, "Now let us see what is inside the fruit."

The thick white flesh inside the woody husk was pried free with a knife and handed to him. After a first cautious bite he ate with alacrity and finished the lot with a burp of satisfaction.

"Your Majesty was absolutely right," he declared. "It is perfectly safe. I can add that it is delicious."

Vijay picked up the fibrous outer covering of the coconut.

"Your Majesty, I wish to take this home. Who knows what delicious tastes lurk here. I will give it to my wife, and if she can cook it I will share it with her and my children."

"Feel free to take it," said the king laughing, "but I doubt if even your good wife's culinary skills will be able to create anything edible out of it."

On this delightfully comic note King Chandraketu adjourned the session of his royal court for the day.

The next morning Chand woke up feeling refreshed. He went through his preparations for the day in a cheerful mood. First, he had a bath, then he offered puja to Shiva and Chandi. His breakfast was cooked in the meantime, and he sat down to eat, and after the meal chewed *paan*.

Soon he was ready to start the day's business. He changed into suitable attire and went to King Chandraketu's court in his palanquin.

They greeted each other cordially, each inquiring affectionately, "How is my namesake today?" The king bade his guest sit beside him.

After the pleasing discovery of the gustatory properties of coconuts, King Chandraketu was eager to do trade with Chand.

"It is our good fortune that you have come to our shores to trade, bringing fourteen tall ships loaded with merchandise and produce. You can conduct your business from here. I would like to see what you have brought; as your host I deserve to have the first choice in buying your commodities. Don't you agree?"

"I would not have it otherwise, dear namesake," Chand graciously agreed.

Chand ordered his servant Tera: "Bring the things we have brought and show them one by one to His Majesty."

Tera rushed off and came back shortly with a load of things. First he put out the coconuts. King Chandraketu handled them appreciatively and handed them to his servants. Tera, whom Chand had appointed his personal assistant in appreciation of his streetwise qualities, humbly joined his palms and said to King Chandraketu, "Your Majesty, don't you think it would be a good idea to conduct trade on the basis of barter— exchanging things of equal value?"

"Yes, of course," the king agreed.

"Right," reiterated Chand. "My namesake and I will exchange one thing for another of equal value."

Chand held up a coconut and gave a sales pitch. "Inside it is a cool liquid, the coconut milk, tasty as ambrosia, and then there's delicious, creamy white flesh inside."

He added, "You must drink the coconut milk, taste the flesh, and give your opinion before we can talk of a barter."

King Chandraketu obliged and pronounced both milk and flesh to be delicious.

"I leave it to you to decide what you will give for each coconut," Chand said.

"How about ten conch shells for each coconut?" Chandraketu asked.

"You are most kind," said Chand. He ordered Tera to take care of the counting and send the shells to the ships.

Chand picked up an orange and gave a spiel. "This brilliantly colored fruit is sweet as manna inside. Each of them is worth a moonstone."

"Done," said Chandraketu.

Tera counted out the oranges and moonstones and sent the latter to the ships.

Chand picked up a large, scented lemon from his stock and sniffing it delicately, said, "If you squeeze the juice of this fruit onto your food, it enhances the taste immensely. I can let you have each lemon for a piece of coral."

"Done," said Chandraketu.

"And when you have finished a meal and had some fruit, my dear friend," said Chand, "it is time for *paan*."

With a flourish he picked up a *paan* leaf and some sliced areca nuts and, applying a patina of water-soaked lime to the leaf, he rolled up the sliced nuts in it.

"Try it, my friend, open your mouth," he said, offering the rolled leaf.

Chandraketu opened his mouth and let his friend put it in. He chewed it, first tentatively, then energetically.

"Hmm, nice," he mumbled.

Chand explained: "You see, my friend, the juice that is forming in your mouth from the combination of *paan* leaf, areca nut, and lime is good for digestion and also has a beneficial effect on the nerves, making you feel equable."

"Yes, I feel happier after chewing it," Chandraketu agreed. "I will give you gemstones in exchange."

Finally, Chand offered the golden jute fiber and said he would swap it for yak hair.

"Done."

Both parties were pleased with the day's transactions and agreed to meet again soon so that the rest of the visitor's cargo could be examined.

◆   ◆   ◆

When Chand returned to his lodgings, Tera began shaking his head and making inarticulate noises of disapproval.

"What is it?" Chand asked.

"Your Majesty," began Tera, "I am an old retainer in your family. I began working for your great father when I was a mere boy. So let me tell you about your father. He traded to make huge profits."

"What's your point?" Chand asked tetchily.

"This voyage is a disaster," Tera cried, striking his forehead with his palm to signify the bad luck that he claimed was their fate. "Instead of making a profit you are at risk of losing your capital."

"Come, come, don't exaggerate," Chand said chidingly.

"Well, you have to remember that we have brought our merchandise to this country facing tremendous dangers, risking life and limb, and spending much time. So the equivalent in value of one of our items is many times what it is back home."

"I'll remember that—it makes sense," Chand conceded.

And so, the next time Chand took his merchandise to Chandraketu's court, he was prepared to give his best as a salesman. He greeted the king with great warmth—which was reciprocated—and declared, "I have brought a wondrous stock of materials for you, my friend."

Picking up a roll of coarse cotton fabric, Chand shook it open with a sharp crackling sound.

"This is a magical material," he announced. "In the sweltering heat of summer you feel cool under it, but in winter it keeps you warm. If you wear it next to the skin, you will itch all over, but you will be purged of all the minor ailments that bother you."

Chandraketu curiously fingered the coarse cloth, then he picked up a roll of fine silken fabric and suggested a swap, one to one. Chand would have agreed if Tera hadn't picked up the silk and said matter-of-factly, "But the two aren't equal."

Tera picked up the silk cloth and without warning tore it into two. He tried to do the same to the coarse cotton: it was impossible.

"See!" he declared triumphantly. "The two cannot be considered equal."

Chand stepped in and, with the air of a wise man suggesting a compromise, declared, "Very well then, one roll of cotton is equivalent to ten rolls of silk." Turning to Chandraketu he added, "What do you say, my friend?"

Chandraketu was too startled to say anything and let the transaction proceed. A large number of rolls of the finest silk were sent to Chand's ships.

Chand offered the leaves of the jute plant next. "If you eat these as a vegetable," he said, "your body will function well. Any imbalance due to an excess of phlegm or bile in the system will be rectified and you will experience a state of well-being. My friend, you can have these if you give pearls in exchange."

"Very well," said Chandraketu.

"Work out the equation and send the pearls to the ships," Chand ordered Tera.

Now Chand picked up a radish and declared: "One cannot praise this vegetable too highly. Eaten raw, it relieves the discomfort from overeating, and it is very tasty when cooked."

"I will take it," said Chandraketu. "Tell me what you want in exchange for this and whatever else you have."

"An elephant's tusk for each radish," Chand decided. Now that he had been given carte blanche, he didn't take long to complete the barter of his entire cargo, though he didn't neglect to give a sales pitch for each item.

For cumin Chand took diamonds; saffron for turmeric; a rare gem for the plum; fine shawls for jute sacking; golden pots and pitchers for his earthen ones: he spieled, rightly, that food cooked in earthen pots tasted better and that drinking water kept in earthen pitchers became very cool.

With that Chand's barter trade with Chandraketu was completed. Back in his lodgings Chand asked Tera, "How did I do today?"

"Not too badly, Master."

THE RETURN VOYAGE

THE DAYS PASSED PLEASANTLY in Kanakpaton. Chand became a valuable adviser to Chandraketu and could have led an easy life for the rest of his days if thoughts of home and his responsibilities to his family and kingdom didn't keep occurring with increasing frequency. One day he decided it was time to embark on the return voyage. Chandraketu was sorry to hear about it and tried to tempt him into staying on permanently.

"We two namesakes form a wonderful partnership," Chandraketu said, "you help me run the country and when we have leisure we enjoy ourselves immensely. One couldn't ask for more congenial circumstances."

"Agreed, but . . ."

"Listen, my friend, I will get you a beautiful young *padmini* to marry—you know, the cynosure of womanhood according to the great sage Vatsayana's *Kama Sutra*. Raise a big, happy family here, be one of us."

At the mention of a happy family Chand remembered his family life in his native Bengal, how it had been blighted by tragedy because of Padma's animosity, and his face clouded over. He remembered that his wife

Sonaka was dead set against this expedition and wept inconsolably when he bade goodbye. Was she still waiting for him or had she given him up for dead? He burned with longing to go home.

"My friend," he said, "it's twelve years since I arrived in your country. You have given me a second home, otherwise I couldn't have stayed away from my own home so long. Now permit me to go back and pray that I find peace and happiness there."

Chandraketu realized that it would be pointless—and graceless—to continue the argument, that it was natural and inevitable that his friend should wish to take leave.

"I wish you godspeed, my friend," he said to Chand. "Have a joyous homecoming. I will always remember our friendship and the good times we've had together."

"So will I, my friend."

Chandraketu loaded his friend's ships with precious gifts and prepared to give him a spectacular send-off at the quay, with musicians, jugglers, and dancers and acrobats.

Chand had a purificatory bath and sat down to offer puja to Shiva and Chandi. He had just opened his mouth to invoke the divine couple when, with a crash of cymbals, Padma appeared before him and demanded: "Offer puja to me—overcome your animosity . . ."

"Here's my animosity," Chand thundered, picking up his *hintala* staff and brandishing it. "How dare you make such a demand after using lies in a dream to make me suffer pain and humiliation!" As the painful memories came back to Chand he lost all self-control and swung his staff at Padma: it sliced through air; Padma had vanished, with a resounding laugh, leaving Chand quivering with rage.

Chand took a few deep breaths to compose himself and began the puja again. This time there was no hitch and as soon as he invoked his adored divinities, Chandi appeared amid the swirling incense, and the cymbals and drums quickened their beat.

"Set sail, my son," she said, "I will safely guide you home. If danger threatens, I will personally take over the navigation of the fleet."

"When you are with me, I fear nothing," Chand said in passionate tones, tears of gratitude coursing down his cheeks.

Soon it was time to cast off. A cheering crowd had gathered on the quay to wave farewell to the visitors from distant Bengal who had lived in their midst as friends for twelve long years. Some of the sailors had lovers among the port's demimondaines; they came, all decked out, to see off their beaux. Chand and Chandraketu embraced and expressed a hope that they would meet again. Then Chand boarded the *Madhukar*. The music grew deafeningly loud, crackers went off, and with the rhythmic dip and rise of oars the fleet trooped out of the dock and unfurled its sails on the open sea.

It was spring, and a gentle southerly breeze held steady as the ships made their way home. The men attended to their duties conscientiously but were otherwise pensive, filled with memories of Kanakpaton and anticipatory ruminations about home; that is, they were partly nostalgic and partly excited and anxious: they would meet their families, friends, relatives after so many years. Was everyone alive and well? Who had died? Who was ill?

Excitement became the dominant feeling as the ships neared the coast of Bengal and sailed past familiar islands and places, now in reverse order. The first inhabited island they sailed past was the one where Chand had demolished Padma's puja altar. Chand laughed heartily as he recalled the incident; Padma watched from her invisible chariot.

Soon after came the conch-shell-infested stretch; then the mangrove forest where everyone got goose bumps of fear as the tigers roared. The rowers didn't dally here a moment; nor did they when they came to the crab-infested waters. When they reached the cowrie-rich stretch, they dug up the quantities of cowries they had stashed away while Lanka bound. They hurried through the stretches of riverway filled with prawns and leeches and reached Kalidaha. Here Chand called a halt. They alighted, lit fires on the bank to do their cooking, and picnicked. Chand bathed and offered puja to Shiva and Chandi.

Unseen, Padma had an urgent tête-à-tête with Neta.

"Chand's fourteen ships must be sunk," Padma said. "Tell me how I can do it."

"Kalidaha is part of a river and our stepmother Ganga is the goddess who controls all rivers. Go to her and seek her help."

Ganga had always been the good stepmother, a welcome contrast to the jealous, mean-minded Chandi; so when Padma went to her the reception was cordial, even affectionate. But as Padma explained what she wanted, Ganga balked. She knew that Chandi was giving protection to

Chand and at that moment was in fact captaining the *Madhukar*. Ganga did not want to cross Chandi—was wary, and even a little scared of her. But what would she tell Padma?

"You know, my dear," she began softly, "Chand's ships are all quite huge, I'm not sure if I know how to sink them."

Padma was crestfallen, but she rallied instantly and dealt with the situation in her characteristic manner, using the direct, aggressive approach that she had at times applied to Chandi and even to her father.

"I am sorry to see that you have been cowed by my other stepmother," Padma began, and added: "Now I'll have no alternative but to poison your waters. A million nagas will disgorge their venom into the rivers. The poison will travel upstream during high tide and downstream during the neap tide. After a few deaths people will avoid touching the water and will curse you roundly."

"Now, now, my dear, you are becoming too excited," Ganga said placatingly. "I was just trying to point out the difficulties involved."

"Then can you tell me how these difficulties may be overcome?"

"The waters at Kalidaha must be deepened," said Ganga. "Get all the other great rivers to come to Kalidaha so that there is a towering tidal wave that will sink any ship."

"Now we are getting somewhere, Mother, but the rivers won't listen to me. You must command them to come."

Since there was no getting away from it, Ganga buckled down to the task, took a deep breath and let out a deep-throated call. Then she waited, one ear cupped, the better to be able to hear any response. Within moments there was a distant rumble, coming from many directions, and steadily growing louder.

The rivers roared toward Kalidaha: the Bhagirathi, Padma, Karotoa, Saraswati, Damodar, Chandrabhaga, Jamuna, Kantabati, Prabha, Shashadhar, Narmada, Godavari, Bhaluka, Bangeswar, Mandakini, Brahmaputra, and of course the mighty Ganges.

As these rivers encountered the salty tide from the sea, the waters rose to mountain height with a terrifying roar and the sky darkened, letting loose a deadly hailstorm.

The ships were tossed about like paper boats, their moorings snapped like old thread, a tumult of desperate cries rose from the sailors. Padma watched from her invisible perch on her flying chariot, at first with satisfaction, but soon with chagrin, for the ships, under Chandi's protection, seemed proof against sinking, as if they were made of cork.

"This is insufferable!" fumed Padma. "What do you suggest, Neta? I feel like striking Chand dead."

"As I've explained, whatever happens, don't kill Chand. If you do, he'll die a hero's death, for he'll have defied you at the cost of his life. No, our dear mother must be neutralized with father's help. Go to him, beg him to make his wife go home and sit quietly while we have our way."

Padma didn't waste a moment and in no time was at her father's place—at his feet. Shiva tried to brush her off with a show of petulance.

"Stop bothering me again and again with this sticky problem of yours. I feel like abandoning everything and going into endless meditation. I am caught in the middle with your mother pulling from one side and you pulling from the other, and down there in the human world is this stubborn fellow Chand, whose devotion to me is a hundred percent, and because of that I can't be rude to him." The thought of Chand's devotion mellowed Shiva's mood. "He is really the most ardent of all my worshippers and would be terribly hurt if I scolded him."

"Such divine vanity!" chided Padma, and decided to be petulant in her turn. "How can you withdraw into meditation and forgo the pleasure of basking in absolute adoration? Instead let me leap into an inferno. My stepmother will be happy to be rid of me, and you can lead a normal life."

"Now, now, don't be impetuous, I have told you Chand will come around, and you have worked out a strategy that will do the trick," Shiva said.

"Splendid! But to make the strategy work one of the tactical moves is to sink the fourteen ships of Chand's fleet."

"Hanuman can do that," said Shiva. At his summons Hanuman appeared instantly and awaited orders.

"Go with the wind to Kalidaha and sink the fourteen ships moored there," said Shiva. "You go along and watch the action," he said to Padma.

She got on her swan-drawn chariot in high spirits and followed Hanuman.

As soon as he reached Kalidaha, Hanuman swooped down and without wasting a moment spun the ships one by one so that they whirled around like potters' wheels. Chand, taken by surprise, reeled with giddiness and begged for Chandi's help.

"Don't worry," Chandi reassured him, taking hold of the tiller of the *Madhukar*, "nothing will happen to you. Just watch the fun."

Hanuman sank thirteen ships one by one, all except the *Madhukar*, which Chandi's presence rendered invulnerable. A cry of despair escaped Chand's lips as he saw his thirteen ships vanish without a trace.

"Now watch," said Chandi, invoking Kshetrapala, the earth god.

Kshetrapala brought the thirteen ships to the surface, dripping but intact. Hanuman sank them again, with loud plops and splashes. Again, Kshetrapala produced the ships out of the depths. Chand knew that this could go on indefinitely, and yet Hanuman wouldn't be able to destroy the ships. He danced on the deck of the *Madhukar*, jeering at the great ape god. Padma frowned and clenched her teeth on her airborne chariot.

"Go to Father again and make him call our dear mother home," advised Neta.

This time Padma fell at Shiva's feet, hugging them as she cried loudly. "O Father," she sobbed, "do you want to hear what Chand says about me? If he is truly devoted to you how can he insult your daughter? He called me . . ."

"Now, now, you don't have to repeat filthy words uttered in fits of folly," said Shiva.

"You see, you know what horrid things he says, for you are all-knowing. Isn't he insulting you? And now, after you ordered Hanuman to sink the ships, your wife is defying you. After this, who will revere you as the greatest of gods?"

Shiva bestirred himself, albeit unwillingly, for there was no getting away from direct action now.

"Come with me, my child," he said, "and we'll take care of this little problem."

Shiva, dressed in tiger skins, mounted his bull-drawn chariot with Padma, while Nandi went alongside, and in a moment arrived at Kalidaha. There stood Chandi in all her glory on the *Madhukar*, with Chand capering excitedly beside her. Shiva took her by the hand and said, "Come, let's go home. The children need you. Let Padma have her way."

Chandi bristled. "So it has come to this," she said. "You are making yourself a laughingstock among gods, for you won't stand by your greatest devotee. Look at what happened to Ravana. He sacrificed his ten heads to you, and you let him perish at Rama's hand over the Sita affair. Another of your ardent devotees was King Bana—Krishna cut off his hand. King Bali was yet another loyal devotee of yours—Rama finished him off. Today none is more devoted to you than Chand, and you are abandoning him. Can anyone in their right senses worship you after all this?"

"Calm down and just listen for a minute," said Shiva. He then outlined the whole strategy involving Usha and Aniruddha to bring the trouble with Chand to a satisfactory conclusion. For that strategy to be smoothly implemented, the ships would have to be sunk for the time being.

As Chandi listened with a skeptical frown, Padma whispered into her ear: "If you don't go home at once I'll kill your sons Ganesha and Kartikeya, even though I love them, for they are my brothers."

Chandi didn't stay a moment after that.

Chand found himself all alone and helpless. Pavana, the wind god, who is Hanuman's father, hurled the ships this way and that. Chand desperately invoked Chandi, but his mantras evoked no response.

"Why have you abandoned me, O great goddess, O mother of the cosmos?" an anguished Chand cried to the heavens. He flopped down and holding his head in his hands lamented: "I took these ships all the way to distant Kanakpaton, I used trickery in the barter trade to make a fabulous profit, only to see everything devoured by the water of Kalidaha. And I may perish without seeing Sonaka and my friends again!"

"O great goddess," Chand apostrophized Chandi, "my ships are sinking—save them, for only you can do so. You are all divinities combined in one, only you can save me from my one-eyed foe."

But there was no sign of Chandi. She was back home with Shiva, feeding her children and serving her husband's meal like a good mother and wife.

Chand's sailors, both the *bhagis,* those who would have got a share of the profits, and the *shagis,* who worked for wages, were critical of their master. They said, "The gods and goddesses are ultimately one and indivisible. One cannot separate them. Shiva and Chandi and Padma are of the same divine substance. Our master has brought disaster on himself and on us by defying Padma."

As they spoke Hanuman sank the mountain-tall ships with fancy names one by one, the last to go down being the *Madhukar*. It took a while to send this one down. For while Chand stood on it Hanuman's might was of no avail. Hanuman rocked it, jumped on it, but it wouldn't go down. Chand jeered at him: "How can you with your ugly face sink my beautiful ship?" Padma, hovering invisibly whispered into Hanuman's ear the reason why he was unsuccessful: "Chand's father obtained a boon whereby a ship carrying Chand would be unsinkable."

"Aha!" cried Hanuman, knocking Chand into the water with a lightning swipe.

Chand went down, gulped water, came up gasping, while Padma, now making herself visible, laughed uproariously. Hanuman capered on the deck of the *Madhukar*, rocking it violently, and with a mighty thrust sent it down to the bottom.

Neta flung Chand a raft made of banana trees. He reached for it with both hands and hauled himself up. She flung edible lotus—*padma*—blossoms down to him. He scowled, saying, "Yuk! These have the same name as the one-eyed bitch," and taking some water into his mouth squirted it on the floating flowers. Then picking up his *hintala* staff, which had floated up to him, he smashed it down on the bobbing blossoms. Padma sent a violent wave crashing on the raft; it carried away the *hintala* staff. She swooped down and with her left hand squeezed the whole of Chand's body.

"Padma!" cautioned Neta. "Don't kill him and make him a hero. You want him to live and worship you."

Padma let go. She went to Ganga and said, "Mother, please save Chand and let him safely reach the bank." The gentle Ganga was pleased to hear this from her fiery stepdaughter and guided Chand's raft to safety. One end of it slid up the gently sloping bank while the other end bobbed up and down with the lapping waves.

Chand tried to get up and step onto firm land, but he was too weak. He had been tossed about in the raft for nine days, and when he tried to stand up his knees shook. He clambered onto the bank somehow and lay down. He was completely naked, Padma having ensured that wind and water in violent motion left him so. She chuckled to herself at the sight and dropped a loincloth. Not far from it he saw a banana peel. His mouth watered at the sight. After so many days without a bite the peel seemed like a delicacy. He wanted to make a proper meal of it and took a dip in the river. He wrapped the loincloth around his waist and with a silent prayer of gratitude to Shiva and Chandi turned to pick up the banana peel. Before bathing he had washed it and placed it on clean grass.

But it wasn't there. Padma had quietly removed it. Invisible in her chariot, she was looking at the peel in her hand and giggling. Chand has really lost his marbles, she thought; he will eat anything.

His stomach blazing with hunger, his limbs hardly able to stir, Chand slowly shuffled along. Padma assumed the form of a yogini and sat cross-legged in meditation at a spot that lay on his path. He stopped when he came up to her and said, "Where have you come from, yogini, and what are you doing here?"

"Why do you want to know about me? You have no business asking a yogini about her home and her movements. Go wherever you are headed and don't waste my time."

Chand saluted the yogini with joined palms and said, "Please hear my sad tale. My name is Chandradhara and I am a devoted slave of the great god Shiva. My home is in Champaknagar, which I left years ago to go on a trading mission to Lanka. I was returning with my fleet of fourteen ships loaded with precious commodities when they sank in Kalidaha because of the machinations of the one-eyed upstart. She could have her way because the great god and his consort withdrew their support. If you can give me the directions to Champaknagar, I'll be on my way. You know, once I broke the one-eyed bitch's hip bone with a blow of my *hintala* staff. Just see what I do if I can lay my hands on her once more."

The yogini clucked her tongue and warned him: "You are really a barbarous beast to tangle with a deity in this fashion. You should humbly offer puja to Padma; then you will receive all manner of boons and blessings."

Chand started at her words. "I know who you are," he cried. "You have put on a disguise to canvas your case. It's no use. I'll see what you can do!" He waved his feeble fists at the calmly smiling yogini, who vanished before his eyes.

Padma dropped Chand's *hintala* staff in the Gungari River near Champaknagar. It drifted up to the ghat where Sonaka came with her lady friends and her widowed daughters-in-law to offer puja to Ganga. She recognized her husband's staff as soon as she spotted it and swooned with a cry of despair. Everyone reached out to prevent her from falling on the hard platform of the ghat and hurting herself. She sat down and picked up the bobbing staff. Clutching it to her breast, she broke into a dirge. "Oh my husband," she cried, stabbing her breast with the staff, "you went to make a fortune in trade and lost your capital and your life."

Sonaka rolled on the ground; her clothes came off, but she was indifferent. "How could you nurture such animosity toward a goddess?" she cried. "You have paid with your life for your stupidity, and now we will never see you and you will never see your new son.

Word of the discovery of Chand's *hintala* staff and the inference naturally drawn from it spread like wildfire and gave rise to loud mourning among the citizens of Champaknagar. They made their way to the ghat in thousands, beating their breasts, tearing their hair, sobbing uncontrollably. The wiser and better educated of the citizens muttered mantras and wondered if their fears could be confirmed.

The schoolteacher Pandit Somai went to Sonaka and asked her to consider the matter calmly and not jump to conclusions.

"It is well known in all three realms that Chandradhara is Shiva's favorite, his most ardent devotee," the pandit pointed out. "It is therefore inconceivable that anyone would dare kill him. If you accept this reasoning you will surmise that a peculiar concatenation of circumstances has brought the *hintala* staff here. What those circumstances are we do not know, but we do know that prayers to Shiva are ever on Chand's lips and he can be sure of the great god's protection."

Sonaka composed herself sufficiently to go through the puja offered to Ganga and then returned home to shed silent tears. Padma watched from above and had a good laugh.

And she laughed too as she watched Chand walk slowly away from the banks of the Kalidaha. His stomach was still completely empty, his mind overburdened with anxiety. He shuffled along, fearful that he might collapse and not be able to get up again. The fields he walked through were barren, without a single tree or plant that might offer him something edible. There wasn't a single soul in sight either. His eyes were alert: surely someone would cross his path.

Suddenly someone did materialize—in the distance, on a rough track, coming toward him. Chand tried to speed up to hasten the encounter but couldn't: he began panting and slowed down to a shuffle again.

The stranger had also spotted him and spoke when they were within hailing distance. "Namaskar, stranger, where are you from and what is your name?"

Chand stopped and tried to gather enough strength to answer clearly. The stranger, without waiting for a reply, continued: "I am Dhanpati, a merchant, and I live in a village not far from here."

Chand managed to utter his name at last and went on to describe his family background and the unhappy circumstances that had brought him here. He concluded: "I am lucky to have come through the ordeal alive. But I am so weak from hunger that I won't be able to walk much farther. It is surely my good karma that has brought me to you."

"My village isn't very far," said Dhanpati. "You will have a good meal as soon as we get there. I am beginning to like you and if you will allow me I would like to make a proposal to you."

"Feel free to tell me about it, I will do whatever you suggest," said Chand.

"Then listen," said Dhanpati. "I have an unmarried daughter at home. I haven't been able to find a husband for her so long because she has a few drawbacks."

"Like what?" asked Chand, less out of curiosity than just to keep the conversation going. He had already decided that he would do whatever was asked just to be able to eat proper meals.

"She isn't good-looking," said Dhanpati.

"There are many girls who aren't good-looking but are happily married," said Chand.

"That's true, that's true," agreed Dhanpati with a telling sigh.

"Is your daughter very ugly?"

"Perhaps, perhaps."

"Does she have pale green eyes like a cat."

"Why, yes."

"Does she have thinning hair?"

"Umm, yes."

"Is she hunched?"

"You could say so."

"Does she have a sooty complexion, does she bend in three places when she walks?"

"People have said so."

"Does she have sores on her hands?"

Dhanpati nodded.

"Does she have callused fingers, is she blind in one eye and deaf in one ear?"

Dhanpati didn't reply. Instead he said, "If you marry her you will want nothing."

"What's the use of beauty?" said Chand. "Your daughter is to my mind the equal of a talented and beautiful celestial being. My body is about to collapse from hunger. Beauty can't keep me alive, only a proper meal can."

"Here we are," said Dhanpati. "We have arrived." He gave a fresh loin-cloth to Chand and asked him to have a bath in the pond so that they could sit down to a meal.

Chand ate with relish. The grains of rice were like manna on his tongue. He had his fill and rubbed his distended belly with satisfaction. A pleasurable numbness stole over his body, and he yawned, ready to fall asleep. Dhanpati showed him to a bed in one of the outer rooms and said, "I will talk to the priest tomorrow to determine an auspicious hour for the happy event." Chand fell asleep wondering how he would make his escape before the happy event could take place.

Dhanpati talked to his wife about the accidental meeting with Chand as a result of which they would be relieved of the burden of having an unmarried daughter.

Later, as Dhanpati fell asleep, Padma appeared in a dream and re-buked him for pampering Chand.

"Just because Chand will marry your daughter, will you support him as if he were a child? Put him to work. Let him work for the family and not live like a drone. Send him out in the morning to cut firewood."

So in the morning Dhanpati handed Chand a dao, a curved machete, and said, "It isn't right to let you eat without working. Go and cut some firewood before you have your morning meal."

Chand took the dao and went out, muttering to himself, "I can sense the one-eyed bitch's machinations behind this as well."

He went into the forest in the company of a couple of woodcutters, jolly fellows who befriended him, swapping amusing stories as they went. The woodcutters stopped in a clearing, shared their *paan* with Chand and, girding up their loins, began chopping wood. Chand joined in but found he had no knack for the job. The sun neared the zenith and yet Chand hadn't cut enough wood to make a single bundle. The woodcutters prepared to go home, tying up their bundles of wood.

"Won't you go home?" they asked Chand.

"I haven't even got enough wood to make one bundle," said Chand. "I fear Dhanpati will have second thoughts about marrying his daughter to me and will kick me out without giving me any food."

The woodcutters felt sorry for Chand, who had told them the whole story of his misfortunes and the strange proposal from Dhanpati.

"Here, take one bundle from us," they said, "if that will help."

"You are most kind," enthused Chand. "I will be able to make up one bundle. With two bundles I should be able to placate my prospective father-in-law."

The woodcutters left. Chand hacked away at dry branches. In one of the trees he noticed something bulbous that he would be able to reach if he climbed onto one of the lower branches. A jackfruit, he thought. It was indeed a jackfruit tree, and he was by now hungry again; a jackfruit would be a delight to eat in the heat of the afternoon. Let me tie up my bundle, he thought, then eat before setting off.

But the jackfruit he saw wasn't a jackfruit; it was a delusion foisted on him by Padma. When he climbed the tree and reached for it he realized what it was in reality: a hornet's nest. They stung him in the face and he fell from the tree and rolled on the earth in agony.

"It's the one-eyed bitch again," he groaned. From above came Padma's mocking laughter.

After a while, when the pain of the stings had subsided, Chand picked up the two bundles of firewood and set off for the nearest village with the intention of selling one of them and buying some clothes with the money.

"Firewood! Firewood!" he called like a common vendor.

A potter stopped him and asked the price of a bundle.

"An ounce of gold," said Chand.

"You are a crook and a swindler!" cried the potter. His friends came and pounced on Chand, kicking and butting him. The potter snatched away the bundle of firewood and threw some cowries at Chand's feet.

Chand picked up the cowries and thought: I'll spend half the cowries on clothes and the other half on the ferry that will take me back to Dhanpati. He went to a village of weavers and cried out: "Who wants to sell clothes?" Thinking that a merchant had come to buy his supplies wholesale, the weavers crowded round Chand. The one who got to him first took him by the hand and led him home. The weaver displayed his wares, mentioning prices, which ranged from ten to twenty rupees.

Chand felt foolish. "I have these cowries," he said, adding by way of a joke, "will you give me anything in exchange?"

The weaver wasn't amused. He started abusing Chand, calling him a cheat and a thief. The shouts drew the other weavers who ringed Chand and roughed him up. He fell down, hurting his ribs, then got up and ran for his life.

Padma chuckled. "The poor fellow has lost his common sense," she said in mock commiseration.

Chand still managed to cling to one bundle of firewood. On reaching Dhanpati's home he dropped it in the doorway. The firewood metamorphosed into hundreds of serpents that hissed and slithered all over the place. People dropped everything and ran, many tripped and were divested of their clothes.

Dhanpati cried out: "This fellow is an *ojha*. I won't have him in my family." He threw Chand out by the scruff of his neck. Humiliated and famished, Chand went away, tears coursing down his face.

He stopped at a pond to drink; water was all he had been able to ingest that day. Not far away there were some men working in a rice field, weeding it. In such cases the landowner was usually ready to employ extra laborers to get the work done quickly. Chand went and asked if he could work too. The landowner gave him some cowries as an advance on his wages and some food as well by way of a midday meal. Chand gratefully opened his hands to accept the food. When he had eaten, the landowner gave him a weeder and asked him to get going.

Rejuvenated by the food, Chand began weeding the field, but to his dismay found himself inadvertently cutting off the rice plants instead of the weeds. Try as he might he couldn't do otherwise. The landowner ran toward him, shouting and gesticulating. He snatched away the weeder, took back the cowries and with a few wild kicks drove Chand away.

Chand trudged on disconsolately, observed from on high by Padma. When the merchant was utterly exhausted and ready to drop, she sent five nagas who had put on the appearance of dervishes. They were outlandishly attired and behaved like drunks or drug addicts. Their appearance heightened Chand's anxiety. The dervishes encircled Chand and scrutinized him. One of them said, "It's good that we've found a Hindu to join our group." He said to Chand, "Here is a skullcap, put it on your head and come with us. We'll go around begging, the six of us." Chand was in no position to say no.

The dervishes pushed Chand to the front of the group when they came to a house to beg. Sometimes the householder threw stale rice at him. If the householder happened to have had his meal he would take a sip of water and squirt it out of his mouth at Chand. While Chand suffered these indignities a dervish behind him would knock off his cap, another would put it back on, and when the distraught merchant mumbled the name of his beloved god Shiva in supplication, a third dervish would shout at him: "Why do you take the name of a *bhuta*? Take the name of the holy prophet instead!" Then, suddenly, as if at the wave of a magic wand, the five dervishes vanished. Chand collapsed in tears, trembling with rage against the one-eyed foe who was amusing herself at his expense.

Chand walked on alone, feeling like a homeless vagabond. He began to feel hungry again. But he perked up when he found himself in familiar surroundings: Bijoynagar lay ahead, and he had an old friend there, a namesake, Chandradhara. The two friends embraced with tears of joy at their reunion. The Chandradhara from Champaknagar accompanied the Bijoynagar Chandradhara to the latter's home, telling once again the story of his many adventures and misadventures.

The wife of the Bijoynagar Chandradhara cooked a range of dishes for dinner—leafy vegetables, shredded and fried; fried vegetable cakes; small fry in gravy, with jute leaves; fish in sour gravy; diced bottle-gourd in a spicy gravyless curry; the prized *rui* carp in a hot curry. And, of course, boiled rice of the finest quality.

Chand sat down with his friend and host. Servants served them large helpings, but Padma would not allow her antagonist the pleasure of eating to his satisfaction. She sent an elusive, magical rat that gobbled up whatever was put on Chand's plate before he could taste even a morsel. His host, unaware of this strange phenomenon, ate his fill. Once again Chand (from Champaknagar) had to spend the night on an empty stomach.

In the morning the Bijoynagar Chandradhar found his house teeming with fierce nagas of various shapes and sizes. Having heard everything from his namesake about the ongoing struggle with Padma, he knew the reason behind this dangerous invasion. He woke up his friend and told him about it.

"It's that one-eyed bitch! If I only had my *hintala* staff with me, I'd show her!"

The host looked grim and annoyed. "My friend," he said, "I fear for the lives of my wife and children. It would be unfair to make them suffer because of your stubborn animosity toward the goddess. Your attitude is foolish and wrong. I must ask you to leave at once and go home to Champaknagar. My men will escort you to the road that will take you home."

Going home as soon as possible was also our Chand's desire, but to be given an unceremonious shove was not pleasant. It would rankle; Padma had damaged an old friendship. Anyway, he put these thoughts behind him and concentrated on what lay ahead. Once he hit the high road, Champaknagar was a few hours' walk away. He was a king returning to his capital, but what a sorry sight he had become. If he made his appearance in his present state he would feel terribly embarrassed. Worse, people would titter; he would become the joke of his own kingdom. What should he do then, he wondered.

As Chand advanced with slow steps and with furrowed brow, Padma arrived in Champaknagar and, almanac in hand, strolled the city in the guise of an astrologer. Sonaka, who now spent as much time as she could gazing at the road—for her hopes of seeing her husband come home alive had been rekindled—spotted the astrologer and sent a servant to summon her.

Sonaka respectfully greeted the astrologer, offered her a comfortable seat, and asked her to give a reading.

"My husband is missing," Sonaka said, "and I am naturally anxious. Please consult your books and charts and tell me what you find."

The astrologer confidently declared, "Your husband Chand is alive and is on his way home."

Sonaka clutched the astrologer's hand, as if she wanted some guarantee that the prediction was dependable.

"No harm will come to him, he is alive and well. I will burn my books if I'm proved wrong."

Sonaka sighed with relief.

"However," continued the astrologer, "you can expect a small problem. A thief will try to break into your house, so instruct servants and guards to be alert."

"I will ask them to be on the lookout round the clock," said Sonaka, gratefully pressing gold coins into the astrologer's hands.

"Listen," said the astrologer by way of parting advice, "make sure there are sticks and stones handy so that you can round upon the thief and give him a drubbing as you capture him."

Sonaka passed on these instructions with doubled seriousness, and so whoever passed by the palace ran the risk of being stopped as a suspected thief.

Chand arrived at his palace in the evening. Because of his shabby attire he did not enter through the main door but made a detour and sneaked into the inner quarters under cover of darkness.

One of the maids, sent to cut banana leaves to be used on the brass plates for eating the evening meal, noticed that there was a strange man skulking among the banana trees. She withdrew quietly and reported to Sonaka: "There is a thief hiding in the banana grove." The information was passed on to the guards, who surrounded the grove and closed in. At a signal they rushed at the "thief," aiming stones as they advanced, and then attacking their quarry with their sticks.

Poor Chand! He was covered in wounds and bruises, he bled in a number of places. He made a sudden dash to escape and was chased by a motley crowd of armed guards, servants, maids. He slipped and fell and hurt his knees and hands. His pursuers were immediately upon him. He was now a bearded man: all these days of his ordeal he had neither the time nor the opportunity to shave or trim his growth. The attackers tugged at his beard. They aimed slaps and blows at his face and body. They took hold of his hair and dragged him indoors. He collapsed on the floor.

The ladies of the house joined in. The six widowed daughters-in-law kicked him from behind and then brought flaming brands with which they torched his beard and mustache. An unpleasant odor rose with the smoke. Sonaka came, lamp in hand, to have a look at the "thief" and gave a cry of shock.

She fell at Chand's feet, crying, "My lord, O my lord! What has brought you to such a pass? It's years since you left home to trade in distant Lanka, and it seems you have lost everything, your ships, your capital, your men, all because of your animosity toward Padma."

"Let me tell you what happened," said Chand. And he gave a detailed account once again of the voyage, how he had cheated the Lankans and made huge profits, and how the one-eyed Padma had reduced him to his present state.

Sonaka spoke with great concern and sympathy, but she was none-theless firm in censuring her husband.

"You have set fire to your own house," she said. "You have courted disaster by opposing Manasa-devi."

Chand spoke softly to calm her down. "Don't cry, it's all right now. I have come home in spite of all the obstacles and dangers. What can the bitch do now? We will live quietly, you and I, and if Shiva and Chandi are kind they will bless us with children who will take the places of the departed ones. We will not lack for wealth either. All my sorrows vanished the moment I saw you. Now I would like you to cook me a hearty meal, for I am famished."

Sonaka took heart from Chand's calm, confident speech. She wiped her tears and went to the kitchen to prepare a sumptuous meal. Chand had a bath and changed into freshly, laundered attire and sat down to eat. After a hearty meal he rinsed his mouth and chewed *paan*. It was wonderful to be back home, going through the usual activities of a normal household. He anticipated a restful night's sleep, for the first time in days.

Chand went into the royal bedchamber that he shared with his wife. He stopped short after stepping in. A youth lay asleep in the bed.

"Sonaka! Sonaka!" he yelled.

Sonaka dropped everything and came, wondering why the urgent summons that too had an undertone of rage.

"Who is sleeping in our bed?" Chand demanded. "Have you lost your senses at this mature age? You have disgraced yourself, your family, your caste. Who is this lusty young fellow sleeping in your bed? You never strayed in young age, but now you have ruined the reputation of the merchant community. You are my lawfully wedded wife, known to be of good character, chaste, devoted to your husband. Why have you ruined your reputation? Is there such delight in sin that you can throw away your good name?"

Sonaka burst into laughter; Chand gaped at her.

"Meet our son Lakshmindar, a handsome, strapping young fellow," Sonaka said.

Chand slumped on the bed, a sheepish look on his face.

"If you have any doubts, my lord," said Sonaka, "read the declaration you signed before leaving for Lanka."

She threw the note on the bed. Chand picked it up and read what he had written, and everything came back to him, Sonaka handing him pen and palm leaf at the last moment and telling him she was pregnant, which he didn't quite believe at the time, for he knew that false pregnancies were common in aging women who craved children.

Chand woke up the sleeping boy and surprised him by taking him in his arms and kissing him on his cheeks and forehead.

"Your father," said Sonaka to Lakshmindar. The boy smiled, rubbing his eyes.

"You will have to sleep in your own room," said Sonaka. Lakshimdar got up and left, hugging his pillow to his chest.

"Sonaka, our son is a young man," said Chand. "Where's his wife? Or hasn't he married yet?"

"How could I think of his marriage when there's a dire prediction that he will be bitten by a venomous serpent on his wedding night?"

"Who are you afraid of?" said Chand. "If we are cautious and take all precautions, there will be nothing to fear from nagas. They will be quite powerless. Now that I'm home, I'll get him married with due pomp. Tomorrow morning I'll send for the matchmaker and find out who is the best match for him."

"No, no, I beg you," Sonaka implored. "I don't want to lose my sole surviving son. I have told him about the warning and persuaded him that it's best if he stays celibate."

Nothing that Chand said would make Sonaka budge. Listening in on the conversation from up above, Padma frowned. If Lakshmindar didn't marry, her grand plan would stall. Something had to be done and done quickly. Padma went to Neta and had a whispered conference to decide on the next step.

Lakshmindar had a maternal uncle who lived in Champaknagar with his beautiful young wife Kausalya. Uncle and aunt were extremely fond of their nephew, whose unfortunate circumstances elicited their sympathy and concern and induced them to lavish their affection on him. Kausalya, who had a cheerful, lively personality, was particularly close to Lakshmindar and would often joke with him about getting him a beautiful wife. Lakshmindar, though bashful, secretly enjoyed being teased by his comely aunt.

Kausalya is an attractive wench, thought Padma; I will enjoy watching a sexual intrigue involving her. Neta had suggested a dramatic ploy to force Lakshmindar's mother to change her mind.

As Lakshmindar slept alone in his room, Padma sent an apsara to impersonate Kausalya in a dream. She was at her most seductive as she sidled up to the youth and, putting her arms around him, whispered huskily, "Don't you know why I joke with you about girls and getting you married? It is because I find you attractive. Aren't you attracted to me? Look at my lips, they are full and sensuous. Wouldn't you love to kiss them? I'd love it if you did. Go ahead."

"This is only a dream," muttered Lakshmindar.

"Of course, but I want you to come to me when we are both awake."

Lakshmindar sat up, wide awake but with the dream indelibly imprinted on his consciousness. He couldn't go back to sleep; he had just been taken over by an obsession. In the morning he knew what he must do. He knew all the habits of his aunt; he knew that she went to bathe in a pond at a certain hour when the place was deserted. Had she got into this habit so that she could have assignations there if she wanted? Well, she would have her first assignation with him at the pond.

Lakshmindar surprised Kausalya as she prepared to step into the pond. "Here I am," he said, "just as you wanted."

"Oh, it's you!" said Kausalya. "What are you talking about?"

"Don't act innocent, you were quite forthright in the dream."

"You are talking in riddles."

"Just like the typical woman—a tease. I know what you want and I will give it to you."

Lakshmindar was on her, tearing off her sari, wrestling her to the ground, forcing himself into her. He was like one possessed, and when the fit had passed, stole off like a wild cat that had wrung a chicken's neck and carried it in its mouth.

When she had recovered sufficiently from the brutal assault, Kausalya got up, covered her face with the tattered edge of her sari, and staggered to her sister-in-law's house. Avoiding everyone, she sneaked in through a side entrance and went straight to Sonaka.

"Who is it?" Sonaka asked.

Kausalya fell sobbing at her feet.

"What has happened?" Sonaka asked, "why are your clothes torn, why are you sobbing?"

Kausalya sobbed out her story. Sonaka was stunned. Just then Chand came in and stared in disbelief. His sister-in-law in tears and in tatters, his wife in a state of shock—something horrendous must have happened. He didn't need to hear every detail; he soon knew that his son had violated Kausalya.

"Sonaka," he said, "put Kausalya to bed. She has suffered a terrible ordeal."

Kausalya said, "We will go back to our village home. It is impossible for me or my husband to live in Champaknagar any longer."

It was not a decision with which anyone could argue. But Chand and Sonaka had to live with their son, and something had to be done about him. Chand said firmly, "Sonaka, he must marry or else he will become a wild beast. I am not afraid of that one-eyed bitch. Did she say he will be killed on his wedding night? I will build an airtight steel chamber where he will spend the night. After that the curse will have no validity."

The next morning the royal court of Champaknagar assembled for the first time in over twelve years. Chand appeared in full regalia and addressed a full house. His military commanders were there, and his ministers, councillors, and advisers. Venerable Brahmins sat chanting mantras and offering blessings to the king; florists came and garlanded him; and astrologers made optimistic predictions. Singers and dancers gave a performance to welcome the king back home.

Chand gave a brief account of his voyage and then broached a new subject. "My son Lakshmindar is of marriageable age, so I appeal to you all to help me find a bride for him."

A venerable Brahmin pandit called Sringi stood up and said, "The magnificent city of Manikyapaton has a wealthy inhabitant called Harihar, and he has an exquisitely lovely daughter, five years of age, who would make an excellent match."

"Too young," said Chand." In fact I know that Chandradhar, from Kanchanpaton, has an eight-year-old daughter, but even her I would consider too young for Lakshmindar. If anyone can think of someone older, let him speak.

Again Sringi stood up, "There is an incredibly beautiful girl in Ujaninagar, daughter of the king, whose name is Sahé. She is twelve years old, extraordinarily beautiful, a true *padmini* type. There is none lovelier in the three realms."

"Yes," said Chand, "she is just the girl for my Lakshmindar. Now let us send a proposal and get everything ready for a grand wedding."

THE MARRIAGE OF BEHULA
AND LAKSHMINDAR

FATHER AND SON set off in great pomp for Ujaninagar. Chand took a large box filled with the five legendary precious stones to give as a gift to the prospective bride. These are ruby, sapphire, diamond, pearl, and coral. He put the box in the care of a trustworthy aide. Lakshmindar rode an elephant, as was fitting for a virile, young prince. Chand chose to travel in a palanquin, whose motion caused the least strain among the various modes of transport. An armed escort on horses and chariots, along with conch-blowers, pipers, and drummers, accompanied the king and the prince. And there were two Brahmins who had key roles to play, Jashai, the astrologer, and Sringi, the sage.

The party reached Ujaninagar safely and at Chand's suggestion camped by a pleasant lake known as Madansagar, which means "the sea of erotic love" and had been so named because of its popularity as a trysting place for lovers.

As Chand's men put up tents in a pleasant grove with many champak and *nageswara* plants, Padma hurried to the house of Sahé, the merchant king. Behula had had her midday meal and was deep in a siesta. Padma passed on to her an exciting message in a dream.

"You've had enough rest, my dear," Padma told her. "Go to Madan-sagar on the pretext of having a swim and get a glimpse of your lord and husband. He is a handsome youth called Lakshmindar, son of Chan-dradhara, merchant king of Champaknagar."

Behula's eyes opened wide; a strange excitement gripped her. She called her nurse and took her along to ask for her mother's permission.

"Mother," she said to Sumitra with joined palms. "I want to go for a dip in Madansagar with my friends. The weather is warm and a swim is just what one needs to feel fresh after a nap."

"I don't know why you want to swim in that lake," said Sumitra with a frown. "After marriage your husband will be responsible for you, but now you are in our care, and you are a princess. Is it proper that you should go to that lake?"

"Mother," Behula pouted, "I am not an irresponsible girl, am I? And Nurse is coming along. Do say yes. Please, please, please."

"All right," Sumitra relented. "But don't take too long and come straight back home."

"Promise."

And so Behula and her friends went to Madansagar and began mer-rily sporting in the water.

A Brahmin widow too went for a bath and got into the lake close to where the giggling, high-spirited girls were splashing water at each other. Behula kicked at the water to splash her friends, and some of the water fell on the widow.

The old woman angrily looked up and recognizing Behula as the cul-prit told her, "That's not a nice thing you've done. Aren't you afraid of what might happen if you insult an old Brahmin widow in such a manner?"

The widow's anger got the better of her and she quivered all over as she delivered a curse: "A snake will kill your husband on your wedding night."

Behula took issue with the old woman over this. "You are cruel and unfeeling," she said. "I admit I splashed you with water, but only inad-vertently. In such cases it is humane to be forgiving. Instead you have hurled at me a terrible curse. But let me tell you how I will deal with it. I will bring the dead back to life and earn recognition as an exemplary wife. Since you have cursed me I should reciprocate and put a curse on you."

Before Behula could go any further, the old woman vanished. She was of course none other than Padma.

Did Behula catch a glimpse of her partner? In the altercation with the widow she had forgotten all about him, nor would she have seen him if she hadn't: he was enjoying a long siesta. But Behula, unbeknownst to herself, had attracted the attention of the young fellow's father.

Chand noticed the beautiful Behula as soon as she appeared on the ghat of Madansagar. Here is an embodiment of ideal feminine beauty, he thought. And when he saw a demonstration of her feisty spirit he knew that she would make an ideal wife.

Chand called Sringi the sage and said, "This is the girl I would like my son to marry. Go and find out her family background."

After a while Sringi came back chuckling.

"It was very easy to find out the girl's particulars," he said. "She is Behula, daughter of Sahé, the merchant king of Ujaninagar."

Chand laughed with delight. He and his party spent the night in their lakeside camp. The next morning Chand called on Sahé; he was accompanied by Pandit Sringi and a few close aides. They found Sahé holding court.

Chand greeted his royal counterpart and signaled an aide to present the box containing the five varieties of precious stones. Sahé inquired about his visitor's personal particulars. Pandit Sringi said, "One of the great kingdoms of the world is Champaknagar. Its founder was King Katiswara, of the merchant caste. My master is his son, Chandradhara. He is famed for his wealth and power, as well as his charity and spiritual accomplishments."

Sahé nodded slightly to acknowledge that Chand's fame had preceded him. Pandit Sringi continued: "Having learned that you have a marriageable daughter, King Chandradhara has traveled to your kingdom to ask for her hand for his son."

Chand nodded to signify that the pandit had put things across accurately. Sahé stood up and invited Chand to a seat beside his.

Chand sat down and said, "You are an honor to the merchant caste and it is my earnest desire that our two houses be united by marriage."

Sahé replied: "To enter into such ties with your family would be greatly desirable, but I have to confess that I find an impediment in your conflict with Padma. Because of that I cannot assent to your proposal."

"Why are you scared of nagas?" expostulated Chand. "I have Shiva's blessings, thanks to which I can if I want conquer the world. Who acknowledges Padma as a deity? I broke her hip with a blow from my *hintala* staff. She is blind in one eye—who has ever heard of a one-eyed deity? If she is a powerful goddess, why doesn't she cure her blind eye? She has no standing among the great gods and goddesses and avoids them for fear of being slighted. A sage married her, being told she is Shiva's daughter, but soon realized his blunder and abandoned her. That tells you something about her character."

Sahé became agitated and began berating his guest: "You are an ignorant barbarian. Or else how can you talk like this about the mother of Astika, the sage, and the sister of Vasuki, the serpent king? With her venomous glance she felled both Shiva and Chandi. She is Shiva's daughter and the mother of the universe. How dare you speak ill of her, forgetting what she has dealt out to you? She has killed six of your sons and will kill the seventh as well. You have ruined your life by defying Manasa-devi."

Sahé turned to the gathered assembly and, standing up in his agitation, declared: "The fellow has abused Padma in my presence and deserves to be kicked out of here."

Sahé's retainers rounded upon Chand and with blows and buffets drove him out.

"Why did I come here with the marriage proposal?" Chand ruefully lamented, nursing his injuries as he set off for home.

Padma decided to remedy this setback to her plans. She adopted the disguise of a Brahmin widow—of course, not the one who had squabbled with Behula by the lake. Padma appeared in this guise before Behula and told her about Chand's aborted mission. "Chand is king of Champaknagar," Padma said, "and his only living son Lakshmindar is handsome as a demigod and would make a fit bridegroom for one as lovely and accomplished as you are. Your father insulted and expelled Chand over a minor difference of views."

Behula called her nurse and asked her if she knew anything about the incident. The nurse summed up what had happened. Behula was critical of her father for his impetuosity.

"What is decided by fate regarding one's life and marriage on the day of the Sasthi ritual cannot be altered by anyone," Behula declared. "When parents have a daughter, all they can do is give her a good upbringing. Whether she will get a good man for her husband or a good-for-nothing is determined by her karma. I want you to go to Mother and tell her what has happened and also what I have told you."

The nurse went to Sumitra and did as asked. Sumitra was very pleased with Behula's attitude and told her husband about it. By now Sahé's temper had cooled and hearing what Behula thought made him rue his impetuosity.

"I have been quite thoughtless," Sahé said to his wife. "When the word spreads, all my acquaintances will laugh at me. This embarrassing story will keep away prospective suitors in the future."

Sahé grew worried and called his court priests and instructed them to persuade Chand to return to Ujaninagar and resume negotiations for his son's marriage.

The priests caught up with Chand's homeward-bound party. They said to him, "We have been sent by King Sahé. He is full of regrets for his behavior and requests you to return and resume the talks. Anger in noble persons is always short-lived and he apologizes for giving way to it."

But Chand, sore from the roughing up, felt piqued.

"How can I go back after such humiliation?" he asked.

Pandit Somai, one of the Brahmin priests in Sahé's court, soothed his hurt feelings by quoting words of wisdom from the scriptures and persuaded him to turn back.

Sahé was waiting to welcome Chand back. With admirable humility Sahé said in the presence of the large number of people—courtiers, court officials, and ordinary citizens—who had gathered: "I beg forgiveness for having wronged you. It was done unthinkingly. I sincerely wish to see our two families united through matrimony and if you have no objection you may ask your astrologer to cast horoscopes and confirm the compatibility of the two young persons and to determine the most auspicious day and time for the wedding."

Chand called his court astrologer to do the calculations; it was found that the match would be a perfect one, and the fourth night of the tenth lunar month was the best time for the wedding to take place. Both prospective in-laws were pleased to hear this.

Sahé said, "You have seen my daughter, but I am yet to see your son."

Chand replied, "I will send for him straightaway. Your daughter is lovely as the full moon, and I think you will find my son handsome enough to make the two of them a very good-looking couple."

Chand sent Pandit Sringi to fetch Lakshmindar. The pandit got Lakshmindar to change quickly into a splendid attire in which he looked like a demigod and took him to Sahé's court.

Lakshmindar respectfully greeted his father-in-law-to-be, bending down to touch Sahé's feet. Sahé took him by his arms and embraced him warmly; none could have hoped for a handsomer son-in-law. The three men sat down together and ate *paan* out of a golden tray. Sumitra spied on them through a window and was greatly taken with the handsome youth; so were the other women in the royal household.

Sahé invited Chand and his party to spend the night at his palace.

"My men will show you to your quarters," Sahé said, "so that you may wash and relax. We will meet again at dinner, for which I'll give instructions to my wife and daughter, for they are in charge of the kitchen."

"There is a small problem though," Chand said. "Drinking saltwater during my trading mission to Lanka has had a peculiar effect on my stomach. Now I can only eat iron grains boiled like rice. I have a supply of iron grains with me. I'll give them to you and I'll be much obliged it you ensure that they are properly cooked."

Sahé was puzzled by this strange request but took the grains and gave them to Sumitra, explaining what needed to be done. Sumitra too was bewildered and wondered aloud how iron grains could be boiled till they became soft as boiled rice.

Behula volunteered to cook the iron grains. She spoke with such confidence that Sahé went to Chand and said, "Go, take a bath and come to dinner. It will soon be ready: my daughter is cooking the iron grains."

Behula heated ghee in a copper pot and put in the grains steeped in water. She kept stoking the hearth with fresh firewood, but to no avail. The iron grains showed no sign of softening. Her efforts were doomed, it seemed. The consequences were staggering. It wasn't just a question of cooking something, Behula's position as a woman and wife-to-be was at stake. By voluntarily undertaking the task she had put herself to a test. If she failed it, she might as well immolate herself.

While such dire thoughts passed through her mind she seemed to hear a voice asking her to invoke Padma's help.

As soon as she did so Padma appeared and granted her a boon: iron would cook to a delicious soft consistency at her hands. Behula cooked the iron grains, served them on a *thala* with five accompanying vegetarian dishes and sent for her father-in-law-to-be.

Sahé led Chand to the dining room and they sat down to dinner.

"Here is your special rice, cooked by Behula," Sahé told Chand.

"Wonderful!" exclaimed Chand. "Cooking iron grains is the ultimate test for a housewife, and your daughter has passed with flying colors. I am lucky to have been able to forge ties of marriage with your family."

The next morning Chand and his entourage returned to Champaknagar. Chand told Sonaka about the arrangements made so far and the difficult test that Behula had passed with distinction. Sonaka smiled as she listened—it was an ambiguous smile, compounded of joy and apprehension.

"We have lost six sons," she said, "and there is the danger of losing the son we were lucky to have in our declining years. The threat of a naga attack on his wedding night hangs over him. What is the point of marrying if one can't enjoy a long life?"

"There is also no point in giving in to fear. We'll have our son married, and he'll spend his wedding night with his bride in a steel chamber no snake can enter. Tomorrow morning I'll order the construction of the steel chamber."

The next day Chand summoned Binode, the architect and builder, to the court.

"Have a *paan* and listen carefully," Chand said. "I want you to build a steel chamber that will be absolutely airtight."

Binode went home to get the necessary materials and equipment from his workshop, brooding as he went on his predicament: he could not refuse a royal commission, but accepting it meant angering Padma. At home his wife noticed Binode's anxious expression and asked what was bothering him. He explained. His wife thought for a moment and said, "Build the chamber but leave a hairbreadth chink that no one will notice." Binode breathed a sigh of relief at this simple solution to a serious problem.

Binode set to work, measuring out sheets of steel, putting up rows of steel pillars, fashioning a door and hinges, building an inner bedroom, which was installed with a gold bedstead. Gems like emeralds, pearls, and coral were used to decorate the structure, and yellow and vermilion dye were used to paint charming pictures on the walls. A hairbreadth chink was left at an inconspicuous spot and filled up with vermilion paste. The king came to see and was very pleased; Binode and his workers were paid in gold and silver.

Word reached Padma that the steel chamber had been built. She flew into a rage and sought Neta's advice.

"Visit Binode," Neta counseled. "He will tremble with fear when he sees you. Ask him to leave a little chink in the steel structure."

Padma went, bedecked with writhing serpents, and called Binode. He nearly fainted when he saw her.

She would have gone on and boasted about her prowess—how she had knocked out her own father and stepmother, not to mention a host of lesser beings. But it proved unnecessary.

Binode said, "O great goddess, mother of the universe, I took care to ensure that the king's purpose wouldn't be served by the steel chamber: I left a hairbreadth chink and covered it with vermilion paste that can be removed when necessary." Padma went away, pleased with the cunning of the man and also his loyalty to her.

Chand meanwhile asked Pandit Jashai to make astrological calculations and determine the best time for the wedding ceremony. The pandit gave the answer before long. Chand then wrote to Sahé informing him of the astrologer's findings. Both families began preparations for the prenuptial purificatory rites, first for the bridegroom and then for the bride. The events took place in the evening. Relatives, friends, acquaintances, Brahmins were invited and fed, while loud music played. There was a delegation from the bride's side at the groom's rites; and vice versa. The bride and the groom were given a bath by married womenfolk after their bodies were massaged with herbal preparations and scrubbed with loofahs. After the bath the young people put on new clothes and sat down while their family priests went through rituals for good luck. A pitcher with mango twigs was placed before them and Vedic rites were performed. At Behula's rites, a chaplet of flowers was placed on her head.

Now came the wedding. Chand declared at the morning assembly of his royal court that all preparations were to be made to go in a mammoth procession to Ujaninagar. Richly caparisoned elephants with ornate howdahs, horses with decorated saddles and tinkling bells around their necks, palanquins with cushioned seats, musicians playing a variety of instruments, contingents of armed escorts, all were swiftly marshaled.

Lakshmindar touched his mother's feet and received her blessings. He then turned to his mother's "aunt," who had been staying off and on with them for years. The old widow, who was of course none other than Padma, placed a hand on Lakshmindar's head and solemnly said, "May my blessings bear fruit. May a naga get you on your wedding night. Get going at an auspicious moment so that your woman carries your dead body in her arms."

Sonaka was shocked and remonstrated with her "aunt": "Surely, this is old-age dementia. You couldn't in your right mind curse my only living son. How could you wish him killed by snakes on his wedding night?"

"Oh!" exclaimed the "aunt." "I don't know what I said. Silly me!"

Lakshmindar mounted the richly decorated elephant set aside for him, Chand climbed into a large palanquin, courtiers, pundits, relatives got into carriages and palanquins and mounted horses and elephants. Quantities of supplies were carried in bullock carts, including dairy products, flowers, various foodstuffs, *paan* condiments, sweets. Armed escorts marched ahead, alongside, and behind the main body. At a steady pace the procession traversed mountains, valleys, and caverns. When they passed through towns, there was a wholesale flight of people. Old people hobbled away with the help of staffs, men girded their loincloths and ran, women ran in panic, oblivious of their unraveling clothing.

"This is strange," said Chand. Then, realizing what the matter was, he ordered wedding music to be played when they came near habitation. They were being mistaken for an invading army! The wedding music drew cheering crowds; Chand ordered that sweets be distributed among them. Thus the procession reached Ujaninagar in a cheerful mood.

Sahé's five sons rode out accompanied by a disciplined contingent of troops and a group of friends and relatives to welcome the groom's party. The five brothers greeted Chand, reverentially touching his feet, and affectionately embraced Lakshmindar. The soldiers from the two kingdoms saluted each other and marched side by side. The music from the bands, the one from Champaknagar and another from Ujaninagar, was deafening. People in a celebratory mood came flocking and shrilled with joy.

The procession wended its way through the localities inhabited by the different castes. In all of them, the stunningly handsome appearance of Lakshmindar had an electrifying effect: women forgot themselves and cast coquettish looks and flashed their tits at him. It was a tough job for commanders to prevent their troops from going berserk and to keep them moving in a more or less straight line.

The five sons of Sahé guided the procession to a large and pleasant mansion not far from the royal palace. Chand sat down with his councillors and said to the five princes of Ujaninagar, "Please convey my greetings to your revered father and tell him that I think dusk is the best time to start the wedding rituals."

The king, on hearing the message, ordered the preparations for the festivities to be completed. Rows of banana trees lined the path leading to the main venue. Silken buntings embroidered with jasmine designs fluttered in the breeze, and yak's-tail fans waved beneath ochre awnings. At the ceremonial spot a votive pitcher was placed; and King Sahé placed fresh leaves on it. Above stretched four awnings of a sky-blue material. A mandala depicting the earth marked the place assigned to musicians. They played nonstop, and dancers from Ujaninagar cavorted tirelessly. Queen Sumitra sent young married women, carrying baskets of *paan* on their hips, to go from house to house inviting people to the wedding. Women put on attractive saris to come and join the festivities.

Behula's friends came one by one, a bevy of beautiful girls, with faces lovely as the full moon, doe-eyed, ample-hipped, and with pretty names to match, Padmavati and Chandravati and Chandramukhi and Padma-ankhi and Arundhati and Bhagavati and Bimala and Kamala and Madhumati and Jambrati and Satyavati and Malavati and Kulavati and Bhavani and Srivani and Saraswati and Leelavati and Gangavati and Kanta and Shantavati and Sukeshi and Urvashi and Katyayani and Satyabhama and Tilottama and Gauri and Shyama and Abhirama and Jaya and Bijoya and Narayani and Taravati and Lakshmi and Khema and Ahalya and Kausalya and Mandodari and Chintavati and Ratnavati and Ganga and Durga and Bhadravati and Savitri and Parvati and Maheswari and Hasyamukhi and Chandralekha and Ushapani and Chitrarekha and Malini and Jamini and Mandakini and Kalavati and Chhayavati and Sita and Sati and Shobhavati and Kamakhya and Kalindi and Subadini. Delighted that their friend Behula was getting married, they came to Sahé's palace all decked out and giggly.

The married women among the guests, both young and mature, came attractively attired and bejeweled and sat down around the spot where Behula would have her purificatory bath. Attendants offered them *paan* on a golden tray. Others brought the substances needed for the bath: oil, *sindur,* sandalwood paste, musk, saffron paste, alkaline earth. The key role would be played by a professional washerman: in this case, a man called Bijoy, the palace dhobi.

Behula sat on a low wooden stool. Bijoy, the dhobi, took two handfuls of alkaline earth and, touching it lightly to her head, threw it away. Then he touched her with a loofah smeared with a medicinal herbal paste. The women shrilled with joy, rapidly jiggling their tongues inside their pursed mouths. The dhobi carried Behula and made seven perambulations around the ceremonial pitcher, while music played at a smart tempo. Two jasmine blossoms were dropped on the earth, and Behula had to crush them underfoot. A stone was placed on her head and oil poured in a stream over it. The dhobi was handsomely rewarded with quality clothes and jewelry and sent on his way. The married women proceeded to give Behula a scrub and bath, after which she began donning her elaborate bridal attire and ornaments.

Meanwhile Queen Sumitra went around the localities inhabited by the various castes, Brahmin, Kshatriya, Vaishya, Sudra, seeking the goodwill of their womenfolk. They signified the show of goodwill by offering a drink of water, which is known as *sohagpani*—"the water of affection."

Behula put on jewelry on every limb—gold, gems, pearls, coral. Flowers bedecked her hair, which fell in a thick braid over her back. Her nails were beautifully manicured, her teeth sparkled, her eyes rimmed with collyrium. While her sari was of heavily worked silk, her bodice was out of this world: it was embroidered with representations of various things and the names of numerous powerful beings. All three realms—this world, the celestial sphere, the underworld—were represented. The stars and planets were drawn, the great gods, Brahma, Vishnu, Shiva; the great goddesses, Lakshmi, Saraswati, Chandi, and, of course, Padma, whose victory was proclaimed in writing: Jai Brahmani. Indra and his son, the ten avatars of Vishnu, Krishna and his brother Balarama, Ganesha and Kartikeya, demigods like the good-looking, musically talented *vidyadharas,* demons like Ravana and Kumbhkarna, Bali and Sugreeb, demonesses, snakes, the heroic Hanuman, all were mentioned; and the great sages, Jaratkaru—who was none other than Padma's husband—Narada, Kasyapa, Bharvaga, Parasara, Jamadagni, Gautama, Vasistha, Vishwamitra, Sonaka, Sanatana, Jaimini, Sukhdev, Vyasa, Padma's son Astika. The divine couple whose purview is love—Kama and Rati—of course had to be there. Then there were the flora and fauna, the tiger, buffalo, rhino, deer, boar, the susu, and the crocodile, and various flowers and plants and their foliage. In short the magnificent bodice, tailored by Sumitra, was a microcosm of the whole universe and its divine, demonic, human, animal, and vegetational occupants.

Lakshmindar too had a bath and put on his wedding weeds and ornaments: gems on every limb, a crown of gem-studded gold, earrings with gems, a garland of jasmine around the neck, a veil of threaded blossoms that fell shimmering over the face.

Lakshmindar set off for the wedding venue on an elephant, accompanied by musicians and an escort of foot soldiers. Pennants fluttering, drums beating, pipes playing, friends dancing around the bridegroom's elephant, the groom attracted admiring glances as the party moved forward.

As it was nearly time for the wedding service to start, Behula asked her mother to excuse her for a while as she wished to offer puja to Manasa-devi and receive her blessings. Sumitra demurred; leaving the venue at this stage was unheard of.

"Just look about you," Sumitra said. "All the guests are here, waiting for the groom to arrive and the rituals to begin. How can you disappear now?'

Behula broke into tears.

"You don't understand. Padma's blessings will mean assurance of safety. Do I have to remind you of the threat that hangs over us?"

Sumitra fell silent. She had been trying to lose herself in the excitement of the festivities in order to forget about the imminent danger.

"Go," she said softly to Behula. "Go and get her blessings."

Behula hurried to the puja altar dedicated to Padma. She concentrated all her mind on the prayers and offered sweet-smelling flowers and incense and lit votive lamps. But unlike other days, today Padma did not promptly appear before her devotee. Behula began to worry.

"O great goddess, you are my refuge," Behula said. "It was on your advice that I agreed to marry Lakshmindar. If you try to deceive me now, I will take my own life and the blame will be yours."

The naga guarding the entrance to the puja altar said to Behula, "The goddess isn't present, and it is pointless to pray in an empty prayer room. Go to your own room and come back when the goddess returns. She has gone with Neta and a naga host to visit Shiva."

Behula was dismayed at this trick played by Manasa. But she wasn't one to wait and do nothing. She continued to pray, concentrating hard, while tears coursed down her cheeks.

She sacrificed sheep and goats and buffaloes, but there was no sign of the goddess.

She gouged out her own eyes and offered them to the goddess: no response from the goddess.

She cut off her breasts: still no response.

She raised the machete to cut off her tongue. Before the blade could touch the tongue, Padma appeared.

"Why do you wish to die by dismembering yourself?" Padma demanded. "Put your eyes and breasts back on."

"O divine mother," Behula appealed, "give me a boon so that my husband will be invincible and immortal."

"What you are saying cannot be countenanced," said Padma. "I am bound by an oath to take your husband's life."

Behula broke down in tears.

"Then you will be responsible for my death."

Padma became nervous about further complications that would arise from a suicide; her grand strategy would be shaken. She whispered the Mahamantra, the Great Mantra, into Behula's ear and said, "Forget such dire thoughts; all will come right in the end. With the mantra I have given you, you will be able to bring your husband back to life three times."

Delighted with this assurance and little suspecting a trick, Behula returned to the wedding venue, where her mother was becoming impatient. The bridegroom's party had arrived, and Lakshmindar had taken his assigned seat on a podium. Women from all sides scrutinized him appreciatively; they said unanimously, "Isn't Behula lucky!" Irrespective of age, they were irresistibly attracted to the handsome youth. The young ones felt they had been pierced all over by the arrows of desire; only shame or fear restrained them. The mature ones hugged Lakshmindar and derived what satisfaction they could from the contact. The old women brooded over the realization that they would never be young again. Any woman who dies without having made love to this young man, they thought, has lived in vain. A toothless eighty-year-old woman who lived in Sahé's household said, "If my young days came back I'd make love to Lakshmindar round the clock." Another old woman of indeterminate age massaged raw turmeric paste on her body to brighten her complexion and came hobbling on a walking stick to catch a glimpse of the bridegroom. Lakshmindar couldn't contain his laughter on seeing her. A white-haired woman wearing *sindur* shook her large earrings as she danced provocatively—such was the desire burning in her heart on seeing Lakshmindar.

King Sahé sat down with holy *kusha* grass in one hand, facing the Brahmin priests who would conduct the wedding rites. The objects that would be needed for the ritual of giving away the bride were placed before Sahé. The priests chanted Vedic mantras, while the musicians played tirelessly. Pandit Somai, the royal priest, said to King Sahé: "In order to formally receive the bridegroom, you have to face south, Your Majesty. The groom will be to your west and in that position you will receive him with presents of clothing, jewelry, and scented flowers."

Pandit Sringi burst into laughter. "You've got things the wrong way round," he crowed. "And you are supposed to be a royal priest! When the lord of the mountains gave his daughter Parvati to Lord Shiva, he stood facing north, with the groom on the east. In that position the lord of the mountains presented Shiva with clothes and jewelry. This has since become the inviolable rule."

The procedural matters being settled, the ritual proceeded as divinely ordained. Lakshmindar sat on a gem-studded seat, under a gem-studded umbrella. Behula, veiled and dressed in bridal finery, went and sat facing him. She parted the veil to salute him with joined palms. He put a *bindi* mark on her forehead with his finger and applied collyrium—the color of love—to her eyes. She handed her looking glass to him and took the one he was holding. Lakshmindar slipped a garland of flowers over Behula's head. Yak's-tail fans waved and ochre-colored silken pennants fluttered merrily all around. Lakshmindar picked up flowers by the handful and scattered them over the guests. Behula got up and with her palms joined in a namaskar slowly circumambulated Lakshmindar seven times. Her gaze was lowered but from time to time she would involuntarily raise her eyes to see the man standing tall at the center—and smile with joy. The guests cheered; the ladies shrilled *ulu-lu-lu*, flicking their tongues inside their mouths. Lakshmindar kept showering flowers all around.

Suddenly his eyes fell on the heavy braid of hair swinging over Behula's back.

"Snake! Snake!" he screamed and collapsed on the floor. Everyone stood up.

"Dead!" rose a cry from the crowd.

Behula took Lakshmindar in her arms, recited the Mahamantra that Padma had taught her a short while back, and slapped him on his back. At once his eyelids fluttered and he sat up.

The machete and rolled up banana leaf had fallen from his hand; Behula had picked up the tube-like banana leaf. Its reflection fell on the looking glass that was now lying on the floor. Lakshmindar saw this reflection and again collapsed screaming, "Snake! Snake!"

Behula again applied the Mahamantra, with a thump on Lakshmindar's back. "Where have you seen the snake?" she asked, puzzled.

Lakshmindar couldn't say where, only that he was convinced he had seen one. He stood up and Behula resumed her perambulations around him. His eyes fell on her bodice, that gorgeous creation of the couturier's art, embellished with intricate designs that incorporated, as has been already mentioned, everything significant in the universe. Lakshmindar stared in fascination and saw something come slitheringly alive.

"Snake! Snake!" Lakshmindar screamed once again and collapsed.

For the third time Behula whispered the Mahamantra into Lakshmindar's ear, thumped him on the back, and had him back on his feet.

How wonderful, thought Chand, that my daughter-in-law knows the great mantra that can revive the dead. A terrible weight lifted off his mind, and he got up and danced with his arms waving above his head while the music grew louder, reflecting the ecstatic mood of the crowd that had witnessed the miraculous revival of the bridegroom three times in succession. This would be a wedding to remember.

Now came the last phase of the ceremony—the formal giving away of the bride. King Sahé's men carried Lakshmindar to their master's presence. There were loud cheers as the groom was borne away. The women followed with the symbolic objects necessary for the remaining rituals—pots, pitcher, ear of rice, *durba* grass.

The groom was brought together with the bride. The bride's father sat holding a bundle of *kusha* grass in one hand. Pandit Somai lit a sacrificial fire and recited Vedic mantras invoking good luck for the newlyweds. King Sahé took the ends of the attire of bride and groom and tied the corners together. The priest took the right hand of Behula and placed it in Lakshmindar's right hand. Their two families were now linked by holy matrimony.

King Sahé announced what he was giving as dowry: quantities of precious stones of various sorts; a thousand horses, all harnessed, saddled, and richly caparisoned; a hundred handpicked elephants, together with howdahs; hundreds of milk cows; a beautiful bed, with luxurious pillows, mattresses, and sheets; gold and silver crockery; slaves and slave girls, all with a supply of clothing; an estate comprising five villages and the agricultural land attached to them; gold and pearls in plenty. The five sons of Sahé also presented the newlyweds with precious stones.

Lakshmindar and Behula were now taken to their sitting room. A clutch of women stood around them as they played dice. Queen Sumitra came in and hinted that it was time for the guests to go home. They took the hint, and the newlyweds could relax. Lakshmindar took off his crown with relief.

Sumitra called her daughters-in-law and asked them to serve dinner to their new brother-in-law. There were numerous dishes of vegetables and fish, cooked in ghee with appropriate spices and condiments. But for a joke, as is common at weddings, there were a few fake dishes, which Lakshmindar had to spit out amid laughter from his sisters-in-law. The upshot was that he remained hungry.

The newlyweds were taken to their bedchamber and bid goodnight. Lakshmindar and Behula were finally together all by themselves. They sat on a golden bed with silk sheets. Unbeknownst to them, Sumitra and some of her close friends took turns peering through a gap in a window. They nudged each other and had a difficult time suppressing their giggles. After a few minutes they withdrew, pleased with what they had seen: clearly, judging from their expressions and their body language, there was an exciting chemistry between them.

Indeed, poets declared that Lakshmindar and Behula at this moment were like Kama and Rati; or Shashadhar, the moon god, and Rohini; or Indra and Sachi, when they were newlyweds.

Lakshmindar put his arms around Behula and kissed her. The soft, warm touch of her body and the sweet scents that came from her hair, her body, and her clothes inflamed his desire. He wanted to prolong the embrace and explore further but she gently separated herself. It wasn't a rejection, rather an entreaty that he should wait till she was ready. He took a *paan* and wanted to put it in her mouth. At first she resisted gently, putting her restraining hand on his. He coaxed her into taking the *paan* from his hand. They chatted for a while before Lakshmindar fell asleep. Not so Behula. She picked up a machete and sat on guard.

Padma consulted with Neta and decided to dispatch naga assassins to Ujaninagar. She sent one and waited. She sent one after another at intervals, four in all. None came back. They all suffered the same fate, in this manner: as soon as the naga sneaked into the bridal chamber it found the bride waiting, machete in hand, and hung its head in apprehension. Behula calmly greeted it with these words: "Why didn't you come to see the wedding? You have come to see the bridegroom at night, when he is asleep. Anoint yourself with sandalwood essence, wear one of these floral garlands, and have your fill of milk and bananas, and then sleep in one of these wooden boxes. You can see the groom when he wakes up in the morning and go home satisfied."

The naga ate and drank and entered a box; at once Behula snapped it shut. After trapping four nagas Behula wondered how she would get through the night. It was still the first watch and none could tell what the rest of the night would bring. Tiredness might get the better of her at some point, or Padma might send a horde of nagas against which she would have no defense. She decided to wake up Lakshmindar.

But how? If she nudged him he might open his eyes and get the wrong idea. She blushed at the thought. That wouldn't do. She thought for a moment, then dipped her fingers in sandalwood essence and flicked it at his face. He stirred, opened his eyes, and sat up.

"I had just dozed off. Why have you woken me up now, my darling?"

Behula blushed. What was he thinking? She had to explain everything quickly.

Her account stirred Lakshmindar into action. He called Baghai, one of the most dependable of his father's retainers and told him what had happened. Baghai woke up his master, passed on the news, and forcefully suggested: "Go back to Champaknagar at once, my lord, and put the newlyweds in the steel chamber. Tonight's the fateful night. If they survive it the threat will be lifted. It is too dangerous to stay here."

Chand woke up Sahé, told him everything and asked for his permission to take leave. Sahé was too stunned by the account to reply at once. He went to Sumitra and gave her the news. She became so distraught as to be irrational.

"Didn't I tell you this Chandradhara fellow is in a weird tangle with snakes? You have courted disaster by marrying our daughter with his son. There's nothing to be done now, of course. Let them go without delay and spend the rest of the night in their steel chamber. They'll be safe inside, and if they can survive till morning the danger may pass."

Sahé bade farewell to Chand, counseling extreme caution for the rest of the night.

Lakshmindar took leave of his in-laws, touching the feet of his wife's parents, and warmly embracing her brothers. Sahé and Sumitra commended their daughter to his care.

A girl's departure from her parent's home after her wedding is one of the saddest occasions one comes across in the Indian subcontinent. Behula fell sobbing at her mother's feet. Sumitra raised her to her feet and hugged her. "This will become a desolate place," she said. "I don't know how I can live here without seeing you. Who knows when we will meet again?"

On a more practical note Sumitra advised Behula to be awake and alert all night. The chief purpose of her life was to serve her husband and tonight she would serve him best by staying alert and awake.

Sumitra wailed, rolling in the dust, and had to be helped up. Sahé bit on his scarf to control his sobs. The five brothers, however, wept unrestrainedly.

Behula went with Lakshmindar and got into a palanquin, which was considered the safest mode of transport under the present circumstances. An elephant, by contrast, was quite exposed. Soldiers, who were on all four sides of the main party, carried hundreds of lamps. Sahé accompanied the party some way on horseback. He stopped at a bend, bade everyone a last farewell, and as the lights disappeared in the distance, sadly made his way home.

Chand ordered a forced march in order to reach Champaknagar as quickly as possible. A messenger rode ahead to warn Sonaka of the return, and so she was ready with a group of married women to receive the bride.

Lakshmindar and Behula alighted from the palanquin and walked to the door. He carried her across the threshold while the women shrilled *lu-lu-lulu*. Sonaka presented the bride with the five precious stones and kissed her over and over on her forehead.

Chand called to her to stop and take Behula and Lakshmindar into the safety of the steel chamber. Sonaka did so without wasting another moment. She shut the iron door after the newlyweds and went in. Then the door was locked and the key taken by Chand and secreted into a safe box. A hundred guards stood around the chamber, with strict instructions to stay awake. *Ojhas* with reputations comparable to what Dhanvantari's had been, were in attendance round the clock. Hundreds of lamps rendered it impossible for any creature to approach the chamber without being seen.

DEATH IN THE STEEL CHAMBER

LAKSHMINDAR AND BEHULA CURIOUSLY EXPLORED the interior of the safe house. It was not as dark as they had expected. Sunstone on the walls reflected and intensified whatever light was there. There was a large golden bed with silk sheets. Lakshmindar and Behula sat down on it; he slipped a garland of flowers over her head and drew her to him.

She yielded, but only up to that point. Nor did he pursue further; he laughed instead—she wondered why—and said, "My darling, you must do something for me." Oh no, she thought, and then, I wonder what.

"I couldn't eat properly at Ujaninagar," he said, "what with my shyness and the jokes at my expense. Now I'm famished." He looked into her eyes, like an imploring child. "Do you think you could rustle up something? It would help me sleep well."

"Let me see, I'll cook something."

Lakshmindar looked around and found some rice; he handed it to Behula, lay down and within seconds began snoring.

Behula gathered together the foodstuffs kept in the chamber and decided what to do. In order to light a fire she dipped silk sheets in ghee and improvised a burner. She cooked a sweet dish with crushed sesame and coconut, and boiled the rice in a golden bowl.

Behula sat waving a hand fan over Lakshmindar's head, then after pondering the matter for a moment, again used a sprinkling of sandal-wood essence to wake him up. He got up, rubbing his eyes and asked, "Why have you woken me up—I'd just dozed off."

"My lord, your repast is ready," she said.

First she served rice mingled with ghee, then milk, yogurt, sandesh, and bananas. He ate with relish, rinsed his mouth, and popped into his mouth a *paan* that Behula rolled for him. Thanks to the nap and the wholesome meal, Lakshmindar felt rejuvenated—and, soon, sexually aroused.

"You are my beautiful beloved and I, your very own husband. It's only natural that we should make love. Kama, the god of love, has shot his arrows right through my heart, and my mind can't remain steady even for a moment. Your beauty will enchant all three realms. Let us give our-selves up to lusty lovemaking."

Behula sat with bowed head throughout Lakshmindar's passionate declaration. She shed silent tears worrying that her master would feel rejected. She collected her thoughts and spoke slowly: "Why are you asking me to do something ill-advised? It's not considered decent to have sex on one's wedding night. Friends who come to know will tease us, which would be quite embarrassing. You are an experienced man of the world, I am still a girl whose body is not fully developed. A bee will not find satisfaction in an unopened bud. It must wait for the bud to blossom."

Lakshmindar felt ashamed and realized the virtue of self-control in certain circumstances. He held Behula affectionately, wiped her tears, and said, "You have taught me an important lesson. There is a time for everything, and patience can enrich an experience when it comes at the right time." Husband and wife lay down side by side, calm and happy, and were soon fast asleep.

✦   ✦   ✦

"Neta, the second watch of the night is drawing to a close, and the job of finishing off Lakshmindar is still unfinished," said Padma irritably.

"Send a naga at once, now that Lakshmindar and Behula are asleep."

It turned out to be easier said than done. Much to Padma's exasperation, the nagas were loath to venture into Champaknagar, such was the terror Chand had struck in their hearts.

"The nagas have turned into sheep and foxes," Padma said. "The night is running out and my oath has so far been in vain. Our grand strategy will come to naught if Lakshmindar isn't eliminated before sunrise."

"Get Kalnagini, the black cobra, from Kalidaha and send her," said Neta.

Padma sent the harmless snake Dhamna with her message. Dhamna went to Kalidaha and called Kalnagini. From her home in the depths of Kalidaha, Kalnagini thought she heard the call of the serpent-devouring king of birds, Garuda. She kept quiet. Dhamna shouted, "You have nothing to fear. I've come with a message from Padma."

Kalnagini surfaced cautiously.

"Padma wants you to come at once."

Kalnagini reported to Padma, who explained to her the mission she had to undertake and its significance.

"My prestige is at stake—and that means the prestige of the entire naga race."

"I can do it," said Kalnagini, "but I'm out of venom. If you refill my poison fangs I'll get going."

The fresh supply of extra-potent venom with which Padma refilled Kalnagini's fangs gave her a burst of confidence. She declared, "Padma, your enemy will go straight to the underworld."

"No, not there," Padma corrected her. "I'll keep this one myself. Now go and get him."

Kalnagini disappeared and came back after some time.

"Mission accomplished?"

"No, I found the steel chamber but not the hairbreadth chink, though I looked all around."

"Let's go to the blacksmith Binode and get precise instructions," said Neta.

Padma called out Binode, the builder-architect, who dutifully gave precise instructions: "At the northern end of the chamber there are two emeralds. Between them is the chink, concealed by vermilion paste. The fire of venom will melt the paste, and the way will be clear."

Padma dispatched Kalnagini. This time she had no difficulty finding the chink or getting in. She found the young couple sleeping side by side and took a good look at the husband, her target. What a good-looking man. Kalnagini was smitten. How could she bring herself to kill such a man. He had gone to bed with his beautiful bride in a romantic mood. If Kalnagini killed him, what curses wouldn't she bring upon her head from the lovely widow! On the other hand, if she didn't kill the fellow, Padma would come down heavily on her. And Padma was her goddess, and had a lot riding on this mission. Kalnagini moved around her target, considering him from various angles. His arm, raised in sleep—perhaps in a dream—fell on her. Now, she could hold this against him: people had been killed for less. She went to the foot of the bed. He moved a leg, his foot fell on her head. Now, that was a grave provocation. She had better get the job done and get away. She chose the spot under the nail of the little toe and dug in her fangs.

"Papa! Papa! Help!" screamed Lakshmindar, sitting up with a jerk. He saw the snake slithering away and picking up the machete that had featured in the wedding rituals, he hurled it at the villain, nicking off a bit of her tail.

Lakshmindar collapsed, incapacitated by pain. He could barely move his arms. He picked up two leaves of some plant that came with the flowers strewn on the bed and scratched a note addressed to Behula: "I have been bitten by a naga. I called you but you didn't awake. Still, it is some consolation that as I lie dying my eyes are on you, my darling. You will of course keep your splendid oath—to find what has been lost, to revive the dead. When you bring your husband back from the dead, you will be universally hailed as the ideal wife."

Lakshmindar barely managed to keep the note in a box when his body seized up through the action of the venom and he gave up the ghost.

At once Chitralekha, whose job as Yama's assistant is keeping track of the longevity of all beings as well as their karmic account sheet, shouted that it was time to send an emissary to Champaknagar to fetch the spirit of Lakshmindar who had just died. Yama sent Suchimukhi, one of his many minions, and shortly he was inside the steel chamber. He entered Lakshmindar's body and laid about with a cudgel to separate out his *prana*, his life spirit, which he then tied up with thongs. Leaving the dead body where it lay, Suchimukhi headed for the underworld with Lakshmindar's spirit. On the way he ran into the sage Narada. With characteristic curiosity, Narada asked who was being carried away. Having learned that it was Lakshmindar, he went straight to Padma and told her that she ought to keep Lakshmindar herself.

Padma flew into a mighty rage and ordered a general mobilization of nagas, but Neta induced her to postpone it.

"There's no point giving Yama and his servants another thrashing. Go to Father and ask him to straighten out Yama."

Padma went and told Shiva what had happened: "Yama sent for Lakshmindar's spirit a second time!"

"He's being childish," said Shiva. "He wants to get even. I'll send Hanuman to bring Lakshmindar back."

Hanuman carried out a spectacular raid single-handed, knocking out Yama's minions with his lashing tail, and carried Lakshmindar back. Yama sulkily complained to Shiva, who told him bluntly: "Get this straight. Things are now different. Snakebite victims go to Padma. You can have them if she passes them on to you, not otherwise."

"If you say so," said Yama, swallowing his pride.

✦   ✦   ✦

Behula had a nightmare: she was surrounded by snakes. She woke up in a sweat and saw Lakshmindar lying lifeless beside her.

"My lord!" she cried, nudging the body.

Her eyes fell on the leaves and an anguished perusal of the message on them made everything clear. She found the chopped off inches of the Kalnagini's tail and a drop of blood. Examining Lakshmindar's body she found a drop of blood and fang marks on a little toe. Her grief exploded like a bursting dam.

"Why have you left me, my lord?" she wailed. "You went without even saying goodbye. Padma has prematurely widowed me: how luckless I am! How sinful of the *nagini* to kill my husband on the wedding night. Is there any nightwatchman who can hear me? Tell the master of the house that his son is no more. Cut down some full-grown banana trees and make a raft. I will drift away with my lord."

Behula's cries, though muffled by the walls of steel, reached Sonaka's ears. She woke up Chand. He tried to reassure her that it wasn't what she thought.

"Have you forgotten what you did when you were a newlywed wife?" Chand said. "These are not the cries of mourning but the cries of lovemaking."

"I don't agree with you," said Sonaka. "She is not yet ready for that, she is still too young. I tell you something is wrong."

Just then the sky began to lighten, presaging dawn, and Behula's pet crow began cawing.

Behula called out to the crow: "My beautiful gem of a bird, fly at once and tell my parents that my lord has died inside the steel chamber."

The crow said, "Last night I had two babies. They neither know their parents nor can they eat by themselves. How can I leave them, they will die."

"Don't worry, I'll look after them with motherly affection, and when they grow up I'll gild their beaks and decorate their wings with pearls. Now take wing, I beg you, and fly with the speed of the wind."

The crow took off and flew to Sahé's bedroom. It started to caw and call Queen Sumitra. The queen came out and the crow said, "A *nagini* has killed Lakshmindar inside the steel chamber. By now Behula may be on a raft, with the dead body."

✦ ✦ ✦

Sonaka, convinced that the muffled cries of Behula betokened disaster, got out of bed and without bothering to change rushed to the steel chamber. The guards ringing the chamber were at some distance; most were dozing, oblivious of the voice inside. Sonaka went to the door and put her ear to it to listen better. There was no doubt about it: Behula was lamenting piteously, and there wasn't another voice.

Sonaka beat upon the door and shouted, "Open up! Open up!"

Hearing her mother-in-law's voice, Behula cried louder as she came to the door and beat against it. There was no time to look for the key. Sonaka ordered the door to be forced open. She burst in crying. She beat her breast, rolled on the ground, and cried out between sobs: "What use were guards against the venomous attackers? How can I live without my son?" She cradled the dead body in her arms and cried in despair: "I'll drink poison or jump into the flames. I told his father there was no point getting him married because Padma would get him on his wedding night. My husband has brought on this disaster. Our lives are desolate."

Chand, finding his wife gone and hearing the commotion that had begun around the steel chamber, could no longer delude himself into thinking nothing was amiss. He ran to the chamber, found the door open and rushed in: his wife and daughter-in-law were keening over a lifeless Lakshmindar. His grief fueled his rage at his archenemy.

"That bitch has done it!" he said. "Let me catch up with her, she'll have to pay for her evil deeds. I broke her hip, now I'll smash her head with my *hintala* staff."

Behula tore her hair, oblivious of the disarray of her attire. She smashed the conch-shell bracelets, the symbol of marriage, against the wall. She tore away her necklace and other ornaments like one demented. No more words came from her mouth, only a ceaseless cry that rose from the depths of her being.

Word of the disaster spread like wildfire, and the sound of lamentation rose from all over the city. Lakshmindar was a much-loved prince and everyone—especially the women and girls—felt bereaved. Sages stopped meditating to vent their grief at the news; yogis came out of their yogic postures; the koel cried louder; leaves fell from trees, as if winter had suddenly struck.

BEHULA'S RIVER JOURNEY

CHAND COMPOSED HIMSELF to deal with the practicalities of disposing of the dead body. He ordered a raft to be specially made for Lakshmindar. The usual practice is to lash a number of banana trees together, place the dead body on it, and set it adrift. Chand had a much larger raft made, with many banana trees linked to each other with iron chains and locks. He hired a builder to put up a cabin on the raft, with strong pillars, four doors, and a wooden roof. The body would consequently be protected from sun, rain, and hailstorms.

Chand said to Sonaka, "Pull yourself together, stop crying. What is ordained cannot be prevented. Crying will only increase Padma's glee. Wise men say that one should try to overcome grief. Let us accept what has happened and cannot be undone. We have to get on with our lives. If we can win their favor, the gods will grant us more children and multiply our wealth. Go home now and take our daughter-in-law with you. I will place our son on the raft and let him go."

Sonaka turned to Behula and said, "Come, my child, let's go home. Let the men take care of the disposal of the dead."

"No, Mother dear, that cannot be. How can I turn my back on my husband? I will drift with my lord on the river. Of what value is a woman's life in this world when her husband is dead? When a woman's husband dies her duty is to continue serving him. I will drift from village to village with my lord in my lap. If I cannot bring him back to life, I will leap into a fire and die. Put my husband on the raft, I will accompany him."

Chand had grave objections to Behula's decision. "Who has ever heard of the dead being brought back to life in this world?" he declared. "And who has ever accompanied a dead body? Listen to me, give up the absurd plan, or else you will only bring disgrace upon yourself. You are of noble lineage, and the scandal will be all the greater on that account. Be sensible, go home with Sonaka, that's where you belong. Your sisters-in-law will help you and look after you."

But Behula was not to be dissuaded or consoled. She replied: "Steady your mind, Father. If I have been a truly chaste and devoted wife—in word, thought, and deed—I will certainly resurrect the lord of my life. I ask for your blessings before bidding farewell."

Behula touched the feet of her parents-in-law. Sonaka embraced her and cried. The six sisters-in-law clung to Behula's neck, sobbing. Chand called the men to carry Lakshmindar's body to the raft. Behula followed and sat down in the cabin with Lakshmindar's head in her lap. Men got into the water and heaved to set the raft in motion down the waters of the Gungari River. Behula mentally saluted Padma's feet, concentrating her attention on the great goddess in whom she put absolute trust, no matter how arduous the journey leading to a happy resolution.

Mourning crowds lined the banks of the Gungari River as the raft began its uncharted voyage. Sonaka and the six daughters-in-law watched through tear-dimmed eyes till the raft floated out of sight.

While the sad and protracted farewell was taking place, another bizarre side drama was enacted between Padma and Chand. The goddess, while remaining invisible, from her aerial perch urged Chand to offer puja to her. "In exchange you will recover all you have lost, wealth, goods, sons, daughter-in-law," Padma promised.

"You are wicked and unfeeling," Chand shouted. "You are compounding my sorrow by mocking and teasing me. I'll live happily without a son, I'll gladly embrace death, yet I'll not offer puja to you."

For once Sonaka forgot her unquestioning adoration of Padma and exploded: "May you be destroyed and suffer endless torments in hell. For what fault of his have you taken my beautiful son?"

Chand turned to the gathered mourners. "Don't cry, dear citizens of Champaknagar. It's true I have lost seven sons, and a daughter-in-law too is as good as lost. But who lives forever? Those who are born must die sooner or later."

And yet, when the citizens saluted him and sadly took their leave, Chand broke down and cried like a child.

+ + +

Behula's raft soon left Champaknagar behind and approached Simadaha, not far from her parents' kingdom. Her brothers, who had got word of the tragedy and the strange fate chosen by their sister, came riding in chariots and met up with her at Simadaha. The brothers wept at the sight of Behula cradling the dead body. They tried to dissuade her from pursuing the mission.

"Who can resurrect someone dead of snakebite?" they said. "You are still a child, how can you face the dark night all alone with a dead body? It's enough to make one die of fright. The hot sun in summer, rain, thunderstorms, hailstorms, the numbing cold of winter—how will you face these on this little raft? Father and Mother are sick with worry on your account. Forget this foolhardy mission, come home, dear sister."

Behula wept profusely on seeing her brothers because she wanted to share her grief with them. But her resolve remained unshakable.

"I will drift from village to village with my lord. If I can't revive him, what will my life be worth? Ask Father and Mother to give me their blessings so that I can return with my lord and have a grand reunion."

Behula asked her brothers to give her raft a forceful shove. They sent it skimming over the waves and waved, weeping, at their little sister. When they went home and told their parents about the meeting. Queen Sumitra cried and cursed the day they agreed to marry their daughter to the son of "that snake-eating fellow." King Sahé rolled on the ground in grief.

+ + +

Behula's raft carried on down the meandering river. She prayed continuously to Padma and surveyed the passing scenes: men, women, children bathing or giving cattle a bath, washing clothes, filling pitchers with water to take home; men working on the agricultural plots on the bank or grazing cattle and goats in the fields; white-blossomed reeds growing wild on the banks. The river flowed into another, and then into another, and so on, changing names as it went along, until Behula didn't know what river she was on.

But at a number of the bends she passed, Behula had strange, unforeseen, and unforeseeable encounters that showed her life in its terrifying, disgusting, grotesque, shocking aspects, so that when she reached the end of her journey she was no longer an innocent child but—so to speak—a battle-hardened veteran.

Along a stretch of forestland the river flowed past a bend that was a notorious haunt of tigers. Padma asked Neta to assume the shape of a hungry tigress and give Behula a scare. Neta made a very convincing tigress as she ran out of the forest roaring and stood facing the raft as it rounded the bend.

"I'm famished, I haven't eaten in seven days," the tigress announced. "I've been drawn by the smell of dead flesh. Give up the dead body and go home."

"Why eat a dead body when you can have fresh flesh?" interjected Behula. "I'll cut off my flesh and give it to you."

The tigress gave a grunt of annoyance. "If you refuse to let me have the dead body, I'll take it by force and you along with it."

The tigress gnashed its teeth, lashed its tail, and glared, to no avail. Behula gathered her courage and said calmly, "In case you try to touch me, I appeal to Padma to avenge me."

The tigress decided to leap back into the forest and end this trial of Behula.

The raft pushed off and continued at a steady pace till another prominent bend came into view. This was known to all as Goda's Bend, haunt of an eponymous character unique for grotesquerie. Goda was this character's nickname; it means "fat" or "swollen," appropriate in this instance because of the character's elephantiasis.

Goda sat on the riverbank, with a fishing rod trailing its line in the water. On seeing the raft bearing down upon the bend, Goda became excited.

"What a radiant beauty is headed this way! She must be coming with the intention of satisfying my wishes."

Goda began jumping up and down on the riverbank.

"Stop over here, my beauty. Abandon that useless corpse and be my companion. We are well matched in beauty and age. You are young, I'm only seventy. You are lovely as a mermaid, I'm an expert in the erotic arts. My legs and feet are huge and rounded because of elephantiasis. My feet are like a pair of pumpkins. It is destiny that has brought you to me. Come live with me in my straw-roofed reed huts—I have five of them by the river. I fish with my rod and earn over five thousand cowries. There's bitter vegetable and boiled rice in plenty and jute sacking to spread on the mud floor and lie like a king. I will give you ghee with your rice and you will sit with me and rub oil on my swollen parts."

"You have nothing between your ears," said Behula. "You are a dwarf that reaches for the sky, a wretched fisherman who can't handle a net. You not only have elephantiasis, you are also hunchbacked. Live happily with your old wife."

"I'll get rid of her," shouted Goda.

Behula hurried the raft past the wretch. He ran alongside, shouting, "I'll fall at your feet. Have mercy."

He jumped into the river to swim to the raft. Behula put a curse that sent him to the bottom. He could barely make his way up to the surface, swallowing water, spluttering. He made his way somehow to the bank and got up panting.

"I'm lucky to have come out alive," he said.

◆   ◆   ◆

Behula continued on her way, with a sense of relief at having shaken off the comically bizarre Goda. She kept praying fervently to Padma: her faith was unshakable though her prayers had borne no fruit. Before long she came to a bend with a cremation ground on it; but to her it would come to be identified as the Gambler's Bend.

Here's the background to her third strange encounter. A wealthy merchant called Dhanpati had a son who had gone to the dogs and become addicted to gambling. He lost all his money and fell into despair. He found a cowrie and was again seized with the gambling fever. He thought: I will recoup my fortune with this single cowrie. He lost it within seconds and sat down with his head in his hands. He thought: I need more cowries. He went looking for them on the cremation ground by the river. That is when he saw a beautiful young woman on a raft, cradling a dead body. He thought a divine boon had come his way and, proudly introducing himself, made a brazen proposition.

"I am the merchant Dhanpati's son; my pedigree is impeccable, so why don't you throw that stinking corpse overboard and come with me? My personal wealth is of vast potential; if I gamble with a single cowrie, I may win a king's ransom. We will have a jolly time together; you will simply adore me, I'm sure."

"Your brain has become addled, you good-for-nothing," said Behula. "Your indecent proposal merits summary punishment. On my way back I'll stamp on your head with my heel, just you wait and see."

The wind picked up, sending the raft skimming over the waves. Behula prayed to Padma, imagining herself prostrated at the goddess's feet. Presently the raft approached a bend where two brothers, Dhona and Mona—not to be confused with the *ojha* Dhanvantari's sons—liked to hang out. The brothers were surprised to see a raft with a cabin on it and a beautiful young woman cradling a decomposing body. Their desire was immediately inflamed and they began calling out to her.

"You can't go any farther, come to the bank and tie up your raft."

Behula silently prayed to Padma to save her from the two scoundrels.

"You are the ultimate source of succor for one as helpless as I am."

Padma was pleased and solved Behula's problem by fomenting a conflict between the two brothers. They had got into a swift dinghy and were paddling furiously toward Behula's raft. Suddenly Mona paused and said, "You are my elder brother, Dhona, and you have a wife. I am still a bachelor, and I am desperate to have female company, so this woman is rightfully mine."

Dhona replied, "I am your senior, Mona, and it is my prerogative to have this woman for my own enjoyment."

Hot words were exchanged, followed by blows, kicks, and freestyle wrestling. The dinghy overturned and the two combatants were sucked into a whirlpool. It took all their strength and stamina to extricate themselves from the swirling water and reach the bank. By then Behula's raft had been driven out of sight by a favorable wind.

No sooner had Behula reached a clear stretch of water and begun to feel composed than she came upon another bend at which the stream narrowed, making it difficult to steer clear of the banks. The raft seemed to pause of its own accord at a ferry ghat where Apna Dom sat in his house on stilts. In order to make small talk Apna asked Behula about her family particulars: caste, parents, hometown, in-laws, and so on.

"Who are you to put such questions to me?" Behula retorted and proudly described her lineage. She made a point of describing the purpose of her journey. Apna brushed aside her speech and said, "Get rid of the stinking body and come with me. I will make you the chief of my wives. I will wash your feet and cook your meals, if only you will share my bed."

By now Behula had become quite experienced at dealing with this sort of sexual harassment, and without batting an eye she rendered him unconscious with a curse.

Like the tiger there were other creatures interested in the dead body rather than the attractive living woman. The wind drove Behula's raft to a narrow stream where scavengers roamed the banks.

A vixen, with vicious-looking teeth and daggerlike nails bluntly demanded Lakshmindar's dead body: "Give me your dead husband's body and go home!"

Behula sent up a silent prayer to Padma who inspired her to gather her courage, pick up a stick and drive away the pest.

Likewise, at another bend came flocks of vultures, which is only natural if a dead body is floating by. But these were no ordinary vultures. Padma instructed Neta to take the form of a vulture, and turn a large number of serpents as well into vultures and crows, and then harass Behula. The birds demanded Lakshmindar's dead body as their natural right and backed off only when Behula invoked Padma's help.

But all these ordeals at various river bends would pale in comparison to the encounter with a man called Narayan Dani. The surname means "munificent," and Narayan habitually showed his generosity to people of all kinds. He was sitting with bags of money, which he was giving away to whoever applied for a largesse. This was his leisure activity. Just then Behula's raft hove into view, and the man who was happily giving wealth away experienced an anguished desire for the lovely young woman he saw.

The words of solicitation he used were not crude like those of some men Behula had encountered—indeed, they were quite poetic—but the purport was the same: throw away the dead body and come live with me.

Words of mutual introduction were also exchanged, and it transpired that Narayan was Sonaka's brother.

"Forgive me, I have said sinful things," he said, averting his eyes in embarrassment and blushing. But the next moment he went on in his original vein: "How much longer will you continue with the dead body, which has almost completely disintegrated. Let it drift by itself and come home with me. Let us enjoy life while we can."

"You astonish me," expostulated Behula. "You felt no remorse for making a sinful proposition. As for me, I know that my husband is my greatest wealth, my lord and master, and without him my life is worthless. I will therefore go to the abode of the gods and bring him back to life and also his brothers."

"Such admirable devotion! But are you sure your husband deserves it?"

Narayan's tone became acerbic. "How well do you know your husband? Are you sure he has not committed heinous crimes and sins?"

"Everyone makes mistakes."

"I don't mean those—not little misdemeanors, but grave sins."

"My lord is a man of principle, noble, virtuous, high-minded."

"What if I were to tell you that he lost all self-control in the throes of lust and violated a woman he should have respected and loved like his mother."

"What nonsense you are talking!"

Narayan Dani was now quivering with anger and shouting.

"He raped his mother's brother's wife—my wife—your aunt—his aunt."

Behula put her hands to her ears, shaking her head.

"You may shake your head but you know I'm not lying."

But Behula wasn't thinking anything. Emptying her mind of all thought and passion she prayed calmly to Padma: "I take refuge in you, only you."

Padma came to her rescue, induced Narayan to calm down and withdraw and helped Behula resume her arduous voyage. At night Padma came to her in a dream and explained how she had manipulated Lakshmindar into raping his aunt so that her grand design would be served.

"Things should not be seen in isolation or in a narrow, moralistic way."

Behula did not argue with Padma or even say anything, but she woke up in the morning a sadder and a wiser person.

The raft sped on, day and night, the river was wider now; the waves higher, wilder; the currents swifter. It reached the Triveni Sangam, the confluence of three great rivers, where from the middle of the stream the banks become invisible. Behula was frightened, she felt lost, helpless. This was very different from the strange problems encountered at constricted bends.

"How will I cross this vast expanse of water," Behula cried in anguish, "I cannot see the banks, there is only water as far as the eye can reach, the waves dance wildly and touch the sky. Huge birds circle overhead and the crocodiles and sharks swimming around could devour the entire raft. If Shiva's mighty daughter doesn't help me there is no hope."

Padma heard Behula's lament and instructed Neta to go and take a hand in the unfolding drama.

Neta went to Triveni in the guise of a celestial washerwoman who had to clean the raiment of gods and goddesses. With her was her young son Dhananjaya. Neta kept the clothes in a pile and began washing them. The washed, clean clothes she kept in another place. The playful Dhananjaya started dancing on the washed clothes, dirtying them, so that Neta had to wash them again. But could a child be trusted to obey an injunction not to do something that was fun?

"You naughty child," said Neta, "you'd better lie down dead while I do my work." At once the child collapsed and lay inert. Behula watched all this with fascination. She was struck by the weird symmetry in their situations. On the one hand was Behula with her dead husband; on the other, this extraordinary washerwoman who had put her son to death with a wish. Behula waited to see what happened next.

When all the clothes had been washed and tied in a neat bundle Neta picked up her lifeless son, whispered something into his ear—no doubt the Mahagyan, the great occult mantra—and the next moment the boy was his usual spritely self.

Behula felt that she had come to the end of her quest. She moored the raft on the bank and leapt into the water. Swimming underwater, she came up thrice for air, and found Neta's feet, which she embraced with desperate energy. Neta, startled, fell down and cried out. Dhananjaya came running and pulled out Neta. Behula got out of the water but wouldn't let go of Neta's legs.

Neta asked Behula for her personal particulars; once again Behula said who she was and why she was there.

"Have mercy on me and bring my husband back to life," begged Behula. "I saw you put down and then resurrect your son. You are Shiva's daughter, aren't you? You can help me."

Neta said, "Listen to me patiently. You have wasted your energy and time—six months, you say—for none can resurrect someone who has died of snakebite. There is no *ojha* anywhere who can do that."

Behula would not take no for an answer. She hung on to Neta's legs and didn't let up on her sobs and tears. Neta relented: the tears and the grip on her legs were too much to bear; she was touched.

She said, "Stop crying, dear girl, I'll find a way to have your lord Lakshmindar revived. First, wash his bones, then come with me to the divine realm."

Behula felt hope rise in her breast. She busied herself washing the bones in the waters of Triveni. A large *boal* fish, attracted by the smell of dead flesh, swam up and swallowed a kneecap. Neta saw this and gave chase to catch the fish and, invoking the authority of Padma, entrusted the bone to its care.

"You must bring it back when Padma revives Lakshmindar. For Shiva's sake take good care of it. If it's damaged in any way, you'll see what happens."

Behula gathered the bones she had washed on one end of her sari and happily accompanied Neta.

THE RESOLUTION

ON THE WAY TO THE DIVINE realm Neta magically devised a cat-walk of sharp-edged diamonds over a stream and told Behula that she would have to cross it barefoot as a test of character. If she was truly chaste, she would be able to walk across with no difficulty. If not, the walk would be fatal.

Behula silently prayed to Padma and stepped on the walkway. Even a fly falling on it was sliced instantly. Nothing happened to Behula. Her chastity was proven; Neta continued with her toward the heavens.

Behula was delighted to see Amaravati, Indra's celestial home, once again. Neta asked her to wait at Neta's place while she went to inform Padma.

"Behula is here," Neta told Padma. "Now resurrect Chand's son and he will worship you all his life."

Padma curtly replied, "You've got things mixed up, Neta. How can I revive Lakshmindar when he has gone to Yamapur, the underworld realm? Tell Sahé's daughter to go home."

Lakshmindar, of course, hadn't been confined in the underworld. Padma was fibbing—for a purpose; so Neta went to Behula and solemnly told her that Padma wouldn't revive Lakshmindar and that she should go home.

Behula began crying again.

Neta said, "Stop crying, I'll find a solution. Go and meet your old *vidyadhari* friends, especially Chandramukhi. Then give a performance before Shiva. If he is pleased with the performance, he may resuscitate Lakshmindar."

Behula went to meet the *vidyadharis* and had a happy reunion.

"Usha has come home," the *vidyadharis* cried exultantly. They wanted to know where Aniruddha was, and Behula told them the whole story of their travails.

"But my sorrow has dispersed, now that I have met you, my friends," Behula said. "Only one thing remains to make everything perfect: reviving Aniruddha."

The *vidyadharis* were of the same mind as Neta. If Behula could please Shiva with her songs and dance, he would no doubt grant her prayers. The *vidyadharis* dressed and made up Behula in the most alluring of forms, one that would enchant all three realms. With the flowers, jewels, ivory, gold, pearls, and coral, *kajal* for the eyes, makeup for the skin, sandalwood essence, gorgeous saris, hair done up and exquisitely braided, eyebrows finely painted, anklets that sound like a chortling stream, Behula was ready to give the performance of her life.

The sage Narada turned up just then and, seeing Behula, asked the apsara Menaka what was going on. Menaka told him everything about her travails. Then Narada went to Shiva and told him that an exquisitely beautiful danseuse, a universal enchantress, had arrived and would like to perform before him. Shiva, who was getting bored, welcomed the prospect of some entertainment. He instructed Nandi to invite all the gods and goddesses. They all came, each on their special mounts and vehicles, and sat in a glorious assembly.

Behula entered the assembly hall accompanied by the *vidyadharis,* her accompanists. She began by paying homage to all the gathered gods and goddesses and sages.

The *vidyadhari* Chitrasena struck up on the mridanga drums, others sang with koel-sweet voices, and Behula, the center of attraction, commenced dancing. Her movements were ethereal, she didn't seem to touch feet to the ground but seemed to float and fly and make intricate movements in air. When her eyes shot a glance at someone, he was at once pierced by love's arrows.

Shiva was delighted at the performance and promised Behula any boon she wanted. In gratitude she fell at his feet in a full *pranam*. Then she recounted her whole story in brief and concluded: "Without her husband a woman's life is fruitless. The boon I desire is that you restore my husband's life."

Shiva said to Nandi, "Go and fetch Padma. All the gods and goddesses have come here to watch Behula's show. What keeps her in her own home? Tell her I have asked her to come."

Nandi went and found Padma at home. He gave Shiva's message—to no avail. She said, "I've got a headache, I don't feel like watching a dance or listening to music. Please pay my respects to Father and explain why I can't come."

Nandi reported back to Shiva. The great god turned to Narada: "Go and get Padma without delay." Narada called on Padma and was respectfully received, but when he conveyed Shiva's message, she responded as she had to Nandi. But Narada was not to be easily shaken off by the excuse of a "splitting headache." He pointed out gently but firmly that Shiva was probably more powerful than any other deity and it would be unwise to cross him without a good reason. Padma went along and made a *pranam* at her father's feet and sat down beside him after greeting the gods and goddesses, including her stepmother Chandi.

"Why were you alone at home when all the other deities were here to watch the dance?" asked Shiva. He added with a chuckle, "How's your health?"

Padma solemnly replied, "I've been under the weather the past four days. I have a splitting headache and aches and pains all over the body. I've come only because it's your wish."

Shiva touched her head by way of giving his blessings.

"Sit down and watch the dance."

As Behula began dancing again, Padma said to her angrily, "Do you call this dancing? You have artfully painted your face to attract gods and demons alike." Then turning to Shiva: "How can you, lord of three realms, fall for such cheap cavorting?"

Shiva said in annoyance, "You are out of line, Padma. Usha and Aniruddha are star performers, and you used all sorts of machinations to take them to earth, where your nagas killed Aniruddha."

Shiva asked Behula to tell the whole story for the benefit of the gathered assembly. When Behula reached the part where nagas start killing Chand's children, Padma rudely interjected: "My nagas did not kill any of Chand's children. In fact Chand was so vindictive toward snakes that they steered clear of Champaknagar."

Behula, flabbergasted, asked what was the point of the lies. She said, "Here is proof of the depredations of the nagas." She produced the snipped off tips of nagas' tails, explaining how she had stayed awake to catch the snakes. But on the fateful night Lakshmindar was killed while Behula slept, exhausted by the long-drawn wedding rituals and the strain of keeping awake.

Behula's account was cogent and convincing; Padma countered it by throwing a tantrum: "Father, see how she slights me and right in front of you."

Chandi joined in the fray, siding with Behula and slandering Padma's character: "Your husband deserted you because of your unsavory character."

Padma hit back: "Look at yourself before you slander me. As a maiden you went with Kama to a flower garden in order to pray for a husband; and it was because of you that Kama was reduced to ashes."

"Don't make me tell more about you, Padma, you will become the laughingstock of heaven."

Shiva intervened to bring order. "If mother and daughter carry on squabbling like this I feel ashamed."

The two ladies fell silent.

"I was pleased with Behula's performance and promised to have her husband resurrected. Don't let my words come to nothing, Padma. Bring Lakshmindar back to life before this assembly."

"Father, you will have to forgive me. Chand is continuously abusing me. He smashes the pitchers for my puja wherever he comes across them. He is jealous of the power of my nagas. He is a mere mortal, a *baniya* in origin. He will worship all the other goddesses in the three realms but not me. His animosity toward me is increasing all the time. How can you expect me to resurrect his son?"

Shiva said solemnly, "Resurrect Behula's husband and your fame will spread through the three realms. People will worship you with true devotion. Don't let my promise remain unfulfilled."

Behula fell at Padma's feet, crying piteously and with joined palms entreating the goddess to help mankind across the sea of sorrow that is life. She sang a heartfelt paean to Padma and again begged her to give her back her husband.

Neta lent her voice to make Padma relent. "When people see that you have given back Lakshmindar his life, more and more people will worship you," she said. Neta clasped her sister's legs and begged her to be generous. It made Padma burst out laughing. She raised Neta to her feet. Then she took Behula by the hand and said, "Stop crying. I will bring your husband back presently."

+ + +

First, Lakshmindar's skeleton had to be reconstructed. "Bring me all the bones you've got," Padma said to Behula. Behula brought the sari, one end of which had been used to make a bundle for the bones, and handed it to Padma. Padma sat down like a child at play and put the bones together at the various joints. The joints were then fixed, all except the knee joints—because the kneecaps were missing.

"Where could they have gone?" asked Behula. "I slung them from a string round my neck."

"When you cleaned the bones they fell into the water and were swallowed up by a giant *boal* fish," Neta said. "I asked the fish to take care of them, and I will presently go and retrieve them."

So Neta went and called the fish to come and deliver the kneecaps.

"I swallowed them but I don't know what happened to them," said the fish.

"In that case we will have to cut open your belly."

"Very well," said the fish and turned over. The kneecaps were indeed inside. The fish lay dead while the kneecaps were fitted, completing the skeleton.

Next Padma ordered the nagas to fetch water from the seven seas. Seven species of nagas sped away to the seven seas. Padma asked Neta to bring twigs from a hundred varieties of flowering plants. Padma sat down to recreate Lakshmindar. She recited a mantra and splashed water over the bones. A covering of flesh formed and the joints clicked into place. More mantras, twigs, water, and blood and skin were created. More subtle mantras brought back the delicate features of the face, the lips, nose, eyelashes, ears.

But even with his body complete once again, Lakshmindar lay lifeless—because the poison was still active. It was the *kalkuta* poison, produced in the churning of the seas. Padma waved the twigs and chanted mantras and sprinkled water to neutralize the poison. Slowly Lakshmindar regained consciousness, but he was still too weak to stand up and move about and speak. The first elaborate speech he made was a eulogy for Padma.

"Ask me for a boon," said Padma.

"I want to see the brothers whom I have never seen, and Shankha-Dhanvantari and Dhona and Mona."

Happy introductions followed, and people spontaneously began to celebrate. Padma offered Behula a boon too.

"Bring back the fourteen ships of my father-in-law's fleet together with the crew and passengers."

"But how?" remonstrated Padma. "The ships are sunk deep in Kalidaha."

"You are the great goddess, nothing is impossible for you."

Padma asked for Hanuman's help and a unique salvage operation took place. Hanuman wrapped his giant tail round a ship and swung it up to the surface. When all the ships were up on the surface, the crews were resurrected. They looked as if they had woken from a dream. Padma asked that an inventory of everything on the ships be taken to see if anything was missing. Only one item was not found, a pot of lime, giving rise to some jocularity: which among the creatures of the deeps were addicted to *paan*?

Behula and Lakshmindar were eager to go back to their celestial home and assume their old identities as Usha and Aniruddha. But first they had to return to Champaknagar and bring their earthly life to a satisfactory end. When they bade farewell to Padma they gave their assurance that Chand would finally bow down before her. In anticipation, a puja pitcher was placed on the *Madhukar*. At Neta's request Padma gave away gifts to everyone—clothes, rings, gold nuggets—to Behula, Lakshmindar, Lakshmindar's six brothers, Dhanvantari, Chand's cunning factotum Tera, all the Brahmin pandits.

The grand fleet of fourteen ships carrying all the newly resurrected people sailed upriver toward Champaknagar. They sailed past the bends that marked Behula's varied trials, now in reverse order. Lakshmindar showed great protective concern as Behula pointed out the spots and described the disturbing or even traumatic encounters. Some of the unsavory characters aroused Lakshmindar's wrath, and he anchored and got off the ship to mete out summary punishment to them—to the brothers Dhona and Mona, for instance. Goda aroused laughter, the gambler aroused contempt; the tiger, vulture, and vixen elicited fear. As they neared the tiger's bend the crew of the ships got off and cleared a swath of forest on both banks. At Narayan Dani's bend Lakshmindar acted in high dudgeon, seriously proposing that he take some men, apprehend his lecherous uncle, shave his head, and paint his face with black ink and white chalk. But Behula mysteriously commented that such scandalous behavior was more common than people believed, and there were nephews who harassed aunts. Lakshmindar blushed and looked away,; neither he nor Behula referred to the subject again.

"Let bygones be bygones," Behula wisely said.

Eventually the fleet neared Champaknagar and excitement ran high among the crew and passengers. At the bend in the Gungari River just outside the town Behula came up with the idea for a strange experiment. "You all stay on the ships for some time, while I reconnoiter the town and Lakshmindar's family home in the guise of a Dom maiden.

"Make me some palm leaf hand fans," Behula told her friends. "I'll put on copper jewelry, tie up my hair in typical Dom fashion, and peddle the fans."

Behula stitched on a cloth fringe on the fans embroidered mottoes— like "Victory to Padma"—and signed her name, "Behula Sundari." There were some embroidered pictures: Padma standing victorious, with Chand beneath her feet, while his seven sons and Dhanvantari looked on.

Behula cried like a peddler, "Fan anyone?" and was stopped by one of Sonaka's maids, who wanted to buy a fan. She was struck by the vendor's looks, which bore a lifelike resemblance to Sonaka's missing daughter-in-law. The maid ran to tell Sonaka about the strange peddler. Sonaka looked at the peddler and her wares and knew at once who she was. They embraced with tears in their eyes.

But Sonaka had some unpleasant questions. Where was Lakshmindar—or rather his body? Why did Behula become a Dom woman? Was it through marrying one of that lowly caste? How did Behula's much-vaunted mission to resurrect Lakshmindar turn out?

Sonaka at least limited her onslaught to words. Chand came charging with his *hintala* staff, hurling abuse at Behula. Behula ran and narrated the encounters in great detail to Chand's seven sons—who had a good laugh.

Dulai Kandari, one of the pilots in the fleet, and the Brahmin pandit Sridhar called on Chand and found him fulminating against Behula. They calmly told him that his fourteen ships had been salvaged and were moored not far away.

"You are a lucky man, Chandradhara," said Pandit Sridhar, "lucky to have a son like Lakshmindar and a daughter-in-law like Behula. It is through her efforts that you have got the ships back, absolutely intact, with all the men alive again. It is Padma's power that brought them, your sons, and Dhanvantari back from the dead. You must offer sincere puja to Padma."

Chand set off at once to see his sons. Sonaka went with her six daughters-in-law. When Chand saw that the reported miracles were all true he danced with his *hintala* staff on his shoulder. Lakshmindar told him: "All this has been possible because of Padma. Forget the old antagonism and fall at her feet."

Chand bristled. "How can I offer puja to her with the same hand that I use to worship Shiva and Chandi?"

Dhanvantari put forward forceful arguments in favor of Padma worship.

"Listen, man, Padma knocked out Shiva and Chandi. She can kill and revive men as well as gods. It is folly to defy her."

Chand, realizing that his staunchest allies were now converted to the Padma cult, was forced to agree to offer her puja. Still, he tried one last trick of subversion.

"You know, Pandit Sridhar, if you insist that I offer puja to Padma, I'll do it by offering a bowl of flowers with my left hand."

"Don't be childish, that is no puja at all. In fact it's asking for trouble, and you've had enough for one lifetime. Why don't you pray to Shiva and Chandi and do as they suggest?"

Chand accepted the suggestion. He prayed to Shiva, cutting open a vein and offering his own blood to the god. Shiva smiled with satisfaction and said, "Now go and offer puja to Padma."

After so much drama Chand's puja to Padma, Manasa-devi, might appear to be an anticlimax, but it was the happiest religious occasion in Champaknagar in living memory.

Padma appeared in person, in her celestial chariot, accompanied by the eight fabled nagas. Once Chand joined palms before her, he found it was quite natural to do so. All his devotional sentiments poured out, directed now at the mysterious and volatile new goddess in the pantheon. Padma, with characteristic generosity, gave the best of boons, including the great occult mantra, to Chand. She smiled, and so did Chand, as they remembered how the wily serpent goddess had robbed him of it. Every household in Champaknagar resounded with eulogies to Padma, with puja drums and occult chants.

But the resolution to the drama would not be complete without Behula and Lakshmindar resuming their true form. Before that they had to take their places in Chand's family once again, however briefly. And here a problem arose that required a drastic solution. By embarking on her river journey Behula had placed herself beyond the pale. For her to occupy again the position she had in society she had to prove that her purity, her chastity, had not been compromised. It was Lakshmindar, of all people, who said she had to undergo a test. Chand said he would not be a party to it; as far as he was concerned the girl had behaved admirably. Behula herself then insisted on a trial by fire. A trench was dug and filled with firewood. Pitchers of ghee were poured over it and a tremendous conflagration lit up. Behula saluted the elders with joined palms and made this declaration: "In life after life my lord and master has been Lakshmindar. If another man has touched me let this fire consume me." With those words she circumambulated the fire seven times and leapt into the heart of the flames. Everyone gasped and stood up to look into the flames. There was Behula, all intact, inside the flames. The flames died down. Behula walked out; not a hair had been singed. Murmurs of praise rose from all sides.

Not long after, a celestial chariot arrived to convey Behula and Lakshmindar—or rather, Usha and Aniruddha—to their heavenly abode in Amaravati. Champaknagar mourned their departure with long faces and muffled sobs and copious tears. Pandit Sringi said, "Just think, they went to heaven in their everyday bodies. Is that something to mourn or to make us happy?" The pandit's impeccable logic had the desired impact. Everyone settled down to a peaceful existence under the potent aegis of the great goddess Padma and retained fond memories of the ravishing demigod and demigoddess who acted out their divinely ordained roles in their midst.

NOTES

INTRODUCTION

1. Jean Philippe Vogel, *Indian Serpent Lore* (London: Arthur Probsthain, 1926), 39–42.

2. *Atharva Veda* (with the commentary of Sayana), ed. Vishva Bandhu et al., Vishveshvaranand Indological Series 13–17 (Hoshiarpur: Vishveshvaranand Vedic Research Institute, 1960–1964), 5.13.4.

3. Edward C. Dimock, Jr., "The Goddess of Snakes in Medieval Bengali Literature," part 1, *History of Religions* 1, no. 2 (Winter 1962): 307–321; here 318.

4. Asutosh Bhattacarya, "The Serpent in Folk-Belief in Bengal," *Indian Folklore* 1, no. 2 (1956): 25.

5. Dimock, "The Goddess of Snakes," part 1, p. 318.

6. Ibid., 311.

7. Ibid., 321, citing *Atharva Veda* 4.6.1.

8. Wendy Doniger O'Flaherty, *Asceticism and Eroticism in the Mythology of Siva* (Oxford: Oxford University Press, 1973).

9. John Watson McCrindle, *Ancient India as Described in Classical Literature* (1901; repr., Amsterdam: Philo Press, 1971), 145.

10. Diana L. Eck, *Banaras, City of Light* (Princeton, N.J.: Princeton University Press, 1984), 264.

11. Edward C. Dimock, Jr., "The Theology of the Repulsive: The Myth of the Goddess Sitala," in *The Divine Consort: Radha and the Goddess of India,* ed. John Stratton Hawley and Donna Marie Wulff (Berkeley, Calif.: Berkeley Religious Studies Series, 1982), 184–203.

12. *Rig Veda* 10.16.6, in Wendy Doniger O'Flaherty, ed. and trans., *The Rig Veda: An Anthology* (Harmondsworth: Penguin Classics, 1981). All citations here from the *Rig Veda* are my own.

13. *Rig Veda* 1.32 and 1.2.

14. E.g., *Rig Veda* 1.52.2, 1.52.6, 2.14.2.

15. *Rig Veda* 10.32.

16. Richard Gombrich, *How Buddhism Began* (London: Athlone Press, 1996), 72.

17. *Ashvalayana Grihyasutra* (with the commentary of Gargya Narayana), ed. Ramanaryana Vidyaratna and Anandachandra Vedantavagisa (Calcutta: Asiatic Society of Bengal, 1874), 2.1.9.

18. *Tandya (Panchavimsha) Brahmana*, 2 vols., ed. Cinnaswami Sastri and Pattachirama Sastri, Kashi Sanskrit Series, no. 105 (Benares: Sanskrit Series Office, 1935), 25.15.1–4.

19. *Mahabharata* 1.31.4–18; 1.52.3–22. This and all subsequent references are to the critical (Poona) edition of the *Mahabharata: Mahabharata*, ed. V. S. Sukthankar et al. (Poona: Bhandarkar Oriental Research Institute, 1933–1969). I have summarized rather than translated the passages cited from the *Mahabharata*.

20. J. A. B. van Buitenen, ed. and trans., *The Mahabharata*, vol. 1, *Book 1: The Book of the Beginning* (Chicago: University of Chicago Press, 1973), 4.

21. *Mahabharata* 1.47.6–7.

22. *Mahabharata* 1.2.3–6.

23. Madeleine Biardeau, *Études de mythologie hindoue* (Paris: École française d'Extrême Orient, 1981); Alf Hiltebeitel, *The Ritual of Battle: Krishna in the Mahabharata* (Ithaca, N.Y.: Cornell University Press, 1976).

24. See *Kamasutra* 5.6.24–25: "He makes his shadow and his body disappear by means of the magic trick of the 'pocket–no pocket.' The technique for this is: He cooks the heart of a mongoose, the fruits of a fenugreek plant and a long gourd, and snake eyes, over a fire that does not smoke. Then he rubs into this the same measure of the collyrium used as eye makeup. When he has smeared his eyes with this, he can move about without a shadow or a body." In *Kamasutra*, trans. Wendy Doniger and Sudhir Kakar (Oxford: Oxford University Press, 2002).

25. Van Buitenen, *Book of the Beginning*, 12.

26. Ibid., 439.

27. *Mahabharata* 1.18.

28. *Mahabharata* 1.1.20–210, 1.2.1–243.

29. *Mahabharata* 1.2.73–74.

30. *Mahabharata* 1.44.19–20.

31. Wendy Doniger, "The Concept of Heresy in Hinduism," in *On Hinduism,* ed. Wendy Doniger (Delhi: Aleph Book Company, 2013), 36–69.

32. Claude Lévi-Strauss, "The Story of Asdiwal," in *The Structural Study of Myth and Totemism,* ed. Edmund Leach (London: Tavistock, 1967), 1–48.

33. *Mahabharata* 1.15–17.

34. This story is also retold later, to Astika, at *Mahabharata* 1.49.

35. *Mahabharata* 1.14–30.

36. *Mahabharata* 1.32.1–25.

37. *Suparnadhyaya* 3.2, cited by Jarl Charpentier, *Die Suparnasage: Untersuchungen zur altindischen Literatur- und Sagengeschichte* (Uppsala: Akademiska Bokhandeln; Leipzig: Harrassowitz, 1920), 218–219.

38. *Mahabharata* 1.32.1–25, 10.16.1–15, 14.66–70.

39. *Mahabharata* 1.36–40.

40. *Mahabharata* 1.46.26–27.

41. Sadashiv Ambadas Dange, *Legends in the Mahabharata* (Delhi: Motilal Banarsidass, 1969), 354.

42. *Mahabharata* 1.8–12.

43. *Mahabharata* 1.34–35.

44. *Mahabharata* 1.13.9–45.

45. *Mahabharata* 1.42–45.

46. *Mahabharata* 1.36.5.

47. *Vipradasa's Manasa-vijaya,* ed. Sukumar Sen (Calcutta: Asiatic Society, 1953), xxxii.

48. Cited by Dimock, "The Goddess of Snakes," part 1, p. 315.

49. *Mahabharata* 1.11.17.

50. Kalidasa, *Raghuvamsha,* ed. M. R. Kale (Delhi: Motilal Banarsidass, 1971), 16.72–88.

51. *Bhuridatta Jataka* in *The Jataka Together with Its Commentary,* ed. Viggo Fausbøll (London: Luzac, 1963).

52. Vogel, *Indian Serpent Lore,* 36–37.

53. Laurie Cozad, *Sacred Snakes: Orthodox Images of Indian Snake Worship* (Aurora, Colo.: Davies Group, 2004), 72.

54. *Mahabharata* 1.3.1–18.

55. *Mahabharata* 1.3.85–195.

56. *Mahabharata* 1.3.139–146.

57. *Mahabharata* 1.47–53.

58. *Mahabharata* 1.215–225.

59. *Mahabharata* 3.63.

60. *Mahabharata* 1.14–30.

61. *Bhagavata Purana* 10.15–17, trans. Wendy Doniger O'Flaherty, in *Hindu Myths: A Sourcebook* (Harmondsworth: Penguin Classics, 1975), 221–228. Summarized here.

62. *Mahabharata* 1.34.9–10.

63. *Mahabharata* 1.61.90.

64. *Mahabharata* 1.32.1–25.

65. *Mahabharata* 1.48.9–26

66. *Mahabharata* 1.52.4–91.

67. *Mahavagga*, trans. I. B. Horner, ed. Hermann Oldenberg, vol. 1, of the Pali Text Society's *Vinaya Pitakam* (London: Luzac, 1969), 1.3.1–3.

68. James Fergusson, *Tree and Serpent Worship* (London: India Museum, 1868), plate 76.

69. Reginald Ray, *Buddhist Saints in India* (Oxford: Oxford University Press, 1994), 75.

70. *Mahavagga* 1.63.1–2, 4–5.

71. Gombrich, *How Buddhism Began*, 73.

72. *Mahavastu*, ed. Émile Senart (Paris: Imprimeri Nationale, 1876), vol. 1, 102–103.

73. Edward C. Dimock, Jr., and A. K. Ramanujan, "The Goddess of Snakes in Medieval Bengali Literature," part 2, *History of Religions* 3, no. 2 (Winter 1964): 300–322; here 319–321.

74. Ibid., 320.

75. Ibid., 321.

76. Ibid.

77. A. K. Ramanujan, *The Collected Essays of A. K. Ramanujan*, ed. Vinay Dharwadker (Delhi: Oxford University Press, 1999), p. 185.

78. Wendy Doniger, "How to Escape the Curse," review of John Smith, trans., *The Mahabharata*, for the *London Review of Books*, October 8, 2009.

PROLOGUE

1. For an authoritative treatment of the subject, see Perween Hasan, *Sultans and Mosques: The Early Muslim Architecture of Bangladesh* (London: I. B. Tauris, 2007).

2. Sukumar Sen, *Bangla Sahityer Itihash* [History of Bengali Literature], rev. ed., vol. 1 (1959; Kolkata: Ananda, 2009), 81–82.

3. For a selection sensitively translated and introduced, see Edward C. Dimock, Jr., and Denise Levertov, trans., *In Praise of Krishna: Songs from the Bengali* (London: Jonathan Cape, 1968).

4. Edward C. Dimock, Jr., *The Place of the Hidden Moon: Erotic Mysticism in the Vaisnava-Sahajiya Cult of Bengal* (Chicago: University of Chicago Press, 1966), 249–270.

5. Tony K. Stewart, *Fabulous Females and Peerless Pirs: Tales of Mad Adventure in Old Bengal* (New York: Oxford University Press, 2004).

6. Clinton B. Seely, *Barisal and Beyond: Essays on Bangla Literature* (Delhi: Chronicle Books, 2008), 7.

7. Ibid., 34–46.

8. David L. Curley, *Poetry and History: Bengali Mangal-kabya and Social Change in Precolonial Bengal* (Delhi: Chronicle Books, 2008).

9. Kumkum Chatterjee, "Goddess Encounters: Mughals, Monsters and the Goddess in Bengal," *Modern Asian Studies* 47, no. 5 (2013): 1435–1487.

10. Ashutosh Bhattacharya, *Bangla Mangal Kavyer Itihash* [History of Bengali *Mangalkavya*] (Calcutta: Mukherjee, 1975), 183–245.

11. Sukumar Sen, ed., *Vipradasa's Manasa-vijaya* (Calcutta: Asiatic Society, 1953), xvi.

12. Muhammad Shahjahan Mian, *Sreerai Binod: Kavi O Kavya* [Sri Ray Binod: The Poet and His Poetry] (Dhaka: Bangla Academy, 1991).

13. Tantrabibhuti, *Manasapuran,* ed. Ashutosh Das, 2 vols. (Calcutta: Calcutta University Press, 1980).

14. Sen, *Vipradasa's Manasa-vijaya.*

15. Ketakadas-Kshemananda, *Manasa-Mangal,* ed. Jatindramohan Bhattacharya (Calcutta: Calcutta University Press, 1943).

16. Vijaya Gupta, *Manasamangal (Padmapuran),* ed. Pandit Kalikishore Vidyavinode (Calcutta: Benimadhab Sheel's Library, n.d.).

17. Narayan Dev, *Padmapuran,* ed. Tamonash Dasgupta (Calcutta: Calcutta University Press, 1942).

18. Ray Binod, *Padmapuran,* ed. Muhammad Shahjahan Mian (Dhaka: Dhaka University Press, 1993).

19. Radhanath Raychaudhuri, *Padmapuran (Manasamangal)* (Calcutta: Deb Sahitya Kutir, 1992).

20. Baishkobi, *SriSri Padmapuran* (Kolkata: Rajendra Library, n.d.).

21. Sen, *Vipradasa's Manasa-vijaya,* p. ii.

22. *The Collected Essays of A. K. Ramanujan,* ed. Vinay Dharwadker (Delhi: Oxford University Press, 1999), 377–397.

23. Sen, *Vipradasa's Manasa-vijaya,* p. xxix.

24. Richard M. Eaton, *The Rise of Islam and the Bengal Frontier, 1204–1760* (Delhi: Oxford University Press, 1994), 207.

25. Syed Jamil Ahmed, *Acinpakhi Infinity: Indigenous Theatre of Bangladesh* (Dhaka: University Press, 2000), 113.

26. Eaton, *Rise of Islam*, 281.

27. Ibid., 49.

28. Bhattacharya, *Bangla Mangal Kavyer Itihash*, 278–279.

29. T. W. Clark, "Evolution of Hinduism in Medieval Bengali Literature: Siva, Candi, Manasa," *Bulletin of the School of Oriental and African Studies* (University of London) 17, no. 3 (1955): 509; cited in Ahmed, *Acinpakhi Infinity*, 113.

30. Mian, *Sreerai Binod*, 305.

31. Ahmed, *Acinpakhi Infinity*, 111–157.

32. Stewart, *Fabulous Females*, 6.

33. See, for instance, Saumitra Chakravarty, "Defeating Patriarchal Politics: The Snake Woman as Goddess; A Study of the *Manasa Mangal Kavya* of Bengal," *Intersections: Gender and Sexuality in Asia and the Pacific* 30 (August 2012).

34. "Baby Name Meanings: Behula," www.sheknows.com/baby-names /name/behula, accessed March 8, 2015.

35. Sen, *Vipradasa's Manasa-vijaya*, p. xxxv.

SOURCES

This retelling of the Manasa legends is based on the following Bengali versions:

Binod, Ray. *Padmapuran* [seventeenth century]. Edited by Muhammad Shahjahan Mian. Dhaka: Dhaka University Press, 1993.

Gupta, Vijay. *Manasamangal (Padmapuran)* [fifteenth century]. Edited by Pandit Kalikishore Vidyavinode. Calcutta: Benimadhab Seal's Library, n.d.

Raychaudhuri, Radhanath. *Padmapuran (Manasamangal)* [nineteenth century]. Calcutta: Deb Sahitya Kutir, 1992.

Tantrabibhuti, *Manasapuran* [sixteenth century]. Edited by Ashutosh Das. 2 vols. Calcutta: Calcutta University Press, 1980.

Vipradasa. *Manasa-vijaya* [fifteenth century]. Edited by Sukumar Sen. Calcutta: Asiatic Society, 1953.

In addition, I have taken the cue for a particular detail from each of the following two texts:

Ahmed, Jamil. *Behular Bhasan*. Unpublished text of play based on the Manasa legends, 2011.

Radice, William. *Myths and Legends of India*. Delhi: Viking Penguin, 2001.

SOURCES FOR INDIVIDUAL CHAPTERS

Part I: In the Divine Realm

Creation (Binod, pp. 11, 13; Raychaudhuri, pp. 36–43)
The Revenge of the Valakhilyas (Raychaudhuri, pp. 43–52)
The Menace of Taraka (Raychaudhuri, p. 52)
The Birth of Parvati and Her Marriage with Shiva (Raychaudhuri, pp. 53–63)
The Birth of Ganesha and Kartikeya (Raychaudhuri, pp. 63–64)
The Slaying of Taraka the Asura (Raychaudhuri, pp. 65–66)
The Birth of Chandradhara (Raychaudhuri, pp. 66–69)
Shiva's Dalliances (Binod, pp. 19–23; Vipradasa, p. 11)
The Birth of Manasa (Raychaudhuri, pp. 74–83; Binod, pp. 43–44)
Manasa's Forest Exile (Binod, pp. 71–74; Tantrabibhuti, pp. 25–26, 33–34; Vipradasa, pp. 17–18)
The Churning of the Seas (Vipradasa, pp. 21–29; Radice, p. 64)
The Marriages of Manasa and Neta (Vipradasa, pp. 39–45)
The Sarpa Satra (Vipradasa, pp. 46–56)
Looking Earthward (Vipradasa, pp. 56–58; Tantrabibhuti, pp. 63–65)

Part II: In the Realm of the Merchant King

Winning over Cowherds (Binod, pp. 109–113; Vipradasa, p. 63)
The Battle with Hassan and Hossein (Vipradasa, pp. 63–86)
Jalu and Malu (Vipradasa, pp. 86–88)
Neutralizing Chand's Occult Power (Gupta, pp. 90–95)
The Slaying of Shankha-Dhanvantari (Vipradasa, pp. 94–115; Binod, pp. 156–159)
The Killing of Dhona and Mona (Vipradasa, pp. 116–124)
Eliminating Chand's Six Sons (Vipradasa, pp. 125–128; Gupta, pp. 95–101)
Usha and Aniruddha Press-Ganged by Padma (Binod, pp. 164–184)
The Birth of Lakshmindar and Behula (Binod, pp. 185–191, 195–200)
The Adventures and Misadventures of Chand the Merchant King (Binod, pp. 192–195, 200–219)
The Return Voyage (Binod, pp. 219–246, 249–250; Vipradasa, pp. 163–164; Tantrabibhuti, pp. 240–247)
The Marriage of Behula and Lakshmindar (Binod, pp. 247–284)
Death in the Steel Chamber (Binod, pp. 284–299)
Behula's River Journey (Binod, pp. 300–316; Ahmed, n.p.)
The Resolution (Binod, pp. 316–355)

GLOSSARY

Aishiki: mythic weapon to counter enemy missiles.

Alpana: drawings using traditional motifs on floors and walls with pigment prepared from rice powder; believed to be auspicious, they are commonly seen at weddings and religious and other festivals.

Amaravati: Indra's celestial capital; his palace therein.

Amlaki: small, sour, marble-sized tropical fruit; *Emblica officinalis.*

Aniruddha: Krishna's grandson, husband of Usha.

Apsara: one of the stunningly beautiful celestial nymphs dwelling in Amaravati; Menaka, Tilottama, Urvashi are celebrated examples.

Artha: wealth, worldly possessions; also, worldly affairs, politics, and the like. Another, unrelated, meaning is "meaning."

Ashar: first of the two monsoon months, mid-June to mid-July.

Asura: powerful supernatural being; asuras are enemies of gods.

Baniya: the merchant caste; a member thereof.

Bhagis: in a business venture bhagis receive a share *(bhag)* of the profits as remuneration, while shagis are wage-earners.

Bhairava: one of the forms assumed by Shiva; some of the lookalikes accompanying him in the story assume this form.

Bhuta: commonly equated with "ghost," one of the spirits attending on Shiva.

Bighatiya: literally, a handspan; hence, (deadly) snake of that length.

Brahmastra: mythic weapon charged with Brahma's power.

Chira: flattened rice.

Dharma: what is right according to one's position in life; the god Dharma is the guardian of righteousness.

Dhora: a harmless water snake; the episode featuring Dhora explains in mythic fashion how it became harmless.

Durba: kind of long grass considered sacred and used in rituals; also known as *kusha.*

Dwapar Yuga: the brazen age, after the "golden" Satya Yuga and the "silver" Treta Yuga, and before the current dark age, Kali Yuga.

Gandharva: one of the handsome celestial males who take apsaras as wives; gandharvas are gifted musicians and accompany apsara dancers at Indra's court.

Women fall in love with them at first sight; hence, a gandharva marriage is one in which a woman gives herself to a man without bothering about rites. A gandharva missile is a mythic weapon.

Ganga: goddess identified with the river that bears her name.

Guhyaka: yaksha attendant of Kubera, god of wealth.

Hanuman: the monkey god, son of the wind god Pavana (Vayu); also, generic term for monkeys.

Hintala: Elate paludosa, a variety of palm; a staff fashioned out of it is commonly believed to scare away snakes.

Kajal: collyrium.

Kal-bikal: a highly venomous snake duo.

Kalkuta: the most potent of poisons, final product of the churning of the seas.

Kalpataru: celestial tree in Indra's domain possessing the power to grant a devotee's wish.

Karamcha: small tropical fruit, crimson when ripe and sour to taste; *Carissa carandas.*

Kazi: judge in a Muslim kingdom.

Ketaki: a tropical flower, also known as *keya; Pandanus fascicularis.*

Kinnara: one of a class of celestial beings with singing talent, physically composite, with human bodies and horses' heads.

Kinshuk: a pretty but scentless red flower; *Butea monosperma.*

Kirata: an aboriginal ethnic group in India.

Kumkum: women's cosmetic made from saffron juice.

Kusha: same as *durba* (q.v.).

Lota: small brass pot for carrying water.

Mahamaya: primal Shakti or female superpower, variously manifested as Shiva's consort Sati, or Parvati, Durga, Chandi, Kali.

Maqtab: school for religious instruction attached to a mosque.

Matrika: one of a group of sixteen female deities.

Maulana: Muslim religious scholar.

Moksha: spiritual liberation as the ultimate end of life.

Nagar: town or city, e.g., Hassan-nagar.

Nageswara: also *Nag-kesara,* a flowering tree valued for health-giving properties; *Mesua ferrea.*

Namaskar: also *namaste,* the Hindu salute made by vertically joining palms.

Niranjan: literally, the immaculate one, the supreme deity.

Ojha: medicine man specializing in treating snakebite.

Paan: betel leaf, chewed along with lime, areca nut, and a tobacco preparation; can be habit forming, if not addictive.

Pir: Muslim saint; Sufi preceptor.

Pisacha: evil spirit that feeds on corpses.

Pranam: obeisance made by bending and touching the feet of a person or by prostrating oneself at the person's feet.

Preta: ghoul.

Purusa and Prakriti: two opposed yet complementary forces supposed to operate in the universe, identified with Man and Nature, or the masculine and feminine principles.

Rajasuya: special sacrifice performed by a king in order to impose dominion over other rulers.

Rakshasa: flesh-eating demon; not to be confused with asura.

Samadhi: a state of mystic ecstasy.

Sarpa Satra: snake sacrifice.

Shagis: see bhagis.

Shankha naga: the king cobra.

Shastra: Hindu scripture.

Siddhi: state of spiritual enlightenment.

Sija: plant sacred to Manasa; *Euphorbia nivulia.*

Sindur: vermilion mark in hair parting above the forehead, worn by married Hindu women.

Sraddha: Hindu ritual accompanied by feasting to mark end of mourning period.

Syed: South Asian Muslim claiming descent from the Prophet Muhammad, and hence considered spiritually enlightened.

Thala: flat circular brass plate with low, vertical edge.

Toggor: small, usually white flower; *Tabernaemontana coronaria.*

Triveni Sangam: confluence of three rivers, the Ganges, Yamuna, and the mythic Saraswati, supposed to flow underground.

Udaykala naga: a venomous snake.

Usha: asura princess, daughter of Bana, and wife of Aniruddha, like whom she is attached to Indra's court.

Vaikuntha: celestial home of Vishnu.

Vaitarani: river in the underworld that spirits of the dead must cross, Indian counterpart of the Styx.

Vetalas: class of zombie-like bhutas.

Vidyadharas (m.) *and Vidyadharis* (fem.): class of good-looking celestial beings with extraordinary musical talent.

Yaksha: celestial beings whose special function is to guard treasure.

ACKNOWLEDGMENTS

Dr. Sharmila Sen, executive editor-at-large of Harvard University Press, has been as inspirational as Saraswati, goddess of arts and letters, and deserves a devotee's gratitude. Professor Wendy Doniger's magisterial introduction has greatly enriched the book by filling in the Sanskrit background to the Bengali Manasa legends. Several friends and colleagues have helped with information, suggestions, and the loan or gift of books; I should like to mention in particular Professor Anisuzzaman, Professor Bashabi Fraser, Professor Syed Jamil Ahmed, and Professor Shahjahan Mian. My brother Shahnoor Haq, a lapsed Bengali scholar, fished out a number of useful books from his moldering collection. The book's final shape owes much to the meticulous critique of the anonymous readers and the scrupulous attention of the copyeditor. Heather Hughes, assistant editor for Humanities at Harvard University Press, has been helpful throughout. And the dedicatees, who share my life through thick and thin, have been as always quietly supportive.